THE PILGRIM'S PROGRESS

THE
PILGRIM'S PROGRESS

From this world to that which is to come, delivered under the similitude of a dream : wherein is discovered the manner of his setting out, his dangerous journey and safe arrival at the desired country : by

JOHN BUNYAN

BAKER BOOK HOUSE
Grand Rapids, Michigan

Reprinted 1984 by Baker Book House Company
from the edition issued by Charles Scribner's Sons

ISBN: 0-8010-0732-1

Twelfth printing, September 1994

Printed in the United States of America

THE AUTHOR'S APOLOGY FOR HIS BOOK

WHEN at the first I took my pen in hand
Thus for to write, I did not understand
That I at all should make a little book
In such a mode; nay, I had undertook
To make another; which when almost done,
Before I was aware I this begun.

And thus it was: I, writing of the way
And race of saints, in this our gospel day,
Fell suddenly into an allegory
About their journey, and the way to glory,
In more than twenty things which I set down;
This done, I twenty more had in my crown,
And they again began to multiply,
Like sparks that from the coals of fire do fly.
Nay, then, thought I, if that you breed so fast,
I 'll put you by yourselves, lest you at last
Should prove *ad infinitum*, and eat out
The book that I already am about.

Well, so I did; but yet I did not think
To show to all the world my pen and ink
In such a mode; I only thought to make
I knew not what: nor did I undertake
Thereby to please my neighbour: no, not I;
I did it mine own self to gratify.

Neither did I but vacant seasons spend
In this my scribble; nor did I intend
But to divert myself in doing this
From worser thoughts, which make me do amiss.

Thus I set pen to paper with delight,
And quickly had my thoughts in black and white.
For having now my method by the end,
Still as I pull'd, it came; and so I penn'd
It down, until at last it came to be
For length and breadth the bigness which you see.

Well, when I had thus put mine ends together,
I show'd them others, that I might see whether
They would condemn them, or them justify:
And some said, Let them live; some, Let them die;
Some said, John, print it; others said, Not so;
Some said, It might do good; others said, No.

Now was I in a strait, and did not see
Which was the best thing to be done by me:
At last I thought, Since you are thus divided,
I print it will, and so the case decided.

For, thought I, Some, I see, would have it done,
Though others in that channel do not run.
To prove, then, who advised for the best,
Thus I thought fit to put it to the test.

I further thought, if now I did deny
Those that would have it thus, to gratify;
I did not know but hinder them I might
Of that which would to them be great delight.

For those that were not for its coming forth,
I said to them, Offend you I am loth,
Yet since your brethren pleased with it be,
Forbear to judge, till you do further see.

If that thou wilt not read, let it alone;
Some love the meat, some love to pick the bone:
Yea, that I might them better palliate,
I did too with them thus expostulate:

May I not write in such a style as this?
In such a method too, and yet not miss
My end,—thy good? Why may it not be done?
Dark clouds bring waters, when the bright bring none.

Yea, dark or bright, if they their silver drops
Cause to descend, the earth, by yielding crops,
Gives praise to both, and carpeth not at either,
But treasures up the fruit they yield together;
Yea, so commixes both, that in her fruit
None can distinguish this from that: they suit
Her well, when hungry; but if she be full,
She spues out both, and makes their blessings null.

    You see the ways the fisherman doth take
To catch the fish; what engines doth he make!
Behold how he engageth all his wits;
Also his snares, lines, angles, hooks, and nets:
Yet fish there be, that neither hook, nor line,
Nor snare, nor net, nor engine can make thine;
They must be groped for, and be tickled too,
Or they will not be catch'd, whate'er you do.

    How doth the fowler seek to catch his game
By divers means, all which one cannot name?
His gun, his nets, his lime-twigs, light, and bell;
He creeps, he goes, he stands; yea, who can tell
Of all his postures? Yet there's none of these
Will make him master of what fowls he please.
Yea, he must pipe and whistle to catch *this*;
Yet, if he does so, *that* bird he will miss.

    If that a pearl may in a toad's head dwell,
And may be found too in an oyster-shell;
If things that promise nothing do contain
What better is than gold; who will disdain,
That have an inkling of it, there to look,
That they may find it? Now my little book
(Though void of all those paintings that may make
It with this or the other man to take)
Is not without those things that do excel
What do in brave, but empty notions dwell.

    Well, yet I am not fully satisfied,
That this your book will stand, when soundly tried.

Why, what's the matter? It is dark. What tho'?
But it is feigned : What of that, I trow ?
Some men, by feigning words as dark as mine,
Make truth to spangle, and its rays to shine.
But they want solidness. Speak man thy mind.
They drown'd the weak ; metaphors make us blind.
Solidity, indeed, becomes the pen
Of him that writeth things divine to men ;
But must I needs want solidness, because
By metaphors I speak ? Were not God's laws,
His gospel laws, in olden time held forth
By types, shadows, and metaphors ? Yet loth
Will any sober man be to find fault
With them, lest he be found for to assault
The highest wisdom. No, he rather stoops,
And seeks to find out what by pins and loops,
By calves and sheep, by heifers and by rams,
By birds and herbs, and by the blood of lambs,
God speaketh to him. And happy is he
That finds the light and grace that in them be.
Be not too forward, therefore, to conclude
That I want solidness,—that I am rude :
All things solid in show, not solid be ;
All things in parables despise not we,
Lest things most hurtful lightly we receive,
And things that good are of our souls bereave.
My dark and cloudy words they do but hold
The truth, as cabinets enclose the gold.
The prophets used much by metaphors
To set forth truth ; yea, whoso considers
Christ, His apostles too, shall plainly see
That truths to this day in such mantles be.
Am I afraid to say that holy writ,
Which for its style and phrase puts down all wit,
Is everywhere so full of all these things—
Dark figures, allegories ? Yet there springs

From that same book that lustre, and those rays
Of light, that turns our darkest nights to days.
Come, let my carper to his life now look,
And find there darker lines than in my book
He findeth any; yea, and let him know,
That in his best things there are worse lines too.
May we but stand before impartial men,
To his poor one I dare adventure ten,
That they will take my meaning in these lines
Far better than his lies in silver shrines.
Come, truth, although in swaddling-clouts, I find,
Informs the judgment, rectifies the mind,
Pleases the understanding, makes the will
Submit; the memory too it doth fill
With what doth our imagination please;
Likewise it tends our troubles to appease.
Sound words I know Timothy is to use,
And old wives' fables he is to refuse;
But yet grave Paul him nowhere did forbid
The use of parables; in which lay hid
That gold, those pearls, and precious stones that were
Worth digging for, and that with greatest care.
Let me add one word more, O Man of God!
Art thou offended? Dost thou wish I had
Put forth my matter in another dress,
Or that I had in things been more express?
Three things let me propound, then I submit
To those that are my betters, as is fit.
1. I find not that I am denied the use
Of this my method, so I no abuse
Put on the words, things, readers; or be rude
In handling figure or similitude,
In application; but, all that I may,
Seek the advance of truth this or that way.
Denied, did I say? Nay, I have leave
(Example too, and that from them that have

God better pleased by their words or ways,
Than any man that breatheth nowadays)
Thus to express my mind, thus to declare
Things unto thee, that excellentest are.

    2. I find that men (as high as trees) will write
Dialogue-wise; yet no man doth them slight
For writing so: indeed if they abuse
Truth, cursed be they, and the craft they use
To that intent; but yet let Truth be free
To make her sallies upon thee and me,
Which way it pleases God. For who knows how,
Better than He that taught us first to plough,
To guide our mind and pens for His design?
And He makes base things usher in divine.

    3. I find that holy writ, in many places,
Hath semblance with this method, where the cases
Do call for one thing, to set forth another:
Use it I may, then, and yet nothing smother
Truth's golden beams; nay, by this method may
Make it cast forth its rays as light as day.

    And now, before I do put up my pen,
I 'll show the profit of my book, and then
Commit both thee and it unto that Hand
That pulls the strong down, and makes weak ones stand.

    This book, it chalketh out before thine eyes
The man that seeks the everlasting prize:
It shows you whence he comes, whither he goes,
What he leaves undone, also what he does:
It also shows you how he runs, and runs
Till he unto the gate of glory comes.

    It shows, too, who set out for life amain,
As if the lasting crown they would attain;
Here also you may see the reason why
They lose their labour, and like fools do die.

    This book will make a traveller of thee,
If by its counsel thou wilt ruled be;

It will direct thee to the Holy Land,
If thou wilt its directions understand :
Yea, it will make the slothful active be ;
The blind also delightful things to see.
Art thou for something rare and profitable?
Wouldest thou see a truth within a fable?
Art thou forgetful? Wouldest thou remember
From New-year's day to the last of December?
Then read my fancies, they will stick like burrs,
And may be, to the helpless, comforters.
This book is writ in such a dialect
As may the minds of listless men affect :
It seems a novelty, and yet contains
Nothing but sound and honest gospel strains.
Wouldst thou divert thyself from melancholy?
Wouldst thou be pleasant, yet be far from folly?
Wouldst thou read riddles, and their explanation?
Or else be drowned in thy contemplation?
Dost thou love picking meat? Or wouldst thou see
A man i' th' clouds, and hear him speak to thee?
Wouldst thou be in a dream, and yet not sleep?
Or wouldst thou in a moment laugh and weep?
Wouldest thou lose thyself, and catch no harm,
And find thyself again without a charm?
Wouldst read thyself, and read thou know'st not what,
And yet know whether thou are blest or not,
By reading the same lines? O then come hither,
And lay my book, thy head, and heart together.

JOHN BUNYAN

THE PILGRIM'S PROGRESS

IN THE SIMILITUDE OF A DREAM

THE FIRST PART

As I walked through the wilderness of this world, I lighted on a certain place where was a den, and The Gaol. laid me down in that place to sleep; and, as I slept, I dreamed a dream. I dreamed, and, behold, I saw a man clothed with rags, standing in a certain place, Isa. lxiv. 6. with his face from his own house, a book in his Luke xiv. 33. Ps. xxxviii. 4. hand, and a great burden upon his back. I looked, Hab. ii. 2. Acts xvi. 31. and saw him open the book, and read therein; and, as he read, he wept and trembled; and not being able longer to contain, he brake out with a lamentable cry, saying, 'What shall I do?' His outcry.

In this plight therefore he went home, and Acts ii. 37. refrained himself as long as he could, that his wife and children should not perceive his distress; but he could not be silent long, because that his trouble increased. Wherefore at length he brake his mind to his wife and children; and thus he began to talk to them: O my dear wife, said he, and you the children of my bowels, I, your dear friend, am in myself undone, by reason of a burden that lieth hard upon me; moreover, I am for certain informed

This world. that this our city will be burnt with fire from heaven;
in which fearful overthrow, both myself, with thee
my wife, and you my sweet babes, shall miserably
He knew no come to ruin, except (the which yet I see not) some
way of escape way of escape can be found, whereby we may be
as yet. delivered. At this his relations were sore amazed;
not for that they believed that what he had said to
them was true, but because they thought that some
frenzy distemper had got into his head; therefore, it
drawing towards night, and they hoping that sleep
might settle his brains, with all haste they got him
to bed. But the night was as troublesome to him
as the day; wherefore, instead of sleeping, he spent
it in sighs and tears. So, when the morning was
come, they would know how he did; he told them,
Worse and worse. He also set to talking to them
again; but they began to be hardened. They also
Carnal physic thought to drive away his distemper by harsh and
for a sick surly carriages to him; sometimes they would
soul. deride, sometimes they would chide, and sometimes
they would quite neglect him. Wherefore he
began to retire himself to his chamber to pray for
and pity them, and also to condole his own misery;
he would also walk solitarily in the fields, sometimes
reading, and sometimes praying : and thus for some
days he spent his time.

Now I saw, upon a time, when he was walking in
the fields, that he was, as he was wont, reading in
his book, and greatly distressed in his mind; and as
he read, he burst out, as he had done before, crying,
Acts xvi. 30, 31. 'What shall I do to be saved?'

I saw also that he looked this way and that way,

as if he would run; yet he stood still, because, as I perceived, he could not tell which way to go. I looked then, and saw a man named Evangelist coming to him,[1] and asked, Wherefore dost thou cry? He answered, Sir, I perceive by the book in my hand that I am condemned to die, and after that to come to judgment; and I find that I am not willing to do the first, nor able to do the second. Heb. ix. 27. Job xvi. 21, 22. Ezek. xxii. 14.

Then said Evangelist, Why not willing to die, since this life is attended with so many evils? The man answered, Because I fear that this burden that is upon my back will sink me lower than the grave, and I shall fall into Tophet. And, sir, if I be not Isa. xxx. 33. fit to go to prison, I am not fit, I am sure, to go to judgment, and from thence to execution; and the thoughts of these things make me cry.

Then said Evangelist, If this be thy condition, why standest thou still? He answered, Because I Conviction of know not whither to go. Then he gave him a the necessity of flying. parchment roll, and there was written within, ' Fly Matt. iii. 7. from the wrath to come.'

The man therefore read it, and looking upon Evangelist very carefully, said, Whither must I fly? Then said Evangelist, pointing with his finger over a very wide field, Do you see yonder Wicket-gate? The man said, No. Then said the other, Do Matt. vii. 13,14. you see yonder shining light? He said, I think I Ps. cxix. 105. 2 Pet. i. 19. do. Then said Evangelist, Keep that light in your

---

[1] Christian no sooner leaves the world but meets
Evangelist, who lovingly him greets
With tidings of another; and doth show
Him how to mount to that from this below.

Christ and the way to Him cannot be found without the Word.

eye, and go up directly thereto: so shalt thou see the gate; at which, when thou knockest, it shall be told thee what thou shalt do.

So I saw in my dream that the man began to run. Now he had not run far from his own door, but his wife and children, perceiving it, began to cry after him to return; but the man put his fingers in his ears, and ran on, crying, Life! life! eternal life! So he looked not behind him, but fled towards the middle of the plain.

Luke xiv. 26.

Gen. xix. 17.

They that fly from the wrath to come are a gazing-stock to the world. Jer. xx. 10.

The neighbours also came out to see him run; and as he ran, some mocked, others threatened, and some cried after him to return; and among those that did so, there were two that resolved to fetch him back by force. The name of the one was Obstinate, and the name of the other Pliable. Now, by this time, the man was got a good distance from them; but, however, they were resolved to pursue him, which they did, and in a little time they overtook him. Then said the man, Neighbours, wherefore are you come? They said, To persuade you to go back with us. But he said, That can by no means be; you dwell, said he, in the City of Destruction, the place also where I was born: I see it to be so; and, dying there, sooner or later, you will sink lower than the grave, into a place that burns with fire and brimstone: be content, good neighbours, and go along with me.

Obstinate and Pliable follow him.

Obstinate.

OBST. What! said Obstinate, and leave our friends and our comforts behind us?

Christian.
2 Cor. iv. 18.

CHR. Yes, said Christian (for that was his name), because that all which you shall forsake is not worthy to be compared with a little of that that I am seeking to enjoy; and if you will go along with me, and hold it, you shall fare as I myself; for there, where I go, is enough and to spare. Come away, and prove my words. *Luke xv. 17.*

OBST. What are the things you seek, since you leave all the world to find them?

CHR. I seek an inheritance incorruptible, undefiled, and that fadeth not away; and it is laid up in heaven, and safe there, to be bestowed, at the time appointed, on them that diligently seek it. Read it so, if you will, in my book. *1 Pet. i. 4.* *Heb. xi. 16.*

OBST. Tush! said Obstinate, away with your book; will you go back with us, or no?

CHR. No, not I, said the other; because I have laid my hand to the plough. *Luke ix. 62.*

OBST. Come, then, Neighbour Pliable, let us turn again, and go home without him; there is a company of these crazed-headed coxcombs that, when they take a fancy by the end, are wiser in their own eyes than seven men that can render a reason.

PLI. Then said Pliable, Don't revile; if what the good Christian says is true, the things he looks after are better than ours: my heart inclines to go with my neighbour.

OBST. What! more fools still? Be ruled by me, and go back; who knows whither such a brain-sick fellow will lead you? Go back, go back, and be wise.

CHR. Nay, but do thou come with me, Neighbour Pliable; there are such things to be had which I spoke of, and many more glories besides. If you *Christian and Obstinate pull for Pliable's soul.*

believe not me, read here in this book ; and for the truth of what is expressed therein, behold, all is confirmed by the blood of Him that made it.

Heb. ix. 17-21.
Chap. xiii. 20,
21.

PLI. Well, Neighbour Obstinate, said Pliable, I begin to come to a point; I intend to go along with this good man, and to cast in my lot with him : but, my good companion, do you know the way to this desired place?

Pliable contented to go with Christian.

CHR. I am directed by a man, whose name is Evangelist, to speed me to a little gate that is before us, where we shall receive instruction about the way.

PLI. Come, then, good neighbour, let us be going.

Then they went both together.

Obstinate goes railing back.

OBST. And I will go back to my place, said Obstinate; I will be no companion of such misled, fantastical fellows.

Talk between Christian and Pliable.

Now I saw in my dream, that when Obstinate was gone back, Christian and Pliable went talking over the plain ; and thus they began their discourse :

CHR. Come, Neighbour Pliable, how do you do? I am glad you are persuaded to go along with me. Had even Obstinate himself but felt what I have felt of the powers and terrors of what is yet unseen, he would not thus lightly have given us the back.

PLI. Come, Neighbour Christian, since there is none but us two here, tell me now further, what the things are, and how to be enjoyed, whither we are going?

God's things unspeakable.

CHR. I can better conceive of them with my mind than speak of them with my tongue: but yet, since you are desirous to know, I will read of them in my book.

PLI. And do you think that the words of your book are certainly true?

CHR. Yes, verily; for it was made by Him that cannot lie.   Tit. i. 2.

PLI. Well said: what things are they?

CHR. There is an endless kingdom to be inhabited, Isa. xlv. 17. and everlasting life to be given us, that we may John x. 27, 28, 29. inhabit that kingdom for ever.

PLI. Well said; and what else?

CHR. There are crowns of glory to be given us, 2 Tim. iv. 8. and garments that will make us shine like the sun Rev. iii. 4. Matt. xiii. 43. in the firmament of heaven.

PLI. This is excellent; and what else?

CHR. There shall be no more crying, nor sorrow; Isa. xxv. 8. for He that is owner of the place will wipe all tears Rev. vii. 16, 17. Chap. xxi. 4. from our eyes.

PLI. And what company shall we have there?

CHR. There we shall be with seraphims and Isa. vi. 2. cherubims, creatures that will dazzle your eyes to look on them.   There also you shall meet with thousands and ten thousands that have gone before 1 Thess. iv. 16, 17. us to that place; none of them are hurtful, but Rev. v. 11. loving and holy; every one walking in the sight of God, and standing in His presence with acceptance for ever.   In a word, there we shall see the elders Rev. iv. 4. with their golden crowns; there we shall see the Chap. xiv. 1-5. holy virgins with their golden harps; there we shall see men that by the world were cut in pieces, burnt John xii. 25. in flames, eaten of beasts, drowned in the seas, for the love that they bare to the Lord of the place,

Cor. v. 2, 3, 5. all well, and clothed with immortality as with a garment.

PLI. The hearing of this is enough to ravish one's heart. But are these things to be enjoyed? How shall we get to be sharers thereof?

Isa. lv. 1, 2.
John vii. 37.
Chap. vi. 37.
Rev. xxi. 6.
Chap. xxii. 17. CHR. The Lord, the Governor of that country, hath recorded that in this book; the substance of which is, If we be truly willing to have it, he will bestow it upon us freely.

PLI. Well, my good companion, glad am I to hear of these things. Come on, let us mend our pace.

CHR. I cannot go so fast as I would, by reason of this burden that is upon my back.

Now I saw in my dream, that just as they had ended this talk, they drew near to a very miry The Slough of Despond. slough, that was in the midst of the plain; and they being heedless, did both fall suddenly into the bog. The name of the slough was Despond. Here therefore they wallowed for a time, being grievously bedaubed with the dirt; and Christian, because of the burden that was on his back, began to sink in the mire.

PLI. Then said Pliable, Ah, Neighbour Christian, where are you now?

CHR. Truly, said Christian, I do not know.

PLI. At that Pliable began to be offended, and angrily said to his fellow, Is this the happiness you have told me all this while of? If we have such ill speed at our first setting out, what may we expect It is not enough to be pliable. betwixt this and our journey's end? May I get out again with my life, you shall possess the brave country alone for me. And with that he gave a desperate struggle or two, and got out of the mire on that side of the slough which was next to his own house. So away he went, and Christian saw him no more.

Wherefore Christian was left to tumble in the Slough of Despond alone : but still he endeavoured to struggle to that side of the slough that was still further from his own house, and next to the Wicket-gate ; the which he did, but could not get out, because of the burden that was upon his back. But I beheld in my dream that a man came to him, whose name was Help, and asked him what he did there. *Christian, in trouble, seeks still to get farther from his own house.*

CHR. Sir, said Christian, I was bid go this way by a man called Evangelist, who directed me also to yonder gate, that I might escape the wrath to come ; and as I was going thither, I fell in here.

HELP. But why did you not look for the steps ? *The promises.*

CHR. Fear followed me so hard that I fled the next way, and fell in.

HELP. Then, said he, give me thy hand ! So he gave him his hand, and he drew him out, and set him upon sound ground, and bid him go on his way. *Help lifts him out. Ps. xl. 2.*

Then I stepped to him that plucked him out, and said, Sir, wherefore (since over this place is the way from the City of Destruction to yonder gate) is it that this plat is not mended, that poor travellers might go thither with more security ? And he said unto me, This miry slough is such a place as cannot be mended ; it is the descent whither the scum and filth that attends conviction for sin doth continually *What makes the Slough of Despond.*

run, and therefore it is called the Slough of Despond ; for still as the sinner is awakened about his lost condition, there ariseth in his soul many fears, and doubts, and discouraging apprehensions, which all of them get together, and settle in this place. And this is the reason of the badness of this ground.

Isa. xxxv. 3, 4. It is not the pleasure of the King that this place should remain so bad. His labourers also have, by the direction of His Majesty's surveyors, been for above this sixteen hundred years employed about this patch of ground, if perhaps it might have been mended : yea, and to my knowledge, said he, here hath been swallowed up at least twenty thousand cart-loads, yea, millions of wholesome instructions, that have at all seasons been brought from all places of the King's dominions (and they that can tell say they are the best materials to make good ground of the place), if so be it might have been mended ; but it is the Slough of Despond still, and so will be, when they have done what they can.

The promises of forgiveness and acceptance to life by faith in Christ. True, there are, by the direction of the Lawgiver, certain good and substantial steps, placed even through the very midst of this slough ; but at such time as this place doth much spue out its filth, as it doth against change of weather, these steps are hardly seen ; or if they be, men, through the dizziness of their heads, step besides ; and then they are bemired to purpose, notwithstanding the steps be there ; but the ground is good, when they are once

1 Sam. xii. 23. got in at the gate.

Pliable got home Now I saw in my dream, that by this time Pliable was got home to his house again. So his neigh-

bours came to visit him ; and some of them called
him wise man for coming back, and some called him
fool for hazarding himself with Christian: others,
again, did mock at his cowardliness ; saying, Surely,
since you began to venture, I would not have been
so base as to have given out for a few difficulties.
So Pliable sat sneaking among them.   But at last he
got more confidence, and then they all turned their
tails, and began to deride poor Christian behind his
back.   And thus much concerning Pliable.

and is visited
of his
neighbours.

His enter-
tainment by
them at his
return.

Now as Christian was walking solitarily by himself, he espied one afar off come crossing over the
field to meet him ; and their hap was to meet just
as they were crossing the way of each other.   The
gentleman's name that met him was Mr. Worldly-
Wiseman : he dwelt in the town of Carnal-Policy,
a very great town, and also hard by from whence
Christian came.   This man then meeting with
Christian, and having some inkling of him,—for
Christian's setting forth from the City of Destruction was much noised abroad, not only in the
town where he dwelt, but also it began to be the
town-talk in some other places,—Mr. Worldly-
Wiseman therefore, having some guess of him, by
beholding his laborious going, by observing his
sighs and groans, and the like, began thus to enter
into some talk with Christian.

Mr. Worldly-
Wiseman
meets with
Christian.

WORLD. How now, good fellow, whither away
after this burdened manner ?

CHR. A burdened manner indeed, as ever I
think poor creature had.   And whereas you ask
me, Whither away ? I tell you, sir, I am going

Talk betwixt
Mr. Worldly-
Wiseman and
Christian.

to yonder Wicket-gate before me; for there, as I am informed, I shall be put into a way to be rid of my heavy burden.

WORLD. Hast thou a wife and children?

CHR. Yes, but I am so laden with this burden that I cannot take that pleasure in them as formerly: methinks I am as if I had none.

1 Cor. vii. 29.

WORLD. Wilt thou hearken to me if I give thee counsel?

CHR. If it be good, I will; for I stand in need of good counsel.

Mr. Worldly-Wiseman's counsel to Christian.

WORLD. I would advise thee, then, that thou with all speed get thyself rid of thy burden; for thou wilt never be settled in thy mind till then; nor canst thou enjoy the benefits of the blessing which God hath bestowed upon thee till then.

CHR. That is that which I seek for, even to be rid of this heavy burden; but get it off myself I cannot, nor is there a man in our country that can take it off my shoulders; therefore am I going this way, as I told you, that I may be rid of my burden.

WORLD. Who bid thee go this way to be rid of thy burden?

CHR. A man that appeared to me to be a very great and honourable person; his name, as I remember, is Evangelist.

Mr. Worldly-Wiseman condemned Evangelist's counsel.

WORLD. I beshrew him for his counsel: there is not a more dangerous and troublesome way in the world than is that into which he hath directed thee; and that thou shalt find, if thou wilt be ruled by his counsel. Thou has met with something (as I perceive) already; for I see the dirt of the Slough of Despond is upon thee; but that slough is the beginning of the sorrows that do attend those that go on in that way. Hear me, I am older than thou! thou art like to meet with, in the way which thou goest, wearisomeness, pain-fulness, hunger, perils, nakedness, sword, lions, dragons, darkness, and, in a word, death, and what not? These things are certainly true, having been confirmed by many testimonies. And why should a man so carelessly cast away himself, by giving heed to a stranger?

CHR. Why, sir, this burden upon my back is more terrible to me than are all these things which you have mentioned; nay, methinks I care not what I meet with in the way, so be I can also meet with deliverance from my burden.

The frame of the heart of young Christians.

WORLD. How camest thou by thy burden at first?

CHR. By reading this book in my hand.

WORLD. I thought so; and it is happened unto thee as to other weak men, who, meddling with things too high for them, do suddenly fall into thy distractions; which distractions do not only unman men (as thine I perceive has done thee), but they run them upon desperate ventures, to obtain they know not what.

Worldly-Wiseman does not like that men should be serious in reading the Bible.

CHR. I know what I would obtain; it is ease for my heavy burden.

WORLD. But why wilt thou seek for ease this way, seeing so many dangers attend it? Especially since (hadst thou but patience to hear me) I could

direct thee to the obtaining of what thou desirest,
without the dangers that thou in this way wilt
run thyself into; yea, and the remedy is at hand.
Besides, I will add, that instead of these dangers,
thou shalt meet with much safety, friendship, and
content.

Whether
Mr. Worldly
prefers
Morality
before the
Strait Gate.

CHR. Pray, sir, open this secret to me.

WORLD. Why, in yonder village (the village is
named Morality) there dwells a gentleman, whose
name is Legality, a very judicious man, and a man
of a very good name, that has skill to help men
off with such burdens as thine are, from their
shoulders: yea, to my knowledge he hath done
a great deal of good this way; ay, and besides,
he hath skill to cure those that are somewhat
crazed in their wits with their burdens. To him,
as I said, thou mayest go, and be helped presently.
His house is not quite a mile from this place,
and if he should not be at home himself, he hath
a pretty young man to his son, whose name is
Civility, that can do it (to speak on) as well as
the old gentleman himself; there, I say, thou
mayest be eased of thy burden; and if thou art
not minded to go back to thy former habitation,
as indeed I would not wish thee, thou mayest send
for thy wife and children to thee to this village,
where there are houses now stand empty, one of
which thou mayest have at reasonable rates; provision is there also cheap and good; and that
which will make thy life the more happy is, to be
sure there thou shalt live by honest neighbours, in
credit and good fashion.

Now was Christian somewhat at a stand, but presently he concluded : If this be true which this gentleman hath said, my wisest course is to take his advice : and with that he thus further spoke :

Christian snared by Mr. Worldly-Wiseman's words.

CHR. Sir, which is my way to this honest man's house ?

WORLD. Do you see yonder high hill ?

Mount Sinai.

CHR. Yes, very well.

WORLD. By that hill you must go, and the first house you come at is his.

So Christian turned out of his way to go to Mr. Legality's house for help ; but behold, when he was got now hard by the hill, it seemed so high, and also that side of it that was next the wayside did hang so much over, that Christian was afraid to venture further, lest the hill should fall on his head ; wherefore there he stood still, and he wot not what to do. Also his burden, now, seemed heavier to him than while he was in his way. There came also flashes of fire out of the hill, that made Christian afraid that he should be burned. Here therefore he sweat, and did quake for fear. And now he began to be sorry that he had taken Mr. Worldly-Wiseman's counsel. And with that he saw Evangelist coming to meet him ; at the sight also of whom he began to blush for shame. So Evangelist drew nearer and nearer ; and coming up to him, he looked upon him with a severe and dreadful countenance, and thus began to reason with Christian :

Christian afraid that Mount Sinai would fall on his head.

Exod. xix. 18. Ver. xvi.

Heb. xii. 21.

Evangelist findeth Christian under Mount Sinai, and looketh severely upon him.

Evangelist reasons afresh with Christian.

EVAN. What doest thou here, Christian ? said he: at which words Christian knew not what to answer : wherefore at present he stood speechless before him. Then said Evangelist further, Art not thou the man that I found crying without the walls of the City of Destruction ?

CHR. Yes, dear sir, I am the man.

EVAN. Did not I direct thee the way to the little Wicket-gate ?

CHR. Yes, dear sir, said Christian.

EVAN. How is it then that thou art so quickly turned aside ? for thou art now out of the way.

CHR. I met with a gentleman so soon as I had got over the Slough of Despond, who persuaded me that I might, in the village before me, find a man that could take off my burden.

EVAN. What was he ?

CHR. He looked like a gentleman, and talked much to me, and got me at last to yield ; so I came hither : but when I beheld this hill, and how it hangs over the way, I suddenly made a stand, lest it should fall on my head.

EVAN. What said that gentleman to you ?

CHR. Why, he asked me whither I was going; and I told him.

EVAN. And what said he then?

CHR. He asked me if I had a family ; and I told him. But, said I, I am so loaden with the burden that is on my back that I cannot take pleasure in them as formerly.

EVAN. And what said he then ?

CHR. He bid me with speed get rid of my burden ; and I told him 'twas ease that I sought. And said I, I am therefore going to yonder gate, to receive further direction how I may get to the place of deliverance. So he said that he would show me a better way, and short, not so attended with difficulties as the way, sir, that you set me; which way, said he, will direct you to a gentleman's house that hath skill to take off these burdens. So I believed him, and turned out of that way into this, if haply I might be soon eased of my burden. But when I came to this place, and beheld things as they are, I stopped for fear (as I said) of danger : but I now know not what to do.

EVAN. Then, said Evangelist, stand still a little, that I may show thee the words of God. So he stood trembling. Then said Evangelist, 'See that ye refuse not him that speaketh ; for if they escaped not who refused him that spake on earth, much more shall not we escape, if we turn away from him that speaketh from heaven.' He said moreover, 'Now the just shall live by faith ; but if any man draws back, my soul shall have no pleasure in him.' He also did thus apply them : Thou art the man that art running into this misery, thou hast begun to reject the counsel of the Most High, and to draw back thy foot from the way of peace, even almost to the hazarding of thy perdition.

Then Christian fell down at his foot as dead, crying, Woe is me, for I am undone! At the sight of which, Evangelist caught him by the right hand, saying, All manner of sin and blasphemies shall be forgiven unto men. Be not faithless, but believing. Then did Christian again a little revive, and stood up trembling, as at first, before Evangelist.

Heb. xii. 25.

Evangelist convinces Christian of his error.
Chap. x. 38.

Matt. xii. 31.
Mark iii. 28.

Then Evangelist proceeded, saying, Give more earnest heed to the things that I shall tell thee of.

Mr. Worldly-Wiseman described by Evangelist.

1 John iv. 5.

Gal. vi. 12.

Evangelist discovers the deceit of Mr. Worldly-Wiseman.

Luke xiii. 24.

Matt. vii. 13, 14.

I will now show thee who it was that deluded thee, and who it was also to whom he sent thee. The man that met thee is one Worldly-Wiseman, and rightly is he so called : partly, because he favoureth only the doctrine of this world (therefore he always goes to the town of Morality to church) ; and partly, because he loveth that doctrine best, for it saveth him from the Cross. And because he is of this carnal temper, therefore he seeketh to pervert my ways, though right. Now there are three things in this man's counsel that thou must utterly abhor :

1. His turning thee out of the way.

2. His labouring to render the Cross odious to thee.

3. And his setting thy feet in that way that leadeth unto the administration of death.[1]

First, Thou must abhor his turning thee out of the way ; yea, and thine own consenting thereto : because this is to reject the counsel of God for the sake of the counsel of a Worldly-Wiseman. The Lord says, 'Strive to enter in at the strait gate,' the gate to which I sent thee ; for, ' strait is the gate that leadeth unto life, and few there be that find it.' From this little Wicket-gate, and from the way thereto, hath this wicked man turned

[1] When Christians unto carnal men give ear,
Out of their way they go, and pay for 't dear ;
For Master Worldly-Wiseman can but show
A saint the way to bondage and to woe.

thee, to the bringing of thee almost to destruction ; hate therefore his turning thee out of the way, and abhor thyself for hearkening to him.

Secondly, Thou must abhor his labouring to render the Cross odious unto thee : for thou art to prefer it ' before the treasures in Egypt.' Besides, the King of Glory hath told thee, that ' he that will save his life shall lose it ' : and ' he that comes after him, and hates not his father, and mother, and wife, and children, and brethren, and sisters, yea, and his own life also, he cannot be my disciple.' I say therefore, for a man to labour to persuade thee, that that shall be thy death, without which the truth hath said thou canst not have eternal life ; This doctrine thou must abhor.

Heb. xi. 25, 26.
Mark viii. 35.
John xii. 25.
Matt. x. 39.
Luke xiv. 26.

Thirdly, Thou must hate his setting of thy feet in the way that leadeth to the ministration of death. And for this thou must consider to whom he sent thee, and also how unable that person was to deliver thee from thy burden.

He to whom thou wast sent for ease being by name Legality, is the son of the bond-woman which now is, and is in bondage with her children ; and is, in a mystery, this Mount Sinai, which thou hast feared will fall on thy head. Now if she with her children are in bondage, how canst thou expect by them to be made free ? This Legality therefore is not able to set thee free from thy burden. No man was as yet ever rid of his burden by him, no, nor ever is like to be ; ye cannot be justified by the works of the law ; for by the deeds of the law no man living can be rid of his burden ; there-

The bond-woman.
Gal. iv. 21-27.

fore, Mr. Worldly-Wiseman is an alien, and Mr. Legality a cheat; and for his son Civility, notwithstanding his simpering looks, he is but a hypocrite, and cannot help thee. Believe me, there is nothing in all this noise, that thou hast heard of these sottish men, but a design to beguile thee of thy salvation, by turning thee from the way in which I had set thee. After this Evangelist called aloud to the heavens for confirmation of what he had said; and with that there came words and fire out of the mountain under which poor Christian stood, that made the hair of his flesh stand up. The words were thus pronounced, 'As many as are of the works of the law are under the curse; for it is written, Cursed is every one that continueth not in all things which are written in the book of the law to do them.'

Gal. iii. 10.

Now Christian looked for nothing but death, and began to cry out lamentably, even cursing the time in which he met with Mr. Worldly-Wiseman, still calling himself a thousand fools for hearkening to his counsel: he also was greatly ashamed to think that this gentleman's arguments, flowing only from the flesh, should have that prevalency with him, to forsake the right way. This done, he applied himself again to Evangelist in words and sense as follows:

Christian inquired if he may yet be happy.

CHR. Sir, what think you? is there hopes? may I now go back and go up to the Wicket-gate? Shall I not be abandoned for this, and sent back from thence ashamed? I am sorry I have hearkened to this man's counsel: but may my sin be forgiven?

Evan. Then said Evangelist to him, Thy sin is very great, for by it thou hast committed two evils: thou hast forsaken the way that is good, to tread in forbidden paths; yet will the man at the gate re- *Evangelist* ceive thee, for he has good will for men; only, said *comforts him.* he, take heed that thou turn not aside again, ' lest Ps. ii. *last.* thou perish from the way, when his wrath is kindled but a little.' Then did Christian address himself to go back; and Evangelist, after he had kissed him, gave him one smile, and bid him God-speed. So he went on with haste, neither spake he to any man by the way; nor if any asked him, would he vouchsafe them an answer. He went like one that was all the while treading on forbidden ground, and could by no means think himself safe, till again he was got into the way which he left to follow Mr. Worldly-Wiseman's counsel. So in process of time Christian got up to the gate. Now over the gate there was written, ' Knock and it shall be opened Matt. vii. unto you.' He knocked therefore, more than once or twice,[1] saying :

> May I now enter here?   Will he within
> Open to sorry me, though I have been
> An undeserving rebel?   Then shall I
> Not fail to sing his lasting praise on high.

At last there came a grave person to the gate named Good-will, who asked who was there? and whence he came? and what he would have?

---

[1] He that will enter in must first without
Stand knocking at the gate, nor need he doubt
That is a knocker but to enter in ;
For God can love him, and forgive his sin.

CHR. Here is a poor burdened sinner. I come from the city of Destruction, but am going to Mount Zion, that I may be delivered from the wrath to come. I would therefore, sir, since I am informed that by this gate is the way thither, know if you are willing to let me in.

GOOD-WILL. I am willing with all my heart, said he; and with that he opened the gate.

So when Christian was stepping in, the other gave him a pull. Then said Christian, What means that? The other told him, A little distance from this gate, there is erected a strong castle, of which Beelzebub is the captain; from thence both he and them that are with him shoot arrows at those that come up to this gate, if haply they may die before they can enter in. Then said Christian, I rejoice and tremble. So when he was got in, the man of the gate asked him who directed him thither.

CHR. Evangelist bid me come hither and knock (as I did); and he said that you, sir, would tell me what I must do.

GOOD-WILL. An open door is set before thee, and no man can shut it.

CHR. Now I begin to reap the benefits of my hazards.

GOOD-WILL. But how is it that you came alone?

CHR. Because none of my neighbours saw their danger, as I saw mine.

GOOD-WILL. Did any of them know of your coming?

CHR. Yes, my wife and children saw me at the first, and called after me to turn again; also some

The gate will be opened to broken-hearted sinners.

Satan envies those that enter the Strait Gate.

Christian entered the gate with joy and trembling.

Talk between Good-will and Christian.

of my neighbours stood crying, and calling after me to return; but I put my fingers in my ears, and so came on my way.

GOOD-WILL. But did none of them follow you, to persuade you to go back?

CHR. Yes, both Obstinate and Pliable; but when they saw that they could not prevail, Obstinate went railing back, but Pliable came with me a little way.

GOOD-WILL. But why did he not come through?

CHR. We indeed came both together, until we came at the Slough of Despond, into the which we also suddenly fell. And then was my neighbour Pliable discouraged, and would not adventure further. Wherefore getting out again on that side next to his own house, he told me I should possess the brave country alone for him; so he went his way, and I came mine: he after Obstinate, and I to this gate.

A man may have company when he sets out for heaven, and yet go thither alone.

GOOD-WILL. Then said Good-will, Alas! poor man, is the celestial glory of so small esteem with him that he counteth it not worth running the hazards of a few difficulties to obtain it?

CHR. Truly, said Christian, I have said the truth of Pliable; and if I should also say all the truth of myself, it will appear there is no betterment 'twixt him and myself. 'Tis true, he went back to his own house, but I also turned aside to go in the way of death, being persuaded thereto by the carnal arguments of one Mr. Worldly-Wiseman.

Christian accuseth himself before the man at the gate.

GOOD-WILL. Oh, did he light upon you? What! he would have had you a sought for ease at the hands of Mr. Legality. They are both of them a very cheat; but did you take his counsel?

CHR. Yes, as far as I durst: I went to find out Mr. Legality, until I thought that the mountain that stands by his house would have fallen upon my head; wherefore there I was forced to stop.

GOOD-WILL. That mountain has been the death of many, and will be the death of many more; 'tis well you escaped being by it dashed in pieces.

CHR. Why, truly I do not know what had become of me there, had not Evangelist happily met me again, as I was musing in the midst of my dumps: but 'twas God's mercy that he came to me again, for else I had never come hither. But now I am come, such a one as I am, more fit indeed for death by that mountain than thus to stand talking with my Lord; but oh, what a favour is this to me, that yet I am admitted entrance here!

Christian comforted again. John vi. 37.

GOOD-WILL. We make no objections against any, notwithstanding all that they have done before they come hither, they in no wise are cast out; and therefore, good Christian, come a little way with me, and I will teach thee about the way thou must go. Look before thee; dost thou see this narrow way? THAT is the way thou must go; it was cast up by the patriarchs, prophets, Christ, and his apostles; and it is as straight as a rule can make it: This is the way thou must go.

Christian directed yet on his way.

CHR. But, said Christian, are there no turnings nor windings by which a stranger may lose the way?

Christian afraid of losing his way.

GOOD-WILL. Yes, there are many ways BUTT

down upon this, and they are crooked, and wide;
but thus thou mayest distinguish the right from
the wrong, The right only being straight and
narrow. Matt. vii. 14.

Then I saw in my dream that Christian asked him
further if he could not help him off with his burden
that was upon his back; for as yet he had not got
rid thereof, nor could he by any means get it off
without help.

Christian weary of his burden.

He told him, As to thy burden, be content to
bear it, until thou comest to the place of deliverance; for there it will fall from thy back itself.

Then Christian began to gird up his loins, and to
address himself to his journey. So the other told
him that by that he was gone some distance from
the gate, he would come at the house of the Interpreter, at whose door he should knock, and he would
show him excellent things. Then Christian took
his leave of his friend, and he again bid him God-
speed.

There is no deliverance from the guilt and burden of sin but by the death and blood of Christ.

Then he went on till he came at the house of
the Interpreter, where he knocked over and over;
at last one came to the door, and asked Who was
there?

Christian comes to the house of the Interpreter.

CHR. Sir, here is a traveller, who was bid by an
acquaintance of the good-man of this house to call
here for my profit; I would therefore speak with the
master of the house. So he called for the master
of the house, who after a little time came to
Christian, and asked him what he would have.

CHR. Sir, said Christian, I am a man that am
come from the city of Destruction, and am going to

the Mount Zion; and I was told by the man, that stands at the gate, at the head of this way, that if I called here, you would show me excellent things, such as would be a help to me in my journey.

He is entertained.

INTER. Then said the Interpreter, Come in, I will show thee that which will be profitable to thee. So he commanded his man to light the candle, and bid Christian follow him : so he had him into a private room, and bid his man open a door; the which when he had done, Christian saw the picture of a very grave person hang up against the wall; and this was the fashion of it: It had eyes lifted up to heaven, the best of books in his hand, the law of truth was written upon his lips, the world was behind his back; it stood as if it pleaded with men, and a crown of gold did hang over its head.

Illumination.

Christian sees a brave picture. The fashion of the picture.

CHR. Then said Christian, What means this?

INTER. The man whose picture this is, is one of a thousand; he can beget children, travail in birth with children, and nurse them himself when they are born. And whereas thou seest him with his eyes lift up to heaven, the best of books in his hand, and the law of truth writ on his lips, it is to show thee that his work is to know and unfold dark things to sinners; even as also thou seest him stand as if he pleaded with men; And whereas thou seest the world as cast behind him, and that a crown hangs over his head, that is to show thee that slighting and despising the things that are present, for the love that he hath to his Master's service, he is sure in the world that comes next to have glory for his reward. Now, said the Interpreter, I have showed thee this

1 Cor. iv. 15. Gal. iv. 19. 2 Thess. ii. 7.

The meaning of the picture.

picture first, because the man whose picture this Why he showed him the picture first. is, is the only man whom the Lord of the place whither thou art going hath authorised to be thy guide in all difficult places thou mayest meet with in the way; wherefore take good heed to what I have showed thee, and bear well in thy mind what thou hast seen, lest in thy journey thou meet with some that pretend to lead thee right, but their way goes down to death.

Then he took him by the hand, and led him into a very large parlour that was full of dust, because never swept; the which, after he had reviewed a little while, the Interpreter called for a man to sweep. Now when he began to sweep, the dust began so abundantly to fly about, that Christian had almost therewith been choked. Then said the Interpreter to a damsel that stood by, Bring hither the water, and sprinkle the room; the which when she had done, it was swept and cleansed with pleasure.

CHR. Then said Christian, What means this?

INTER. The Interpreter answered, This parlour is the heart of a man that was never sanctified by the sweet grace of the gospel: the dust is his original sin, and inward corruptions that have defiled the whole man. He that began to sweep at first, is the Law; but she that brought water, and did sprinkle it, is the Gospel. Now, whereas thou sawest that so soon as the first began to sweep, the dust did so fly about that the room by him could not be cleansed, but that thou wast almost choked therewith; this is to show thee, that the Law, instead of cleansing the

Rom. vii. 6.
1 Cor. xv. 56.
Rom. v. 20.
heart (by its working) from sin, doth revive, put strength into, and increase it in the soul, even as it doth discover and forbid it, but doth not give power to subdue.

Again, as thou sawest the damsel sprinkle the room with water, upon which it was cleansed with pleasure; that is to show thee that when the gospel comes in the sweet and precious influences thereof to the heart, then I say, even as thou sawest the John xv. 3.
Eph. v. 26.
Acts xv. 9.
Rom. xvi. 25, 26.
John xv. 13. damsel lay the dust by sprinkling the floor with water, so is sin vanquished and subdued, and the soul made clean, through the faith of it, and consequently fit for the King of Glory to inhabit.

I saw moreover in my dream, that the Interpreter took him by the hand, and had him into a little room, where sat two little children, each one in his chair. The name of the eldest was Passion, and the He showed him Passion and Patience. name of the other Patience. Passion seemed to be much discontent; but Patience was very quiet. Then Christian asked, What is the reason of the discontent of Passion? The Interpreter answered, Passion will have all now. Patience is for waiting. The governor of them would have him stay for his best things till the beginning of the next year; but he will have all now, but Patience is willing to wait.

Passion has his desire. Then I saw that one came to Passion, and brought him a bag of treasure, and poured it down at his feet, the which he took up and rejoiced therein; and withal, laughed Patience to scorn. But I beheld And quickly lavishes all away. but a while, and he had lavished all away, and had nothing left him but rags.

CHR. Then said Christian to the Interpreter, Expound this matter more fully to me.

INTER. So he said, These two lads are figures: The matter expounded. Passion, of the men of *this* world; and Patience, of the men of *that* which is to come; for as here thou seest, Passion will have all now, this year, that is to say, in this world; so are the men of this world: they must have all their good things now, they cannot stay till next year, that is, until the next world, for their portion of good.   That proverb, ' A The worldly man for a bird in the hand. bird in the hand is worth two in the bush,' is of more authority with them than are all the divine testimonies of the good of the world to come.   But as thou sawest that he had quickly lavished all away, and had presently left him nothing but rags, so will it be with all such men at the end of this world.

CHR. Then said Christian, Now I see that Patience has the best wisdom, and that upon many Patience had the best wisdom. accounts.   (1) Because he stays for the best things; (2) and also because he will have the glory of his, when the other hath nothing but rags.

INTER. Nay, you may add another, to wit, the glory of the next world will never wear out; but these are suddenly gone.   Therefore Passion had not so much reason to laugh at Patience, because he had his good things first, as Patience will have to laugh at Passion, because he had his best things last; for first must give place to last, because last Things that are first must give place; but things that are last are lasting. must have his time to come: but last gives place to nothing, for there is not another to succeed.   He therefore that hath his portion first, must needs have a time to spend it; but he that has his portion last, must have it lastingly.   Therefore it is said of

Luke xvi.
Dives had
his good
things first.

Dives, 'In thy lifetime thou receivedst thy good things, and likewise Lazarus evil things; but now he is comforted, and thou art tormented.'

CHR. Then I perceive 'tis not best to covet things that are now, but to wait for things to come.

2 Cor. iv. 18.
The first
things are
but temporal.

INTER. You say truth: 'For the things that are seen are temporal; but the things that are not seen are eternal.' But though this be so, yet since things present, and our fleshly appetite, are such near neighbours one to another; and again, because things to come, and carnal sense, are such strangers one to another: therefore it is that the first of these so suddenly fall into amity, and that distance is so continued between the second.

Then I saw in my dream, that the Interpreter took Christian by the hand and led him into a place where was a fire burning against a wall, and one standing by it always, casting much water upon it, to quench it; yet did the fire burn higher and hotter.

Then said Christian, What means this?

The Interpreter answered, This fire is the work of grace that is wrought in the heart; he that casts water upon it, to extinguish and put it out, is the devil; but if that thou seest the fire notwithstanding burn higher and hotter, thou shalt also see the reason of that. So he had him about to the backside of the wall, where he saw a man with a vessel of oil in his hand, of the which he did also continually cast, but secretly, into the fire.

Then said Christian, What means this? The Interpreter answered, This is Christ, who con-

tinually, with the oil of His grace, maintains the
work already begun in the heart: by the means of
which, notwithstanding what the devil can do, the
souls of His people prove gracious still.   And in ² Cor. xii. 9.
that thou sawest that the man stood behind the
wall to maintain the fire, this is to teach thee that
it is hard for the tempted to see how this work of
grace is maintained in the soul.

I saw also that the Interpreter took him again by
the hand, and led him into a pleasant place, where
was builded a stately palace, beautiful to behold; at
the sight of which Christian was greatly delighted.
He saw also upon the top thereof certain persons
walking, who were clothed all in gold.   Then said
Christian, May we go in thither?   Then the Interpreter took him, and led him up toward the door of
the palace; and behold, at the door stood a great
company of men, as desirous to go in, but durst
not.   There also sat a man, at a little distance from
the door, at a table-side, with a book, and his ink-
horn before him, to take the name of him that
should enter therein.   He saw also, that in the
doorway stood many men in armour to keep it,
being resolved to do to the men that enter
what hurt and mischief they could.   Now was
Christian somewhat in amaze.   At last, when every
man started back for fear of the armed men,
Christian saw a man of a very stout countenance The valiant
come up to the man that sat there to write, saying, man.
Set down my name, sir: the which when he had
done, he saw the man draw his sword, and put a
helmet upon his head, and rush toward the door

upon the armed men, who laid upon him with deadly force; but the man, not at all discouraged, fell to cutting and hacking most fiercely. So, after he had received and given many wounds to those that attempted to keep him out, he cut his way through them all, and pressed forward into the palace; at which there was a pleasant voice heard from those that were within, even of those that walked upon the top of the palace, saying—

Acts xiv. 22.

> Come in, come in;
> Eternal glory thou shalt win.

So he went in, and was clothed with such garments as they   Then Christian smiled, and said, I think verily I know the meaning of this.

Now, said Christian, let me go hence. Nay, stay, said the Interpreter, till I have showed thee a little more, and after that thou shalt go on thy way. So he took him by the hand again, and led him into a very dark room, where there sat a man in an iron cage.

Despair like an iron cage.

Now the man, to look on, seemed very sad. He sat with his eyes looking down to the ground, his hands folded together; and he sighed as if he would break his heart. Then said Christian, What means this? At which the Interpreter bid him talk with the man.

CHR. Then said Christian to the man, What art thou? The man answered, I am what I was not once.

CHR. What wast thou once?

Luke viii. 13.

MAN. The man said, I was once a fair and flourishing professor, both in mine own eyes, and also in the eyes of others: I once was, as I thought, fair for the Celestial City, and had then even joy at the thoughts that I should get thither.

CHR. Well, but what art thou now?

MAN. I am now a man of despair, and am shut up in it, as in this iron cage. I cannot get out; Oh, *now* I cannot.

CHR. But how camest thou in this condition?

MAN. I left off to watch and be sober; I laid the reins upon the neck of my lusts; I sinned against the light of the Word, and the goodness of God; I have grieved the Spirit, and he is gone; I tempted the devil, and he is come to me; I have provoked God to anger, and he has left me; I have so hardened my heart, that I cannot repent.

Then said Christian to the Interpreter, But is there no hopes for such a man as this? Ask him, said the Interpreter.

CHR. Then said Christian, Is there no hope but you must be kept in this iron cage of despair?

MAN. No, none at all.

CHR. Why? the Son of the Blessed is very pitiful.

MAN. I have crucified him to myself afresh, I have despised his person, I have despised his righteousness, I have counted his blood an unholy thing; I have done despite to the Spirit of Grace: therefore I have shut myself out of all the promises, and there now remains to me nothing but threatenings, dreadful threatenings, fearful threatenings of certain judgment and fiery indignation, which shall devour me as an adversary. Heb. vi. 6. Luke xix. 14. Heb. x. 28, 29.

CHR. For what did you bring yourself into this condition ?

MAN. For the lusts, pleasures, and profits of this world; in the enjoyment of which I did then promise myself much delight; but now every one of those things also bite me, and gnaw me like a burning worm.

CHR. But canst thou not now repent and turn ?

MAN. God hath denied me repentance : his Word gives me no encouragement to believe; yea, himself hath shut me up in this iron cage; nor can all the men in the world let me out. O eternity ! eternity ! how shall I grapple with the misery that I must meet with in eternity !

INTER. Then said the Interpreter to Christian, Let this man's misery be remembered by thee, and be an everlasting caution to thee.

CHR. Well, said Christian, this is fearful; God help me to watch and be sober, and to pray that I may shun the cause of this man's misery. Sir, is it not time for me to go on my way now ?

INTER. Tarry till I shall show thee one thing more, and then thou shalt go on thy way.

So he took Christian by the hand again, and led him into a chamber, where there was one rising out of bed; and as he put on his raiment, he shook and trembled. Then said Christian, Why doth this man thus tremble ? The Interpreter then bid him tell to Christian the reason of his so doing. So he began and said, This night, as I was in my sleep, I dreamed, and behold the heavens grew exceeding black; also it thundered and lightened in most fearful wise, that it put me into an agony. So I looked up in my dream, and saw the clouds racked at an unusual rate, upon which I heard a great sound of a trumpet, and saw also a Man sit upon a cloud, attended with the thousands of heaven: they were all in flaming fire; also the heavens were on a burning flame. I heard then a voice saying, 'Arise, ye dead, and come to judgment'; and with that the rocks rent, the graves opened, and the dead that were therein came forth. Some of them were exceeding glad, and looked upward; and some sought to hide themselves under the mountains. Then I saw the Man that sat upon the cloud open the book, and bid the world draw near. Yet there was, by reason of a fierce flame that issued out and came from before him, a convenient distance betwixt him and them, as betwixt the judge and the prisoners at the bar. I heard it also proclaimed to them that attended on the Man that sat on the cloud, 'Gather together the tares, the chaff, and stubble, and cast them into the burning lake.' And with that, the bottomless pit opened, just whereabout I stood; out of the mouth of which there came in an abundant manner smoke, and coals of fire, with hideous noises. It was also said to the same persons, 'Gather my wheat into the garner.' And with that I saw many catched up and carried away into the clouds, but I was left behind. I also sought to hide myself, but I could not, for the Man that sat upon the cloud still kept his eye upon me: my sins also came into my mind; and my conscience

1 Cor. xv.
1 Thess. iv.
Jude xv.
2 Thess. i. 8.
John v. 28.
Rev. xx. 11-14.
Isa. xxvi. 21.
Mic. vii. 16, 17.

Ps. xcv. 1-3.
Dan. x. 7.

Mal. iii. 2, 3.
Dan. vii. 9, 10.

Matt. iii. 12.
Chap. xiii. 30.
Mal. iv. 1.

Luke iii. 17.

1 Thess. iv. 16, 17.

Rom. ii. 14, 15.

did accuse me on every side. Upon this I awaked from my sleep.

CHR. But what was it that made you so afraid of this sight?

MAN. Why, I thought that the day of judgment was come, and that I was not ready for it; but this frighted me most, that the angels gathered up several, and left me behind; also the pit of hell opened her mouth just where I stood: my conscience, too, afflicted me; and as I thought, the Judge had always his eye upon me, showing indignation in his countenance.

Then said the Interpreter to Christian, Hast thou considered all these things?

CHR. Yes, and they put me in hope and fear.

INTER. Well, keep all things so in thy mind, that they may be as a goad in thy sides, to prick thee forward in the way thou must go. Then Christian began to gird up his loins, and to address himself to his journey. Then said the Interpreter, The Comforter be always with thee, good Christian, to guide thee in the way that leads to the city. So Christian went on his way, saying—

> Here I have seen things rare, and profitable;
> Things pleasant, dreadful, things to make me stable
> In what I have begun to take in hand;
> Then let me think on them, and understand
> Wherefore they showed me was, and let me be
> Thankful, O good Interpreter, to thee.

Now I saw in my dream that the highway up which Christian was to go, was fenced on either side with a wall, and that wall is called Salvation. Up

Isa. xxvi. 1.

this way therefore did burdened Christian run, but not without great difficulty, because of the load on his back.

He ran thus till he came at a place somewhat ascending, and upon that place stood a Cross, and a little below in the bottom, a Sepulchre. So I saw in my dream, that just as Christian came up with the Cross his burden loosed from off his shoulders, and fell from off his back; and began to tumble, and so continued to do, till it came to the mouth of the Sepulchre, where it fell in, and I saw it no more.[1]

Then was Christian glad and lightsome, and said with a merry heart, He hath given me rest by his sorrow, and life by his death. Then he stood still a while, to look and wonder; for it was very surprising to him, that the sight of the Cross should thus ease him of his burden. He looked therefore, and looked again, even till the springs that were in his head sent the waters down his cheeks. Now as he stood looking and weeping, behold three Shining Ones came to him and saluted him with ' Peace be to thee.' So the first said to him, ' Thy sins be forgiven ': the second stripped him of his rags, and clothed him with change of raiment; the third also set a mark in his forehead, and gave him a roll with a seal upon it, which he bid him look on as he ran, and that he should give it in at the Celestial Gate.

When God releases us of our guilt and burden, we are as those that leap for joy.

Zech. xii. 10.

Mark ii. 5.

Zech. iii. 4.

Eph. i. 13.

---

[1] Who's this? the Pilgrim. How! 'tis very true,
Old things are pass'd away, all's become new.
Strange! he's another man, upon my word,
They be fine feathers that make a fine bird.

So they went their way.   Then Christian gave three leaps for joy, and went on singing—

A Christian can sing though alone, when God doth give him the joy of his heart.

Thus far did I come loaden with my sin ;
Nor could aught ease the grief that I was in,
Till I came hither : What a place is this !
Must here be the beginning of my bliss ?
Must here the burden fall from off my back ?
Must here the strings that bound it to me, crack ?
Blest Cross ! blest Sepulchre ! blest rather be
The Man that there was put to shame for me.

I saw then in my dream that he went on thus, even until he came at a bottom, where he saw, a little out of the way, three men fast asleep, with fetters upon their heels.   The name of the one was Simple, another Sloth, and the third Presumption.

Simple, Sloth, and Presumption.

Christian then seeing them lie in this case, went to them, if peradventure he might awake them, and cried, You are like them that sleep on the top of a mast, for the Dead Sea is under you, a gulf that hath no bottom.   Awake therefore and come away ; be willing also, and I will help you off with your irons.   He also told them, If he that goeth about like a roaring lion comes by, you will certainly became a prey to his teeth.   With that they looked upon him, and began to reply in this sort : Simple said, I see no danger ; Sloth said, Yet a little more sleep ; and Presumption said, Every vat must stand upon his own bottom.   And so they lay down to sleep again, and Christian went on his way.

1 Pet. v. 8.

There is no persuasion will do, if God openeth not the eyes.

Yet was he troubled to think that men in that danger should so little esteem the kindness of him that so freely offered to help them, both by awakening of them, counselling of them, and proffering to help them off with their irons.   And as he was troubled thereabout, he espied two men come tumbling over the wall, on the left hand of the narrow way ; and they made up apace to him.   The name of the one was Formalist, and the name of the other Hypocrisy.   So, as I said, they drew up unto him, who thus entered with him into discourse :

CHR. Gentlemen, whence came you, and whither do you go ? *Christian talked with them.*

FORM. and HYP. We were born in the land of Vainglory, and are going for praise to Mount Zion.

CHR. Why came you not in at the gate which standeth at the beginning of the way ?   Know you not that it is written, that ' He that cometh not in by the door, but climbeth up some other way, the same is a thief and a robber ' ? *John x. 1.*

FORM. and HYP. They said, that to go to the gate for entrance was by all their countrymen counted too far about ; and that therefore their usual way was to make a short cut of it, and to climb over the wall, as they had done.

CHR. But will it not be counted a trespass against the Lord of the city whither we are bound, thus to violate his revealed will ?

FORM. and HYP. They told him, that as for that, he needed not to trouble his head thereabout ; for what they did they had custom for ; and could produce, if need were, testimony that would witness it for more than a thousand years. *They that come into the way, but not by the door, think that they can say something in vindication of their own practice.*

CHR. But, said Christian, will your practice stand a trial at law ?

FORM. and HYP They told him, that custom, it being of so long a standing as above a thousand years, would doubtless now be admitted as a thing legal, by an impartial judge ; and besides, said they, if we get into the way, what's matter which way we get in ? if we are in, we are in ; thou art but in the way, who, as we perceive, came in at the gate ; and we are also in the way, that came tumbling over the wall ; wherein now is thy condition better than ours ?

CHR. I walk by the *rule* of my Master ; you walk by the rude working of your fancies. You are counted thieves already, by the Lord of the way ; therefore I doubt you will not be found true men at the end of the way. You come in by yourselves, without his direction ; and shall go out by yourselves, without his mercy.

To this they made him but little answer ; only they bid him look to himself. Then I saw that they went on every man in his way, without much conference one with another ; save that these two men told Christian, that as to laws and ordinances, they doubted not but they should as conscientiously do them as he. Therefore, said they, We see not wherein thou differest from us but by the coat that is on thy back which was, as we trow, given thee by some of thy neighbours, to hide the shame of thy nakedness.

Gal. ii. 16.

CHR. By laws and ordinances you will not be saved, since you came not in by the door. And as for this coat that is on my back, it was given me by the Lord of the place whither I go ; and

that, as you say, to cover my nakedness with. And
I take it as a token of his kindness to me, for I
had nothing but rags before. And besides, thus
I comfort myself as I go : Surely, think I, when
I come to the gate of the City, the Lord thereof
will know me for good, since I have his coat on
my back ; a coat that he gave me freely in the
day that he stripped me of my rags.   I have,
moreover, a mark in my forehead, of which perhaps
you have taken no notice, which one of my Lord's
most intimate associates fixed there in the day that
my burden fell off my shoulders.   I will tell you,
moreover, that I had then given me a roll sealed
to comfort me by reading, as I go on in the way ;
I was also bid to give it in at the Celestial Gate,
in token of my certain going in after it : all which
things I doubt you want, and want them because
you came not in at the gate.

To these things they gave him no answer ; only
they looked upon each other and laughed.   Then
I saw that they went on all, save that Christian
kept before, who had no more talk but with himself, and that sometimes sighingly, and sometimes
comfortably ; also he would be often reading in the
roll that one of the Shining Ones gave him, by
which he was refreshed.

I beheld then that they all went on till they
came to the foot of the Hill Difficulty, at the
bottom of which was a spring.   There was also
in the same place two other ways besides that
which came straight from the gate ; one turned to
the left hand, and the other to the right, at the

Christian
has got his
Lord's coat
on his back,
and is com-
forted there-
with.

He is
comforted
also with his
mark and
his roll.

Christian has
talk with
himself.

He comes
to the Hill
Difficulty.

bottom of the hill; but the narrow way lay right up the hill (and the name of the going up the side of the hill is called Difficulty). Christian now went to the spring, and drank thereof to refresh himself, and then began to go up the hill, saying—

Isa. xlix. 10.

> The hill, though high, I covet to ascend,
> The difficulty will not me offend ;
> For I perceive the way to life lies here :
> Come, pluck up, heart ; let's neither faint nor fear :
> Better, though difficult, the right way to go,
> Than wrong, though easy, where the end is woe.

The other two also came to the foot of the hill. But when they saw that the hill was steep and high, and that there were two other ways to go ; and supposing also that these two ways might meet again with that up which Christian went, on the other side of the hill ; therefore they were resolved to go in those ways. (Now the name of one of those ways was Danger, and the name of the other Destruction.) So the one took the way which is called Danger, which led him into a great wood ; and the other took directly up the way to Destruction, which led him into a wide field full of dark mountains, where he stumbled and fell, and rose no more.[1]

The danger of turning out of the way.

I looked then after Christian, to see him go up the hill, where I perceived he fell from running to going, and from going to clambering upon his

---

[1] Shall they who wrong begin yet rightly end ?
Shall they at all have safety for their friend ?
No, no ; in headstrong manner they set out,
And headlong will they fall at last no doubt.

hands and his knees, because of the steepness of the place. Now about the midway to the top of the hill was a pleasant arbour, made by the Lord of the hill for the refreshing of weary travellers. Thither therefore Christian got, where also he sat down to rest him. Then he pulled his roll out of his bosom, and read therein to his comfort ; he also now began afresh to take a review of the coat or garment that was given him as he stood by the Cross. Thus pleasing himself a while, he at last fell into a slumber, and thence into a fast sleep, which detained him in that place until it was almost night ; and in his sleep his roll fell out of his hand. Now as he was sleeping, there came one to him, and awaked him, saying ' Go to the ant, thou sluggard ; consider her ways, and be wise.' And with that Christian suddenly started up, and sped him on his way, and went apace till he came to the top of the hill.

A ward of grace.

He that sleeps is a loser.

Prov. vi. 6.

Now when he was got up to the top of the hill, there came two men running against him amain ; the name of the one was Timorous, and the other Mistrust ; to whom Christian said, Sirs, what's the matter you run the wrong way ? Timorous answered that they were going to the City of Zion, and had got up that difficult place ; but, said he, the farther we go, the more danger we meet with ; wherefore we turned, and are going back again.

Christian meets with Mistrust and Timorous.

Yes, said Mistrust, for just before us lie a couple of lions in the way, whether sleeping or waking we know not ; and we could not think, if we came within reach, but they would presently pull us in pieces.

CHR. Then said Christian, You make me afraid, but whither shall I fly to be safe? If I go back to mine own country, that is prepared for fire and brimstone, and I shall certainly perish there. If I can get to the Celestial City, I am sure to be in safety there. I must venture: to go back is nothing but death; to go forward is fear of death, and life everlasting beyond it. I will yet go forward. So Mistrust and Timorous ran down the hill, and Christian went on his way. But thinking again of what he heard from the men, he felt in his bosom for his roll, that he might read therein and be comforted; but he felt and found it not. Then was Christian in great distress, and knew not what to do; for he wanted that which used to relieve him, and that which should have been his pass into the Celestial City. Here therefore he began to be much perplexed, and knew not what to do. At last he bethought himself that he had slept in the arbour that is on the side of the hill: and falling down upon his knees, he asked God forgiveness for that his foolish fact, and then went back to look for his roll. But all the way he went back, who can sufficiently set forth the sorrow of Christian's heart? Sometimes he sighed, sometimes he wept, and oftentimes he chid himself for being so foolish to fall asleep in that place which was erected only for a little refreshment for his weariness. Thus therefore he went back, carefully looking on this side and on that, all the way as he

Christian shakes off fear.

Christian missed his roll wherein he used to take comfort.

He is perplexed for his roll.

went, if haply he might find his roll, that had been his comfort so many times in his journey. He went thus till he came again within sight of the arbour where he sat and slept; but that sight renewed his sorrow the more, by bringing again, Christian even afresh, his evil of sleeping into his mind. bewails his foolish Thus therefore he now went on bewailing his sleeping. sinful sleep, saying O wretched man that I am, Rev. ii. 5.
1 Thess. v. 7, 8. that I should sleep in the daytime! that I should sleep in the midst of difficulty! that I should so indulge the flesh as to use that rest for ease to my flesh, which the Lord of the hill hath erected only for the relief of the spirits of pilgrims! How many steps have I took in vain! (Thus it happened to Israel for their sin, they were sent back again by the way of the Red Sea), and I am made to tread those steps with sorrow, which I might have trod with delight, had it not been for this sinful sleep. How far might I have been on my way by this time! I am made to tread those steps thrice over, which I needed not to have trod but once; yea, now also I am like to be benighted, for the day is almost spent. O that I had not slept!

Now by this time he was come to the arbour again, where for a while he sat down and wept; but at last (as Christian would have it), looking sorrowfully down under the settle, there he espied Christian his roll; the which he with trembling and haste findeth his
roll where catched up, and put it into his bosom. But who he lost it. can tell how joyful this man was, when he had gotten his roll again! for this roll was the assurance of his life and acceptance at the desired haven. Therefore he laid it up in his bosom, gave thanks to God for directing his eye to the place where it lay, and with joy and tears betook himself again to his journey. But oh, how nimbly now did he go up the rest of the hill! Yet before he got up, the sun went down upon Christian; and this made him again recall the vanity of his sleeping to his remembrance, and thus he again began to condole with himself: O thou sinful sleep; how for thy sake am I like to be benighted in my journey! I must walk without the sun, darkness must cover the path of my feet, and I must hear the noise of doleful creatures, because of my sinful sleep. Now also he remembered the story that Mistrust and Timorous told him of, how they were frighted with the sight of the lions. Then said Christian to himself again, These beasts range in the night for their prey; and if they should meet with me in the dark, how should I shift them? how should I escape being by them torn in pieces? Thus he went on his way, but while he was thus bewailing his unhappy miscarriage, he lift up his eyes, and behold there was a very stately palace before him, the name of which was Beautiful; and it stood just by the highway-side.

So I saw in my dream that he made haste and went forward, that if possible he might get lodging there; now before he had gone far, he entered into a very narrow passage, which was about a furlong off of the porter's lodge; and looking very narrowly before him as he went, he espied two lions in the way. Now, thought he, I see the dangers that Mistrust and Timorous were driven back by. (The lions were chained, but he saw not the chains.) Then he was afraid, and thought also himself to go back after them, for he thought nothing but death was before him : but the porter at the lodge, <small>Mark xiii. 34.</small> whose name is Watchful, perceiving that Christian made a halt, as if he would go back, cried unto him, saying, Is thy strength so small ? Fear not the lions, for they are chained, and are placed there for trial of faith where it is, and for discovery of those that have none : keep in the midst of the path, and no hurt shall come unto thee.[1]

Then I saw that he went on, trembling for fear of the lions, but taking good heed to the directions of the porter ; he heard them roar, but they did him no harm. Then he clapt his hands, and went on till he came and stood before the gate where the porter was. Then said Christian to the porter, Sir, what house is this ? and may I lodge here to-night ? The porter answered, This house was built by the Lord of the hill, and he built it for the relief and security of pilgrims. The porter also asked whence he was, and whither he was going ?

CHR. I am come from the City of Destruction, and am going to Mount Zion ; but because the sun is now set, I desire, if I may, to lodge here to-night.

POR. What is your name ?

---

[1] Difficulty's behind, fear is before,
Though he's got on the hill, the lions roar ;
A Christian man is never long at ease,
When one fright's gone, another doth him seize.

CHR. My name is now Christian, but my name at the first was Graceless; I came of the race of Japheth, whom God will persuade to dwell in the tents of Shem.

Gen. ix. 27.

POR. But how doth it happen you come so late? The sun is set.

CHR. I had been here sooner, but that, wretched man that I am! I slept in the arbour that stands on the hill-side; nay, I had notwithstanding that been here much sooner, but that in my sleep I lost my evidence, and came without it to the brow of the hill; and then feeling for it, and finding it not, I was forced with sorrow of heart to go back to the place where I slept my sleep, where I found it, and now I am come.

POR. Well, I will call out one of the virgins of this place, who will, if she likes your talk, bring you in to the rest of the family, according to the rules of the house. So Watchful the porter rang a bell, at the sound of which came out at the door of the house a grave and beautiful damsel, named Discretion, and asked why she was called.

The porter answered, This man is in a journey from the City of Destruction to Mount Zion, but being weary and benighted, he asked me if he might lodge here to-night; so I told him I would call for thee, who, after discourse had with him, mayest do as seemeth thee good, even according to the law of the house.

Then she asked him whence he was, and whither he was going; and he told her. She asked him also, how he got into the way; and he told her. Then she asked him what he had seen and met with in the way; and he told her.   And last she asked his name; so he said, It is Christian, and I have so much the more a desire to lodge here to-night, because, by what I perceive, this place was built by the Lord of the hill, for the relief and security of pilgrims.   So she smiled, but the water stood in her eyes; and after a little pause, she said, I will call forth two or three more of the family.   So she ran to the door, and called out Prudence, Piety, and Charity, who, after a little more discourse with him, had him in to the family; and many of them, meeting him at the threshold of the house, said, Come in, thou blessed of the Lord; this house was built by the Lord of the hill, on purpose to entertain such pilgrims in.   Then he bowed his head, and followed them into the house.   So when he was come in and set down, they gave him something to drink, and consented together that, until supper was ready, some of them should have some particular discourse with Christian, for the best improvement of time; and they appointed Piety, and Prudence, and Charity to discourse with him: and thus they began:

PIETY. Come, good Christian, since we have been so loving to you, to receive you into our house this night, let us, if perhaps we may better ourselves thereby, talk with you of all things that have happened to you in your pilgrimage. *Piety discourses him.*

CHR. With a very good will, and I am glad that you are so well disposed.

PIETY. What moved you at first to betake yourself to a pilgrim's life?

How Christian was driven out of his own country.

CHR. I was driven out of my native country by a dreadful sound that was in mine ears: to wit, that unavoidable destruction did attend me, if I abode in that place where I was.

PIETY. But how did it happen that you came out of your country this way?

CHR. It was as God would have it; for when I was under the fears of destruction, I did not know whither to go; but by chance there came a man, even to me (as I was trembling and weeping), whose name is Evangelist, and he directed me to the Wicket-gate, which else I should never have found, and so set me into the way that hath led me directly to this house.

How he got into the way to Zion.

PIETY. But did you not come by the house of the Interpreter?

CHR. Yes, and did see such things there, the remembrance of which will stick by me as long as I live; specially three things: to wit, How Christ, in despite of Satan, maintains his work of grace in the heart; how the man had sinned himself quite out of hopes of God's mercy; and also the dream of him that thought in his sleep the day of judgment was come.

A rehearsal of what he saw in the way.

PIETY. Why, did you hear him tell his dream?

CHR. Yes, and a dreadful one it was. I thought it made my heart ache as he was telling of it; but yet I am glad I heard it.

PIETY. Was that all you saw at the house of the Interpreter?

CHR. No; he took me and had me where he showed me a stately palace, and how the people were clad in gold that were in it; and how there came a venturous man and cut his way through the armed men that stood in the door to keep him out, and how he was bid to come in, and win eternal glory. Methought those things did ravish my heart; I would have stayed at that good man's house a twelvemonth, but that I knew I had further to go.

PIETY. And what saw you else in the way?

CHR. Saw! Why, I went but a little further, and I saw One, as I thought in my mind, hang bleeding upon the tree; and the very sight of him made my burden fall off my back (for I groaned under a very heavy burden), but then, it fell down from off me. 'Twas a strange thing to me, for I never saw such a thing before; yea, and while I stood looking up (for then I could not forbear looking), three Shining Ones came to me. One of them testified that my sins were forgiven me; another stripped me of my rags, and gave me this broidered coat which you see; and the third set the mark which you see, in my forehead, and gave me this sealed roll (and with that he plucked it out of his bosom).

PIETY. But you saw more than this, did you not?

CHR. The things that I have told you were the best; yet some other matters I saw, as, namely, I saw three men, Simple, Sloth, and Presumption, lie asleep a little out of the way as I came, with irons upon their heels; but do you think I could awake them! I also saw Formality and Hypocrisy come tumbling over the wall, to go, as they pretended, to Zion, but they were quickly lost; even as I myself did tell them, but they would not believe : but, above all, I found it hard work to get up this hill, and as hard to come by the lions' mouth ; and truly if it had not been for the good man, the porter that stands at the gate, I do not know but that after all I might have gone back again ; but now I thank God I am here, and I thank you for receiving of me.

Then Prudence thought good to ask him a few questions, and desired his answer to them.

Prudence discourses him.

PRUD. Do you not think sometimes of the country from whence you came ?

Christian's thoughts of his native country.

Heb. xi. 15, 16.

CHR. Yes, but with much shame and detestation : Truly, if I had been mindful of that country from whence I came out, I might have had opportunity to have returned ; but now I desire a better country, that is, a heavenly.

PRUD. Do you not yet bear away with you some of the things that then you were conversant withal ?

Christian distasted with carnal cogitations.

Christian's choice. Rom. vii. 21.

CHR. Yes, but greatly against my will ; especially my inward and carnal cogitations, with which all my countrymen, as well as myself, were delighted ; but now all those things are my grief : and might I but choose mine own things, I would choose never to think of those things more ; but when I would be doing of that which is best, that which is worst is with me.

PRUD. Do you not find sometimes as if those things were vanquished, which at other times are your perplexity ?

Christian's golden hours.

CHR. Yes, but that is but seldom ; but they are to me golden hours in which such things happen to me.

PRUD. Can you remember by what means you find your annoyances at times, as if they were vanquished?

CHR. Yes, when I think what I saw at the Cross, that will do it; and when I look upon my broidered coat, that will do it; also when I look into the roll that I carry in my bosom, that will do it; and when my thoughts wax warm about whither I am going, that will do it.

How Christian gets power against his corruptions.

PRUD. And what is it that makes you so desirous to go to Mount Zion?

CHR. Why, there I hope to see him *alive*, that did hang *dead* on the Cross; and there I hope to be rid of all those things that to this day are in me an annoyance to me; there they say there is no death, and there I shall dwell with such company as I like best. For to tell you truth, I love him, because I was by him eased of my burden, and I am weary of my inward sickness; I would fain be where I shall die no more, and with the company that shall continually cry 'Holy, holy, holy.'

Why Christian would be at Mount Zion.

Isa. xxv. 8.
Rev. xxi. 4.

Then said Charity to Christian, Have you a family? Are you a married man?

Charity discourses him.

CHR. I have a wife and four small children.

CHAR. And why did you not bring them along with you?

CHR. Then Christian wept, and said, Oh how willingly would I have done it, but they were all of them utterly averse to my going on pilgrimage.

Christian's love to his wife and children.

CHAR. But you should have talked to them, and have endeavoured to have shown them the danger of being behind.

Gen. xix. 14.

CHR. So I did, and told them also what God had showed to me of the destruction of our city; but I seemed to them as one that mocked, and they believed me not.

CHAR. And did you pray to God that he would bless your counsel to them?

CHR. Yes, and that with much affection; for you must think that my wife and poor children were very dear unto me.

CHAR. But did you tell them of your own sorrow, and fear of destruction? for I suppose that destruction was visible enough to you?

Christian's fears of perishing might be read in his very countenance.

CHR. Yes, over, and over, and over. They might also see my fears in my countenance, in my tears, and also in my trembling under the apprehension of the judgment that did hang over our heads; but all was not sufficient to prevail with them to come with me.

CHAR. But what could they say for themselves why they came not?

The cause why his wife and children did not go with him.

CHR. Why, my wife was afraid of losing this world, and my children were given to the foolish delights of youth: so what by one thing, and what by another, they left me to wander in this manner alone.

CHAR. But did you not, with your vain life, damp all that you by words used by way of persuasion to bring them away with you?

CHR. Indeed I cannot commend my life; for I am conscious to myself of many failings therein: I know also that a man by his conversation may soon overthrow what by argument or persuasion he doth labour to fasten upon others for their good. Yet this I can say, I was very wary of giving them occasion, by any unseemly action, to make them averse to going on pilgrimage. Yea, for this very thing they would tell me I was too precise, and that I denied myself of things (for their sakes) in which they saw no evil. Nay, I think I may say, that, if what they saw in me did hinder them, it was my great tenderness in sinning against God, or of doing any wrong to my neighbour. *Christian's good conversation before his wife and children.*

CHAR. Indeed, Cain hated his brother, because his own works were evil, and his brother's righteous; and if thy wife and children have been offended with thee for this, they thereby show themselves to be implacable to good, and thou hast delivered thy soul from their blood. *1 John iii. 12. Christian clear of their blood if they perish. Ezek. iii. 19.*

Now I saw in my dream, that thus they sat talking together until supper was ready. So when they had made ready, they sat down to meat. Now the table was furnished with fat things, and with wine that was well refined; and all their talk at the table was about the Lord of the hill; as, namely, about what he had done, and wherefore he did what he did, and why he had builded that house: and, by what they said, I perceived that he had been a great warrior, and had fought with and slain him that had the power of death, but not without great danger to himself,—which made me love him the more. *What Christian had to his supper. Their talk at suppertime. Heb. ii. 14, 15.*

For, as they said, and as I believe (said Christian), he did it with the loss of much blood; but that which put glory of grace into all he did, was, that he did it out of pure love to his country. And besides, there were some of them of the household that said, they had seen and spoke with him since he did die on the Cross; and they have attested, that they had it from his own lips, that he is such a lover of poor pilgrims, that the like is not to be found from the east to the west.

They moreover gave an instance of what they affirmed, and that was, He had stripped himself of his glory that he might do this for the poor; and that they heard him say and affirm, That he would not dwell in the Mountain of Zion alone. They said moreover, That he had made many pilgrims princes, though by nature they were beggars born, and their original had been the dunghill.

Christ makes princes of beggars. 1 Sam. ii. 8. Ps. cxiii. 7.

Thus they discoursed together till late at night, and after they had committed themselves to their Lord for protection, they betook themselves to rest. The pilgrim they laid in a large upper chamber, whose window opened towards the sun rising: the name of the chamber was Peace; where he slept till break of day, and then he awoke and sang—

Christian's bedchamber.

> Where am I now ! Is this the love and care
> Of Jesus, for the men that pilgrims are !
> Thus to provide ! That I should be forgiven !
> And dwell already the next door to heaven !

So in the morning they all got up, and after some more discourse, they told him that he should not depart till they had showed him the rarities of that place. And first they had him into the study, where they showed him records of the greatest antiquity; in which, as I remember my dream,

Christian had into the study, and what he saw there.

they showed him first the pedigree of the Lord of the hill, that he was the son of the Ancient of Days, and came by an eternal generation. Here also was more fully recorded the acts that he had done, and the names of many hundreds that he had taken into his service; and how he had placed them in such habitations that could neither by length of days nor decays of nature be dissolved.

Then they read to him some of the worthy acts that some of his servants had done: as, how they had subdued kingdoms, wrought righteousness, obtained promises, stopped the mouths of lions, quenched the violence of fire, escaped the edge of the sword; out of weakness were made strong, waxed valiant in fight, and turned to flight the armies of the aliens. *Heb. xi. 33, 34.*

Then they read again in another part of the records of the house, where it was showed how willing their Lord was to receive into his favour any, even any, though they in time past had offered great affronts to his person and proceedings. Here also were several other histories of many other famous things, of all which Christian had a view. As of things both ancient and modern: together with prophecies and predictions of things that have their certain accomplishment, both to the dread and amazement of enemies, and the comfort and solace of pilgrims.

The next day they took him and had him into the armoury, where they showed him all manner of furniture, which their Lord had provided for pilgrims, as sword, shield, helmet, breastplate, all- *Christian had into the armoury.*

prayer, and shoes that would not wear out. And there was here enough of this to harness out as many men for the service of their Lord as there be stars in the heaven for multitude.

Christian is made to see ancient things.

They also showed him some of the engines with which some of his servants had done wonderful things. They showed him Moses' rod, the hammer and nail with which Jael slew Sisera, the pitchers, trumpets, and lamps too, with which Gideon put to flight the armies of Midian. Then they showed him the ox's goad wherewith Shamgar slew six hundred men. They showed him also the jaw-bone with which Samson did such mighty feats: they showed him moreover the sling and stone with which David slew Goliath of Gath; and the sword also with which their Lord will kill the man of sin, in the day that he shall rise up to the prey. They showed him besides many excellent things, with which Christian was much delighted. This done, they went to their rest again.

Then I saw in my dream, that on the morrow he got up to go forwards, but they desired him to stay till the next day also; and then, said they, we will,

Christian showed the Delectable Mountains.

if the day be clear, show you the Delectable Mountains, which, they said, would yet further add to his comfort, because they were nearer the desired haven than the place where at present he was: so he consented and stayed. When the morning was up, they had him to the top of the house, and bid him

Isa. xxxiii. 16, 17.

look south; so he did; and behold, at a great distance he saw a most pleasant mountainous country, beautified with woods, vineyards, fruits of all sorts, flowers also, with springs and fountains, very delectable to behold.   Then he asked the name of the country: they said it was Immanuel's Land; and it is as common, said they, as this hill is, to and for all the pilgrims.   And when thou comest there, from thence thou mayest see to the gate of the Celestial City, as the shepherds that live there will make appear.

Now he bethought himself of setting forward, and they were willing he should.   But first, said they, let us go into the armoury.   So they did; and when he came there, they harnessed him from head to foot, with what was of proof, lest perhaps he should meet with assaults in the way. He being therefore thus accoutred walketh out with his friends to the gate, and there he asked the porter if he saw any pilgrims pass by,[1] Then the porter answered, Yes.

Christian sets forward.

Christian sent away armed.

CHR. Pray did you know him? said he.

POR. I asked his name, and he told me it was Faithful.

CHR. Oh, said Christian, I know him; he is my townsman, my near neighbour, he comes from the place where I was born: how far do you think he may be before?

POR. He is got by this time below the hill.

CHR. Well, said Christian, good porter, the Lord be with thee, and add to all thy blessings much

How Christian and the porter greet at parting.

---

[1] Whilst Christian is among his godly friends,
    Their golden mouths make him sufficient 'mends
    For all his griefs ; and when they let him go,
    He's clad with northern steel from top to toe.

increase, for the kindness that thou hast showed
to me.

Then he began to go forward, but Discretion,
Piety, Charity, and Prudence would accompany
him down to the foot of the hill. So they went on
together, reiterating their former discourses till they
came to go down the hill. Then said Christian, As
it was difficult coming up, so (so far as I can see) it
is dangerous going down. Yes, said Prudence, so
it is; for it is a hard matter for a man to go down

The Valley of into the Valley of Humiliation, as thou art now,
Humiliation. and to catch no slip by the way; therefore, said
they, are we come out to accompany thee down the
hill. So he began to go down, but very warily, yet
he caught a slip or two.

Then I saw in my dream, that these good companions, when Christian was gone down to the
bottom of the hill, gave him a loaf of bread, a
bottle of wine, and a cluster of raisins; and then
he went on his way.

But now in this Valley of Humiliation poor
Christian was hard put to it, for he had gone but
a little way before he espied a foul fiend coming
over the field to meet him; his name is Apollyon.
Then did Christian begin to be afraid, and to cast
in his mind whether to go back, or to stand his

Christian ground. But he considered again, that he had no
no armour armour for his back, and therefore thought that to
for his back. turn the back to him, might give him greater

Christian's advantage with ease to pierce him with his darts;
resolution therefore he resolved to venture, and stand his
on the
approach of ground. For, thought he, had I no more in mine
Apollyon.

eye than the saving of my life, 'twould be the best way to stand.

So he went on, and Apollyon met him. Now the monster was hideous to behold: he was clothed with scales like a fish (and they are his pride); he had wings like a dragon, feet like a bear, and out of his belly came fire and smoke; and his mouth was as the mouth of a lion. When he was come up to Christian, he beheld him with a disdainful countenance, and thus began to question with him:

APOL. Whence come you? and whither are you bound?

CHR. I am come from the City of Destruction, which is the place of all evil, and am going to the City of Zion.

Discourse betwixt Christian and Apollyon.

APOL. By this I perceive thou art one of my subjects, for all that country is mine; and I am the prince and god of it. How is it then that thou hast run away from thy king? Were it not that I hope thou mayest do me more service, I would strike thee now at one blow to the ground.

CHR. I was born indeed in your dominions, but your service was hard, and your wages such as a man could not live on, 'for the wages of sin is death'; therefore when I was come to years, I did as other considerate persons do, look out, if perhaps I might mend myself.

Rom. vi. 23.

APOL. There is no prince that will thus lightly lose his subjects, neither will I as yet lose thee: but since thou complainest of thy service and wages, be content to go back; what our country will afford, I do here promise to give thee.

Apollyon's flattery.

CHR. But I have let myself to another, even to the King of princes, and how can I with fairness go back with thee?

Apollyon undervalues Christ's service.

APOL. Thou hast done in this, according to the proverb, changed a bad for a worse; but it is ordinary for those who have professed themselves his servants, after a while to give him the slip, and return again to me. Do thou so too, and all shall be well.

CHR. I have given him my faith, and sworn my allegiance to him; how then can I go back from this, and not be hanged as a traitor?

Apollyon pretends to be merciful.

APOL. Thou didst the same to me, and yet I am willing to pass by all, if now thou wilt yet turn again and go back.

CHR. What I promised thee was in my nonage; and besides, I count that the Prince under whose banner now I stand, is able to absolve me; yea, and to pardon also what I did as to my compliance with thee: and besides (O thou destroying Apollyon), to speak truth, I like his service, his wages, his servants, his government, his company, and country better than thine; and therefore leave off to persuade me further, I am his servant, and I will follow him.

Apollyon pleads the grievous ends of Christians, to dissuade Christian from persisting in his way.

APOL. Consider again when thou art in cold blood, what thou art like to meet with in the way that thou goest. Thou knowest that for the most part, his servants come to an ill end, because they are transgressors against me and my ways. How many of them have been put to shameful deaths! and besides, thou countest his service better than mine, whereas he never came yet from the place where he is, to deliver any that served him out of our hands; but as for me, how many times, as all the world very well knows, have I delivered, either by power or fraud, those that have faithfully served me, from him and his, though taken by them, and so I will deliver thee.

CHR. His forbearing at present to deliver them is on purpose to try their love, whether they will cleave to him to the end: and as for the ill end thou sayest they come to, that is most glorious in their account: For for present deliverance, they do not much expect it; for they stay for their glory, and then they shall have it, when their Prince comes in his, and the glory of the angels.

APOL. Thou hast already been unfaithful in thy service to him, and how dost thou think to receive wages of him?

CHR. Wherein, O Apollyon, have I been unfaithful to him?

APOL. Thou didst faint at first setting out, when thou wast almost choked in the Gulf of Despond; thou didst attempt wrong ways to be rid of thy burden, whereas thou shouldest have stayed till thy Prince had taken it off; thou didst sinfully sleep and lose thy choice thing; thou wast also almost persuaded to go back at the sight of the lions; and when thou talkest of thy journey, and of what thou hast heard and seen, thou art inwardly desirous of vainglory in all that thou sayest or doest.

Apollyon pleads Christian's infirmities against him.

CHR. All this is true, and much more, which thou hast left out; but the Prince whom I serve

and honour is merciful, and ready to forgive;
but besides, these infirmities possessed me in thy
country, for there I sucked them in, and I have
groaned under them, been sorry for them, and have
obtained pardon of my Prince.

APOL. Then Apollyon broke out into a grievous
rage, saying, I am an enemy to this Prince; I hate
his person, his laws, and people; I am come out on
purpose to withstand thee.

CHR. Apollyon, beware what you do, for I am in
the King's highway, the way of holiness, therefore
take heed to yourself.

APOL. Then Apollyon straddled quite over the
whole breadth of the way, and said, I am void of
fear in this matter, prepare thyself to die; for I
swear by my infernal den thou shalt go no further;
here will I spill thy soul.

And with that he threw a flaming dart at his
breast, but Christian had a shield in his hand, with
which he caught it, and so prevented the danger
of that.

Then did Christian draw, for he saw 'twas time
to bestir him; and Apollyon as fast made at him,
throwing darts as thick as hail; by the which, notwithstanding all that Christian could do to avoid it,
Apollyon wounded him in his head, his hand, and
foot.   This made Christian give a little back;
Apollyon, therefore, followed his work amain, and
Christian again took courage, and resisted as man-
fully as he could.   This sore combat lasted for
above half a day, even till Christian was almost
quite spent.   For you must know that Christian,

Apollyon in a rage falls upon Christian.

Christian wounded in his understanding, faith, and conversation.

by reason of his wounds, must needs grow weaker and weaker.

Then Apollyon, espying his opportunity, began to gather up close to Christian, and wrestling with him, gave him a dreadful fall; and with that Christian's sword flew out of his hand. Then said Apollyon, I am sure of thee now! and with that, he had almost pressed him to death, so that Christian began to despair of life. But as God would have it, while Apollyon was fetching of his last blow, thereby to make a full end of this good man, Christian nimbly reached out his hand for his sword, and caught it, saying, 'Rejoice not against me, O mine enemy! when I fall, I shall arise'; and with that gave him a deadly thrust, which made him give back, as one that had received his mortal wound. Christian perceiving that, made at him again, saying, 'Nay, in all these things we are more than conquerors.' And with that Apollyon spread forth his dragon's wings, and sped him away, that Christian saw him no more.[1]

In this combat no man can imagine, unless he had seen and heard as I did, what yelling, and hideous roaring Apollyon made all the time of the fight, he spake like a dragon; and on the other side, what sighs and groans burst from Christian's heart. I never saw him all the while give him so much as one pleasant look, till he perceived he had wounded

Apollyon casteth down to the ground Christian.

Micah vii. 8.

Christian's victory over Apollyon.

Rom. viii. 37.

James iv. 7.

A brief relation of the combat by the spectator.

---

[1] A more unequal match can hardly be:
Christian must fight an angel; but you see
The valiant man by handling sword and shield,
Doth make him, tho' a dragon, quit the field.

Apollyon with his two-edged sword; then indeed he did smile, and look upward; but 'twas the dreadfullest sight that ever I saw.

Christian gives God thanks for deliverance.

So when the battle was over, Christian said, I will here give thanks to him that hath delivered me out of the mouth of the lion; to him that did help me against Apollyon: and so he did, saying—

> Great Beelzebub, the captain of this fiend,
> Design'd my ruin; therefore to this end
> He sent him harness'd out, and he with rage
> That hellish was, did fiercely me engage:
> But blessed Michael helped me, and I,
> By dint of sword, did quickly make him fly;
> Therefore to him let me give lasting praise,
> And thank and bless his holy name always.

Then there came to him a hand, with some of the leaves of the tree of life, the which Christian took, and applied to the wounds that he had received in the battle, and was healed immediately. He also sat down in that place to eat bread, and to drink of the bottle that was given him a little

Christian goes on his journey with his sword drawn in his hand.

before; so being refreshed, he addressed himself to his journey, with his sword drawn in his hand, for he said, I know not but some other enemy may be at hand. But he met with no other affront from Apollyon, quite through this valley.

The Valley of the Shadow of Death.

Now at the end of this valley was another, called the Valley of the Shadow of Death, and Christian must needs go through it, because the way to the Celestial City lay through the midst of it. Now this valley is a very solitary place. The prophet

Jeremiah thus describes it: 'A wilderness, a land _{Jer. ii. 6.} of deserts and of pits, a land of drought, and of the shadow of death; a land that no man' (but a Christian) 'passeth through, and where no man dwelt.'

Now here Christian was worse put to it than in his fight with Apollyon, as by the sequel you shall see.

I saw then in my dream, that when Christian was got to the borders of the Shadow of Death, there met him two men, children of them that The children brought up an evil report of the good land, mak-of the spies go back. ing haste to go back; to whom Christian spake as Numb. xiii. follows:

CHR. Whither are you going?

MEN. They said, Back, back; and we would have you to do so too, if either life or peace is prized by you.

CHR. Why, what's the matter? said Christian.

MEN. Matter! said they; we were going that way as you are going, and went as far as we durst; and indeed we were almost past coming back, for had we gone a little further, we had not been here to bring the news to thee.

CHR. But what have you met with? said Christian.

MEN. Why, we were almost in the Valley of Ps. xliv. 19. the Shadow of Death, but that by good hap we Ps. cvii. 10. looked before us, and saw the danger before we came to it.

CHR. But what have you seen? said Christian.

MEN. Seen! why the valley itself, which is as

dark as pitch; we also saw there the hobgoblins, satyrs, and dragons of the pit: we heard also in that valley a continual howling and yelling, as of a people under unutterable misery, who there sat bound in affliction and irons; and over that valley hung the discouraging clouds of confusion, death also doth always spread his wings over it: in a word, it is every whit dreadful, being utterly without order.

Job iii. 5.
Chap. x. 22.

CHR. Then said Christian, I perceive not yet, by what you have said, but that this is my way to the desired haven.

Jer. ii. 6.

MEN. Be it thy way, we will not choose it for ours. So they parted, and Christian went on his way, but still with his sword drawn in his hand, for fear lest he should be assaulted.

I saw then in my dream, so far as this valley reached, there was on the right hand a very deep ditch; that ditch is it into which the blind have led the blind in all ages, and have both there miserably perished. Again, behold on the left hand, there was a very dangerous quag, into which, if even a good man falls, he can find no bottom for his foot to stand on. Into that quag King David once did fall, and had no doubt therein been smothered, had not He that is able plucked him out.

Ps. lxix. 14.

The pathway was here also exceeding narrow, and therefore good Christian was the more put to it; for when he sought in the dark to shun the ditch on the one hand, he was ready to tip over into the mire on the other; also when he sought to escape the mire, without great carefulness he would be ready to fall into the ditch. Thus he went on, and I heard him here sigh bitterly; for, besides the dangers mentioned above, the pathway was here so dark, that ofttimes when he lift up his foot to set forward, he knew not where, or upon what he should set it next.[1]

About the midst of this valley, I perceived the mouth of hell to be, and it stood also hard by the wayside. Now thought Christian, what shall I do? And ever and anon the flame and smoke would come out in such abundance, with sparks and hideous noises (things that cared not for Christian's sword, as did Apollyon before), that he was forced to put up his sword, and betake himself to another weapon, called All-prayer; so he cried in my hearing, 'O Lord, I beseech thee, deliver my soul.' Eph. vi. 18. Thus he went on a great while, yet still the flames Ps. cxvi. 4. would be reaching towards him: also he heard doleful voices, and rushings to and fro, so that sometimes he thought he should be torn in pieces, or trodden down like mire in the streets. This frightful sight was seen, and these dreadful noises were heard by him for several miles together: and coming to a place where he thought he heard a company of fiends coming forward to meet him, he stopped, and began to muse what he had best to do. Sometimes he had half a thought to go

---

[1] Poor man! where art thou now? thy day is night.
　Good man, be not cast down, thou yet art right:
　Thy way to heaven lies by the gates of hell;
　Cheer up, hold out, with thee it shall go well.

back.   Then again he thought he might be half way through the valley; he remembered also how he had already vanquished many a danger, and that the danger of going back might be much more than for to go forward; so he resolved to go on.   Yet the fiends seemed to come nearer and nearer; but when they were come even almost at him, he cried out with a most vehement voice, ' I will walk in the strength of the Lord God '; so they gave back, and came no further.

One thing I would not let slip, I took notice that now poor Christian was so confounded, that he did not know his own voice.   And thus I perceived it: Just when he was come over against the mouth of the burning pit, one of the wicked ones got behind him, and stepped up softly to him, and whisperingly suggested many grievous blasphemies to him, which he verily thought had proceeded from his own mind. This put Christian more to it than anything that he met with before, even to think that he should now blaspheme him that he loved so much before; yet if he could have helped it, he would not have done it; but he had not the discretion neither to stop his ears, nor to know from whence those blasphemies came.

When Christian had travelled in this disconsolate condition some considerable time, he thought he heard the voice of a man, as going before him, saying, ' Though I walk through the Valley of the Shadow of Death, I will fear none ill, for thou art with me.'

Then was he glad, and that for these reasons:

Christian put to a stand, but for a while.

Christian made believe that he spake blasphemies, when 'twas Satan that suggested them into his mind.

Ps. xxiii. 4.

First, Because he gathered from thence that some who feared God were in this valley as well as himself.

Secondly, For that he perceived God was with them, though in that dark and dismal state; and why not, thought he, with me, though by reason of the impediment that attends this place, I cannot perceive it? *Job ix. 10.*

Thirdly, For that he hoped (could he overtake them) to have company by and by. So he went on, and called to him that was before, but he knew not what to answer, for that he also thought himself to be alone. And by and by the day broke; then said Christian, 'He hath turned the shadow of death into the morning.' *Christian glad at break of day. Amos v. 8.*

Now morning being come, he looked back, not out of desire to return, but to see, by the light of the day, what hazards he had gone through in the dark. So he saw more perfectly the ditch that was on the one hand, and the quag that was on the other; also how narrow the way was which led betwixt them both: also now he saw the hobgoblins, and satyrs, and dragons of the pit, but all afar off; for after break of day they came not nigh; yet they were discovered to him, according to that which is written, 'He discovereth deep things out of darkness, and bringeth out to light the shadow of death.' *Job xii. 22.*

Now was Christian much affected with his deliverance from all the dangers of his solitary way; which dangers, though he feared them more before, yet he saw them more clearly now, because the light of the day made them conspicuous to him.   And about this time the sun was rising, and this was another mercy to Christian; for you must note, that though the first part of the Valley of the Shadow of Death was dangerous, yet this second part which he was yet to go, was, if possible, far more dangerous: for from the place where he now stood, even to the end of the valley, the way was all along set so full of snares, traps, gins, and nets here, and so full of pits, pitfalls, deep holes, and shelvings down there, that had it now been dark, as it was when he came the first part of the way, had he had a thousand souls, they had in reason been cast away; but as I said, just now the sun was rising.   Then said he, 'His candle shineth on my head, and by his light I go through darkness.'

The second part of this valley very dangerous.

Job xxix. 3.

In this light therefore, he came to the end of the valley.   Now I saw in my dream, that at the end of this valley lay blood, bones, ashes, and mangled bodies of men, even of pilgrims that had gone this way formerly: And while I was musing what should be the reason, I espied a little before me a cave, where two giants, Pope and Pagan, dwelt in old time, by whose power and tyranny the men whose bones, blood, ashes, etc., lay there, were cruelly put to death.   But by this place Christian went without much danger, whereat I somewhat wondered; but I have learnt since, that Pagan has been dead many a day; and as for the other, though he be yet alive, he is, by reason of age, and also of the many shrewd brushes that he met with in his younger days, grown so crazy, and stiff in his joints, that he can now do little more than sit in his cave's mouth, grinning at pilgrims as they go by, and biting his nails, because he cannot come at them.

So I saw that Christian went on his way, yet at the sight of the old man that sat in the mouth of the cave, he could not tell what to think, specially because he spake to him, though he could not go after him, saying, You will never mend, till more of you be burned: but he held his peace, and set a good face on 't; and so went by and catched no hurt.   Then sang Christian:

> O world of wonders! (I can say no less)
> That I should be preserved in that distress
> That I have met with here!   O blessed be
> That hand that from it hath deliver'd me!
> Dangers in darkness, devils, hell, and sin
> Did compass me, while I this vale was in:
> Yea, snares, and pits, and traps, and nets did lie
> My path about, that worthless silly I
> Might have been catch'd, entangled, and cast down:
> But since I live, let JESUS wear the crown.

Now as Christian went on his way, he came to a little ascent, which was cast up on purpose that pilgrims might see before them.   Up there therefore Christian went, and looking forward, he saw Faithful before him, upon his journey.   Then said Christian aloud, Ho, ho, so-ho; stay, and I will be your companion.   At that Faithful looked behind him; to whom Christian cried again, Stay, stay, till I come up to you: but Faithful answered, No, I am upon my life, and the avenger of blood is behind me.   At this Christian was somewhat moved, and

Christian
overtakes
Faithful.

putting to all his strength, he quickly got up with Faithful, and did also overrun him, so the last was first. Then did Christian vaingloriously smile, because he had gotten the start of his brother; but not taking good heed to his feet, he suddenly stumbled and fell, and could not rise again, until Faithful came up to help him.

Christian's
fall makes
Faithful
and he go
lovingly
together.

Then I saw in my dream, they went very lovingly on together, and had sweet discourse of all things that had happened to them in their pilgrimage; and thus Christian began:

CHR. My honoured and well-beloved brother Faithful, I am glad that I have overtaken you; and that God has so tempered our spirits, that we can walk as companions in this so pleasant a path.

FAITH. I had thought, dear friend, to have had your company quite from our town, but you did get the start of me; wherefore I was forced to come thus much of the way alone.

CHR. How long did you stay in the City of Destruction before you set out after me on your pilgrimage?

Their talk
about the
country from
whence they
came.

FAITH. Till I could stay no longer; for there was great talk presently after you were gone out, that our city would in short time with fire from heaven be burned down to the ground.

CHR. What! did your neighbours talk so?

FAITH. Yes, 'twas for a while in everybody's mouth.

CHR. What, and did no more of them but you come out to escape the danger?

FAITH. Though there was, as I said, a great talk

thereabout yet I do not think they did firmly believe it. For in the heat of the discourse, I heard some of them deridingly speak of you, and of your desperate journey (for so they called this your pilgrimage), but I did believe, and do still, that the end of our city will be with fire and brimstone from above; and therefore I have made mine escape.

CHR. Did you hear no talk of Neighbour Pliable?

FAITH. Yes, Christian, I heard that he followed you till he came at the Slough of Despond, where, as some said, he fell in; but he would not be known to have so done: but I am sure he was soundly bedabbled with that kind of dirt.

CHR. And what said the neighbours to him?

FAITH. He hath, since his going back, been had greatly in derision, and that among all sorts of people: some do mock and despise him, and scarce will any set him on work. He is now seven times worse than if he had never gone out of the city.

How Pliable was account ed of when he got home.

CHR. But why should they be so set against him, since they also despise the way that he forsook?

FAITH. Oh, they say, Hang him, he is a turncoat, he was not true to his profession. I think God has stirred up even his enemies to hiss at him, and make him a proverb, because he hath forsaken the way.

Jer. xxix. 18, 19.

CHR. Had you no talk with him before you came out?

FAITH. I met him once in the streets, but he leered away on the other side, as one ashamed of what he had done; so I spake not to him.

CHR. Well, at my first setting out, I had hopes of that man; but now I fear he will perish in the overthrow of the city, for it is happened to him according to the true proverb, 'The dog is turned to his vomit again; and the sow that was washed to her wallowing in the mire.'

The dog and sow.
2 Pet. ii. 22.

FAITH. They are my fears of him too: But who can hinder that which will be?

CHR. Well, Neighbour Faithful, said Christian, let us leave him, and talk of things that more immediately concern ourselves. Tell me now, what you have met with in the way as you came; for I know you have met with some things, or else it may be writ for a wonder.

Faithful assaulted by Wanton.

FAITH. I escaped the slough that I perceived you fell into, and got up to the gate without that danger; only I met with one whose name was Wanton, that had like to have done me a mischief.

Gen. xxxix. 11-13.

CHR. 'Twas well you escaped her net; Joseph was hard put to it by her, and he escaped her as you did; but it had like to have cost him his life. But what did she do to you?

FAITH. You cannot think (but that you know something) what a flattering tongue she had; she lay at me hard to turn aside with her, promising me all manner of content.

CHR. Nay, she did not promise you the content of a good conscience.

FAITH. You know what I mean, all carnal and fleshly content.

Prov. xxii. 14.

CHR. Thank God you have escaped her: The abhorred of the Lord shall fall into her ditch.

FAITH. Nay, I know not whether I did wholly escape her or no.

CHR. Why, I trow you did not consent to her desires?

FAITH. No, not to defile myself; for I remembered an old writing that I had seen, which saith, 'Her steps take hold of hell.' So I shut mine eyes, because I would not be bewitched with her looks: then she railed on me, and I went my way.

Prov. v. 5.
Job xxxi. 1.

CHR. Did you meet with no other assault as you came?

FAITH. When I came to the foot of the hill called Difficulty, I met with a very aged man, who asked me what I was, and whither bound. I told him that I was a pilgrim, going to the Celestial City. Then said the old man, Thou lookest like an honest fellow; wilt thou be content to dwell with me for the wages that I shall give thee? Then I asked him his name, and where he dwelt. He said his name was Adam the First, and I dwell in the town of Deceit. I asked him then what was his work, and what the wages that he would give. He told me that his work was many delights: and his wages, that I should be his heir at last. I further asked him what house he kept, and what other servants he had. So he told me that his house was maintained with all the dainties in the world; and that his servants were those of his own begetting. Then I asked how many children he had. He said that he had but three daughters: 'The Lust of the Flesh, the Lust of the Eyes, and the Pride of Life,' and that I should marry them if I would. Then I asked how long time he would have me live with him. And he told me, As long as he lived himself.

He is assaulted by Adam the First.

Eph. iv. 22.

1 John ii. 16.

CHR. Well, and what conclusion came the old man and you to, at last?

FAITH. Why, at first, I found myself somewhat inclinable to go with the man, for I thought he spake very fair; but, looking in his forehead as I talked with him, I saw there written, 'Put off the old man with his deeds.'

CHR. And how then?

FAITH. Then it came burning hot into my mind, whatever he said, and however he flattered, when he got me home to his house, he would sell me for a slave. So I bid him forbear to talk, for I would not come near the door of his house. Then he reviled me, and told me that he would send such a one after me, that should make my way bitter to my soul. So I turned to go away from him; but just as I turned away to go thence, I felt him take hold of my flesh, and give me such a deadly twitch back, that I thought he had pulled part of me after him-

Rom. vii. 24. self. This made me cry, 'O wretched man!' So I went on my way up the hill.

Now when I had got about half way up, I looked behind me, and saw one coming after me, swift as the wind; so he overtook me just about the place where the settle stands.

CHR. Just there, said Christian, did I sit down to rest me; but, being overcome with sleep, I there lost this roll out of my bosom.

FAITH. But, good brother, hear me out. So soon as the man overtook me, he was but a word and a blow; for down he knocked me, and laid me for dead. But when I was a little come to myself again, I asked him wherefore he served me so. He said, Because of my secret inclining to Adam the First; and with that he struck me another deadly blow on the breast, and beat me down backward, so I lay at his foot as dead as before. So when I came to myself again, I cried him mercy ; but he said, I know not how to show mercy; and with that he knocked me down again. He had doubtless made an end of me, but that one came by, and bid him forbear.

CHR. Who was that, that bid him forbear ?

FAITH. I did not know him at first, but as he went by, I perceived the holes in his hands and in his side; then I concluded that he was our Lord. So I went up the hill.

CHR. That man that overtook you was Moses: *The temper of Moses.* he spareth none, neither knoweth he how to show mercy to those that transgress his law.

FAITH. I know it very well; it was not the first time that he has met with me. 'Twas he that came to me when I dwelt securely at home, and that told me he would burn my house over my head if I stayed there.

CHR. But did you not see the house that stood there on the top of that hill, on the side of which Moses met you ?

FAITH. Yes, and the lions too, before I came at it; but for the lions, I think they were asleep, for it was about noon; and because I had so much of the day before me, I passed by the porter, and came down the hill.

CHR. He told me indeed that he saw you go by, but I wish you had called at the house; for they would have showed you so many rarities, that you would scarce have forgot them to the day of your death. But pray tell me, did you meet nobody in the Valley of Humility?

Faithful assaulted by Discontent.

FAITH. Yes, I met with one Discontent, who would willingly have persuaded me to go back again with him; his reason was, for that the valley was altogether without honour. He told me moreover, That there to go, was the way to disobey all my friends, as Pride, Arrogancy, Self-conceit, Worldly-glory, with others, who he knew, as he said, would be very much offended if I made such a fool of myself, as to wade through this valley.

CHR. Well, and how did you answer him?

Faithful's answer to Discontent.

FAITH. I told him, That although all these that he named might claim kindred of me, and that rightly (for indeed they were my relations according to the flesh), yet since I became a pilgrim they have disowned me, as I also have rejected them; and therefore they were to me now no more than if they had never been of my lineage. I told him, moreover, That as to this valley, he had quite misrepresented the thing; for 'before honour is humility,' and 'a haughty spirit before a fall.' Therefore, said I, I had rather go through this valley to the honour that was so accounted by the wisest, than choose that which he esteemed most worthy our affections.

CHR. Met you with nothing else in that valley?

He is assaulted with Shame.

FAITH. Yes, I met with Shame; but of all the men that I met with in my pilgrimage, he I think bears the wrong name. The other would be said nay, after a little argumentation (and somewhat else), but this bold-faced Shame would never have done.

CHR. Why, what did he say to you?

FAITH. What! why, he objected against religion itself; he said it was a pitiful, low, sneaking business for a man to mind religion; he said that a tender conscience was an unmanly thing; and that for a man to watch over his words and ways, so as to tie up himself from that hectoring liberty that the brave spirits of the times accustom themselves unto, would make him the ridicule of the times. He objected also, That but few of the mighty, rich, or wise were ever of my opinion; nor any of them, before they were persuaded to be fools, and to be of a voluntary fondness to venture the loss of all, for nobody else knows what. He moreover objected the base and low estate and condition of those that were chiefly the pilgrims of the times in which they lived; also their ignorance and want of understanding in all natural science. Yea, he did hold me to it at that rate also, about a great many more things than here I relate; as, that it was a shame to sit whining and mourning under a sermon, and a shame to come sighing and groaning home; that it was a shame to ask my neighbour forgiveness for petty faults, or to make restitution where I had taken from any. He said also that religion made a man grow strange to the great, because of a few vices (which he called by finer names), and made him own and respect the base, because of the same religious fraternity. And is not this, said he, a shame?

1 Cor. i. 26.
Chap. iii. 18.

Phil. iii. 7, 8.
John vii. 48.

CHR. And what did you say to him ?

FAITH. Say ! I could not tell what to say at first. Yea, he put me so to it that my blood came up in my face ; even this Shame fetched it up, and had almost beat me quite off. But at last I began to consider, That 'that which is highly esteemed among men, is had in abomination with God.' And I thought again, This Shame tells me what *men* are, but it tells me nothing what God, or the Word of God is. And I thought, moreover, That at the day of doom, we shall not be doomed to death or life according to the hectoring spirits of the world, but according to the wisdom and law of the Highest. Therefore thought I, what God says, is best—indeed is best, though all the men in the world are against it. Seeing then that God prefers His religion, seeing God prefers a tender conscience, seeing they that make themselves fools for the kingdom of heaven are wisest ; and that the poor man that loveth Christ is richer than the greatest man in the world that hates him ; Shame, depart, thou art an enemy to my salvation : shall I entertain thee against my sovereign Lord ? How then shall I look him in the face at his coming ? Should I now be ashamed of his ways and servants, how can I expect the blessing ? But indeed this Shame was a bold villain ; I could scarce shake him out of my company ; yea, he would be haunting of me, and continually whispering me in the ear, with some one or other of the infirmities that attend religion : but at last I told him, 'Twas but in vain to attempt further in this business ; for those things that he disdained, in those did I see most

Luke xvi. 15.

Mark viii. 38.

glory: and so at last I got past this importunate
one.   And when I had shaken him off, then I began
to sing:

> The trials that those men do meet withal
> That are obedient to the heavenly call,
> Are manifold, and suited to the flesh,
> And come, and come, and come again afresh;
> That now, or sometime else, we by them may
> Be taken, overcome, and cast away.
> Oh, let the pilgrims, let the pilgrims then,
> Be vigilant, and quit themselves like men.

CHR. I am glad, my brother, that thou didst
withstand this villain so bravely; for of all, as thou
sayest, I think he has the wrong name; for he is so
bold as to follow us in the streets, and to attempt to
put us to shame before all men; that is, to make us
ashamed of that which is good.   But if he was not
himself audacious, he would never attempt to do as
he does; but let us still resist him; for, notwithstanding all his bravadoes, he promoteth the fool,
and none else.   'The wise shall inherit glory,' said Prov. iii. 35.
Solomon, 'but shame shall be the promotion of
fools.'

FAITH. I think we must cry to him for help
against Shame, that would have us be valiant for
truth upon the earth.

CHR. You say true.   But did you meet nobody
else in that valley?

FAITH. No, not I; for I had sunshine all the
rest of the way through that, and also through the
Valley of the Shadow of Death.

CHR. 'Twas well for you; I am sure it fared far
otherwise with me.   I had for a long season, as soon

almost as I entered into that valley, a dreadful combat with that foul fiend Apollyon; yea, I thought verily he would have killed me, especially when he got me down, and crushed me under him, as if he would have crushed me to pieces. For as he threw me, my sword flew out of my hand; nay, he told me he was sure of me: but I cried to God, and he heard me, and delivered me out of all my troubles. Then I entered into the Valley of the Shadow of Death, and had no light for almost half the way through it. I thought I should have been killed there, over and over; but at last day brake, and the sun rose, and I went through that which was behind with far more ease and quiet.

Moreover, I saw in my dream, that as they went on, Faithful, as he chanced to look on one side, saw a man whose name is Talkative, walking at a distance besides them (for in this place, there was room enough for them all to walk). He was a tall man, and something more comely at a distance than at hand. To this man Faithful addressed himself in this manner:

Talkative described.

FAITH. Friend, whither away? Are you going to the heavenly country?

TALK. I am going to the same place.

FAITH. That is well; then I hope we may have your good company.

TALK. With a very good will, will I be your companion.

Faithful and Talkative enter discourse.

FAITH. Come on then, and let us go together, and let us spend our time in discoursing of things that are profitable.

TALK. To talk of things that are good, to me is very acceptable, with you, or with any other; and I am glad that I have met with those that incline to so good a work. For to speak the truth, there are but few that care thus to spend their time (as they are in their travels), but choose much rather to be speaking of things to no profit; and this hath been a trouble to me.

Talkative's dislike of bad discourse.

FAITH. That is indeed a thing to be lamented; for what things so worthy of the use of the tongue and mouth of men on earth, as are the things of the God of heaven?

TALK. I like you wonderful well, for your sayings are full of conviction; and I will add, What thing is so pleasant, and what so profitable, as to talk of the things of God?

What things so pleasant? (that is, if a man hath any delight in things that are wonderful) for instance: If a man doth delight to talk of the history or the mystery of things; or if a man doth love to talk of miracles, wonders, or signs, where shall he find things recorded so delightful, and so sweetly penned, as in the holy Scripture?

FAITH. That's true; but to be profited by such things in our talk should be that which we design.

TALK. That it is that I said; for to talk of such things is most profitable; for, by so doing, a man may get knowledge of many things; as of the vanity of earthly things, and the benefit of things above (thus in general): but more particularly, by this a man may learn the necessity of the new birth, the insufficiency of our works, the need of

Talkative's fine discourse.

Christ's righteousness, etc.   Besides, by this a man may learn what it is to repent, to believe, to pray, to suffer, or the like; by this, also, a man may learn what are the great promises and consolations of the gospel, to his own comfort.   Further, by this a man may learn to refute false opinions, to vindicate the truth, and also to instruct the ignorant.

FAITH. All this is true; and glad am I to hear these things from you.

TALK. Alas! the want of this is the cause that so few understand the need of faith, and the necessity of a work of grace in their souls, in order to eternal life; but ignorantly live in the works of the law, by which a man can by no means obtain the kingdom of heaven.

FAITH. But, by your leave, heavenly knowledge of these is the gift of God; no man attaineth to them by human industry, or only by the talk of them.

O brave Talkative.

TALK. All this I know very well, for a man can receive nothing except it be given him from heaven; all is of grace, not of works: I could give you a hundred Scriptures for the confirmation of this.

FAITH. Well, then, said Faithful, what is that one thing that we shall at this time found our discourse upon?

O brave Talkative.

TALK. What you will: I will talk of things heavenly, or things earthly; things moral, or things evangelical; things sacred, or things profane; things past, or things to come; things foreign, or things at home; things more essential, or things circumstantial; provided that all be done to our profit.

FAITH. Now did Faithful begin to wonder; and stepping to Christian (for he walked all this while by himself), he said to him (but softly), What a brave companion have we got! Surely this man will make a very excellent pilgrim. Faithful beguiled by Talkative.

CHR. At this Christian modestly smiled, and said, This man with whom you are so taken will beguile with this tongue of his twenty of them that know him not. Christian makes a discovery of Talkative, telling Faithful who he was.

FAITH. Do you know him, then?

CHR. Know him! Yes, better than he knows himself.

FAITH. Pray what is he?

CHR. His name is Talkative; he dwelleth in our town; I wonder that you should be a stranger to him, only I consider that our town is large.

FAITH. Whose son is he? And whereabout doth he dwell?

CHR. He is the son of one Say-well. He dwelt in Prating Row, and he is known of all that are acquainted with him by the name of Talkative in Prating Row; and notwithstanding his fine tongue, he is but a sorry fellow.

FAITH. Well, he seems to be a very pretty man.

CHR. That is, to them that have not thorough acquaintance with him, for he is best abroad; near home he is ugly enough. Your saying, That he is a pretty man, brings to my mind what I have observed in the work of the painter, whose pictures show best at a distance; but very near, more unpleasing.

FAITH. But I am ready to think you do but jest, because you smiled.

CHR. God forbid that I should jest (though I smiled) in this matter, or that I should accuse any falsely; I will give you a further discovery of him: This man is for any company, and for any talk; as he talketh now with you, so will he talk when he is on the ale-bench: and the more drink he hath in his crown, the more of these things he hath in his mouth: Religion hath no place in his heart, or house, or conversation; all he hath, lieth in his tongue, and his religion is to make a noise therewith.

FAITH. Say you so! Then I am in this man greatly deceived.

CHR. Deceived! you may be sure of it. Remember the proverb, 'They say, and do not'; but 'the kingdom of God is not in word, but in power.' He talketh of prayer, of repentance, of faith, and of the new birth; but he knows but only to *talk* of them. I have been in his family, and have observed him both at home and abroad; and I know what I say of him is the truth. His house is as empty of religion as the white of an egg is of savour. There is there, neither prayer nor sign of repentance for sin; yea, the brute in his kind serves God far better than he. He is the very stain, reproach, and shame of religion to all that know him; it can hardly have a good word in all that end of the town where he dwells, through him. Thus say the common people that know him: A saint abroad, and a devil at home: His poor family finds it so; he is such a

Marginal notes:

Matt. xxiii. 3.
1 Cor. iv. 20.

Talkative talks, but does not.

His house is empty of religion.

He is a stain to religion.
Rom. ii. 24, 25.

The proverb that goes of him.

churl, such a railer at, and so unreasonable with his servants, that they neither know how to do for or speak to him. Men that have any dealings with him, say it is better to deal with a Turk than with him, for fairer dealing they shall have at their hands. This Talkative, if it be possible, will go beyond them, defraud, beguile, and over-reach them. Besides, he brings up his sons to follow his steps ; and if he findeth in any of them a foolish timorousness (for so he calls the first appearance of a tender conscience) he calls them fools and blockheads ; and by no means will employ them in much, or speak to their commendations before others. For my part I am of opinion, that he has by his wicked life caused many to stumble and fall ; and will be, if God prevent not, the ruin of many more.

Men shun to deal with him.

FAITH. Well, my brother, I am bound to believe you, not only because you say you know him, but also because like a Christian you make your reports of men. For I cannot think that you speak these things of ill-will, but because it is even so as you say.

CHR. Had I known him no more than you, I might perhaps have thought of him as at the first you did : yea, had he received this report at their hands only that are enemies to religion, I should have thought it had been a slander : (A lot that often falls from bad men's mouths upon good men's names and professions :) But all these things, yea, and a great many more as bad, of my own knowledge I can prove him guilty of. Besides, good men are ashamed of him ; they can neither call him brother nor friend; the very naming of him among them makes them blush if they know him.

FAITH. Well, I see that saying and doing are two things, and hereafter I shall better observe this distinction.

CHR. They are two things indeed, and are as diverse as are the soul and the body; for, as the body without the soul is but a dead carcass, so saying, if it be alone, is but a dead carcass also. The soul of religion is the practick part: 'Pure religion and undefiled, before God and the Father, is this, To visit the fatherless and widows in their affliction, and to keep himself unspotted from the world.' This Talkative is not aware of; he thinks that hearing and saying will make a good Christian, and thus he deceiveth his own soul. Hearing is but as the sowing of the seed; talking is not sufficient to prove that fruit is indeed in the heart and life; and let us assure ourselves, that at the day of doom, men shall be judged according to their fruits. It will not be said then, Did you believe? but, Were you doers, or talkers only? and accordingly shall they be judged. The end of the world is compared to our harvest, and you know men at harvest regard nothing but fruit. Not that anything can be accepted that is not of faith: But I speak this to show you how insignificant the profession of Talkative will be at that day.

FAITH. This brings to my mind that of Moses, by which he describeth the beast that is clean. He is such an one that parteth the hoof, and cheweth the cud; not that parteth the hoof only, or that

The carcass of religion.

James i. 27.
See ver. 22-26.

See Matt. xiii. and chap. xxv.

Lev. xi.
Deut. xiv.

cheweth the cud only. The hare cheweth the cud, but yet is unclean, because he parteth not the hoof. And this truly resembleth Talkative: he cheweth the cud, he seeketh knowledge, he cheweth upon the word; but he divideth not the hoof, he parteth not with the way of sinners; but, as the hare, he retaineth the foot of a dog, or bear, and therefore he is unclean.

Faithful convinced of the badness of Talkative.

CHR. You have spoken, for ought I know, the true gospel sense of those texts, and I will add another thing. Paul calleth some men, yea and those great talkers too, sounding brass, and tinkling cymbals; that is, as he expounds them in another place, 'things without life, giving sound.' Things without life; that is, without the true faith and grace of the gospel; and consequently, things that shall never be placed in the kingdom of heaven among those that are the children of life: Though their sound, by their talk, be as if it were the tongue or voice of an angel.

1 Cor. xiii. 1-3. Chap. xiv. 7.

Talkative like to things that sound without life.

FAITH. Well, I was not so fond of his company at first, but I am sick of it now. What shall we do to be rid of him?

CHR. Take my advice, and do as I bid you, and you shall find that he will soon be sick of your company too, except God shall touch his heart and turn it.

FAITH. What would you have me to do?

CHR. Why, go to him, and enter into some serious discourse about the power of religion: And ask him plainly (when he has approved of it, for that he will), whether this thing be set up in his heart, house, or conversation.

FAITH. Then Faithful stepped forward again, and said to Talkative: Come, what cheer? how is it now?

TALK. Thank you, well. I thought we should have had a great deal of talk by this time.

FAITH. Well, if you will, we will fall to it now; and since you left it with me to state the question, let it be this: How doth the saving grace of God discover itself, when it is in the heart of man?

TALK. I perceive then that our talk must be about the power of things; Well, 'tis a very good question, and I shall be willing to answer you. And take my answer in brief thus: First, where the grace of God is in the heart, it causeth there a great outcry against sin. Secondly——

Talkative's false discovery of a work of grace.

FAITH. Nay hold, let us consider of one at once: I think you should rather say, It shows itself by inclining the soul to abhor its sin.

TALK. Why, what difference is there between crying out against and abhorring of sin?

To cry out against sin, no sign of grace.

FAITH. Oh! a great deal; a man may cry out against sin, of policy; but he cannot abhor it, but by virtue of a godly antipathy against it: I have heard many cry out against sin in the pulpit, who yet can abide it well enough in the heart, and house, and conversation. Joseph's mistress cried out with a loud voice, as if she had been very holy; but she would willingly, notwithstanding that, have committed uncleanness with him. Some cry out against sin, even as the mother cries out against her child in her lap, when she calleth it slut and naughty girl, and then falls to hugging and kissing it.

TALK. You lie at the catch, I perceive.

FAITH. No, not I ; I am only for setting things right. But what is the second thing whereby you would prove a discovery of a work of grace in the heart ?

TALK. Great knowledge of gospel mysteries.

FAITH. This sign should have been first ; but, first or last, it is also false ; for knowledge, great knowledge, may be obtained in the mysteries of the gospel, and yet no work of grace in the soul. Yea, if a man have all knowledge, he may yet be nothing, and so consequently be no child of God. When Christ said, Do you know all these things ? and the disciples had answered, Yes ; he addeth, Blessed are ye if ye do them. He doth not lay the blessing in the knowing of them, but in the doing of them. For there is a knowledge that is not attended with doing : He that knoweth his Master's will, and doth it not. A man may know like an angel, and yet be no Christian ; therefore your sign of it is not true. Indeed to know, is a thing that pleaseth talkers and boasters ; but to do, is that which pleaseth God. Not that the heart can be good without knowledge ; for without that the heart is naught. There is therefore knowledge, and knowledge. Knowledge that resteth in the bare speculation of things, and knowledge that is accompanied with the grace of faith and love, which puts a man upon doing even the will of God from the heart : the first of these will serve the talker ; but without the other the

Great knowledge no sign of grace. 1 Cor. xiii.

Knowledge and knowledge.

True knowledge attended with endeavours. Ps. cxix. 34.

true Christian is not content. 'Give me understanding, and I shall keep thy law; yea, I shall observe it with my whole heart.'

TALK. You lie at the catch again; this is not for edification.

FAITH. Well, if you please propound another sign how this work of grace discovereth itself where it is.

TALK. Not I; for I see we shall not agree.

FAITH. Well, if you will not, will you give me leave to do it?

TALK. You may use your liberty.

One good sign of grace.

FAITH. A work of grace in the soul discovereth itself, either to him that hath it, or to standers-by.

John xvi. 8.
Rom. vii. 24.
John xvi. 9.
Mark xvi. 16.
Ps. xxxviii. 18.
Jer. xxxi. 19.
Gal. ii. 16.
Acts iv. 12.
Matt. v. 6.
Rev. xxi. 6.

To him that hath it, thus: It gives him conviction of sin, especially of the defilement of his nature, and the sin of unbelief (for the sake of which he is sure to be damned, if he findeth not mercy at God's hand by faith in Jesus Christ). This sight and sense of things worketh in him sorrow and shame for sin; he findeth moreover revealed in him the Saviour of the world, and the absolute necessity of closing with him for life, at the which he findeth hungerings and thirstings after him, to which hungerings, etc., the promise is made. Now according to the strength or weakness of his faith in his Saviour, so is his joy and peace, so is his love to holiness, so are his desires to know him more, and also to serve him in this world. But though I say it discovereth itself thus unto him, yet it is but seldom that he is able to conclude that this is a work of grace, because his corruptions now, and his abused reason, make his mind to misjudge in this matter; therefore in him that hath this work, there is required a very sound judgment, before he can with steadiness conclude that this is a work of grace.

To others it is thus discovered:

1. By an experimental confession of his faith in Christ. 2. By a life answerable to that confession; to wit, a life of holiness; heart-holiness, family-holiness (if he hath a family), and by conversation-holiness in the world; which in the general teacheth him, inwardly to abhor his sin, and himself for that in secret, to suppress it in his family, and to promote holiness in the world; not by talk only, as an hypocrite or talkative person may do: but by a practical subjection in faith and love to the power of the word: And now Sir, as to this brief description of the work of grace, and also the discovery of it, if you have aught to object, object; if not, then give me leave to propound to you a second question. *Rom. x. 10. Phil. i. 27. Matt. v. xix. John xiv. 15. Ps. l. 20. Job xlii. 5, 6. Ezek. xxix. 43.*

TALK. Nay, my part is not now to object, but to hear: let me therefore have your second question.

FAITH. It is this: Do you experience the first part of this description of it? and doth your life and conversation testify the same? or standeth your religion in word or in tongue, and not in deed and truth? Pray, if you incline to answer me in this, say no more than you know the God above will say Amen to; and also, nothing but what your conscience can justify you in: For, 'not he that commendeth himself is approved, but whom the Lord commendeth.' Besides, to say I am thus, and thus, when my conversation, and all my neighbours tell me I lie, is great wickedness. *Another good sign of grace.*

TALK. Then Talkative at first began to blush, but recovering himself, thus he replied: You come now to experience, to conscience, and God: and to appeal to him for justification of what is spoken: This kind of discourse I did not expect, nor am I disposed to give an answer to such questions, because I count not myself bound thereto, unless you take upon you to be a catechiser; and, though you should so do, yet I may refuse to make you my judge: But I pray will you tell me, why you ask me such questions?

FAITH. Because I saw you forward to talk, and because I knew not that you had aught else but notion.   Besides, to tell you all the truth, I have heard of you, that you are a man whose religion lies

in talk, and that your conversation gives this your mouth-profession the lie.   They say You are a spot among Christians, and that religion fareth the worse for your ungodly conversation, that some already have stumbled at your wicked ways, and that more are in danger of being destroyed thereby; your religion, and an ale-house, and covetousness, and uncleanness, and swearing, and lying, and vain company-keeping, etc., will stand together.   The proverb is true of you which is said of a whore, to wit, That she is a shame to all women; so you are a shame to all professors.

TALK. Since you are ready to take up reports, and to judge so rashly as you do; I cannot but conclude you are some peevish or melancholy man, not fit to be discoursed with; and so adieu.

CHR. Then came up Christian, and said to his brother, I told you how it would happen, your words and his lusts could not agree; he had rather leave your company than reform his life : but he is gone as I said, let him go ; the loss is no man's but his A good riddance. own, he has saved us the trouble of going from him ; for he continuing (as I suppose he will do) as he is, he would have been but a blot in our company : besides, the apostle says, 'From such withdraw thyself.'

FAITH. But I am glad we had this little discourse with him, it may happen that he will think of it again ; however, I have dealt plainly with him, and so am clear of his blood, if he perisheth.

CHR. You did well to talk so plainly to him as you did, there is but little of this faithful dealing with men now-a-days, and that makes religion to stink so in the nostrils of many as it doth ; for they are these talkative fools whose religion is only in word, and are debauched and vain in their conversation, that (being so much admitted into the fellowship of the godly) do puzzle the world, blemish Christianity, and grieve the sincere. I wish that all men would deal with such as you have done, then should they either be made more conformable to religion, or the company of saints would be too hot for them. Then did Faithful say :

> How Talkative at first lifts up his plumes !
> How bravely doth he speak ! how he presumes
> To drive down all before him ! but so soon
> As Faithful talks of heart-work, like the moon
> That's past the full, into the wane he goes ;
> And so will all, but he that *Heart-work* knows.

Thus they went on talking of what they had seen

by the way, and so made that way easy, which would otherwise, no doubt, have been tedious to them; for now they went through a wilderness.

Now when they were got almost quite out of this wilderness, Faithful chanced to cast his eye back, and espied one come after them, and he knew him. Oh! said Faithful to his brother, who comes yonder? Then Christian looked, and said, It is my good friend Evangelist. Ay, and my good friend too, said Faithful: for 'twas he that set me the way to the gate. Now was Evangelist come up unto them, and thus saluted them:

Evangelist
overtakes
them again.

EVAN. Peace be with you, dearly beloved, and peace be to your helpers.

They are
glad at the
sight of
him.

CHR. Welcome, welcome, my good Evangelist, the sight of thy countenance brings to my remembrance thy ancient kindness, and unwearied labouring for my eternal good.

FAITH. And a thousand times welcome, said good Faithful; Thy company, O sweet Evangelist, how desirable is it to us, poor pilgrims!

EVAN. Then said Evangelist, How hath it fared with you, my friends, since the time of our last parting? *what* have you met with, and *how* have you behaved yourselves?

Then Christian and Faithful told him of all things that had happened to them in the way; and how, and with what difficulty they had arrived to that place.

His exhorta-
tion to them.

EVAN. Right glad am I, said Evangelist; not that you have met with trials, but that you have been victors; and for that you have (notwithstanding many weaknesses) continued in the way to this very day.

I say, right glad am I of this thing, and that for mine own sake and yours; I have sowed, and you have reaped; and the day is coming, when both he that sowed and they that reaped shall rejoice together; that is, if you hold out: for in due season ye shall reap if you faint not. The crown is before you, and it is an incorruptible one; so run, that you may obtain it. Some there be that set out for this crown, and after they have gone far for it, another comes in, and takes it from them; 'hold fast therefore that you have, let no man take your crown.' You are not yet out of the gun-shot of the devil; you have not resisted unto blood, striving against sin; let the kingdom be always before you, and believe steadfastly concerning things that are invisible. Let nothing that is on this side the other world get within you; and above all, look well to your own hearts, and to the lusts thereof, for they are deceitful above all things, and desperately wicked; set your faces like a flint; you have all power in heaven and earth on your side. *John iv. 36. Gal. vi. 9. 1 Cor. ix. 24-27. Rev. iii. 11.*

CHR. Then Christian thanked him for his exhortation, but told him withal, that they would have him speak further to them for their help, the rest of the way; and the rather, for that they well knew that he was a prophet, and could tell them of things that might happen unto them; and also how they might resist and overcome them. To which request Faithful also consented. So Evangelist began as followeth: *They do thank him for his exhortation.*

He predicteth what troubles they shall meet with in Vanity Fair, and encourageth them to steadfastness.

EVAN. My sons you have heard in the words of the truth of the gospel, that you must through many tribulations enter into the kingdom of heaven. And again, that in every city bonds and afflictions abide in you; and therefore you cannot expect that you should go long on your pilgrimage without them, in some sort or other. You have found something of the truth of these testimonies upon you already, and more will immediately follow: for now, as you see, you are almost out of this wilderness, and therefore you will soon come into a town that you will by and by see before you: and in that town you will be hardly beset with enemies, who will strain hard but they will kill you: and be you sure that one or both of you must seal the testimony which you hold, with blood; but be you faithful unto death, and the King will give you a crown of life.

He whose lot it will be there to suffer, will have the better of his brother.

He that shall die there, although his death will be unnatural, and his pains perhaps great, he will yet have the better of his fellow; not only because he will be arrived at the Celestial City soonest, but because he will escape many miseries that the other will meet with in the rest of his journey. But when you are come to the town, and shall find fulfilled what I have here related, then remember your friend, and quit yourselves like men; and commit the keeping of your souls to God in well-doing, as unto a faithful Creator.

Then I saw in my dream, that when they were got out of the wilderness, they presently saw a town before them, and the name of that town is Vanity; and at the town there is a fair kept, called Vanity

Fair. It is kept all the year long, it beareth the name of Vanity Fair because the town where 'tis kept is lighter than vanity; and also because all that is there sold, or that cometh thither, is vanity. As is the saying of the wise, All that cometh is vanity.

Isa. xl. 17.
Eccl. i. ii. 14.
Chap. ii. 11, 17.

This fair is no new-erected business, but a thing of ancient standing; I will show you the original of it.

Almost five thousand years agone, there were pilgrims walking to the Celestial City, as these two honest persons are; and Beelzebub, Apollyon, and Legion, with their companions, perceiving by the path that the pilgrims made, that their way to the city lay through this town of Vanity, they contrived here to set up a fair, a fair wherein should be sold of all sorts of vanity, and that it should last all the year long. Therefore at this fair are all such merchandise sold, as houses, lands, trades, places, honours, preferments, titles, countries, kingdoms, lusts, pleasures and delights of all sorts, as whores, bawds, wives, husbands, children, masters, servants, lives, blood, bodies, souls, silver, gold, pearls, precious stones, and what not.

The antiquity of this fair.

The merchandise of this fair.

And moreover, at this fair there is at all times to be seen jugglings, cheats, games, plays, fools, apes, knaves, and rogues, and that of every kind.

Here are to be seen too, and that for nothing, thefts, murders, adulteries, false-swearers, and that of a blood-red colour.

And as in other fairs of less moment, there are the several rows and streets, under their proper names, where such and such wares are vended; so here likewise, you have the proper places, rows, streets (viz., countries and kingdoms), where the wares of this fair are soonest to be found: Here is the British Row, the French Row, the Italian Row, the Spanish Row, the German Row, where several sorts of vanities are to be sold. But as in other fairs, some one commodity is as the chief of all the fair, so the ware of Rome and her merchandise is greatly promoted in this fair; only our English nation, with some others, have taken a dislike thereat.

The streets of this fair.

Now, as I said, the way to the Celestial City lies just through this town, where this lusty fair is kept; and he that will go to the city, and yet not go through this town, must needs 'go out of the world.' The Prince of princes himself, when here, went through this town to his own country, and that upon a fair-day too: Yea, and as I think, it was Beelzebub, the chief Lord of this fair, that invited him to buy of his vanities; yea, would have made him lord of the fair, would he but have done him reverence as he went through the town. Yea, because he was such a person of honour, Beelzebub had him from street to street, and showed him all the kingdoms of the world in a little time, that he might (if possible) allure that Blessed One, to cheapen and buy some of his vanities. But he had no mind to the merchandise, and therefore left the town, without laying out so much as one farthing upon these vanities. This fair therefore is an ancient thing, of long standing, and a very great fair.

1 Cor. v. 10. Christ went through this fair. Matt. iv. 8. Luke iv. 5, 7.

Christ bought nothing in this fair.

Now these Pilgrims, as I said, must needs go *The pilgrims enter the fair.* through this fair. Well, so they did; but behold, even as they entered into the fair, all the people in the fair were moved, and the town itself as it *The fair in a hubbub about them.* were in a hubbub about them; and that for several reasons: for—

First, The pilgrims were clothed with such kind *The first cause of the hubbub.* of raiment as was diverse from the raiment of any that traded in that fair. The people therefore of the fair made a great gazing upon them: Some said *1 Cor. ii. 7, 8.* they were fools, some they were bedlams, and some they are outlandish men.

Secondly, And as they wondered at their apparel, *Second cause of the hubbub.* so they did likewise at their speech, for few could understand what they said; they naturally spoke the language of Canaan, but they that kept the fair were the men of this world; so that, from one end of the fair to the other, they seemed barbarians each to the other.

Thirdly, But that which did not a little amuse *Third cause of the hubbub.* the merchandisers, was, that these pilgrims set very light by all their wares, they cared not so much as to look upon them; and if they called upon them to buy, they would put their fingers in their ears, and cry, 'Turn away mine eyes from beholding *Ps. cxix. 37.* vanity,' and look upwards, signifying that their trade *Phil. iii. 19, 20.* and traffic was in heaven.

One chanced mockingly, beholding the carriages *Fourth cause of the hubbub.* of the men, to say unto them, What will ye buy? But they, looking gravely upon him, said, 'We buy *Prov. xxiii. 23.* the truth.' At that, there was an occasion taken *They are mocked.* to despise the men the more; some mocking, some taunting, some speaking reproachfully, and some calling upon others to smite them. At last things came to a hubbub and great stir in the fair, insomuch that all order was confounded. Now was word presently brought to the great one of the fair, who quickly came down, and deputed some of his most trusty friends to take these men into examination, about whom the fair was almost overturned. So the men were brought to examination; and they that sat upon them, asked them whence they came, whither they went, and what they did there in such an unusual garb. The men told them that they were pilgrims and strangers in the world, and that they were going to their own country, which was the heavenly Jerusalem; and that they had given no occasion to the men of the town, nor yet to the merchandisers, thus to abuse them, and to let them in their journey. Except it was, for that, when one asked them what they would buy, they said they would 'buy the truth.' But they that were appointed to examine them did not believe them to be any other than Bedlams and mad, or else such as came to put all things into a confusion in the fair. Therefore they took them and beat them, and besmeared them with dirt, and then put them into the cage, that they might be made a spectacle to all the men of the fair. There therefore they lay for some time, and were made the objects of any man's sport, or malice, or revenge, the great one of the fair laughing still at all that befell them. But the men being patient, and not rendering railing for railing, but contrarywise blessing, and giving good

The fair in a hubbub.

They are examined.

They tell who they are and whence they came. Heb. xi. 13-16.

They are not believed.

They are put in the cage.

Their behaviour in the cage.

words for bad, and kindness for injuries done: Some men in the fair that were more observing, and less prejudiced than the rest, began to check and blame the baser sort for their continual abuses done by them to the men: They therefore in angry manner let fly at them again, counting them as bad as the men in the cage, and telling them that they seemed confederates, and should be made partakers of their misfortunes. The other replied, That for aught they could see, the men were quiet, and sober, and intended nobody any harm; and that there were many that traded in their fair that were more worthy to be put into the cage, yea, and pillory too, than were the men that they had abused. Thus, after divers words had passed on both sides (the men behaving themselves all the while very wisely and soberly before them), they fell to some blows among themselves, and did harm one to another. Then were these two poor men brought before their examiners again, and there charged as being guilty of the late hubbub that had been in the fair. So they beat them pitifully, and hanged irons upon them, and led them in chains up and down the fair, for an example and a terror to others, lest any should speak in their behalf, or join themselves unto them. But Christian and Faithful behaved themselves yet more wisely, and received the ignominy and shame that was cast upon them, with so much meekness and patience, that it won to their side (though but few in comparison of the rest) several of the men in the fair. This put the other party yet into a greater rage, insomuch that they concluded

The men of the fair do fall out among themselves about these two men.

They are made the authors of this disturbance.

They are led up and down the fair in chains, for a terror to others.

Some of the men of the fair won to them.

Their
adversaries
resolve to
kill them.
the death of these two men.[1]   Wherefore they
threatened that the cage nor irons should serve
their turn, but that they should die, for the abuse
they had done, and for deluding the men of the fair.

They are
again put
into the cage,
Then were they remanded to the cage again, until
further order should be taken with them.   So they
put them in, and made their feet fast in the stocks.

Here therefore they called again to mind what
they had heard from their faithful friend Evangelist,
and were the more confirmed in their way and
sufferings, by what he told them would happen to
them.   They also now comforted each other, that
whose lot it was to suffer, even he should have the
best on 't ; therefore each man secretly wished that
he might have that preferment : but committing
themselves to the All-wise dispose of him that ruleth
all things, with much content they abode in the
condition in which they were, until they should be
otherwise disposed of.

and after
brought to
trial.
Then a convenient time being appointed, they
brought them forth to their trial in order to their
condemnation.   When the time was come, they
were brought before their enemies and arraigned.
The judge's name was Lord Hate-good.   Their
indictment was one and the same in substance,
though somewhat varying in form ; the contents
whereof was this :

'That they were enemies to, and disturbers of

---

[1] Behold Vanity Fair ! the Pilgrims there
Are chain'd, and ston'd beside ;
Even so it was, our Lord pass'd here,
And on Mount Calvary died.

their trade: that they had made commotions and Their indict-
divisions in the town, and had won a party to their ment.
own most dangerous opinions, in contempt of the
law of their prince.'

Then Faithful began to answer, That he had only Faithful's
set himself against that which had set itself against answer for himself.
him that is higher than the highest. And said he,
As for disturbance, I make none, being myself a
man of peace; the parties that were won to us
were won by beholding our truth and innocence,
and they are only turned from the worse to the
better. And as to the king you talk of, since he is
Beelzebub, the enemy of our Lord, I defy him and
all his angels.[1]

Then proclamation was made, that they that had
aught to say for their lord the king against the
prisoner at the bar, should forthwith appear and give
in their evidence. So there came in three witnesses,
to wit, Envy, Superstition, and Pickthank. They
were then asked, If they knew the prisoner at the
bar? and what they had to say for their lord the
king against him.

Then stood forth Envy, and said to this effect: Envy begins
My lord, I have known this man a long time, and
will attest upon my oath before this honourable
bench, That he is ——

JUDGE. Hold! Give him his oath. So they
sware him. Then he said: My lord, This man,

---

[1] Now Faithful, play the man, speak for thy God:
 Fear not the wicked's malice, nor their rod:
 Speak boldly, man, the truth is on thy side;
 Die for it, and to life in triumph ride.

notwithstanding his plausible name, is one of the vilest men in our country; he neither regardeth prince nor people, law nor custom: but doth all that he can to possess all men with certain of his disloyal notions, which he in the general calls principles of faith and holiness.   And in particular, I heard him once myself affirm, That Christianity and the customs of our town of Vanity were diametrically opposite, and could not be reconciled. By which saying, my lord, he doth at once not only condemn all our laudable doings, but us in the doing of them.

JUDGE. Then did the judge say to him, Hast thou any more to say?

ENVY. My lord, I could say much more, only I would not be tedious to the court.   Yet if need be, when the other gentlemen have given in their evidence, rather than anything shall be wanting that will despatch him, I will enlarge my testimony against him.   So he was bid stand by.   Then they called Superstition, and bid him look upon the prisoner; they also asked, What he could say for their lord the king against him?   Then they sware him; so he began:

Superstition follows.

SUPER. My lord, I have no great acquaintance with this man, nor do I desire to have further knowledge of him; However this I know, that he is a very pestilent fellow, from some discourse that the other day I had with him in this town; for then talking with him, I heard him say, That our religion was naught, and such by which a man could by no means please God: which sayings of his, my lord, your lordship very well knows, what necessarily thence will follow, to wit, That we still do worship in vain, are yet in our sins, and finally shall be damned; and this is that which I have to say.

Then was Pickthank sworn, and bid say what he knew, in behalf of their lord the king against the prisoner at the bar.

PICK. My lord, and you gentlemen all, This fellow I have known of a long time, and have heard him speak things that ought not to be spoke. For he hath railed on our noble prince Beelzebub, and hath spoken contemptibly of his honourable friends, whose names are the Lord Oldman, the Lord Carnal Delight, the Lord Luxurious, the Lord Desire-of-Vain-Glory, my old Lord Lechery, Sir Having Greedy, with all the rest of our nobility; and he hath said moreover, that if all men were of his mind, if possible, there is not one of these noble men should have any longer a being in this town. Besides, he hath not been afraid to rail on you, my lord, who are now appointed to be his judge, calling you an ungodly villain, with many other such like vilifying terms, with which he hath bespattered most of the gentry of our town.

Pickthank's testimony.

Sins are all lords and great ones.

When this Pickthank had told his tale, the judge directed his speech to the prisoner at the bar, saying: Thou runagate, heretic, and traitor, hast thou heard what these honest gentlemen have witnessed against thee?

FAITH. May I speak a few words in my own defence?

JUDGE. Sirrah, Sirrah, thou deservest to live no

longer, but to be slain immediately upon the place; yet that all men may see our gentleness towards thee, let us hear what thou, vile runagate, hast to say.

Faithful's defence of himself.

FAITH. 1. I say then, in answer to what Mr. Envy hath spoken, I never said aught but this, That what rule, or laws, or custom, or people, were flat against the Word of God, are diametrically opposite to Christianity. If I have said amiss in this, convince me of my error, and I am ready here before you to make my recantation.

2. As to the second, to wit, Mr. Superstition, and his charge against me, I said only this, That in the worship of God there is required a divine faith; but there can be no divine faith without a divine revelation of the will of God: therefore whatever is thrust into the worship of God, that is not agreeable to divine revelation, cannot be done but by a human faith; which faith will not be profitable to eternal life.

3. As to what Mr. Pickthank hath said, I say (avoiding terms, as that I am said to rail, and the like) That the prince of this town, with all the rabblement his attendants, by this gentleman named, are more fit for a being in hell than in this town and country: and so the Lord have mercy upon me.

The judge his speech to the jury.

Then the judge called to the jury (who all this while stood by, to hear and observe): Gentlemen of the Jury, you see this man about whom so great an uproar hath been made in this town: you have also heard what these worthy gentlemen have witnessed against him; also you have heard his reply and confession : It lieth now in your breasts to hang him, or save his life; But yet I think meet to instruct you into our law.

There was an act made in the days of Pharaoh the Great, servant to our prince, That lest those of a contrary religion should multiply and grow too strong for him, their males should be thrown into the river.   There was also an act made in the days of Nebuchadnezzar the Great, another of his servants, that whoever would not fall down and worship his golden image, should be thrown into a fiery furnace. There was also an act made in the days of Darius, That whoso, for some time, called upon any God but him, should be cast into the lions' den.   Now the substance of these laws this rebel has broken, not only in thought (which is not to be borne) but also in word and deed; which must therefore needs be intolerable. *Exod. i.* *Dan. iii.* *Dan. vi.*

For that of Pharaoh, his law was made upon a supposition, to prevent mischief, no crime being yet apparent; but here is a crime apparent.   For the second and third, you see he disputeth against our religion; and for the treason he hath confessed, he deserveth to die the death.

Then went the jury out, whose names were: Mr. Blind-man, Mr. No-good, Mr. Malice, Mr. Love-lust, Mr. Live-loose, Mr. Heady, Mr. High-mind, Mr. Enmity, Mr. Liar, Mr. Cruelty, Mr. Hate-light, and Mr. Implacable, who every one gave in his private verdict against him among themselves, and afterwards unanimously concluded to bring him in guilty before the judge.   And first among them- *The jury and their names.* *Every one's private verdict.*

selves, Mr. Blind-man, the foreman, said, I see clearly that this man is an heretic. Then said Mr. No-good, Away with such a fellow from the earth. Ay, said Mr. Malice, for I hate the very looks of him. Then said Mr. Love-lust, I could never endure him. Nor I, said Mr. Live-loose, for he would always be condemning my way. Hang him, hang him, said Mr. Heady. A sorry scrub, said Mr. High-mind. My heart riseth against him, said Mr. Enmity. He is a rogue, said Mr. Liar. Hanging is too good for him, said Mr. Cruelty. Let's despatch him out of the way, said Mr. Hate-light. Then said Mr. Implacable, Might I have all the world given me, I could not be reconciled to him; therefore let us forthwith bring him in guilty of death. And so they did; therefore he was presently condemned, To be had from the place where he was, to the place from whence he came, and there to be put to the most cruel death that could be invented.

They conclude to bring him in guilty of death.

They therefore brought him out, to do with him according to their law; and first they scourged him, then they buffeted him, then they lanced his flesh with knives; after that, they stoned him with stones, then pricked him with their swords; and last of all they burned him to ashes at the stake.[1] Thus came Faithful to his end. Now, I saw that there stood behind the multitude, a chariot and a couple of

The cruel death of Faithful.

---

[1] Brave Faithful, bravely done in word and deed;
Judge, witnesses, and jury, have instead
Of overcoming thee, but shown their rage:
When they are dead, thou'lt live, from age to age.

horses, waiting for Faithful, who (so soon as his adversaries had despatched him) was taken up into it, and straightway was carried up through the clouds, with sound of trumpet, the nearest way to the Celestial Gate.   But as for Christian, he had some respite, and was remanded back to prison, so he there remained for a space: But he that overrules all things, having the power of their rage in his own hand, so wrought it about, that Christian for that time escaped them, and went his way.

And as he went he sang, saying:

> Well, Faithful, thou hast faithfully profest
> Unto thy Lord: with whom thou shalt be blest;
> When faithless ones, with all their vain delights,
> Are crying out under their hellish plights,
> Sing, Faithful, sing; and let thy name survive,
> For though they kill'd thee, thou art yet alive.

Now I saw in my dream, that Christian went not forth alone, for there was one whose name was Hopeful (being made so by the beholding of Christian and Faithful in their words and behaviour in their sufferings at the fair), who joined himself unto him, and, entering into a brotherly covenant, told him that he would be his companion.   Thus, one died to bear testimony to the truth, and another rises out of his ashes to be a companion with Christian in his pilgrimage.   This Hopeful also told Christian that there were many more of the men in the fair that would take their time and follow after.

So I saw that quickly after they were got out of the fair they overtook one that was going before

Marginal notes:
A chariot and horses wait to take away Faithful.
Christian is still alive.
The song that Christian made of Faithful after his death.
Christian has another companion.
There are more of the men of the fair will follow.
They overtake By-ends.

them, whose name was By-ends: so they said to him, What countryman, Sir? and how far go you this way? He told them that he came from the town of Fair-speech, and he was going to the Celestial City (but told them not his name).

Prov. xxvi. 25.

From Fair-speech! said Christian; is there any that be good that lives there?

BY-ENDS. Yes, said By-ends, I hope.

CHR. Pray, Sir, what may I call you? said Christian.

By-ends loth to tell his name.

BY-ENDS. I am a stranger to you, and you to me: if you be going this way, I shall be glad of your company; if not, I must be content.

CHR. This town of Fair-speech I have heard of, and, as I remember, they say it's a wealthy place.

BY-ENDS. Yes, I will assure you that it is; and I have very many rich kindred there.

CHR. Pray, who are your kindred there, if a man may be so bold?

BY-ENDS. Almost the whole town; and, in particular, my Lord Turn-about, my Lord Time-server, my Lord Fair-speech (from whose ancestors that town first took its name): also Mr. Smooth-man, Mr. Facing-both-ways, Mr. Anything; and the parson of our parish, Mr. Two-tongues, was my mother's own brother, by father's side; and to tell you the truth, I am become a gentleman of good quality; yet my great-grandfather was but a water-man, looking one way and rowing another; and I got most of my estate by the same occupation.

CHR. Are you a married man?

BY-ENDS. Yes, and my wife is a very virtuous

woman, the daughter of a virtuous woman; She was my Lady Feigning's daughter, therefore she came of a very honourable family, and is arrived to such a pitch of breeding that she knows how to carry it to all, even to prince and peasant. 'Tis true, we somewhat differ in religion from those of the stricter sort, yet but in two small points: First, we never strive against wind and tide: Secondly, we are always most zealous when Religion goes in his silver slippers; we love much to walk with him in the street, if the sun shines, and the people applaud him. *The wife and kindred of By-ends.* *Where By-ends differs from others in religion.*

Then Christian stepped a little aside to his fellow Hopeful, saying, It runs in my mind that this is one By-ends of Fair-speech, and if it be he, we have as very a knave in our company as dwelleth in all these parts. Then said Hopeful, Ask him; methinks he should not be ashamed of his name. So Christian came up with him again, and said, Sir, you talk as if you knew something more than all the world doth, and if I take not my mark amiss, I deem I have half a guess of you: Is not your name Mr. By-ends of Fair-speech?

BY-ENDS. This is not my name, but indeed it is a nickname that is given me by some that cannot abide me; and I must be content to bear it as a reproach, as other good men have borne theirs before me.

CHR. But did you never give an occasion to men to call you by this name?

BY-ENDS. Never, never! the worst that ever I did to give them an occasion to give me this name *How By-ends got his name.*

was, That I had always the luck to jump in my judgment with the present way of the times, whatever it was, and my chance was to get thereby; but if things are thus cast upon me, let me count them a blessing, but let not the malicious load me therefore with reproach.

CHR. I thought indeed that you were the man that I heard of, and to tell you what I think, I fear this name belongs to you more properly than you are willing we should think it doth.

He desires to keep company with Christian.

BY-ENDS. Well, if you will thus imagine, I cannot help it. You shall find me a fair company-keeper, if you will still admit me your associate.

CHR. If you will go with us, you must go against wind and tide, the which, I perceive, is against your opinion: You must also own Religion in his rags, as well as when in his silver slippers, and stand by him too, when bound in irons, as well as when he walketh the streets with applause.

BY-ENDS. You must not impose, nor lord it over my faith; leave me to my liberty, and let me go with you.

CHR. Not a step further, unless you will do in what I propound, as we.

Then said By-ends, I shall never desert my old principles, since they are harmless and profitable. If I may not go with you, I must do as I did before you overtook me, even go by myself, until some overtake me that will be glad of my company.

By-ends and Christian part.

Now I saw in my dream, that Christian and Hopeful forsook him, and kept their distance before him; but one of them looking back, saw three men

following Mr. By-ends, and behold, as they came
up with him, he made them a very low *congee*, and
they also gave him a compliment.   The men's
names were Mr. Hold-the-world, Mr. Money-love, He has new
and Mr. Save-all; men that Mr. By-ends had for- companions.
merly been acquainted with; for in their minority
they were school-fellows, and taught by one Mr.
Gripe-man, a schoolmaster in Love-gain, which is
a market-town in the county of Coveting, in the
north.   This schoolmaster taught them the art of
getting, either by violence, cozenage, flattery, lying,
or by putting on a guise of religion; and these four
gentlemen had attained much of the art of their
master, so that they could each of them have kept
such a school themselves.

Well, when they had, as I said, thus saluted each
other, Mr. Money-love said to Mr. By-ends, Who
are they upon the road before us? (For Christian
and Hopeful were yet within view.)

BY-ENDS. They are a couple of far countrymen, By-ends'
that after their mode are going on pilgrimage. character
of the
MONEY-LOVE. Alas! why did not they stay, that pilgrims.
we might have had their good company? for they,
and we, and you, Sir, I hope, are all going on a
pilgrimage.

BY-ENDS. We are so indeed, but the men before
us are so rigid, and love so much their own notions,
and do also so lightly esteem the opinions of others,
that let a man be never so godly, yet if he jumps
not with them in all things, they thrust him quite
out of their company.

SAVE-ALL. That's bad; but we read of some,

that are righteous overmuch; and such men's rigidness prevails with them to judge and condemn all but themselves. But I pray, what, and how many, were the things wherein you differed?

BY-ENDS. Why they, after their headstrong manner, conclude that it is duty to rush on their journey all weathers, and I am for waiting for wind and tide. They are for hazarding all for God at a clap, and I am for taking all advantages to secure my life and estate. They are for holding their notions, though all other men be against them; but I am for religion in what, and so far as, the times and my safety will bear it. They are for religion when in rags and contempt; but I am for him when he walks in his golden slippers, in the sunshine, and with applause.

HOLD-THE-WORLD. Ay, and hold you there still, good Mr. By-ends; for, for my part, I can count him but a fool, that, having the liberty to keep what he has, shall be so unwise as to lose it. Let us be wise as serpents: 'tis best to make hay when the sun shines; you see how the bee lieth still all winter, and bestirs her only when she can have profit with pleasure. God sends sometimes rain, and sometimes sunshine; if they be such fools to go through the first, yet let us be content to take fair weather along with us. For my part, I like that religion best that will stand with the security of God's good blessings unto us; for who can imagine, that is ruled by his reason, since God has bestowed upon us the good things of this life, but that he would have us keep them for his sake?

Abraham and Solomon grew rich in religion. And Job says, that a good man shall lay up gold as dust. But he must not be such as the men before us, if they be as you have described them.

SAVE-ALL. I think that we are all agreed in this matter, and therefore there needs no more words about it.

MONEY-LOVE. No, there needs no more words about this matter indeed; for he that believes neither Scripture nor reason (and you see we have both on our side) neither knows his own liberty nor seeks his own safety.

BY-ENDS. My brethren, we are, as you see, going all on pilgrimage; and for our better diversion from things that are bad, give me leave to propound unto you this question:

Suppose a man, a minister or a tradesman, etc., should have an advantage lie before him to get the good blessings of this life, yet so as that he can by no means come by them, except, in appearance at least, he becomes extraordinary zealous in some points of religion that he meddled not with before; may he not use this means to attain his end, and yet be a right honest man?

MONEY-LOVE. I see the bottom of your question, and with these gentlemen's good leave, I will endeavour to shape you an answer. And first to speak to your question as it concerneth a minister himself: Suppose a minister, a worthy man, possessed but of a very small benefice, and has in his eye a greater, more fat and plump by far; he has also now an opportunity of getting of it, yet so as by being more studious, by preaching more frequently and zealously, and, because the temper of the people requires it, by altering of some of his principles; for my part I see no reason but a man may do this (provided he has a call), ay, and more a great deal besides, and yet be an honest man. For why—

1. His desire of a greater benefice is lawful (this cannot be contradicted), since it is set before him by providence; so then, he may get it if he can, making no question for conscience sake.

2. Besides, his desire after that benefice makes him more studious, a more zealous preacher, etc., and so makes him a better man; yea, makes him better improve his parts, which is according to the mind of God.

3. Now as for his complying with the temper of his people, by dissenting, to serve them, some of his principles, this argueth, 1. That he is of a self-denying temper; 2. Of a sweet and winning deportment; 3. And so more fit for the ministerial function.

4. I conclude then, that a minister that changes a small for a great, should not for so doing be judged as covetous; but rather, since he is improved in his parts and industry thereby, be counted as one that pursues his call, and the opportunity put into his hand to do good.

And now to the second part of the question which concerns the tradesman you mentioned: Suppose such an one to have but a poor employ in the world, but by becoming religious, he may mend his market, perhaps get a rich wife, or more and far better customers to his shop; for my part I see no reason but this may be lawfully done. For why—

1. To become religious is a virtue, by what means soever a man becomes so.

2. Nor is it unlawful to get a rich wife, or more custom to my shop.

3. Besides, the man that gets these by becoming religious, gets that which is good, of them that are good, by becoming good himself: so then here is a good wife, and good customers, and good gain, and all these by becoming religious, which is good: therefore to become religious to get all these is a good and profitable design.

This answer, thus made by this Mr. Money-love to Mr. By-ends' question, was highly applauded by them all; wherefore they concluded upon the whole, that it was most wholesome and advantageous. And because, as they thought, no man was able to contradict it, and because Christian and Hopeful were yet within call, they jointly agreed to assault them with the question as soon as they overtook them, and the rather because they had opposed Mr. By-ends before. So they called after them, and they stopped, and stood still till they came up to them; but they concluded as they went, that not Mr. By-ends, but old Mr. Hold-the-world, should propound the question to them, because, as they supposed, their answer to him would be without the remainder of that heat that was kindled betwixt Mr. By-ends and them, at their parting a little before.

So they came up to each other, and after a short

salutation, Mr. Hold-the-world propounded the question to Christian and his fellow, and bid them to answer it if they could.

CHR. Then said Christian, Even a babe in religion may answer ten thousand such questions. For if it be unlawful to follow Christ for loaves, as it is, how much more abominable is it to make of him and religion a stalking-horse, to get and enjoy the world? Nor do we find any other than heathens, hypocrites, devils, and witches, that are of this opinion.

John vi.

1. Heathens: for when Hamor and Shechem had a mind to the daughter and cattle of Jacob, and saw that there was no way for them to come at them but by becoming circumcised, they say to their companions: If every male of us be circumcised, as they are circumcised, shall not their cattle, and their substance, and every beast of theirs, be ours? Their daughter and their cattle were that which they sought to obtain, and their religion the stalking-horse they made use of to come at them. Read the whole story.

Gen. xxxiv. 20-23.

2. The hypocritical Pharisees were also of this religion; long prayers were their pretence, but to get widows' houses was their intent; and greater damnation was from God their judgment.

Luke xx. 46, 47.

3. Judas the devil was also of this religion; he was religious for the bag, that he might be possessed of what was therein; but he was lost, cast away, and the very son of perdition.

4. Simon the witch was of this religion too: for he would have had the Holy Ghost, that he might

have got money therewith, and his sentence from Acts viii. 19-22.
Peter's mouth was according.

5. Neither will it out of my mind, but that that
man that takes up religion for the world, will throw
away religion for the world; for so surely as Judas
designed the world in becoming religious, so surely
did he also sell religion and his Master for the same.
To answer the question therefore affirmatively, as I
perceive you have done, and to accept of as authen-
tic such answer, is both heathenish, hypocritical,
and devilish, and your reward will be according to
your works.   Then they stood staring one upon
another, but had not wherewith to answer Christian.
Hopeful also approved of the soundness of Christian's
answer; so there was a great silence among them.
Mr. By-ends and his company also staggered and
kept behind, that Christian and Hopeful might
outgo them.   Then said Christian to his fellow, If
these men cannot stand before the sentence of men,
what will they do with the sentence of God?   And
if they are mute when dealt with by vessels of clay,
what will they do when they shall be rebuked by
the flames of a devouring fire?

Then Christian and Hopeful outwent them again, *The ease
and went till they came at a delicate plain called *that pilgrims
Ease, where they went with much content; but *little in this
that plain was but narrow, so they were quickly got *life.
over it.   Now at the further side of that plain was
a little hill called Lucre, and in that hill a silver- *Lucre Hill
mine, which some of them that had formerly gone *a dangerous
that way, because of the rarity of it, had turned *hill.
aside to see; but going too near the brink of the

pit, the ground being deceitful under them, broke, and they were slain; some also had been maimed there, and could not to their dying day be their own men again.

Then I saw in my dream, that a little off the road, over against the silver-mine, stood Demas (gentlemanlike) to call to passengers to come and see; who said to Christian and his fellow: Ho, turn aside hither, and I will show you a thing.

CHR. What thing so deserving, as to turn us out of the way?

DEMAS. Here is a silver-mine, and some digging in it for treasure; if you will come, with a little pains you may richly provide for yourselves.

HOPE. Then said Hopeful, Let us go see.

CHR. Not I, said Christian; I have heard of this place before now, and how many have there been slain; and besides, that treasure is a snare to those that seek it, for it hindereth them in their pilgrimage. Then Christian called to Demas, saying, Is not the place dangerous? hath it not hindered many in their pilgrimage?

DEMAS. Not very dangerous, except to those that are careless; but withal, he blushed as he spake.

CHR. Then said Christian to Hopeful, Let us not stir a step, but still keep on our way.

HOPE. I will warrant you, when By-ends comes up, if he hath the same invitation as we, he will turn in thither to see.

CHR. No doubt thereof, for his principles lead him that way, and a hundred to one but he dies there.

DEMAS. Then Demas called again, saying, But will you not come over and see?

CHR. Then Christian roundly answered, saying, Demas, Thou art an enemy to the right ways of the Lord of this way, and hast been already condemned for thine own turning aside, by one of his Majesty's judges; and why seekest thou to bring us into the like condemnation? Besides, if we at all turn aside, our Lord the King will certainly hear thereof, and will there put us to shame, where we would stand with boldness before him.

Christian roundeth up Demas.
2 Tim. iv. 10.

Demas cried again, That he also was one of their fraternity; and that if they would tarry a little, he also himself would walk with them.

CHR. Then said Christian, What is thy name? is it not the same by the which I have called thee?

DEMAS. Yes, my name is Demas, I am the son of Abraham.

CHR. I know you, Gehazi was your great-grandfather, and Judas your father, and you have trod their steps. It is but a devilish prank that thou usest; thy father was hanged for a traitor, and thou deservest no better reward. Assure thyself that when we come to the King, we will do him word of this thy behaviour. Thus they went their way.

2 Kings v. 20.
Matt. xxvi. 14, 15.
Chap. xxvii. 1-5.

By this time By-ends and his companions were come again within sight, and they at the first beck went over to Demas. Now, whether they fell into the pit by looking over the brink thereof, or whether they went down to dig, or whether they were smothered in the bottom, by the damps that commonly arise, of these things I am not certain; But

By-ends goes over to Demas.

this I observed, that they never were seen again in the way.   Then sang Christian :

> By-ends and Silver-Demas both agree ;
> One calls, the other runs, that he may be
> A sharer in his lucre ; so these two
> Take up in this world, and no further go.

Now I saw, that just on the other side of this plain, the pilgrims came to a place where stood an old monument, hard by the highway-side, at the sight of which they were both concerned, because of the strangeness of the form thereof; for it seemed to them as if it had been a woman transformed into the shape of a pillar : here therefore they stood looking, and looking upon it, but could not for a time tell what they should make thereof.   At last Hopeful espied written above upon the head thereof, a writing in an unusual hand ; but he being no scholar, called to Christian (for he was learned) to see if he could pick out the meaning ; so he came, and after a little laying of letters together, he found the same to be this, 'Remember Lot's wife.'   So he read it to his fellow ; after which they both concluded that that was the pillar of salt into which Lot's wife was turned, for her looking back with a covetous heart, when she was going from Sodom for safety.   Which sudden and amazing sight gave them occasion of this discourse :

CHR. Ah, my brother, this is a seasonable sight ; it came opportunely to us after the invitation which Demas gave us to come over to view the Hill Lucre ; and had we gone over as he desired us, and as thou wast inclined to do (my brother), we had,

They see a strange monument.

Gen. xix. 26.

for aught I know, been made ourselves like this woman, a spectacle for those that shall come after to behold.

Hope. I am sorry that I was so foolish, and am made to wonder that I am not now as Lot's wife; for wherein was the difference 'twixt her sin and mine? she only looked back, and I had a desire to go see. Let grace be adored, and let me be ashamed that ever such a thing should be in mine heart.

Chr. Let us take notice of what we see here, for our help for time to come: this woman escaped one judgment, for she fell not by the destruction of Sodom; yet she was destroyed by another; as we see, she is turned into a pillar of salt.

Hope. True, and she may be to us both caution and example; caution that we should shun her sin, or a sign of what judgment will overtake such as shall not be prevented by this caution: so Korah, Dathan, and Abiram, with the two hundred and fifty men that perished in their sin, did also become a sign or example to others to beware: but above all, I muse at one thing, to wit, how Demas and his fellows can stand so confidently yonder to look for that treasure, which this woman, but for looking behind her, after (for we read not that she stepped one foot out of the way) was turned into a pillar of salt; specially since the judgment which overtook her, did make her an example, within sight of where they are: for they cannot choose but see her, did they but lift up their eyes. _Num. xxvi. 9, 10._

Chr. It is a thing to be wondered at, and it argueth that their hearts are grown desperate in the case; and I cannot tell who to compare them to so fitly, as to them that pick pockets in the presence of the judge, or that will cut purses under the gallows. It is said of the men of Sodom, 'that they were sinners exceedingly,' because they were sinners 'before the Lord'; that is, in his eyesight; and notwithstanding the kindnesses that he had showed them, for the land of Sodom was now like the garden of Eden heretofore. This therefore provoked him the more to jealousy, and made their plague as hot as the fire of the Lord out of heaven could make it. And it is most rationally to be concluded, that such, even such as these are, that shall sin in the sight, yea, and that too in despite of such examples that are set continually before them, to caution them to the contrary, must be partakers of severest judgments.

HOPE. Doubtless thou hast said the truth; but what a mercy is it, that neither thou, but especially I, am not made myself this example: this ministereth occasion to us to thank God, to fear before him, and always to remember Lot's wife.

I saw then, that they went on their way to a pleasant river, which David the king called the 'river of God,' but John, the 'river of the water of life.' Now their way lay just upon the bank of the river; here therefore Christian and his companion walked with great delight; they drank also of the water of the river, which was pleasant and enlivening to their weary spirits: besides, on the banks of this river on either side were green trees, that bore all manner of fruit; and the leaves of the trees were

Gen. xiii. 13.

Ver. 10.

A river.

Ps. lxv. 9.
Rev. xxii.
Ezek. xlvii.

Trees by the river.

good for medicine; with the fruit of these trees they were also much delighted; and the leaves they ate to prevent surfeits, and other diseases that are incident to those that heat their blood by travels. On either side of the river was also a meadow, curiously beautified with lilies; and it was green all the year long. In this meadow they lay down and slept, for here they might lie down safely. When they awoke, they gathered again of the fruit of the trees, and drank again of the water of the river, and then lay down again to sleep. Thus they did several days and nights. Then they sang:

The fruit and leaves of the trees.

A meadow in which they lie down to sleep. Ps. xxiii. 2. Isa. xiv. 30.

> Behold ye how these crystal streams do glide
> (To comfort Pilgrims) by the highway-side ;
> The meadows green, besides their fragrant smell,
> Yield dainties for them ; And he that can tell
> What pleasant fruit, yea, leaves, these trees do yield,
> Will soon sell all, that he may buy this field.

So when they were disposed to go on (for they were not, as yet, at their journey's end) they ate and drank, and departed.

Now I beheld in my dream, that they had not journeyed far, but the river and the way, for a time, parted; at which they were not a little sorry, yet they durst not go out of the way. Now the way from the river was rough, and their feet tender by reason of their travels; so the souls of the pilgrims were much discouraged because of the way: Wherefore still as they went on, they wished for better way. Now a little before them, there was on the left hand of the road a meadow, and a stile to go over into it, and that meadow is called By-path

Num. xxi. 4.

By-path
Meadow.

Meadow. Then said Christian to his fellow, If this meadow lieth along by our way-side, let's go over into it. Then he went to the stile to see, and behold a path lay along by the way on the other side of the fence. 'Tis according to my wish, said Christian, here is the easiest going; come, good Hopeful, and let us go over.

One temptation does make way for another.

HOPE. But how if this path should lead us out of the way?

CHR. That's not like, said the other; look, doth it not go along by the way-side? So Hopeful, being persuaded by his fellow, went after him over the stile. When they were gone over, and were got into the path, they found it very easy for their feet: and withal, they looking before them, espied a man walking as they did (and his name was Vain-confidence), so they called after him, and asked him whither that way led? he said, To the Celestial Gate. Look, said Christian, did not I tell you so? by this you may see we are right. So they followed, and he went before them. But behold the night came on, and it grew very dark, so that they that were behind lost the sight of him that went before.

Strong
Christians
may lead
weak ones
out of the
way.

See what it
is too suddenly to fall
in with
strangers.

He therefore that went before (Vain-confidence by name) not seeing the way before him, fell into a deep pit, which was on purpose there made by the Prince of those grounds, to catch vain-glorious fools withal, and was dashed in pieces with his fall.

A pit to
catch the
vain-glorious
in.
Isa. ix. 16.

Now Christian and his fellow heard him fall. So they called, to know the matter, but there was none to answer, only they heard a groaning. Then said

Hopeful, Where are we now ? Then was his fellow Reasoning between Christian and Hopeful. silent, as mistrusting that he had led him out of the way; and now it began to rain, and thunder, and lighten in a very dreadful manner, and the water rose amain.

Then Hopeful groaned in himself, saying, Oh, that I had kept on my way!

CHR. Who could have thought that this path should have led us out of the way?

HOPE. I was afraid on't at the very first, and therefore gave you that gentle caution. I would have spoke plainer, but that you are older than I.

CHR. Good brother, be not offended; I am sorry Christian's repentance for leading of his brother out of the way. I have brought thee out of the way, and that I have put thee into such eminent danger; pray, my brother, forgive me, I did not do it of an evil intent.

HOPE. Be comforted, my brother, for I forgive thee; and believe too that this shall be for our good.

CHR. I am glad I have with me a merciful brother; But we must not stand thus, let's try to go back again.

HOPE. But, good brother, let me go before.

CHR. No, if you please, let me go first; that, if there be any danger, I may be first therein, because by my means we are both gone out of the way.

HOPE. No, said Hopeful, you shall not go first; for your mind being troubled, may lead you out of the way again. Then for their encouragement, they heard the voice of one saying, 'Let thine Jer. xxxi. 21. heart be towards the highway, even the way that

They are in
danger of
drowning as
they go back.
thou wentest; turn again.' But by this time the
waters were greatly risen, by reason of which the
way of going back was very dangerous. (Then I
thought that it is easier going out of the way when
we are in, than going in when we are out.) Yet
they adventured to go back; but it was so dark,
and the flood was so high, that in their going back,
they had like to have been drowned nine or ten
times.

Neither could they, with all the skill they had,
get again to the stile that night. Wherefore, at
last lighting under a little shelter, they sat down
there till the day brake; but, being weary, they
They sleep in
the grounds
of Giant
Despair.
fell asleep.[1] Now there was, not far from the place
where they lay, a castle, called Doubting Castle,
the owner whereof was Giant Despair, and it was
in his grounds they now were sleeping: wherefore
he getting up in the morning early, and walking
He finds
them in his
ground, and
carries them
to Doubting
Castle.
up and down in his fields, caught Christian and
Hopeful asleep in his grounds. Then with a grim
and surly voice he bid them awake, and asked them
whence they were, and what they did in his grounds.
They told him they were pilgrims, and that they
had lost their way. Then said the Giant, You have
this night trespassed on me, by trampling in and
lying on my grounds, and therefore you must go
along with me. So they were forced to go, because
he was stronger than they. They also had but

[1] The Pilgrims now, to gratify the flesh,
   Will seek its ease; but oh! how they afresh
   Do thereby plunge themselves new griefs into!
   Who seek to please the flesh, themselves undo.

little to say, for they knew themselves in a fault.
The giant therefore drove them before him, and
put them into his castle, into a very dark dungeon, The grievous-
nasty and stinking to the spirits of these two men : ness of their
here then they lay, from Wednesday morning till ment.
Saturday night, without one bit of bread, or drop
of drink, or light, or any to ask how they did.
They were therefore here in evil case, and were far Ps. lxxxviii. 18.
from friends and acquaintance. Now in this place,
Christian had double sorrow, because 'twas through
his unadvised counsel that they were brought into
this distress.

Now Giant Despair had a wife, and her name
was Diffidence. So when he was gone to bed, he
told his wife what he had done, to wit, that he had
taken a couple of prisoners, and cast them into his
dungeon, for trespassing on his grounds. Then he
asked her also what he had best to do further to
them. So she asked him what they were, whence
they came, and whither they were bound ; and he told
her. Then she counselled him, that when he arose
in the morning he should beat them, without any
mercy. So when he arose, he getteth him a grievous
crab-tree cudgel, and goes down into the dungeon
to them, and there first falls to rating of them as if
they were dogs, although they gave him never a
word of distaste. Then he falls upon them, and On Thursday,
beats them fearfully, in such sort, that they were Giant Despair
beats his
not able to help themselves, or to turn them upon prisoners.
the floor. This done, he withdraws and leaves
them, there to condole their misery, and to mourn
under their distress : so all that day they spent the

time in nothing but sighs and bitter lamentations. The next night, she, talking with her husband about them further, and understanding that they were yet alive, did advise him to counsel them to make away themselves. So when morning was come, he goes to them in a surly manner as before, and perceiving them to be very sore with the stripes that he had given them the day before, he told them, that since they were never like to come out of that place, their only way would be, forthwith to make an end of themselves, either with knife, halter, or poison: For why, said he, should you choose life, seeing it is attended with so much bitterness? But they desired him to let them go. With that he looked ugly upon them, and rushing to them had doubtless made an end of them himself, but that he fell into one of his fits (for he sometimes in sunshiny weather fell into fits), and lost (for a time) the use of his hand; wherefore he withdrew, and left them (as before), to consider what to do. Then did the prisoners consult between themselves, whether 'twas best to take his counsel or no; and thus they began to discourse:

CHR. Brother, said Christian, what shall we do? The life that we now live is miserable: for my part I know not whether is best, to live thus, or to die out of hand. 'My soul chooseth strangling rather than life,' and the grave is more easy for me than this dungeon: Shall we be ruled by the Giant?

HOPE. Indeed our present condition is dreadful, and death would be far more welcome to me than thus for ever to abide: But yet let us consider, the

Margin notes:

On Friday, Giant Despair counsels them to kill themselves.

The Giant sometimes has fits.

Christian crushed.

Job vii. 15.

Lord of the country to which we are going hath said, Thou shalt do no murder, no, not to another man's person; much more then are we forbidden to take his counsel to kill ourselves. Besides, he that kills another, can but commit murder upon his body; but for one to kill himself, is to kill body and soul at once. And moreover, my brother, thou talkest of ease in the grave; but hast thou for- gotten the hell, whither for certain the murderers go? for, 'no murderer hath eternal life,' etc. And, let us consider, again, that all the law is not in the hand of Giant Despair: Others, so far as I can understand, have been taken by him as well as we; and yet have escaped out of his hand: Who knows, but that God that made the world, may cause that Giant Despair may die; or that at some time or other he may forget to lock us in; or but he may in a short time have another of his fits before us, and may lose the use of his limbs; and if ever that should come to pass again, for my part I am resolved to pluck up the heart of a man, and to try my utmost to get from under his hand. I was a fool that I did not try to do it before; but however, my brother, let's be patient, and endure a while: the time may come that may give us a happy release; but let us not be our own murderers. With these words Hopeful at present did moderate the mind of his brother; so they continued together (in the dark) that day, in their sad and doleful condition.

Hopeful comforts him.

Well, towards evening the giant goes down into the dungeon again, to see if his prisoners had taken his counsel; but when he came there, he found them alive, and truly, alive was all; for now, what for want of bread and water, and by reason of the wounds they received when he beat them, they could do little but breathe: But, I say, he found them alive; at which he fell into a grievous rage, and told them, that seeing they had disobeyed his counsel, it should be worse with them than if they had never been born.

At this they trembled greatly, and I think that Christian fell into a swoon; but coming a little to himself again, they renewed their discourse about the giant's counsel, and whether yet they had best to take it or no.   Now Christian again seemed to be for doing it, but Hopeful made his second reply as followeth:

Christian still dejected.

HOPE. My brother, said he, rememberest thou not how valiant thou hast been heretofore? Apollyon could not crush thee, nor could all that thou didst hear, or see, or feel in the Valley of the Shadow of Death; what hardship, terror, and amazement hast thou already gone through, and art thou now nothing but fear? Thou seest that I am in the dungeon with thee, a far weaker man by nature than thou art: Also this giant has wounded me as well as thee, and hath also cut off the bread and water from my mouth; and with thee I mourn without the light.   But let's exercise a little more patience. Remember how thou playedst the man at Vanity Fair, and wast neither afraid of the chain nor cage; nor yet of bloody death: wherefore let us (at least to avoid the shame, that becomes not a

Hopeful comforts him again, by calling former things to remembrance.

Christian to be found in) bear up with patience as well as we can.

Now night being come again, and the Giant and his wife being in bed, she asked him concerning the prisoners, and if they had taken his counsel. To which he replied, They are sturdy rogues, they choose rather to bear all hardship, than to make away themselves. Then said she, Take them into the castle-yard to-morrow, and show them the bones and skulls of those that thou hast already despatched, and make them believe, ere a week comes to an end, thou also wilt tear them in pieces, as thou hast done their fellows before them.

So when the morning was come, the Giant goes to them again, and takes them into the castle-yard, and shows them as his wife had bidden him. These, said he, were pilgrims as you are, once, and they trespassed in my grounds, as you have done; and when I thought fit, I tore them in pieces, and so within ten days I will do you. Go, get you down to your den again; and with that he beat them all the way thither. They lay therefore all day on Saturday in lamentable case, as before. Now when night was come, and when Mrs. Diffidence and her husband the Giant were got to bed, they began to renew their discourse of their prisoners; and withal, the old Giant wondered, that he could neither by his blows, nor counsel, bring them to an end. And with that his wife replied, I fear, said she, that they live in hope that some will come to relieve them, or that they have pick-locks about them, by the means of which they hope to escape. And, sayest

On Saturday, the Giant threatened that shortly he would pull them in pieces.

thou so, my dear? said the Giant, I will therefore search them in the morning.

Well, on Saturday about midnight they began to pray, and continued in prayer till almost break of day.

Now a little before it was day, good Christian, as one half amazed, brake out in this passionate speech: What a fool, quoth he, am I thus to lie in a stinking dungeon, when I may as well walk at liberty! I have a key in my bosom called Promise, that will, I am persuaded, open any lock in Doubting Castle. Then said Hopeful, That's good news; good brother, pluck it out of thy bosom and try.

Then Christian pulled it out of his bosom, and began to try at the dungeon door, whose bolt (as he turned the key) gave back, and the door flew open with ease, and Christian and Hopeful both came out. Then he went to the outward door that leads into the castle-yard, and with his key opened that door also. After he went to the iron gate, for that must be opened too, but that lock went damnable hard, yet the key did open it; then they thrust open the gate to make their escape with speed, but that gate, as it opened, made such a creaking, that it waked Giant Despair, who hastily rising to pursue his prisoners, felt his limbs to fail, for his fits took him again, so that he could by no means go after them. Then they went on, and came to the King's highway, and so were safe, because they were out of his jurisdiction.

Now when they were gone over the stile, they began to contrive with themselves what they should

A key in Christian's bosom, called Promise, opens any lock in Doubting Castle.

do at that stile, to prevent those that should come after from falling into the hands of Giant Despair. So they consented to erect there a pillar, and to engrave upon the side thereof this sentence, 'Over this stile is the way to Doubting Castle, which is kept by Giant Despair, who despiseth the King of the Celestial Country, and seeks to destroy his holy pilgrims.' Many therefore that followed after, read what was written, and escaped the danger. This done, they sang as follows— *A pillar erected by Christian and his fellow.*

> Out of the way we went, and then we found
> What 'twas to tread upon forbidden ground;
> And let them that come after have a care,
> Lest heedlessness makes them, as we, to fare:
> Lest they, for trespassing, his prisoners are,
> Whose Castle's Doubting, and whose name's Despair.

They went then, till they came to the Delectable Mountains,[1] which mountains belong to the Lord of that hill, of which we have spoken before; so they went up to the mountains, to behold the gardens and orchards, the vineyards, and fountains of water; where also they drank, and washed themselves, and did freely eat of the vineyards. Now there were on the tops of these mountains Shepherds feeding their flocks, and they stood by the highway-side. The pilgrims therefore went to them, and leaning upon their staves (as is common with weary pilgrims, when they stand to talk with any by the way) they *The Delectable Mountains.* *They are refreshed in the mountains.*

[1] Mountains Delectable they now ascend,
Where Shepherds be, which to them do commend
Alluring things, and things that cautious are,
Pilgrims are steady kept by faith and fear.

Talk with
the Shep-
herds.
asked, Whose delectable Mountains are these? and whose be the sheep that feed upon them?

John x. 11.
SHEP. These mountains are Immanuel's Land, and they are within sight of his city; and the sheep also are his, and he laid down his life for them.

CHR. Is this the way to the Celestial City?

SHEP. You are just in your way.

CHR. How far is it thither?

SHEP. Too far for any, but those that *shall* get thither indeed.

CHR. Is the way safe, or dangerous?

Hos. xiv. 9.
SHEP. Safe for those for whom it is to be safe, but transgressors shall fall therein.

CHR. Is there in this place any relief for pilgrims that are weary and faint in the way?

Heb. xiii. 1, 2.
SHEP. The Lord of these mountains hath given us a charge not to be forgetful to entertain strangers; therefore the good of the place is before you.

I saw also in my dream, that when the Shepherds perceived that they were wayfaring men, they also put questions to them (to which they made answer as in other places), as, Whence came you? and, How got you into the way? and, By what means have you so persevered therein? For but few of them that begin to come hither, do show their face on these mountains. But when the Shepherds heard their answers, being pleased therewith, they looked very lovingly upon them, and said, Welcome to the Delectable Mountains!

The Shep-
herds wel-
come them.

The names
of the Shep-
herds.
The Shepherds, I say, whose names were Knowledge, Experience, Watchful, and Sincere, took them by the hand, and had them to their tents,

and made them partake of that which was ready at present. They said moreover, We would that you should stay here a while, to be acquainted with us, and yet more to solace yourselves with the good of these Delectable Mountains. They then told them that they were content to stay; and so they went to their rest that night, because it was very late.

Then I saw in my dream, that in the morning, the Shepherds called up Christian and Hopeful to walk with them upon the mountains: So they went forth with them, and walked a while, having a pleasant prospect on every side. Then said the Shepherds one to another, Shall we show these *They are* pilgrims some wonders? So when they had con- *shown* *wonders.* cluded to do it, they had them first to the top of a hill called Error, which was very steep on the *The Moun-* furthest side, and bid them look down to the *tain of Error.* bottom. So Christian and Hopeful looked down, and saw at the bottom several men dashed all to pieces by a fall that they had from the top. Then said Christian, What meaneth this? The Shepherds answered, Have you not heard of them that were made to err, by hearkening to Hymenæus and Philetus, as concerning the faith of the re- *2 Tim. ii. 17,* surrection of the body? They answered, Yes. *18.* Then said the Shepherds, Those that you see lie dashed in pieces at the bottom of this mountain are they; and they have continued to this day unburied (as you see) for an example to others to take heed how they clamber too high, or how they come too near the brink of this mountain.

Then I saw that they had them to the top of
another mountain, and the name of that is Caution,
and bid them look afar off; which when they did,
they perceived, as they thought, several men walking up and down among the tombs that were there.
And they perceived that the men were blind,
because they stumbled sometimes upon the tombs,
and because they could not get out from among
them. Then said Christian, What means this?

The Shepherds then answered, Did you not see
a little below these mountains a stile that led into
a meadow on the left hand of this way? They
answered, Yes. Then said the Shepherds, From
that stile there goes a path that leads directly to
Doubting Castle, which is kept by Giant Despair;
and these men (pointing to them among the tombs)
came once on pilgrimage, as you do now, even till
they came to that same stile. And because the
right way was rough in that place, they chose to go
out of it into that meadow, and there were taken
by Giant Despair, and cast into Doubting Castle;
where, after they had a while been kept in the
dungeon, he at last did put out their eyes, and led
them among those tombs, where he has left them
to wander to this very day; that the saying of the
wise man might be fulfilled, 'He that wandereth
out of the way of understanding shall remain in the
congregation of the dead.' Then Christian and
Hopeful looked upon one another, with tears gush-
ing out, but yet said nothing to the Shepherds.

Then I saw in my dream, that the Shepherds had
them to another place, in a bottom, where was a

Mount
Caution.

Prov. xxi. 16.

door in the side of a hill; and they opened the door, and bid them look in. They looked in therefore, and saw that within it was very dark, and smoky; they also thought that they heard there a rumbling noise as of fire, and a cry of some tormented, and that they smelt the scent of brimstone. Then said Christian, What means this? The Shepherds told them, This is a by-way to hell, a way that hypocrites go in at; namely, such as sell their birthright, with Esau; such as sell their Master, with Judas; such as blaspheme the gospel, with Alexander; and that lie and dissemble, with Ananias and Sapphira his wife.

A by-way to hell.

HOPE. Then said Hopeful to the Shepherds, I perceive that these had on them, even every one, a show of Pilgrimage, as we have now; had they not?

SHEP. Yes, and held it a long time too.

HOPE. How far might they go on pilgrimage in their day, since they notwithstanding were thus miserably cast away?

SHEP. Some further, and some not so far as these mountains.

Then said the pilgrims one to another, We had need to cry to the Strong for strength.

SHEP. Ay, and you will have need to use it when you have it too.

By this time the pilgrims had a desire to go forwards, and the Shepherds a desire they should; so they walked together towards the end of the mountains. Then said the Shepherds one to another, Let us here show to the pilgrims the gates

The Shepherds' perspective-glass.

The Hill Clear.

of the Celestial City, if they have skill to look through our perspective-glass. The pilgrims then lovingly accepted the motion: So they had them to the top of a high hill, called Clear, and gave them their glass to look.

Then they essayed to look, but the remembrance of that last thing that the Shepherds had showed them, made their hands shake, by means of which impediment they could not look steadily through the glass; yet they thought they saw something like the gate, and also some of the glory of the place. Then they went away and sang this song—

The fruits of servile fear.

> Thus by the Shepherds secrets are reveal'd,
> Which from all other men are kept conceal'd:
> Come to the Shepherds then, if you would see
> Things deep, things hid, and that mysterious be.

When they were about to depart, one of the Shepherds gave them a note of the way. Another of them bid them beware of the Flatterer. The third bid them take heed that they sleep not upon the Enchanted Ground. And the fourth bid them God-speed. So I awoke from my dream.

A two-fold caution.

And I slept, and dreamed again, and saw the same two pilgrims going down the mountains along the highway towards the city. Now, a little below these mountains, on the left hand, lieth the country of Conceit; from which country there comes into the way in which the pilgrims walked a little crooked lane. Here therefore they met with a very brisk lad, that came out of that country, and his name was Ignorance. So Christian asked him from what parts he came, and whither he was going.

The Country of Conceit, out of which came Ignorance.

IGNOR. Sir, I was born in the country that lieth off there, a little on the left hand; and I am going to the Celestial City.

Christian and Ignorance have some talk.

CHR. But how do you think to get in at the gate, for you may find some difficulty there?

IGNOR. As other good people do, said he.

CHR. But what have you to show at that gate, that may cause that the gate should be opened to you?

IGNOR. I know my Lord's will, and I have been a good liver; I pay every man his own; I pray, fast, pay tithes, and give alms, and have left my country for whither I am going.

The ground of Ignorance's hope.

CHR. But thou camest not in at the Wicket-Gate that is at the head of this way; thou camest in hither through that same crooked lane, and therefore I fear, however thou mayest think of thyself, when the reckoning day shall come, thou wilt have laid to thy charge that thou art a thief and a robber, instead of getting admittance into the city.

IGNOR. Gentlemen, ye be utter strangers to me; I know you not: be content to follow the religion of your country, and I will follow the religion of mine. I hope all will be well. And as for the gate that you talk of, all the world knows that that is a great way off of our country. I cannot think that any man in all our parts doth so much as know the way to it; nor need they matter whether they do or no, since we have, as you see, a fine pleasant green lane, that comes down from our country the next way into it.

He saith to every one that he is a fool.

When Christian saw that the man was wise in

his own conceit, he said to Hopeful whisperingly,

Prov. xxvi. 12.
There is more hopes of a fool than of him.   And

Eccles. x. 3.
said moreover, 'When he that is a fool walketh by
the way, his wisdom faileth him, and he saith to

How to
carry it to
a fool.
every one that he is a fool.'   What, shall we talk
further with him? or outgo him at present? and so
leave him to think of what he hath heard already;
and then stop again for him afterwards, and see if
by degrees we can do any good of him?   Then said
Hopeful—

> Let Ignorance a little while now muse
> On what is said, and let him not refuse
> Good counsel to embrace, lest he remain
> Still ignorant of what's the chiefest gain.
> God saith, Those that no understanding have,
> (Although he made them) them he will not save.

HOPE. He further added, It is not good, I think,
to say all to him at once; let us pass him by, if
you will, and talk to him anon, even as he is able
to bear it.

So they both went on, and Ignorance he came
after.   Now when they had passed him a little way,
they entered into a very dark lane, where they met

Matt. xii. 45.
Prov. v. 22.
a man whom seven devils had bound with seven
strong cords, and were carrying of him back to the
door that they saw on the side of the hill.   Now
good Christian began to tremble, and so did Hopeful his companion: Yet as the devils led away the
man, Christian looked to see if he knew him, and he
thought it might be one Turn-away that dwelt in

The destruc-
tion of one
Turn-away.
the town of Apostacy.   But he did not perfectly
see his face, for he did hang his head like a thief

that is found : But being gone past, Hopeful looked after him, and espied on his back a paper with this inscription, ' Wanton professor, and damnable apostate.' Then said Christian to his fellow, Now I call to remembrance that which was told me of a thing that happened to a good man hereabout. The name of the man was Little-faith, but a good man, and he dwelt in the town of Sincere. The thing was this : at the entering in of this passage there comes down from Broadway Gate a lane called Deadman's Lane; so called, because of the murders that are commonly done there. And this Little-faith going on pilgrimage, as we do now, chanced to sit down there and slept. Now there happened, at that time, to come down that lane from Broadway Gate, three sturdy rogues, and their names were Faint-heart, Mistrust, and Guilt (three brothers), and they espying Little-faith where he was, came galloping up with speed : Now the good man was just awaked from his sleep, and was getting up to go on his journey. So they came all up to him, and with threatening language bid him stand. At this, Little-faith looked as white as a clout, and had neither power to fight nor fly. Then said Faint-heart, Deliver thy purse; but he making no haste to do it (for he was loth to lose his money), Mistrust ran up to him, and thrusting his hand into his pocket, pulled out thence a bag of silver. Then he cried out, Thieves, thieves ! With that, Guilt, with a great club that was in his hand, struck Little-faith on the head, and with that blow felled him flat to the ground, where he lay bleeding as one that

Christian telleth his companion a story of Little-faith.

Broadway Gate. Deadman's Lane.

Little-faith robbed by Faint-heart, Mistrust and Guilt.

They got away his silver, and knocked him down.

would bleed to death. All this while the thieves stood by: But at last, they hearing that some were upon the road, and fearing lest it should be one Great-grace that dwells in the city of Good-confidence, they betook themselves to their heels, and left this good man to shift for himself. Now after a while, Little-faith came to himself, and getting up, made shift to scramble on his way. This was the story.

HOPE. But did they take from him all that ever he had?

CHR. No: The place where his jewels were, they never ransacked, so those he kept still; but, as I was told, the good man was much afflicted for his loss, for the thieves got most of his spending money. That which they got not (as I said) were jewels; also he had a little odd money left, but scarce enough to bring him to his journey's end. Nay, if I was not misinformed, he was forced to beg as he went, to keep himself alive, for his jewels he might not sell; but beg, and do what he could, he went (as we say) with many a hungry belly the most part of the rest of the way.

HOPE. But is it not a wonder they got not from him his certificate, by which he was to receive his admittance at the Celestial Gate?

CHR. 'Tis a wonder, but they got not that: though they missed it not through any good cunning of his; for he, being dismayed with their coming upon him, had neither power nor skill to hide anything; so it was more by good providence than by his endeavour, that they missed of that good thing.

Little-faith lost not his best things.

1 Pet. iv. 18.

Little-faith forced to beg to his journey's end.

He kept not his best things by his own cunning.
2 Tim. i. 14.

Hope. But it must needs be a comfort to him that they got not this jewel from him.

Chr. It might have been good comfort to him, had 2 Pet. ii. 9. he used it as he should; but they that told me the story said, That he made but little use of it all the rest of the way, and that because of the dismay that he had in their taking away his money. Indeed, he forgot it a great part of the rest of his journey; and besides, when at any time it came into his mind, and he began to be comforted therewith, then would fresh thoughts of his loss come again upon him, and those thoughts would swallow up all.

Hope. Alas, poor man! this could not but be a He is pitied by both. great grief unto him.

Chr. Grief! Ay, a grief indeed. Would it not have been so to any of us, had we been used as he, to be robbed and wounded too, and that in a strange place, as he was? 'Tis a wonder he did not die with grief, poor heart! I was told that he scattered almost all the rest of the way with nothing but doleful and bitter complaints; telling also to all that overtook him, or that he overtook in the way as he went, where he was robbed, and how; who they were that did it, and what he lost; how he was wounded, and that he hardly escaped with life.

Hope. But 'tis a wonder that his necessity did not put him upon selling or pawning some of his jewels, that he might have wherewith to relieve himself in his journey.

Chr. Thou talkest like one upon whose head is Christian snibbeth his fellow for unadvised speaking. the shell to this very day. For what should he pawn them? or to whom should he sell them? In all that country where he was robbed, his jewels were not accounted of, nor did he want that relief which could from thence be administered to him. Besides, had his jewels been missing at the gate of the Celestial City, he had (and that he knew well enough) been excluded from an inheritance there; and that would have been worse to him than the appearance and villainy of ten thousand thieves.

Heb. xii. 16.

HOPE. Why art thou so tart, my brother? Esau sold his birthright, and that for a mess of pottage, and that birthright was his greatest jewel; and if he, why might not Little-faith do so too?

A discourse about Esau and Little-faith.

CHR. Esau did sell his birthright indeed, and so do many besides, and by so doing, exclude themselves from the chief blessing, as also that caitiff did. But you must put a difference betwixt Esau and Little-faith, and also betwixt their estates. Esau's birthright was typical, but Little-faith's jewels were not so. Esau's belly was his god, but Little-faith's belly was not so. Esau's want lay in his fleshly appetite; Little-faith's did not so. Besides,

Esau was ruled by his lusts. Gen. xxv. 32.

Esau could see no further than to the fulfilling of his lusts: 'For I am at the point to die,' said he, 'and what good will this birthright do me?' But Little-faith, though it was his lot to have but a little faith, was by his little faith kept from such extravagances, and made to see and prize his jewels more than to sell them, as Esau did his birthright. You

Esau never had faith.

read not anywhere that Esau had faith, no, not so much as a little; therefore no marvel, if where the flesh only bears sway (as it will in that man where no faith is to resist), if he sells his birthright, and his soul and all, and that to the devil of hell; for it is with such, as it is with the ass, who in her occasions cannot be turned away. When their minds are set upon their lusts, they will have them whatever they cost. But Little-faith was of another temper, his mind was on things divine; his livelihood was upon things that were spiritual, and from above: Therefore to what end should he that is of such a temper sell his jewels (had there been any that would have bought them) to fill his mind with empty things? Will a man give a penny to fill his belly with hay? or can you persuade the turtle-dove to live upon carrion, like the crow? Though faithless ones can, for carnal lusts, pawn, or mortgage, or sell what they have, and themselves outright to boot; yet they that have faith, saving faith, though but a little of it, cannot do so. Here, therefore, my brother, is thy mistake.

Jer. ii. 24.

Little-faith could not live upon Esau's pottage.

A comparison between the turtle-dove and the crow.

HOPE. I acknowledge it; but yet your severe reflection had almost made me angry.

CHR. Why, I did but compare thee to some of the birds that are of the brisker sort, who will run to and fro in untrodden paths with the shell upon their heads; but pass by that, and consider the matter under debate, and all shall be well betwixt thee and me.

HOPE. But, Christian, these three fellows, I am persuaded in my heart, are but a company of cowards; would they have run else, think you, as they did, at the noise of one that was coming on the road? Why did not Little-faith pluck up a greater heart? He might, methinks, have stood one brush

Hopeful swaggers.

with them, and have yielded when there had been no remedy.

CHR. That they are cowards, many have said, but few have found it so in the time of trial. As for a great heart, Little-faith had none; and I perceive by thee, my brother, hadst thou been the man concerned, thou art but for a brush, and then to yield. And verily, since this is the height of thy stomach now they are at a distance from us, should they appear to thee, as they did to him, they might put thee to second thoughts.

But consider again, they are but journeymen thieves; they serve under the king of the bottomless pit, who, if need be, will come in to their aid himself, and his voice is as the roaring of a lion. I myself have been engaged as this Little-faith was, and I found it a terrible thing. These three villains set upon me, and I beginning like a Christian to resist, they gave but a call, and in came their master: I would, as the saying is, have given my life for a penny; but that, as God would have it, I was clothed with armour of proof. Ay, and yet though I was so harnessed, I found it hard work to quit myself like a man; no man can tell what in that combat attends us, but he that hath been in the battle himself.

HOPE. Well, but they ran, you see, when they did but suppose that one Great-grace was in the way.

CHR. True, they have often fled, both they and their master, when Great-grace hath but appeared; and no marvel, for he is the King's champion. But

No great heart for God where there is but little faith.

We have more courage when out, than when we are in.

1 Pet. v. 8.

Christian tells his own experience in this case.

The King's champion.

I trow you will put some difference between Little-faith and the King's champion. All the King's subjects are not his champions, nor can they, when tried, do such feats of war as he. Is it meet to think that a little child should handle Goliath as David did? or that there should be the strength of an ox in a wren? Some are strong, some are weak; some have great faith, some have little; this man was one of the weak, and therefore he went to the walls.

Hope. I would it had been Great-grace, for their sakes.

Chr. If it had been he, he might have had his hands full: For I must tell you, That though Great-grace is excellent good at his weapons, and has and can, so long as he keeps them at sword's point, do well enough with them; yet if they get within him, even Faint-heart, Mistrust, or the other, it shall go hard but they will throw up his heels. And when a man is down, you know, what can he do?

Whoso looks well upon Great-grace's face, shall see those scars and cuts there, that shall easily give demonstration of what I say. Yea, once I heard that he should say (and that when he was in the combat), 'We despaired even of life': How did these sturdy rogues and their fellows make David groan, mourn, and roar? Yea, Heman, and Hezekiah too, though champions in their day, were forced to bestir them when by these assaulted; and yet, notwithstanding, they had their coats soundly brushed by them. Peter upon a time would go try what he could do; but, though some do say of him that he is the prince of the apostles, they handled him so, that they made him at last afraid of a sorry girl.

Besides, their king is at their whistle, he is never out of hearing; and if at any time they be put to the worst, he, if possible, comes in to help them: and of him it is said, 'The sword of him that layeth at him cannot hold the spear, the dart, nor the habergeon: he esteemeth iron as straw, and brass as rotten wood. The arrow cannot make him fly; slingstones are turned with him into stubble, darts are counted as stubble: he laugheth at the shaking of a spear.' What can a man do in this case? 'Tis true, if a man could at every turn have Job's horse, and had skill and courage to ride him, he might do notable things: for 'his neck is clothed with thunder, he will not be afraid as the grasshopper, the glory of his nostrils is terrible, he paweth in the valley, rejoiceth in his strength, and goeth out to meet the armed men. He mocketh at fear, and is not affrighted, neither turneth back from the sword. The quiver rattleth against him, the glittering spear and the shield. He swalloweth the ground with fierceness and rage, neither believeth he that it is the sound of the trumpet. He saith among the trumpets, Ha, ha! and he smelleth the battle afar off, the thundering of the captains, and the shoutings.'

But for such footmen as thee and I are, let us never desire to meet with an enemy, nor vaunt as if we could do better, when we hear of others that they have been foiled, nor be tickled at the thoughts of our own manhood, for such commonly

Job xli. 26. Leviathan's sturdiness.

Job xxxix. 19. The excellent mettle that is in Job's horse.

come by the worst when tried. Witness Peter, of whom I made mention before. He would swagger, Ay, he would: He would, as his vain mind prompted him to say, do better, and stand more for his Master, than all men ; But who so foiled, and run down by these villains, as he ?

When therefore we hear that such robberies are done on the King's highway, two things become us to do : first to go out harnessed, and to be sure to take a shield with us ; For it was for want of that, that he that laid so lustily at Leviathan could not make him yield. For indeed, if that be wanting, he fears us not at all. Therefore he that had skill, hath said, 'Above all, take the shield of faith, where- *Eph. vi. 16.* with ye shall be able to quench all the fiery darts of the wicked.'

'Tis good also that we desire of the King a convoy, *'Tis good* yea that he will go with us himself. This made *to have a* *convoy.* David rejoice when in the Valley of the Shadow of Death ; and Moses was rather for dying where he *Exod. xxxiii.* stood, than to go one step without his God. O my *15.* brother, if he will but go along with us, what need *Ps. iii. 5-8.* *Ps. xxvii. 1-3.* we be afraid of ten thousands that shall set them- selves against us, but without him, 'the proud *Isa. x. 4.* helpers fall under the slain.'

I for my part have been in the fray before now, and though (through the goodness of him that is best) I am as you see alive ; yet I cannot boast of my manhood. Glad shall I be, if I meet with no more such brunts, though I fear we are not got beyond all danger. However, since the lion and the bear have not as yet devoured me, I hope God will also deliver us from the next uncircumcised Philistine.   Then sang Christian—

> Poor Little-faith ! Hast been among the thieves ?
> Wast robb'd ?   Remember this : Whoso believes
> And gets more faith, shall then a victor be
> Over ten thousand, else scarce over three.

So they went on, and Ignorance followed.   They went then till they came at a place where they saw

A way and a way.

a *way* put itself into their *way*, and seemed withal to lie as straight as the way which they should go : and here they knew not which of the two to take, for both seemed straight before them ; therefore here they stood still to consider.   And as they

The Flatterer finds them.

were thinking about the way, behold a man black of flesh, but covered with a very light robe, came to them and asked them, Why they stood there ? They answered, They were going to the Celestial City, but knew not which of these ways to take.   Follow me, said the man, it is thither that I am going.   So

Christian and his fellow deluded.

they followed him in the way that but now came into the road, which by degrees turned, and turned them so from the City that they desired to go to, that in little time their faces were turned away from it ; yet they followed him.   But by-and-by,

They are taken in a net.

before they were aware, he led them both within the compass of a net, in which they were both so entangled that they knew not what to do ; and with that, the white robe fell off the black man's back ; then they saw where they were.   Wherefore there they lay crying some time, for they could not get themselves out.

CHR. Then said Christian to his fellow, Now do I see myself in an error. Did not the Shepherds bid us beware of the flatterers? As is the saying of the wise man, so we have found it this day: 'A man that flattereth his neighbour spreadeth a net for his feet.'

They bewail their conditions.

Prov. xxix. 5.

HOPE. They also gave us a note of directions about the way, for our more sure finding thereof; but therein we have also forgotten to read, and have not kept ourselves from the paths of the destroyer. Here David was wiser than we; for saith he, 'Concerning the works of men, by the word of thy lips I have kept me from the paths of the destroyer.' Thus they lay bewailing themselves in the net. At last they espied a Shining One coming towards them, with a whip of small cord in his hand. When he was come to the place where they were, he asked them whence they came, and what they did there. They told him, That they were poor pilgrims going to Zion, but were led out of their way by a black man, clothed in white, who bid us, said they, follow him; for he was going thither too. Then said he with the whip, It is Flatterer, a false apostle, that hath transformed himself into an angel of light. So he rent the net, and let the men out. Then said he to them, Follow me, that I may set you in your way again; so he led them back to the way, which they had left to follow the Flatterer. Then he asked them saying, Where did you lie the last night? They said, With the Shepherds upon the Delectable Mountains. He asked them

Ps. xvii. 4.

A Shining One comes to them with a whip in his hand.

Prov. xxix. 5.
Dan. xi. 32.
2 Cor. xi. 13, 14.

They are examined and convicted of forgetfulness.

then, If they had not of those Shepherds a note of direction for the way? They answered, Yes. But did you, said he, when you were at a stand, pluck out and read your note? They answered, No. He asked them, Why? They said they forgot. He asked them moreover, If the Shepherds did not bid them beware of the Flatterer? They answered, Yes; but we did not imagine, said they, that this fine-spoken man had been he.

Then I saw in my dream, that he commanded them to lie down; which when they did, he chastised them sore, to teach them the good way wherein they should walk; and as he chastised them he said, 'As many as I love, I rebuke and chasten; be zealous therefore, and repent.' This done, he bids them go on their way, and take good heed to the other directions of the Shepherds. So they thanked him for all his kindness, and went softly along the right way, singing—

> Come hither, you that walk along the way;
> See how the pilgrims fare, that go astray!
> They catched are in an entangling net,
> 'Cause they good counsel lightly did forget:
> 'Tis true, they rescued were, but yet you see
> They're scourged to boot: Let this your caution be.

Now after a while, they perceived afar off, one coming softly and alone all along the highway to meet them. Then said Christian to his fellow, Yonder is a man with his back toward Zion, and he is coming to meet us.

HOPE. I see him; let us take heed to ourselves now, lest he should prove a Flatterer also. So he

---

Deceivers fine spoken. Rom. xvi. 18.

They are whipped and sent on their way. Deut. xxv. 2. 2 Chron. vi. 26, 27. Rev. iii. 19.

drew nearer and nearer, and at last came up unto them. His name was Atheist, and he asked them whither they were going.

The Atheist meets them.

CHR. We are going to the Mount Zion.

Then Atheist fell into a very great laughter.

CHR. What is the meaning of your laughter?

He laughs at them.

ATHEIST. I laugh to see what ignorant persons you are, to take upon you so tedious a journey; and yet are like to have nothing but your travel for your pains.

CHR. Why man? Do you think we shall not be received?

They reason together.

ATHEIST. Received! There is no such place as you dream of, in all this world.

CHR. But there is in the world to come.

ATHEIST. When I was at home in mine own country, I heard as you now affirm, and, from that hearing went out to see, and have been seeking this City this twenty years: But find no more of it, than I did the first day I set out.

Jer. xxii. 12.
Eccles. x. 15.

CHR. We have both heard and believe that there is such a place to be found.

ATHEIST. Had not I, when at home, believed, I had not come thus far to seek: But finding none (and yet I should, had there been such a place to be found, for I have gone to seek it further than you), I am going back again, and will seek to refresh myself with the things that I then cast away, for hopes of that which I now see is not.

The Atheist takes up his content in this world.

CHR. Then said Christian to Hopeful his fellow, Is it true which this man hath said?

Christian proveth his brother.

HOPE. Take heed, he is one of the Flatterers;

Hopeful's
gracious
answer.

remember what it hath cost us once already for our hearkening to such kind of fellows. What! no Mount Zion? Did we not see from the Delectable Mountains the gate of the City? Also, are we not now to walk by faith? Let us go on, said Hopeful, lest the man with the whip overtake us again. You should have taught me that lesson, which I will round you in the ears withal: 'Cease, my son, to hear the instruction that causeth to err from the words of knowledge.' I say, my brother, cease to hear him, and let us believe to the saving of the soul.

2 Cor. v. 7.
A remem-
brance of
former
chastisements
is a help
against
present
temptations.
Prov. xix. 27.
Heb. x. 39.

CHR. My brother, I did not put the question to thee for that I doubted of the truth of our belief myself, but to prove thee, and to fetch from thee a fruit of the honesty of thy heart. As for this man, I know that he is blinded by the god of this world. Let thee and I go on, knowing that we have belief of the truth, and 'no lie is of the truth.'

A fruit of
an honest
heart.

1 John ii. 21.

HOPE. Now do I rejoice in hope of the glory of God. So they turned away from the man; and he, laughing at them, went his way.

I saw then in my dream, that they went till they came into a certain country whose air naturally tended to make one drowsy, if he came a stranger into it. And here Hopeful began to be very dull and heavy of sleep; wherefore he said unto Christian, I do now begin to grow so drowsy that I can scarcely hold up mine eyes; let us lie down here and take one nap.

They are
come to the
Enchanted
Ground.

Hopeful
begins to be
drowsy.

Christian
keeps him
awake.

CHR. By no means, said the other, lest sleeping we never awake more.

HOPE. Why, my brother?   Sleep is sweet to the labouring man; we may be refreshed if we take a nap.

CHR. Do you not remember that one of the Shepherds bid us beware of the Enchanted Ground? He meant by that, that we should beware of sleeping; Wherefore let us not sleep, as do others; but let us watch, and be sober. *1 Thess v. 6.*

HOPE. I acknowledge myself in a fault; and had I been here alone, I had, by sleeping, run the danger of death.   I see it is true that the wise man saith, 'Two are better than one.'   Hitherto hath thy company been my mercy, 'and thou shalt have a good reward for thy labour.' *He is thankful.* *Eccles. iv. 9.*

CHR. Now then, said Christian, to prevent drowsiness in this place, let us fall into good discourse. *To prevent drowsiness they fall to good discourse.*

HOPE. With all my heart, said the other.

CHR. Where shall we begin? *Good discourse prevents drowsiness.*

HOPE. Where God began with us.   But do you begin, if you please.

CHR. I will sing you first this song—

> When saints do sleepy grow, let them come hither,
> And hear how these two pilgrims talk together:
> Yea, let them learn of them, in any wise,
> Thus to keep ope their drowsy slumb'ring eyes.
> Saints' fellowship, if it be managed well,
> Keeps them awake, and that in spite of hell.

The Dreamers' Note.

CHR. Then Christian began and said, I will ask you a question: How came you to think at first of doing what you do now? *They begin at the beginning of their conversion.*

HOPE. Do you mean, How came I at first to look after the good of my soul?

CHR. Yes, that is my meaning.

HOPE. I continued a great while in the delight of those things which were seen and sold at our fair; things which, I believe now, would have (had I continued in them still) drowned me in perdition and destruction.

CHR. What things were they?

Hopeful's
life before
conversion.

HOPE. All the treasures and riches of the world. Also I delighted much in rioting, revelling, drinking, swearing, lying, uncleanness, Sabbath-breaking, and what not, that tended to destroy the soul. But I found at last, by hearing and considering of things that are divine, which indeed I heard of you, as also of beloved Faithful, that was put to death for his

Rom. vi. 21-23.
Eph. v. 6.

faith and good living in Vanity Fair, that 'the end of these things is death.' And that for these things' sake the wrath of God cometh upon the children of disobedience.

CHR. And did you presently fall under the power of this conviction?

Hopeful at
first shuts his
eyes against
the light.

HOPE. No, I was not willing presently to know the evil of sin, nor the damnation that follows upon the commission of it; but endeavoured, when my mind at first began to be shaken with the Word, to shut mine eyes against the light thereof.

CHR. But what was the cause of your carrying of it thus to the first workings of God's blessed Spirit upon you?

Reasons of
his resisting
of light.

HOPE. The causes were: 1. I was ignorant that this was the work of God upon me. I never thought that by awakenings for sin God at first begins the conversion of a sinner. 2. Sin was yet very sweet to my flesh, and I was loth to leave it. 3. I could not tell how to part with mine old companions, their presence and actions were so desirable unto me. 4. The hours in which convictions were upon me were such troublesome and such heart-affrighting hours, that I could not bear, no not so much as the remembrance of them upon my heart.

CHR. Then as it seems, sometimes you got rid of your trouble?

HOPE. Yes, verily; but it would come into my mind again, and then I should be as bad, nay worse, than I was before.

CHR. Why, what was it that brought your sins to mind again?

HOPE. Many things; as:

1. If I did but meet a good man in the streets; or,
2. If I have heard any read in the Bible; or,
3. If mine head did begin to ache; or,
4. If I were told that some of my neighbours were sick; or,

When he had lost his sense of sin, what brought it again.

5. If I heard the bell toll for some that were dead; or,

6. If I thought of dying myself; or,

7. If I heard that sudden death happened to others;

8. But especially, when I thought of myself, that I must quickly come to judgment.

CHR. And could you at any time with ease get off the guilt of sin, when by any of these ways it came upon you?

HOPE. No, not latterly, for then they got faster hold of my conscience; and then, if I did but think of going back to sin (though my mind was turned against it), it would be double torment to me.

CHR. And how did you do then?

HOPE. I thought I must endeavour to mend my life; for else, thought I, I am sure to be damned.

CHR. And did you endeavour to mend?

HOPE. Yes, and fled from, not only my sins, but sinful company too; and betook me to religious duties, as praying, reading, weeping for sin, speaking truth to my neighbours, etc. These things did I, with many others, too much here to relate.

CHR. And did you think yourself well then?

HOPE. Yes, for a while; but at the last my trouble came tumbling upon me again, and that over the neck of all my reformation.

CHR. How came that about, since you were now reformed?

HOPE. There were several things brought it upon me, especially such sayings as these: 'All our righteousnesses are as filthy rags.' 'By the works of the law no man shall be justified.' 'When you have done all things, say, We are unprofitable': with many more such like. From whence I began to reason with myself thus: If *all* my righteousnesses are filthy rags, if by the deeds of the law, *no* man can be justified; and if, when we have done *all*, we are yet unprofitable, then 'tis but a folly to think of heaven by the law. I further thought thus: If a man runs an £100 into the shopkeeper's debt, and after that shall pay for all that he shall fetch; yet if

Margin notes:

When he could no longer shake off his guilt by sinful courses, then he endeavours to mend.

Then he thought himself well.

Isa. lxiv. 6.

Gal. ii. 16.
Luke xvii. 20.
Reformation at last could not help, and why.

His being a debtor by the law troubled him.

his old debt stand still in the book uncrossed, for that the shopkeeper may sue him, and cast him into prison till he shall pay the debt.

CHR. Well, and how did you apply this to yourself?

HOPE. Why, I thought thus with myself: I have by my sins run a great way into God's Book, and that my now reforming will not pay off that score; therefore I should think still under all my present amendments, But how shall I be freed from that damnation that I brought myself in danger of by my former transgressions?

CHR. A very good application: but pray go on.

HOPE. Another thing that hath troubled me, even since my late amendments, is, that if I look narrowly into the best of what I do now, I still see sin, new sin, mixing itself with the best of that I do; so that now I am forced to conclude, that notwithstanding my former fond conceits of myself and duties, I have committed sin enough in one duty to send me to hell, though my former life had been faultless.

His espying bad things in his best duties, troubled him.

CHR. And what did you do then?

HOPE. Do! I could not tell what to do, till I brake my mind to Faithful, for he and I were well acquainted. And he told me, that unless I could obtain the righteousness of a man that never had sinned, neither mine own, nor all the righteousness of the world could save me.

This made him break his mind to Faithful, who told him the way to be saved.

CHR. And did you think he spake true?

HOPE. Had he told me so when I was pleased and satisfied with mine own amendments, I had called him fool for his pains; but now, since I see my own infirmity, and the sin that cleaves to my best performance, I have been forced to be of his opinion.

CHR. But did you think, when at first he suggested it to you, that there was such a man to be found, of whom it might justly be said, That he never committed sin?

At which he started at present.

HOPE. I must confess the words at first sounded strangely; but after a little more talk and company with him, I had full conviction about it.

CHR. And did you ask him what man this was, and how you must be justified by him?

Heb. x.
Rom. iv.
Col. i.
1 Pet. i.

HOPE. Yes, and he told me it was the Lord Jesus, that dwelleth on the right hand of the Most High. And thus, said he, you must be justified by him, even by trusting to what he hath done by himself in the days of his flesh, and suffered when he did hang on the tree. I asked him further, How that man's righteousness could be of that efficacy, to justify another before God? And he told me, He was the mighty God, and did what he did, and died the death also, not for himself, but for me; to whom his doings, and the worthiness of them should be imputed, if I believed on him.

A more particular discovery of the way to be saved.

CHR. And what did you do then?

He doubts of acceptation.

HOPE. I made my objections against my believing, for that I thought he was not willing to save me.

CHR. And what said Faithful to you then?

Matt. xi. 28.

HOPE. He bade me go to him and see. Then I said it was presumption: he said, No; for I was

invited to come.   Then he gave me a book of Jesus *He is better instructed.*
his inditing, to encourage me the more freely to
come; and he said concerning that book, that every *Matt. xxiv. 35.*
jot and tittle thereof stood firmer than heaven and
earth.   Then I asked him, What I must do when I
came? and he told me, I must entreat upon my *Ps. xcv. 6. Dan. vi. 10.*
knees, with all my heart and soul, the Father to
reveal him to me.   Then I asked him further, How
I must make my supplication to him?   And he said, *Jer. xxix. 12, 13. Exod. xxv. 22. Lev. xvi. 2. Num. vii. 89. Heb. iv. 16.*
Go, and thou shalt find him upon a mercy-seat,
where he sits all the year long, to give pardon and
forgiveness to them that come.   I told him that I
knew not what to say when I came.   And he bid
me say to this effect: God be merciful to me a *He is bid to pray.*
sinner, and make me to know and believe in Jesus
Christ; for I see that if his righteousness had not
been, or I have not faith in that righteousness, I am
utterly cast away; Lord, I have heard that thou art
a merciful God, and hast ordained that thy Son
Jesus Christ should be the Saviour of the world;
and moreover, that thou art willing to bestow him
upon such a poor sinner as I am (and I am a sinner
indeed), Lord, take therefore this opportunity, and
magnify thy grace in the salvation of my soul,
through thy Son Jesus Christ.   Amen.

CHR.   And did you do as you were bidden?

HOPE.   Yes; over, and over, and over. *He prays.*

CHR.   And did the Father reveal his Son to
you?

HOPE.   Not at the first, nor second, nor third, nor
fourth, nor fifth, no, nor at the sixth time neither.

CHR.   What did you do then?

HOPE. What! why I could not tell what to do.

CHR. Had you not thoughts of leaving off praying?

He thought
to leave off
praying.

HOPE. Yes, an hundred times, twice told.

CHR. And what was the reason you did not?

HOPE. I believed that that was true which had been told me, to wit, That without the righteous-

He durst
not leave
off praying,
and why.

ness of this Christ, all the world could not save me; and therefore thought I with myself, If I leave off, I die; and I can but die at the throne of grace.

Hab. ii. 3.

And withal, this came into my mind, 'If it tarry, wait for it, because it will surely come, and will not tarry.' So I continued praying until the Father showed me his Son.

CHR. And how was he revealed unto you?

HOPE. I did *not* see him with my bodily eyes, but with the eyes of mine understanding; and thus it

Eph. i. 18, 19.

was: One day I was very sad, I think sadder than at any one time in my life, and this sadness was through a fresh sight of the greatness and vileness

Christ is
revealed to
him, and
how.

of my sins. And as I was then looking for nothing but hell, and the everlasting damnation of my soul, suddenly, as I thought, I saw the Lord Jesus look

Acts xvi. 30, 31.

down from heaven upon me, and saying, 'Believe on the Lord Jesus Christ, and thou shalt be saved.'

But I replied, Lord, I am a great, a very great

2 Cor. xii. 9.

sinner: and he answered, 'My grace is sufficient for thee.' Then I said, But, Lord, what is believing?

John vi. 35.

And then I saw from that saying ['He that cometh to me shall never hunger, and he that believeth on me shall never thirst'], that believing and coming was all one; and that he that came, that is, ran out in his heart and affections after salvation by Christ, he indeed believed in Christ.   Then the water stood in mine eyes, and I asked further, But, Lord, may such a great sinner as I am be indeed accepted of thee, and be saved by thee?   And I heard him say, John vi. 37. 'And him that cometh to me I will in no wise cast out.'   Then I said, But how, Lord, must I consider of thee in my coming to thee, that my faith may be placed aright upon thee?   Then he said, 'Christ 1 Tim. i. 15. Jesus came into the world to save sinners.'   'He is Rom. x. 4. the end of the law for righteousness to every one that believes.'   'He died for our sins, and rose again Chap. iv. for our justification: He loved us and washed us from our sins in his own blood.'   'He is Mediator' between God and us.   'He ever liveth to make Heb. vii. 24, 25. intercession for us.'   From all which I gathered, that I must look for righteousness in his person, and for satisfaction for my sins by his blood; that what he did in obedience to his Father's law, and in submitting to the penalty thereof, was not for himself, but for him that will accept it for his salvation, and be thankful.   And now was my heart full of joy, mine eyes full of tears, and mine affections running over with love to the name, people, and ways of Jesus Christ.

CHR. This was a revelation of Christ to your soul indeed; but tell me particularly what effect this had upon your spirit.

HOPE. It made me see that all the world, notwithstanding all the righteousness thereof, is in a state of condemnation.   It made me see that God the Father, though he be just, can justly justify the coming sinner. It made me greatly ashamed of the vileness of my former life, and confounded me with the sense of mine own ignorance; for there never came thought into mine heart before now, that showed me so the beauty of Jesus Christ. It made me love a holy life, and long to do something for the honour and glory of the name of the Lord Jesus. Yea, I thought, that had I now a thousand gallons of blood in my body, I could spill it all for the sake of the Lord Jesus.

I saw then in my dream, that Hopeful looked back and saw Ignorance, whom they had left behind, coming after. Look, said he to Christian, how far yonder youngster loitereth behind.

CHR. Ay, ay, I see him; he careth not for our company.

HOPE. But I trow, it would not have hurt him, had he kept pace with us hitherto.

CHR. That's true; but I warrant you he thinketh otherwise.

HOPE. That I think he doth; but, however, let us tarry for him. So they did.

Young Ignorance comes up again. Their talk.

Then Christian said to him, Come away, man, why do you stay so behind?

IGNOR. I take my pleasure in walking alone, even more a great deal than in company, unless I like it the better.

Then said Christian to Hopeful (but softly), Did I not tell you he cared not for our company? But, however, said he, come up, and let us talk away the time in this solitary place. Then, directing his speech to Ignorance, he said, Come, how do you? How stands it between God and your soul now?

IGNOR. I hope well; for I am always full of good motions, that come into my mind, to comfort me as I walk. *Ignorance's hope, and the ground of it.*

CHR. What good motions? Pray tell us.

IGNOR. Why, I think of God and heaven.

CHR. So do the devils and damned souls.

IGNOR. But I think of them, and desire them.

CHR. So do many that are never like to come there. 'The soul of the sluggard desires, and hath nothing.' *Prov. xiii. 4.*

IGNOR. But I think of them, and leave all for them.

CHR. That I doubt, for leaving of all is an hard matter; yea, a harder matter than many are aware of. But why, or by what, art thou persuaded that thou hast left all for God and heaven?

IGNOR. My heart tells me so.

CHR. The wise man says, 'He that trusts his own heart is a fool.' *Prov. xxviii. 26.*

IGNOR. This is spoken of an evil heart, but mine is a good one.

CHR. But how dost thou prove that?

IGNOR. It comforts me in hopes of heaven.

CHR. That may be, through its deceitfulness; for a man's heart may minister comfort to him in the hopes of that thing for which yet he has no ground to hope.

IGNOR. But my heart and life agree together, and therefore my hope is well grounded.

CHR. Who told thee that thy heart and life agree together?

IGNOR. My heart tells me so.

CHR. Ask my fellow if I be a thief! Thy heart tells thee so! Except the Word of God beareth witness in this matter, other testimony is of no value.

IGNOR. But is it not a good heart that has good thoughts, and is not that a good life that is according to God's commandments?

CHR. Yes, that is a good heart that hath good thoughts, and that is a good life that is according to God's commandments; but it is one thing indeed to have these, and another thing only to think so.

IGNOR. Pray, what count you good thoughts, and a life according to God's commandments?

CHR. There are good thoughts of divers kinds, some respecting ourselves, some God, some Christ, and some other things.

What are good thoughts. IGNOR. What be good thoughts respecting ourselves?

CHR. Such as agree with the Word of God.

IGNOR. When do our thoughts of ourselves agree with the Word of God?

CHR. When we pass the same judgment upon ourselves which the Word passes. To explain myself: The Word of God saith of persons in a natural condition, 'There is none righteous, there is none that doth good.' It saith also, 'That every imagination of the heart of man is only evil, and that continually.' And again, 'The imagination of man's heart is evil from his youth.' Now then, when we think thus of ourselves, having sense thereof, then

Rom. iii.

Gen. vi. 5.

are our thoughts good ones, because according to the Word of God.

IGNOR. I will never believe that my heart is thus bad.

CHR. Therefore thou never hadst one good thought concerning thyself in thy life. But let me go on: As the Word passeth a judgment upon our Heart, so it passeth a judgment upon our Ways; and when OUR thoughts of our Hearts and Ways agree with the judgment which the Word giveth of both, then are both good, because agreeing thereto.

IGNOR. Make out your meaning.

CHR. Why, the Word of God saith that man's ways are crooked ways, not good, but perverse. It saith they are naturally out of the good way, that they have not known it. Now when a man thus thinketh of his ways, I say when he doth sensibly, and with heart-humiliation thus think, then hath he good thoughts of his own ways, because his thoughts now agree with the judgment of the Word of God. *Ps. cxxv. 5. Prov. ii. 15. Rom. iii.*

IGNOR. What are good thoughts concerning God?

CHR. Even (as I have said concerning ourselves) when our thoughts of God do agree with what the Word saith of him. And that is, when we think of his being and attributes as the Word hath taught: of which I cannot now discourse at large. But to speak of him with reference to us, Then we have right thoughts of God, when we think that he knows us better than we know ourselves, and can see sin in us, when and where we can see none in ourselves; when we think he knows our inmost thoughts, and that our heart with all its depth is always open unto his eyes: Also when we think that all our righteousness stinks in his nostrils, and that therefore he cannot abide to see us stand before him in any confidence, even in all our best performances.

IGNOR. Do you think that I am such a fool, as to think God can see no further than I? or, that I would come to God in the best of my performances?

CHR. Why, how dost thou think in this matter?

IGNOR. Why, to be short, I think I must believe in Christ for justification.

CHR. How! think thou must believe in Christ, when thou seest not thy need of him! Thou neither seest thy original nor actual infirmities; but hast such an opinion of thyself, and of what thou doest, as plainly renders thee to be one that did never see a necessity of Christ's personal righteousness to justify thee before God: How then dost thou say, I believe in Christ?

IGNOR. I believe well enough for all that.

CHR. How dost thou believe?

The faith of Ignorance.   IGNOR. I believe that Christ died for sinners, and that I shall be justified before God from the curse, through his gracious acceptance of my obedience to his law: Or thus, Christ makes my duties that are religious, acceptable to his Father by virtue of his merits; and so shall I be justified.

CHR. Let me give an answer to this confession of thy faith.

1. Thou believest with a fantastical faith, for this faith is nowhere described in the Word.

2. Thou believest with a false faith, because it

taketh justification from the personal righteousness of Christ, and applies it to thy own.

3. Thy faith maketh not Christ a justifier of thy person, but of thy actions; and of thy person for thy actions' sake, which is false.

4. Therefore this faith is deceitful, even such as will leave thee under wrath in the day of God Almighty; for true justifying faith puts the soul (as sensible of its lost condition by the law) upon flying for refuge unto Christ's righteousness (which righteousness of *his*, is not an act of grace, by which he maketh for justification *thy* obedience accepted with God, but *his* personal obedience to the law in doing and suffering for us, what that required at our hands) —This righteousness, I say, true faith accepteth; under the skirt of which, the soul being shrouded, and by it presented as spotless before God, it is accepted, and acquit from condemnation.

IGNOR. What! would you have us trust to what Christ in his own person has done without us? This conceit would loosen the reins of our lust, and tolerate us to live as we list. For what matter how we live, if we may be justified by Christ's personal righteousness from all, when we believe it?

CHR. Ignorance is thy name, and as thy name is, so art thou; even this thy answer demonstrateth what I say. Ignorant thou art of what justifying righteousness is, and as ignorant how to secure thy soul, through the faith of it, from the heavy wrath of God. Yea, thou also art ignorant of the true effects of saving faith in this righteousness of Christ, which is, to bow and win over the heart to God in

Christ, to love his name, his Word, ways, and people, and not as thou ignorantly imaginest.

HOPE. Ask him if ever he had Christ revealed to him from heaven.

Ignorance jangles with them.

IGNOR. What! you are a man for revelations.   I believe that what both you, and all the rest of you, say about that matter, is but the fruit of distracted brains.

HOPE. Why, man! Christ is so hid in God from the natural apprehensions of the flesh, that he cannot by any man be savingly known, unless God the Father reveals him to them.

He speaks reproachfully of what he knows not.

IGNOR. That is your faith, but not mine; yet mine, I doubt not, is as good as yours, though I have not in my head so many whimsies as you.

CHR. Give me leave to put in a word. You ought not so slightly to speak of this matter; for this I

Matt. xi. 27.
1 Cor. xii. 3.
Eph. i. 18, 19.

will boldly affirm (even as my good companion hath done), that no man can know Jesus Christ but by the revelation of the Father; yea, and faith too, by which the soul layeth hold upon Christ (if it be right) must be wrought by the exceeding greatness of his mighty power; the working of which faith, I perceive, poor Ignorance, thou art ignorant of. Be awakened then, see thine own wretchedness, and fly to the Lord Jesus; and by his righteousness, which is the righteousness of God (for he himself is God), thou shalt be delivered from condemnation.

The talk broke up.

IGNOR. You go so fast I cannot keep pace with you; do you go on before, I must stay awhile behind.

Then they said—

Well, Ignorance, wilt thou yet foolish be,
To slight good counsel, ten times given thee?
And if thou yet refuse it, thou shalt know
Ere long the evil of thy doing so :
Remember, man, in time ; stoop, do not fear,
Good counsel taken well, saves ; therefore hear :
But if thou yet shalt slight it, thou wilt be
The loser (Ignorance), I 'll warrant thee.

Then Christian addressed thus himself to his fellow :

CHR. Well, come my good Hopeful, I perceive that thou and I must walk by ourselves again.

So I saw in my dream, that they went on apace before, and Ignorance he came hobbling after. Then said Christian to his companion, It pities me much for this poor man, it will certainly go ill with him at last.

HOPE. Alas, there are abundance in our town in his condition ; whole families, yea, whole streets (and that of pilgrims too) ; and if there be so many in our parts, how many think you must there be in the place where he was born ?

CHR. Indeed the Word saith, ' He hath blinded their eyes, lest they should see,' etc. But now we are by ourselves, what do you think of such men? Have they at no time, think you, convictions of sin, and so consequently fears that their state is dangerous ?

HOPE. Nay, do you answer that question yourself, for you are the elder man.

CHR. Then I say sometimes (as I think) they may, but they being naturally ignorant, understand not that such convictions tend to their good ; and therefore they do desperately seek to stifle them, and presumptuously continue to flatter themselves in the way of their own hearts.

The good
use of fear.

HOPE. I do believe as you say, that fear tends much to men's good, and to make them right, at their beginning to go on pilgrimage.

Job xxviii. 28.
Ps. cxi. 10.
Prov. i. 7.
Chap. ix. 10.

CHR. Without all doubt it doth, if it be right; for so says the Word, 'The fear of the Lord is the beginning of wisdom.'

Right fear.

HOPE. How will you describe right fear?

CHR. True, or right fear, is discovered by three things:

1. By its rise; it is caused by saving convictions for sin.

2. It driveth the soul to lay fast hold of Christ for salvation.

3. It begetteth and continueth in the soul a great reverence of God, his Word, and ways, keeping it tender, and making it afraid to turn from them, to the right hand or to the left, to anything that may dishonour God, break its peace, grieve the Spirit, or cause the enemy to speak reproachfully.

HOPE. Well said; I believe you have said the truth. Are we now almost got past the Enchanted Ground?

CHR. Why, are you weary of this discourse?

HOPE. No verily, but that I would know where we are.

Why ignorant
persons stifle
convictions.
1. In general.

CHR. We have not now above two miles further to go thereon. But let us return to our matter. Now the ignorant know not that such convictions that tend to put them in fear, are for their good, and therefore they seek to stifle them.

HOPE. How do they seek to stifle them?

CHR. 1. They think that those fears are wrought by the devil (though indeed they are wrought of God); and thinking so, they resist them as things that directly tend to their overthrow. 2. They also think that these fears tend to the spoiling of their faith (when, alas for them, poor men that they are, they have none at all), and therefore they harden their hearts against them. 3. They presume they ought not to fear, and therefore, in despite of them, wax presumptuously confident. 4. They see that these fears tend to take away from them their pitiful old self-holiness, and therefore they resist them with all their might. *2. In particular.*

HOPE. I know something of this myself; for before I knew myself it was so with me.

CHR. Well, we will leave at this time our neighbour Ignorance by himself, and fall upon another profitable question.

HOPE. With all my heart; but you shall still begin.

CHR. Well then, did you not know about ten years ago, one Temporary in your parts, who was a forward man in religion then? *Talk about one Temporary.*

HOPE. Know him! yes; he dwelt in Graceless, a town about two miles off of Honesty, and he dwelt next door to one Turn-back. *Where he dwelt.*

CHR. Right; he dwelt under the same roof with him. Well, that man was much awakened once: I believe that then he had some sight of his sins, and of the wages that was due thereto. *He was towardly once.*

HOPE. I am of your mind, for (my house not

being above three miles from him) he would oft-times come to me, and that with many tears. Truly I pitied the man, and was not altogether without hope of him; but one may see it is not every one that cries, 'Lord, Lord.'

CHR. He told me once, that he was resolved to go on pilgrimage, as we go now; but all of a sudden he grew acquainted with one Save-self, and then he became a stranger to me.

HOPE. Now, since we are talking about him, let us a little inquire into the reason of the sudden backsliding of him and such others.

CHR. It may be very profitable; but do you begin.

HOPE. Well then, there are in my judgment four reasons for it.

Reasons why towardly ones go back.

1. Though the consciences of such men are awakened, yet their minds are not changed: there-fore, when the power of guilt weareth away, that which provoketh them to be religious ceaseth. Wherefore they naturally turn to their own course again, even as we see the dog that is sick of what he hath eaten, so long as his sickness prevails, he vomits and casts up all; not that he doth this of a free mind (if we may say a dog has a mind) but because it troubleth his stomach; but now, when his sickness is over, and so his stomach eased, his desires being not at all alienate from his vomit, he turns him about and licks up all; and so it is true

2 Pet. ii. 22.

which is written, 'The dog is turned to his own vomit again.' Thus I say, being hot for heaven by virtue only of the sense and fear of the torments of hell, as their sense of hell and the fears of damnation chills and cools, so their desires for heaven and salvation cool also. So then it comes to pass, that when their guilt and fear is gone, their desires for heaven and happiness die, and they return to their course again.

2. Another reason is, they have slavish fears that do overmaster them: I speak now of the fears that they have of men, 'For the fear of men bringeth a snare.' Prov. xxix. 25. So then, though they seem to be hot for heaven so long as the flames of hell are about their ears, yet when that terror is a little over, they betake themselves to second thoughts; namely, that 'tis good to be wise, and not to run (for they know not what) the hazard of losing all; or at least, of bringing themselves into unavoidable and unnecessary troubles: and so they fall in with the world again.

3. The shame that attends religion lies also as a block in their way; they are proud and haughty, and religion in their eye is low and contemptible; therefore, when they have lost their sense of hell and wrath to come, they return again to their former course.

4. Guilt, and to meditate terror, are grievous to them. They like not to see their misery before they come into it; though perhaps the sight of it first, if they loved that sight, might make them fly whither the righteous fly and are safe. But because they do, as I hinted before, even shun the thoughts of guilt and terror, therefore, when once they are rid of their awakenings about the terrors and wrath of God, they harden their hearts gladly, and choose such ways as will harden them more and more.

CHR. You are pretty near the business, for the bottom of all is, for want of a change in their mind and will. And therefore they are but like the felon that standeth before the judge, he quakes and trembles, and seems to repent most heartily, but the bottom of all is the fear of the halter: not that he hath any detestation of the offence, as is evident, because, let but this man have his liberty, and he will be a thief, and so a rogue still; whereas, if his mind was changed, he would be otherwise.

HOPE. Now I have showed you the reasons of their going back, do you show me the manner thereof.

CHR. So I will willingly.

How the apostate goes back.

1. They draw off their thoughts, all that they may, from the remembrance of God, death, and judgment to come.

2. Then they cast off by degrees private duties, as closet-prayer, curbing their lusts, watching, sorrow for sin, and the like.

3. Then they shun the company of lively and warm Christians.

4. After that, they grow cold to public duty, as hearing, reading, godly conference, and the like.

5. Then they begin to pick holes, as we say, in the coats of some of the godly, and that devilishly; that they may have a seeming colour to throw religion (for the sake of some infirmity they have spied in them) behind their backs.

6. Then they begin to adhere to, and associate themselves with, carnal, loose and wanton men.

7. Then they give way to carnal and wanton

discourses in secret; and glad are they if they can see such things in any that are counted honest, that they may the more boldly do it through their example.

8. After this, they begin to play with little sins openly.

9. And then, being hardened, they show themselves as they are. Thus being launched again into the gulf of misery, unless a miracle of grace prevent it, they everlastingly perish in their own deceivings.

Now I saw in my dream, that by this time the pilgrims were got over the Enchanted Ground, and entering in the country of Beulah, whose air was *Isa. lxii. 4.* very sweet and pleasant, the way lying directly through it, they solaced themselves there for a season. Yea, here they heard continually the *Cant. ii. 10-12.* singing of birds, and saw every day the flowers appear in the earth, and heard the voice of the turtle in the land. In this country the sun shineth night and day; wherefore this was beyond the Valley of the Shadow of Death, and also out of the reach of Giant Despair, neither could they from this place so much as see Doubting Castle. Here they were within sight of the city they were going to; also here met them some of the inhabitants thereof; *Angels.* for in this land the Shining Ones commonly walked, because it was upon the borders of heaven. In this land also the contract between the Bride and the Bridegroom was renewed; yea here, ' As the bride- *Isa. lxii. 5.* groom rejoiceth over the bride, so did their God rejoice over them.' Here they had no want of corn *Ver. 8.* and wine; for in this place they met with abundance of what they had sought for in all their pilgrimage. Here they heard voices from out of the city, loud Ver. 11. voices, saying, 'Say ye to the daughter of Zion, Behold, thy salvation cometh! behold, his reward is with him!' Here all the inhabitants of the country Ver. 12. called them 'The holy people, The redeemed of the Lord, Sought out,' etc.

Now as they walked in this land, they had more rejoicing than in parts more remote from the kingdom to which they were bound; and drawing near to the city, they had yet a more perfect view thereof. It was builded of pearls and precious stones, also the street thereof was paved with gold; so that by reason of the natural glory of the city, and the reflection of the sunbeams upon it, Christian with desire fell sick, Hopeful also had a fit or two of the same disease. Wherefore here they lay by it a while, crying out because of their pangs, 'If you see my Beloved, tell him that I am sick of love.'

But being a little strengthened, and better able to bear their sickness, they walked on their way, and came yet nearer and nearer, where were orchards, vineyards, and gardens, and their gates opened into the highway. Now as they came up to these places, behold, the gardener stood in the way, to whom the pilgrims said, Whose goodly vineyards Deut. xxiii. 24. and gardens are these? He answered, they are the King's, and are planted here for his own delights, and also for the solace of pilgrims. So the gardener had them into the vineyards, and bid them refresh themselves with dainties. He also showed them there the King's walks, and the arbours where he delighted to be: and here they tarried and slept.

Now I beheld in my dream, that they talked more in their sleep at this time than ever they did in all their journey; and being in a muse thereabout, the gardener said even to me, Wherefore musest thou at the matter? It is the nature of the fruit of the grapes of these vineyards to go down so sweetly as to cause the lips of them that are asleep to speak.

So I saw that when they awoke, they addressed themselves to go up to the city. But, as I said, the reflection of the sun upon the city (for the city was pure gold) was so extremely glorious, that they could not, as yet, with open face behold it, but through an instrument made for that purpose. So I saw, that as they went on, there met them two men, in raiment that shone like gold, also their faces shone as the light. Rev. xxi. 18. Cor. iii. 18.

These men asked the pilgrims whence they came; and they told them. They also asked them where they had lodged, what difficulties and dangers, what comforts and pleasures they had met in the way; and they told them. Then said the men that met them, You have but two difficulties more to meet with, and then you are in the city.

Christian then and his companion asked the men to go along with them, so they told them they would. But, said they, you must obtain it by your own faith. So I saw in my dream that they went on together till they came in sight of the gate.

Death.

Now I further saw, that betwixt them and the gate was a river, but there was no bridge to go over; the river was very deep. At the sight, therefore, of this river the pilgrims were much stounded; but the men that went with them said, You must go through, or you cannot come at the gate.

Death is not welcome to nature, though by it we pass out of this world into glory. 1 Cor. xv. 51, 52.

The pilgrims then began to inquire if there was no other way to the gate; to which they answered, Yes; but there hath not any, save two, to wit, Enoch and Elijah, been permitted to tread that path, since the foundation of the world, nor shall, until the last trumpet shall sound. The pilgrims then, especially Christian, began to despond in their minds, and looked this way and that, but no way could be found by them by which they might escape the river. Then they asked the men if the waters were all of a depth. They said, No; yet

Angels help us not comfortably through death.

they could not help them in that case; for said they, You shall find it deeper or shallower, as you believe in the King of the place.

They then addressed themselves to the water; and entering, Christian began to sink, and, crying out to his good friend Hopeful, he said, I sink in deep waters; the billows go over my head, all his waves go over me! Selah.

Then said the other, Be of good cheer, my brother; I feel the bottom, and it is good. Then

Christian's conflict at the hour of death.

said Christian, Ah, my friend, the sorrows of death have compassed me about; I shall not see the land that flows with milk and honey. And with that, a great darkness and horror fell upon Christian, so

that he could not see before him. Also here he in
great measure lost his senses; so that he could
neither remember nor orderly talk of any of those
sweet refreshments that he had met with in the
way of his pilgrimage. But all the words that he
spake still tended to discover that he had horror
of mind, and heart-fears that he should die in that
river, and never obtain entrance in at the gate.
Here also, as they that stood by perceived, he
was much in the troublesome thoughts of the
sins that he had committed, both since and before
he began to be a pilgrim. It was also observed
that he was troubled with apparitions of hobgoblins and evil spirits; for ever and anon he
would intimate so much by words. Hopeful
therefore here had much ado to keep his brother's
head above water; yea, sometimes he would be
quite gone down, and then, ere a while, he would
rise up again half dead. Hopeful also would
endeavour to comfort him, saying, Brother, I see
the gate, and men standing by to receive us; but
Christian would answer, It is you, it is you they
wait for; you have been *hopeful* ever since I knew
you. And so have you, said he to Christian. Ah,
brother! said he, surely if I was right, he would
now arise to help me; but for my sins he hath
brought me into the snare, and hath left me.
Then said Hopeful, My brother, you have quite
forgot the text where it is said of the wicked,
'There is no band in their death, but their strength Ps. lxxiii. 4, 5.
is firm; they are not troubled as other men, neither
are they plagued like other men.' These troubles

and distresses that you go through in these waters are no sign that God hath forsaken you; but are sent to try you, whether you will call to mind that which heretofore you have received of his goodness, and live upon him in your distresses.

Then I saw in my dream, that Christian was in a muse a while. To whom also Hopeful added this word, 'Be of good cheer, Jesus Christ maketh thee whole.' And with that Christian brake out with a loud voice, Oh, I see him again! and he tells me, 'When thou passest through the waters, I will be with thee; and through the rivers, they shall not overflow thee.' Then they both took courage, and the enemy was after that as still as a stone until they were gone over. Christian therefore presently found ground to stand upon; and so it followed that the rest of the river was but shallow. Thus they got over. Now, upon the bank of the river, on the other side, they saw the two Shining Men again, who there waited for them. Wherefore, being come out of the river, they saluted them, saying, We are ministering spirits, sent forth to minister for those that shall be heirs of salvation. Thus they went along towards the gate. Now you must note that the city stood upon a mighty hill; but the pilgrims went up that hill with ease, because they had these two men to lead them up by the arms: also they had left their mortal garments behind them in the river; for, though they went in with them, they came out without them. They therefore went up here with much agility and speed, though

Christian delivered from his tears in death.

Isa. xliii. 2.

The angels do wait for them as soon as they are passed out of this world.

They have put off mortality.

the foundation upon which the city was framed was higher than the clouds; they therefore went up through the regions of the air, sweetly talking as they went, being comforted, because they safely got over the river, and had such glorious companions to attend them.

The talk they had with the Shining Ones was about the glory of the place, who told them that the beauty and glory of it was inexpressible. There, said they, is the Mount Zion, the heavenly Jerusalem, the innumerable company of angels, *Heb. xii. 22-24.* and the spirits of just men made perfect. You are going now, said they, to the paradise of God, *Rev. ii. 7.* wherein you shall see the tree of life, and eat of *Rev. iii. 4.* the never-fading fruits thereof; and when you come there, you shall have white robes given you, and your walk and talk shall be every day with the King, even all the days of eternity. There you shall not see again such things as you saw when you were in the lower region upon the earth, to wit, sorrow, sickness, affliction, and death; 'for the former things are passed away.' *Chap. xxi. 4, 5.* You are going now to Abraham, to Isaac, and *Isa. lvii. 1, 2.* Jacob, and to the prophets; men that God hath *Chap. lxv. 17.* taken away from the evil to come, and that are now resting upon their beds, each one walking in his righteousness. The men then asked, What must we do in the holy place? To whom it was answered, You must there receive the comfort of all your toil, and have joy for all your sorrow; you must reap what you have sown, even the *Gal. vi. 7.* fruit of all your prayers and tears, and sufferings for the King by the way. In that place you must wear crowns of gold, and enjoy the perpetual sight and visions of the Holy One; for there 'you shall see him as he is.' There also you shall serve him continually with praise, with shouting and thanksgiving, whom you desired to serve in the world, though with much difficulty, because of the infirmity of your flesh. There your eyes shall be delighted with seeing, and your ears with hearing the pleasant voice of the Mighty One. There you shall enjoy your friends again that are gone thither before you; and there you shall with joy receive even every one that follows into the holy place after you. There also you shall be clothed with glory and majesty, and put into an equipage fit to ride out with the King of Glory. When he shall come with sound of trumpet in the clouds, as upon the wings of the wind, you shall come with him; and when he shall sit upon the throne of judgment, you shall sit by him; yea, and when he shall pass sentence upon all the workers of iniquity, let them be angels or men, you also shall have a voice in that judgment, because they were his and your enemies. Also, when he shall again return to the city, you shall go too, with sound of trumpet, and be ever with him.[1]

Now while they were thus drawing towards the gate, behold, a company of the heavenly host came

Margin notes: 1 John iii. 2. — 1 Thess. iv. 13-16. Jude 14. Dan. vii. 9, 10. 1 Cor. vi. 2, 3.

---

[1] Now, now look how the holy pilgrims ride,
Clouds are their chariots, angels are their guide:
Who would not here for him all hazards run,
That thus provides for his when this world's done?

out to meet them; to whom it was said by the
other two Shining Ones, These are the men that
have loved our Lord when they were in the world,
and that have left all for his holy name; and he
hath sent us to fetch them, and we have brought
them thus far on their desired journey, that they
may go in and look their Redeemer in the face
with joy. Then the heavenly host gave a great
shout saying, 'Blessed are they that are called to Rev. xix. 9.
the marriage supper of the Lamb.' There came
out also at this time to meet them several of the
King's trumpeters, clothed in white and shining
raiment, who, with melodious noises, and loud,
made even the heavens to echo with their sound.
These trumpeters saluted Christian and his fellow
with ten thousand welcomes from the world; and
this they did with shouting, and sound of trumpet.

This done, they compassed them round on every
side; some went before, some behind, and some on
the right hand, some on the left (as 'twere to guard
them through the upper regions), continually sounding as they went, with melodious noise, in notes
on high: so that the very sight was to them that
could behold it, as if heaven itself was come down
to meet them. Thus therefore they walked on together; and as they walked, ever and anon these
trumpeters, even with joyful sound, would, by mixing their music with looks and gestures, still signify
to Christian and his brother how welcome they were
into their company, and with what gladness they
came to meet them. And now were these two men,
as 'twere in heaven, before they came at it, being

swallowed up with the sight of angels, and with hearing of their melodious notes.   Here also they had the city itself in view, and they thought they heard all the bells therein to ring, to welcome them thereto.   But above all, the warm and joyful thoughts that they had about their own dwelling there, with such company, and that for ever and ever.   Oh! by what tongue or pen can their glorious joy be expressed!—Thus they came up to the gate.

Now when they were come up to the gate, there was written over it in letters of gold, 'BLESSED ARE THEY THAT DO HIS COMMANDMENTS, THAT THEY MAY HAVE RIGHT TO THE TREE OF LIFE, AND MAY ENTER IN THROUGH THE GATES INTO THE CITY.'

Rev. xxii. 14.

Then I saw in my dream, that the Shining Men bid them call at the gate; the which when they did, some from above looked over the gate, to wit, Enoch, Moses, and Elijah, etc., to whom it was said, These pilgrims are come from the City of Destruction, for the love that they bear to the King of this place: and then the pilgrims gave in unto them each man his certificate, which they had received in the beginning; those, therefore, were carried in to the King, who, when he had read them, said, Where are the men?   To whom it was answered, They are standing without the gate.   The King then commanded to open the gate, 'That the righteous nation,' said he, 'that keepeth truth may enter in.'

Isa. xxvi. 2.

Now I saw in my dream, that these two men went in at the gate; and lo, as they entered, they were transfigured, and they had raiment put on that shone like gold.   There was also that met them with harps and crowns, and gave them to them; the harps to praise withal, and the crowns in token of honour. Then I heard in my dream that all the bells in the city rang again for joy, and that it was said unto them, 'Enter ye into the joy of your Lord.' I also heard the men themselves, that they sang with a loud voice, saying, 'Blessing, honour, glory, and power be to him that sitteth upon the throne, and to the Lamb, for ever and ever.' *Rev. v. 13, 14.*

Now just as the gates were opened to let in the men, I looked in after them; and behold, the city shone like the sun; the streets also were paved with gold, and in them walked many men, with crowns on their heads, palms in their hands, and golden harps to sing praises withal.

There were also of them that had wings, and they answered one another without intermission, saying, 'Holy, holy, holy, is the Lord.' And after that they shut up the gates; which, when I had seen, I wished myself among them.

Now while I was gazing upon all these things, I turned my head to look back, and saw Ignorance come up to the river-side; but he soon got over, and that without half that difficulty which the other two men met with. For it happened that there was then in that place one Vain-hope, a ferryman, that with his boat helped him over; so he, as the other I saw, did ascend the hill to come up to the gate, only he came alone; neither did any man meet him with the least encouragement. When he was come up to the gate, he looked up to *Ignorance comes up to the river.*

Vain-hope does ferry him over.

the writing that was above, and then began to knock, supposing that entrance should have been quickly administered to him; but he was asked by the men that looked over the top of the gate, Whence came you? and what would you have? He answered, I have eat and drank in the presence of the King, and he has taught in our streets. Then they asked him for his certificate, that they might go in and show it to the King. So he fumbled in his bosom for one, and found none. Then said they, Have you none? But the man answered never a word. So they told the King, but he would not come down to see him, but commanded the two Shining Ones that conducted Christian and Hopeful to the city, to go out and take Ignorance and bind him hand and foot, and have him away. Then they took him up, and carried him through the air, to the door that I saw in the side of the hill, and put him in there. Then I saw that there was a way to hell even from the gates of heaven, as well as from the City of Destruction.

So I awoke, and behold, it was a dream.

THE CONCLUSION

Now, Reader, I have told my Dream to thee;
See if thou canst interpret it to me,
Or to thyself, or neighbour; but take heed
Of misinterpreting; for that, instead
Of doing good, will but thyself abuse:
By misinterpreting; evil ensues.
   Take heed also, that thou be not extreme
In playing with the outside of my Dream:
Nor let my figure or similitude
Put thee into a laughter or a feud;
Leave this for boys and fools; but as for thee,
Do thou the substance of my matter see.
   Put by the curtains, look within my veil;
Turn up my metaphors, and do not fail
There, if thou seekest them, such things to find,
As will be helpful to an honest mind.
   What of my dross thou findest there, be bold
To throw away, but yet preserve the gold;
What if my gold be wrapped up in ore?—
None throws away the apple for the core:
But if thou shalt cast all away as vain,
I know not but 'twill make me dream again.

THE PILGRIM'S PROGRESS

FROM THIS WORLD TO THAT WHICH IS TO COME:

The Second Part

DELIVERED UNDER THE SIMILITUDE OF A DREAM: WHEREIN IS SET FORTH THE MANNER OF THE SETTING OUT OF CHRISTIAN'S WIFE AND CHILDREN, THEIR DANGEROUS JOURNEY, AND SAFE ARRIVAL AT THE DESIRED COUNTRY:

BY

JOHN BUNYAN

I have used Similitudes.—Hos. xii. **10.**

THE AUTHOR'S WAY OF SENDING FORTH
HIS SECOND PART OF THE PILGRIM

Go now, my little Book, to every place
Where my first Pilgrim has but shown his face;
Call at their door.   If any say, Who's there?
Then answer thou, Christiana is here.
If they bid thee come in, then enter thou,
With all thy boys; and then, as thou know'st how,
Tell who they are, also from whence they came;
Perhaps they'll know them by their looks or name.
But if they should not, ask them yet again
If formerly they did not entertain
One Christian, a Pilgrim?   If they say
They did, and were delighted in his way;
Then let them know that those related were
Unto him, yea, his wife and children are.
   Tell them, that they have left their house and home,
Are turned Pilgrims, seek a world to come;
That they have met with hardships in the way;
That they do meet with troubles night and day;
That they have trod on serpents, fought with devils;
Have also overcome a many evils.
Yea, tell them also of the next, who have
Of love to pilgrimage been stout and brave
Defenders of that way, and how they still
Refuse this world, to do their Father's will.
   Go, tell them also of those dainty things
That Pilgrimage unto the Pilgrim brings.

Let them acquainted be, too, how they are
Beloved of their King, under his care;
What goodly mansions for them he provides,
Tho' they meet with rough winds and swelling tides,
How brave a calm they will enjoy at last,
Who to their Lord, and by his ways hold fast.
    Perhaps with heart and hand they will embrace
Thee, as they did my firstling, and will grace
Thee, and thy fellows, with such cheer and fare,
As show will they of Pilgrims lovers are.

I. OBJECT

But how if they will not believe of me
That I am truly thine; 'cause some there be
That counterfeit the Pilgrim and his name,
Seek by disguise to seem the very same,
And by that means have wrought themselves into
The hands and houses of I know not who?

ANSWER

'Tis true, some have of late, to counterfeit
My Pilgrim, to their own my title set;
Yea others, half my name and title too
Have stitched to their book, to make them do;
But yet they, by their features, do declare
Themselves not mine to be, whose'er they are.
    If such thou meet'st with, then thine only way
Before them all, is, to say out thy say,
In thine own native language, which no man
Now useth, nor with ease dissemble can.
If, after all, they still of you shall doubt,
Thinking that you, like gipsies, go about
In naughty wise the country to defile,
Or that you seek good people to beguile

With things unwarrantable; send for me,
And I will testify you Pilgrims be;
Yea, I will testify that only you
My Pilgrims are; and that alone will do.

2. OBJECT

But yet, perhaps, I may inquire for him,
Of those that wish him damned, life and limb.
What shall I do, when I at such a door
For Pilgrims ask, and they shall rage the more?

ANSWER

Fright not thyself, my Book, for such bugbears
Are nothing else but ground for groundless fears.
My Pilgrim's book has travell'd sea and land,
Yet could I never come to understand
That it was slighted, or turn'd out of door
By any kingdom, were they rich or poor.
    In France and Flanders, where men kill each other,
My Pilgrim is esteem'd a friend, a brother.
    In Holland too, 'tis said, as I am told,
My Pilgrim is with some worth more than gold.
    Highlanders and wild Irish can agree
My Pilgrim should familiar with them be.
    'Tis in New England under such advance,
Receives there so much loving countenance,
As to be trimm'd, new clothed, and deck'd with gems,
That it may show its features and its limbs,
Yet more; so comely doth my Pilgrim walk,
That of him thousands daily sing and talk.
    If you draw nearer home, it will appear
My Pilgrim knows no ground of shame or fear;
City and country will him entertain
With, Welcome, Pilgrim; yea, they can't refrain

From smiling, if my Pilgrim be but by,
Or shows his head in any company.

Brave gallants do my Pilgrim hug and love,
Esteem it much, yea, value it above
Things of a greater bulk; yea, with delight,
Say, My lark's leg is better than a kite.

Young ladies, and young gentlewomen too,
Do no small kindness to my Pilgrim show;
Their cabinets, their bosoms, and their hearts
My Pilgrim has, 'cause he to them imparts
His pretty riddles in such wholesome strains,
As yield them profit double to their pains
Of reading: yea, I think I may be bold
To say, some prize him far above their gold.

The very children that do walk the street,
If they do but my holy Pilgrim meet,
Salute him will, will wish him well, and say,
He is the only stripling of the day.

They that have never seen him, yet admire
What they have heard of him, and much desire
To have his company, and hear him tell
Those Pilgrim stories which he knows so well.

Yea, some who did not love him at the first,
But call'd him fool and noddy, say they must,
Now they have seen and heard him, him commend,
And to those whom they love, they do him send.

Wherefore, my Second Part, thou need'st not be
Afraid to show thy head; none can hurt thee,
That wish but well to him that went before,
'Cause thou com'st after with a second store
Of things as good, as rich, as profitable,
For young, for old, for stagg'ring, and for stable.

3. OBJECT

But some there be that say, he laughs too loud;
And some do say his head is in a cloud.

Some say, his words and stories are so dark,
They know not how, by them, to find his mark.

ANSWER

One may (I think) say, Both his laughs and cries
May well be guess'd at by his watery eyes.
Some things are of that nature as to make
One's fancy checkle, while his heart doth ache.
When Jacob saw his Rachel with the sheep,
He did at the same time both kiss and weep.

Whereas some say, A cloud is in his head,
That doth but show how wisdom's covered
With its own mantles, and to stir the mind
To a search after what it fain would find:
Things that seem to be hid in words obscure,
Do but the godly mind the more allure;
To study what those sayings should contain,
That speak to us in such a cloudy strain.

I also know a dark similitude
Will on the fancy more itself intrude,
And will stick faster in the heart and head,
Than things from similes not borrowed.

Wherefore, my Book, let no discouragement
Hinder thy travels.   Behold thou art sent
To friends, not foes; to friends that will give place
To thee, thy Pilgrims, and thy words embrace.

Besides, what my first Pilgrim left conceal'd,
Thou, my brave second Pilgrim, hast reveal'd;
What Christian left lock'd up, and went his way,
Sweet Christiana opens with her key.

4. OBJECT

But some love not the method of your first:
Romance they count it; throw't away as dust.

If I should meet with such, what should I say?
Must I slight them as they slight me, or nay?

ANSWER

My Christiana, if with such thou meet,
By all means in all loving wise them greet;
Render them not reviling for revile;
But if they frown, I prithee on them smile;
Perhaps 'tis nature, or some ill report,
Has made them thus despise, or thus retort.
Some love no cheese, some love no fish, and some
Love not their friends, nor their own house or home;
Some start at pig, slight chicken, love not fowl,
More than they love a cuckoo or an owl;
Leave such, my Christiana, to their choice,
And seek those who to find thee will rejoice;
By no means strive, but in humble-wise
Present thee to them in thy Pilgrim's guise.
Go then, my little Book, and show to all
That entertain, and bid thee welcome shall,
What thou shalt keep close, shut up from the rest,
And wish what thou shalt show them may be blest
To them for good, may make them choose to be
Pilgrims, better by far, than thee or me.
Go then, I say, tell all men who thou art,
Say, I am Christiana, and my part
Is now, with my four sons, to tell you what
It is for men to take a Pilgrim's lot:
Go also tell them who, and what they be,
That now do go on pilgrimage with thee:
Say, here's my neighbour Mercy, she is one
That has long time with me a Pilgrim gone.
Come, see in her virgin face, and learn
'Twixt idle ones and Pilgrims to discern.

Yea, let young damsels learn of her to prize
The world which is to come, in any wise.
When little tripping maidens follow God,
And leave old doting sinners to his rod;
'Tis like those days wherein the young ones cried
Hosanna! to whom old ones did deride.

Next tell them of old Honest, who you found
With his white hairs treading the Pilgrim's ground.
Yea, tell them how plain-hearted this man was,
How after his good Lord he bare his cross;
Perhaps with some grey head this may prevail
With Christ to fall in love, and sin bewail.

Tell them also how Master Fearing went
On pilgrimage, and how the time he spent
In solitariness, with fears and cries,
And how at last he won the joyful prize.
He *was* a good man, though much down in spirit,
He *is* a good man, and doth life inherit.

Tell them of Master Feeble-mind also,
Who, not before, but still behind would go;
Show them also how he had like been slain,
And how one Great-heart did his life regain:
This man was true of heart, tho' weak in grace,
One might true godliness read in his face.

Then tell them of Master Ready-to-halt,
A man with crutches, but much without fault;
Tell them how Master Feeble-mind and he
Did love, and in opinions much agree.
And let all know, tho' weakness was their chance,
Yet sometimes one could sing, the other dance.

Forget not Master Valiant-for-the-truth,
That man of courage, though a very youth.
Tell every one his spirit was so stout,
No man could ever make him face about,
And how Great-heart and he could not forbear,
But put down Doubting Castle, slay Despair.

Overlook not Master Despondency,
Nor Much-afraid, his daughter, tho' they lie
Under such mantles as may make them look
(With some) as if their God had them forsook.
They softly went, but sure, and at the end
Found that the Lord of Pilgrims was their Friend.
When thou hast told the world of all these things,
Then turn about, my Book, and touch these strings,
Which, if but touched, will such music make,
They 'll make a cripple dance, a giant quake.

These riddles that lie couch'd within thy breast,
Freely propound, expound ; and for the rest
Of thy mysterious lines, let them remain
For those whose nimble fancies shall them gain.

Now may this little Book a blessing be
To those that love this little Book and me :
And may its buyer have no cause to say,
His money is but lost or thrown away ;
Yea, may this second Pilgrim yield that fruit,
As may with each good Pilgrim's fancy suit
And may it persuade some that go astray,
To turn their foot and heart to the right way.

Is the hearty prayer

of the Author,

JOHN BUNYAN

THE PILGRIM'S PROGRESS

IN THE SIMILITUDE OF A DREAM

THE SECOND PART

COURTEOUS companions, some time since, to tell you my dream that I had of Christian the Pilgrim, and of his dangerous journey toward the Celestial Country, was pleasant to me, and profitable to you. I told you then also what I saw concerning his wife and children, and how unwilling they were to go with him on pilgrimage, insomuch that he was forced to go on his progress without them; for he durst not run the danger of that destruction which he feared would come by staying with them in the City of Destruction. Wherefore, as I then showed you, he left them and departed.

Now it hath so happened, through the multiplicity of business, that I have been much hindered and kept back from my wonted travels into those parts whence he went, and so could not till now obtain an opportunity to make further inquiry after whom he left behind, that I might give you an account of them. But having had some concerns that way of late, I went down again thitherward. Now, having taken up my lodgings in a wood, about a mile off the place, as I slept I dreamed again.

And as I was in my dream, behold, an aged gentleman came by where I lay; and because he was to go some part of the way that I was travelling, methought I got up and went with him. So as we walked, and as travellers usually do, I was as if we fell into discourse, and our talk happened to be about Christian and his travels; for thus I began with the old man:

Sir, said I, what town is that there below, that lieth on the left hand of our way?

Then said Mr. Sagacity (for that was his name), It is the City of Destruction, a populous place, but possessed with a very ill-conditioned and idle sort of people.

I thought that was that city, quoth I; I went once myself through that town, and therefore know that this report you give of it is true.

SAG. Too true, I wish I could speak truth in speaking better of them that dwell therein.

Well, Sir, quoth I, then I perceive you to be a well-meaning man; and so one that takes pleasure to hear and tell of that which is good. Pray, did you never hear what happened to a man some time ago in this town (whose name was Christian) that went on pilgrimage up towards the higher regions?

SAG. Hear of him! Ay, and I also heard of the molestations, troubles, wars, captivities, cries, groans, frights, and fears that he met with, and had in his journey. Besides, I must tell you, all our country rings of him; there are but few houses that have heard of him and his doings but have sought after and got the records of his pilgrimage; yea, I think I may say that that his hazardous journey has got a many well-wishers to his ways; for though, when he was here, he was fool in every man's mouth, yet, now he is gone, he is highly commended of all. For, 'tis said he lives bravely where he is; yea, many of them that are resolved never to run his hazards, yet have their mouths water at his gains. *Christians are well spoken of when gone, tho' called fools while they are here.*

They may, quoth I, well think, if they think anything that is true, that he liveth well where he is; for he now lives at and in the Fountain of Life, and has what he has without labour and sorrow, for there is no grief mixed therewith.

SAG. Talk! the people talk strangely about him. Some say that he now walks in white, that he has a chain of gold about his neck, that he has a crown of gold, beset with pearls, upon his head. Others say that the Shining Ones, that sometimes showed themselves to him in his journey, are become his companions, and that he is as familiar with them in the place where he is, as here one neighbour is with another. Besides, 'tis confidently affirmed concerning him, that the King of the place where he is has bestowed on him already a very rich and pleasant dwelling at court; and that he every day eateth and drinketh, and walketh, and talketh with him; and receiveth of the smiles and favours of him that is Judge of all there. Moreover, it is expected of some, that his Prince, the Lord of that country, will shortly come into these parts, and will know the reason, if they can give any, why his neighbours set so little by him, and had him so much in derision when they *Rev. iii. 4. Chap. vi. 11.* *Zech. iii. 7.* *Luke xiv. 15.*

perceived that he would be a pilgrim. For they say, that now he is so in the affections of his Prince, and that his Sovereign is so much concerned with the indignities that were cast upon Christian when he became a pilgrim, that he will look upon all as if done unto himself ; and no marvel, for 'twas for the love that he had to his Prince that he ventured as he did.

I dare say, quoth I, I am glad on 't ; I am glad for the poor man's sake, for that now he has rest from his labour, and for that he now reapeth the benefit of his tears with joy ; and for that he has got beyond the gunshot of his enemies, and is out of the reach of them that hate him. I also am glad for that a rumour of these things is noised abroad in this country ; who can tell but that it may work some good effect on some that are left behind ? But pray, Sir, while it is fresh in my mind, do you hear anything of his wife and children ? Poor hearts, I wonder in my mind what they do !

SAG. Who ? Christiana and her sons ? They are like to do as well as did Christian himself ; for though they all played the fool at the first, and would by no means be persuaded by either the tears or entreaties of Christian, yet second thoughts have wrought wonderfully with them ; so they have packed up, and are also gone after him.

Better and better, quoth I : but what ! wife and children and all ?

SAG. 'Tis true : I can give you an account of the matter, for I was upon the spot at the instant, and was thoroughly acquainted with the whole affair.

Then, said I, a man it seems may report it for a truth ?

SAG. You need not fear to affirm it, I mean that they are all gone on pilgrimage, both the good woman and her four boys. And being we are, as I perceive, going some considerable way together, I will give you an account of the whole matter.

This Christiana (for that was her name from the day that she with her children betook themselves to a pilgrim's life) after her husband was gone over the river, and she could hear of him no more, her thoughts began to work in her mind. First, for that she had lost her husband, and for that the loving bond of that relation was utterly broken betwixt them. For you know, said he to me, nature can do no less but entertain the living with many a heavy cogitation in the remembrance of the loss of loving relations. This therefore of her husband did cost her many a tear. But this was not all, for Christiana did also begin to consider with herself, whether her unbecoming behaviour towards her husband was not one cause that she saw him no more, and that in such sort he was taken away from her. And upon this came into her mind, by swarms, all her unkind, unnatural, and ungodly carriages to her dear friend ; which also clogged her conscience, and did load her with guilt. She was moreover much broken with calling to remembrance the restless groans, brinish tears, and self-bemoanings of her husband, and how she did harden her heart against all his entreaties, and loving persuasions (of her and her sons) to go with him ; yea, there was not any-

Part I. page 194.

Mark this, you that are churls to your godly relations.

thing that Christian either said to her, or did before her, all the while that his burden did hang on his back, but it returned upon her like a flash of lightning, and rent the caul of her heart in sunder.

Part i. page 10.

Specially that bitter outcry of his, 'What shall I do to be saved?' did ring in her ears most dolefully.

Then said she to her children, Sons, we are all undone. I have sinned away your father, and he is gone: he would have had us with him; but I would not go myself, I also have hindered you of life. With that the boys fell all into tears, and cried out to go after their father. Oh! said Christiana, that it had been but our lot to go with him, then had it fared well with us beyond what 'tis like to do now; for though I formerly imagined concerning the troubles of your father, that they proceeded of a foolish fancy that he had, or for that he was overrun with melancholy humours; yet now 'twill not out of my mind but that they sprang from another

James i. 23-25.

cause, to wit, for that the Light of light was given him, by the help of which, as I perceive, he has escaped the snares of death. Then they all wept again, and cried out, Oh! woe worth the day!

The next night Christiana had a dream; and

Christiana's dream. Luke xviii. 13.

behold, she saw as if a broad parchment was opened before her, in which were recorded the sum of her ways; and the times, as she thought, looked very black upon her. Then she cried out aloud in her sleep, 'Lord have mercy upon me, a sinner'; and the little children heard her.

After this she thought she saw two very ill-favoured ones standing by her bedside, and saying,

What shall we do with this woman? for she cries out for mercy waking and sleeping; if she be suffered to go on as she begins, we shall lose her as we have lost her husband. Wherefore we must, by one way or other, seek to take her off from the thoughts of what shall be hereafter, else all the world cannot help it but she will become a pilgrim.

Mark this, this is the quintessence of hell.

Now she awoke in a great sweat, also a trembling was upon her, but after a while she fell to sleeping again. And then she thought she saw Christian her husband in a place of bliss among many immortals, with a harp in his hand, standing and playing upon it before One that sat on a throne with a rainbow about his head. She saw also as if he bowed his head with his face to the paved-work that was under the Prince's feet, saying, I heartily thank my Lord and King for bringing of me into this place. Then shouted a company of them that stood round about, and harped with their harps; but no man living could tell what they said, but Christian and his companions.

Help against discouragement.

Next morning when she was up, had prayed to God, and talked with her children a while, one knocked hard at the door, to whom she spake out, saying, If thou comest in God's name, come in. So he said, Amen, and opened the door, and saluted her with Peace be to this house. The which when he had done, he said, Christiana, knowest thou wherefore I am come? Then she blushed and trembled, also her heart began to wax warm with desires to know whence he came, and what was his errand to her. So he said unto her, my name is Secret, I

Convictions seconded with fresh tidings of God's readiness to pardon.

dwell with those that are high. It is talked of where I dwell, as if thou hadst a desire to go thither; also there is a report that thou art aware of the evil thou hast formerly done to thy husband, in hardening of thy heart against his way, and in keeping of these thy babes in their ignorance. Christiana, the Merciful One has sent me to tell thee that he is a God ready to forgive, and that he taketh delight to multiply to pardon offences. He also would have thee know that he inviteth thee to come into his presence, to his table, and that he will feed thee with the fat of his house, and with the heritage of Jacob thy father.

There is Christian thy husband, *that was*, with legions more his companions, ever beholding that face that doth minister life to beholders; and they will all be glad when they shall hear the sound of thy feet step over thy Father's threshold.

Christiana at this was greatly abashed in herself, and bowing her head to the ground, this Visitor proceeded and said, Christiana, here is also a letter for thee, which I have brought from thy husband's King. So she took it and opened it, but it smelt after the manner of the best perfume, also it was written in letters of gold. The contents of the letter was: 'That the King would have her do as did Christian her husband; for that was the way to come to his city, and to dwell in his presence with joy for ever.' At this the good woman was quite overcome; so she cried out to her Visitor, Sir, will you carry me and my children with you, that we also may go and worship this King?

Song i. 3.

Christiana quite overcome.

Then said the Visitor, Christiana, the bitter is Further instruction to Christiana. before the sweet: thou must through troubles, as did he that went before thee, enter this Celestial City. Wherefore I advise thee to do as did Christian thy husband. Go to the Wicket-gate yonder, over the plain, for that stands in the head of the way up which thou must go, and I wish thee all good speed. Also I advise that thou put this letter in thy bosom; that thou read therein to thyself and to thy children, until you have got it by root-of-heart, for it is one of the songs that thou must sing while Ps. cxix. 54. thou art in this house of thy pilgrimage; also this thou must deliver in at the *further* gate.

Now I saw in my dream, that this old gentleman, as he told me this story, did himself seem to be greatly affected therewith. He moreover proceeded and said, So Christiana called her sons together, and began thus to address herself unto them: My sons, Christiana prays well for her Journey. I have, as you may perceive, been of late under much exercise in my soul about the death of your father; not for that I doubt at all of his happiness, for I am satisfied now that he is well. I have also been much affected with the thoughts of mine own state and yours, which I verily believe is by nature miserable. My carriages also to your father in his distress, is a great load to my conscience; for I hardened both my own heart and yours against him, and refused to go with him on pilgrimage.

The thoughts of these things would now kill me outright, but that for a dream which I had last night, and but that for the encouragement that this stranger has given me this morning. Come, my children, let

us pack up, and begone to the gate that leads to the
Celestial Country, that we may see your father, and
be with him and his companions in peace, according
to the laws of that land.

Then did her children burst out into tears for joy
that the heart of their mother was so inclined. So
their Visitor bid them farewell; and they began to
prepare to set out for their journey.

But while they were thus about to be gone, two
of the women that were Christiana's neighbours
came up to her house and knocked at her door.
To whom she said as before, If you come in God's
name, come in. At this the women were stunned,
for this kind of language they used not to hear, or
to perceive to drop from the lips of Christiana.
Yet they came in: but, behold, they found the
good woman a-preparing to be gone from her
house.

So they began and said, Neighbour, pray what is
your meaning by this?

Christiana answered and said to the eldest of
them, whose name was Mrs. Timorous, I am preparing for a journey. (This Timorous was daughter
to him that met Christian upon the Hill Difficulty,
and would a had him gone back for fear of the
lions.)

Tim. For what journey, I pray you?

Chris. Even to go after my good husband. And
with that she fell a-weeping.

Tim. I hope not so, good neighbour; pray, for
your poor children's sakes, do not so unwomanly
cast away yourself.

Christiana's
new language
stuns her old
neighbours.

Part 1.
page 51.

Timorous
comes to visit
Christiana,
with Mercy,
one of her
neighbours.

CHRIS. Nay, my children shall go with me; not one of them is willing to stay behind.

TIM. I wonder, in my very heart, what, or who has brought you into this mind.

CHRIS. O neighbour, knew you but as much as I do, I doubt not but that you would go with me.

TIM. Prithee, what new knowledge hast thou got, that so worketh off thy mind from thy friends, and that tempteth thee to go nobody knows where?

CHRIS. Then Christiana replied, I have been sorely afflicted since my husband's departure from me, but specially since he went over the river.   But that *Death.* which troubleth me most, is my churlish carriages to him when he was under his distress.   Besides, I am *now* as he was *then*; nothing will serve me but going on pilgrimage.   I was a-dreaming last night that I saw him.   O that my soul was with him! He dwelleth in the presence of the King of the country, he sits and eats with him at his table, he is become a companion of immortals, and has a house now given him to dwell in, to which the best palaces *2 Cor. v. 1-4.* on earth, if compared, seem to me to be but as a dunghill.   The Prince of the place has also sent for me, with promise of entertainment if I shall come to him; his messenger was here even now, and has brought me a letter, which invites me to come.   And with that she plucked out her letter, and read it, and said to them, What now will ye say to this?

TIM. Oh the madness that has possessed thee and thy husband, to run yourselves upon such difficulties!   You have heard, I am sure, what your *Part i.* husband did meet with, even in a manner at the *pages 12-17.*

first step that he took on his way, as our Neighbour Obstinate can yet testify, for he went along with him; yea, and Pliable too, until they, like wise men, were afraid to go any farther. We also heard over and above, how he met with the lions, Apollyon, the Shadow of Death, and many other things. Nor is the danger that he met with at Vanity Fair to be forgotten by thee; for if he, though a man, was so hard put to it, what canst thou, being but a poor woman, do? Consider also that these four sweet babes are thy children, thy flesh and thy bones. Wherefore, though thou shouldest be so rash as to cast away thyself, yet, for the sake of the fruit of thy body, keep thou at home.

The reasonings of the flesh.

But Christiana said unto her, Tempt me not, my neighbour. I have now a price put into mine hand to get gain, and I should be a fool of the greatest size if I should have no heart to strike in with the opportunity. And for that you tell me of all these troubles that I am like to meet with in the way, they are so far off from being to me a discouragement, that they show I am in the right. The bitter must come before the sweet, and that also will make the sweet the sweeter. Wherefore, since you came not to my house in God's name, as I said, I pray you to be gone, and not to disquiet me further.

A pertinent reply to fleshly reasonings.

Then Timorous also reviled her, and said to her fellow, Come, Neighbour Mercy, let's leave her in her own hands, since she scorns our counsel and company. But Mercy was at a stand, and could not so readily comply with her neighbour, and that for a twofold reason. First, her bowels yearned over Christiana: so she said within herself, If my neighbour will needs be gone, I will go a little way with her and help her. Secondly, her bowels yearned over her own soul (for what Christiana had said had taken some hold upon her mind). Wherefore she said within herself again, I will yet have more talk with this Christiana, and if I find truth and life in what she shall say, myself with my heart shall also go with her. Wherefore Mercy began thus to reply to her Neighbour Timorous:

Mercy's bowels yearn over Christiana.

MERCY. Neighbour, I did indeed come with you to see Christiana this morning; and since she is, as you see, a-taking of her last farewell of her country, I think to walk this sunshine morning a little way with her to help her on the way. But she told her not of her second reason, but kept that to herself.

Timorous forsakes her, but Mercy cleaves to her.

TIM. Well, I see you have a mind to go a-fooling too, but take heed in time and be wise: while we are out of danger, we are out: but when we are in, we are in. So Mrs. Timorous returned to her house, and Christiana betook herself to her journey. But when Timorous was got home to her house, she sends for some of her neighbours, to wit, Mrs. Bat's-eyes, Mrs. Inconsiderate, Mrs. Light-mind, and Mrs. Know-nothing. So when they were come to her house, she falls to telling of the story of Christiana and of her intended journey. And thus she began her tale:

Timorous acquaints her friends what the good Christiana intends to do.

TIM. Neighbours, having had little to do this morning, I went to give Christiana a visit; and when I came at the door, I knocked, as you know 'tis our custom. And she answered, If you come in God's name, come in. So in I went, thinking all was well. But when I came in, I found her preparing herself to depart the town, she and also her children. So I asked her what was her meaning by that; and she told me in short, that she was now of a mind to go on pilgrimage, as did her husband. She told me also a dream that she had, and how the King of the country where her husband was, had sent her an inviting letter to come thither.

Mrs. Know-nothing.

Then said Mrs. Know-nothing, And what! do you think she will go?

TIM. Ay, go she will, whatever come on 't: and methinks I know it by this, for that which was my great argument to persuade her to stay at home (to wit, the troubles she was like to meet with in the way) is one great argument with her to put her forward on her journey. For she told me in so many words, The bitter goes before the sweet; yea, and forasmuch as it so doth, it makes the sweet the sweeter.

Mrs. Bat's-eyes.

MRS. BAT'S-EYES. Oh this blind and foolish woman! said she; will she not take warning by her husband's afflictions? For my part, I see, if he was here again, he would rest him content in a whole skin, and never run so many hazards for nothing.

Mrs. Inconsiderate.

Mrs. Inconsiderate also replied, saying: Away with such fantastical fools from the town! A good riddance, for my part, I say, of her. Should she stay where she dwells and retain this her mind, who could live quietly by her? for she will either be dumpish or unneighbourly, or talk of such matters as no wise body can abide: Wherefore, for my part, I shall never be sorry for her departure; let her go, and let better come in her room: 'twas never a good world since these whimsical fools dwelt in it.

Then Mrs. Light-mind added as followeth: Come, put this kind of talk away. I was yesterday at Madam Wanton's, where we were as merry as the maids. For who do you think should be there, but I and Mrs. Love-the-flesh, and three or four more, with Mr. Lechery, Mrs. Filth, and some others. So there we had music and dancing, and what else was meet to fill up the pleasure. And I dare say my lady herself is an admirably well-bred gentlewoman, and Mr. Lechery is as pretty a fellow.

By this time Christiana was got on her way, and Mercy went along with her. So as they went, her children being there also, Christiana began to discourse. And, Mercy, said Christiana, I take this as an unexpected favour, that thou shouldest set foot out of doors with me, to accompany me a little on my way.

MERCY. Then said young Mercy (for she was but young), If I thought it would be to purpose to go with you, I would never go near the town any more.

CHRIS. Well, Mercy, said Christiana, cast in thy lot with me: I well know what will be the end of our pilgrimage; my husband is where he would not but be for all the gold in the Spanish mines. Nor shalt thou be rejected, though thou goest but upon my invitation. The King who hath sent for me

Mrs. Light-mind.

Madam Wanton, she that had like to have been too hard for Faithful in time past. Part I. page 84.

Discourse betwixt Mercy and Good Christiana.

Mercy inclines to go.

Christiana would have her neighbour with her.

and my children is one that delighteth in mercy. Besides, if thou wilt, I will hire thee, and thou shalt go along with me as my servant; yet we will have all things in common betwixt thee and me; only go along with me.

MERCY. But how shall I be ascertained that I also shall be entertained? Had I this hope, but from one that can tell, I would make no stick at all, but would go, being helped by him that can help, though the way was never so tedious.

CHRIS. Well, loving Mercy, I will tell thee what thou shalt do: Go with me to the Wicket-gate, and there I will further inquire for thee; and if there thou shalt not meet with encouragement, I will be content that thou shalt return to thy place. I also will pay thee for thy kindness which thou showest to me and my children, in thy accompanying of us in our way, as thou dost.

MERCY. Then will I go thither, and will take what shall follow; and the Lord grant that my lot may there fall, even as the King of heaven shall have his heart upon me.

Christiana then was glad at her heart, not only that she had a companion, but also for that she had prevailed with this poor maid to fall in love with her own salvation. So they went on together, and Mercy began to weep. Then said Christiana, Wherefore weepeth my sister so?

MERCY. Alas! said she, who can but lament that shall but rightly consider what a state and condition my poor relations are in, that yet remain in our sinful town? And that which makes my grief the

more heavy, is, because they have no instructor, nor
any to tell them what is to come.

CHRIS. Bowels becometh pilgrims; and thou dost Christian's prayers were answered for his relations after he was dead.
for thy friends as my good Christian did for me when
he left me; he mourned for that I would not heed
nor regard him, but his Lord and ours did gather up
his tears and put them into his bottle; and now both
I, and thou, and these my sweet babes, are reaping
the fruit and benefit of them.   I hope, Mercy, these
tears of thine will not be lost; for the truth hath
said, that 'They that sow in tears shall reap in joy,' Ps. cxxvi. 5, 6.
in singing.   And 'he that goeth forth and weepeth,
bearing precious seed, shall doubtless come again
with rejoicing, bringing his sheaves with him.'

Then said Mercy:

> Let the Most Blessed be my guide,
>   If't be his blessed will,
> Unto his gate, into his fold,
>   Up to his holy hill.
> And let him never suffer me
>   To swerve or turn aside
> From his free grace and holy ways,
>   Whate'er shall me betide.
> And let him gather them of mine,
>   That I have left behind;
> Lord, make them pray they may be thine,
>   With all their heart and mind.

Now my old friend proceeded and said: But when
Christiana came up to the Slough of Despond, she Part I. pages 16-18.
began to be at a stand; for, said she, This is the
place in which my dear husband had like to have
been smothered with mud.   She perceived also,
that notwithstanding the command of the King to

Their own carnal conclusions instead of the Word of Life.

make this place for pilgrims good, yet it was rather worse than formerly. So I asked if that was true? Yes, said the old gentleman, too true; for that many there be that pretend to be the King's labourers, and that say they are for mending the King's highways, that bring dirt and dung instead of stones, and so mar instead of mending. Here Christiana therefore, with her boys, did make a stand. But said Mercy, Come, let us venture, only let us be wary. Then they looked well to the steps, and made a shift to get staggeringly over.

Mercy the boldest at the Slough of Despond.

Yet Christiana had like to have been in, and that not once nor twice. Now they had no sooner got over, but they thought they heard words that said unto them, 'Blessed is she that believeth, for there shall be a performance of the things that have been told her from the Lord.'

Luke i. 45.

Then they went on again; and said Mercy to Christiana, Had I as good ground to hope for a loving reception at the Wicket-gate as you, I think no Slough of Despond would discourage me.

Well, said the other, you know *your sore*, and I know *mine*; and, good friend, we shall all have enough evil before we come at our journey's end.

For can it be imagined, that the people that design to attain such excellent glories as we do, and that are so envied that happiness as we are, but that we shall meet with what fears and scares, with what troubles and afflictions they can possibly assault us with, that hate us?

And now Mr. Sagacity left me to dream out my dream by myself. Wherefore, methought I saw

Christiana, and Mercy, and the boys, go all of them up to the gate; to which, when they were come, they betook themselves to a short debate about how they must manage their calling at the gate, and what should be said to him that did open to them. So it was concluded, since Christiana was the eldest, that she should knock for entrance, and that she should speak to him that did open, for the rest. So Christiana began to knock, and as her poor husband did, she knocked, and knocked again. But instead of any that answered, they all thought that they heard as if a dog came barking upon them; a dog, and a great one too, and this made the women and children afraid; nor durst they for a while to knock any more, for fear the mastiff should fly upon them. Now, therefore, they were greatly tumbled up and down in their minds, and knew not what to do. Knock they durst not, for fear of the dog; go back they durst not, for fear that the Keeper of that gate should espy them as they so went, and should be offended with them. At last they thought of knocking again, and knocked more vehemently than they did at the first. Then said the Keeper of the gate, Who is there? So the dog left off to bark, and he opened unto them.

Then Christiana made low obeisance, and said, Let not our Lord be offended with his handmaidens for that we have knocked at his princely gate. Then said the Keeper, Whence come ye, and what is that you would have?

Christiana answered, We are come from whence Christian did come, and upon the same errand as

Prayer should be made with consideration and fear, as well as in faith and hope. Part i. page 29.

The dog, the devil, an enemy to prayer.

Christiana and her companions perplexed about prayer.

he; to wit, to be, if it shall please you, graciously admitted by this gate, into the way that leads to the Celestial City.   And I answer, my Lord, in the next place, that I am Christiana, once the wife of Christian, that now is gotten above.

With that the Keeper of the gate did marvel, saying, What! is she become now a pilgrim, that but a while ago abhorred that life? Then she bowed her head, and said, Yes, and so are these, my sweet babes, also.

How Christiana is entertained at the gate.

Then he took her by the hand, and let her in, and said also, 'Suffer the little children to come unto me'; and with that he shut up the gate.   This done, he called to a trumpeter that was above over the gate, to entertain Christiana with shouting and sound of trumpet for joy.   So he obeyed and sounded, and filled the air with his melodious notes.

Luke xv. 7.

Now all this while poor Mercy did stand without, trembling and crying for fear that she was rejected. But when Christiana had gotten admittance for herself and her boys, then she began to make intercession for Mercy.

Christiana's prayer for her friend Mercy.

CHRIS. And she said, My Lord, I have a companion of mine that stands yet without, that is come hither upon the same account as myself; one that is much dejected in her mind, for that she comes, as she thinks, without sending for, whereas I was sent to by my husband's King to come.

The delays make the hungering soul the ferventer.

Now Mercy began to be very impatient, for each minute was as long to her as an hour, wherefore she prevented Christiana from a fuller interceding for her, by knocking at the gate herself. And she knocked *then* so loud, that she made Christiana to start. Then said the Keeper of the gate, Who is there? and said Christiana, It is my friend.

So he opened the gate, and looked out; but Mercy was fallen down without, in a swoon, for she fainted, and was afraid that no gate would be opened to her. Mercy faints.

Then he took her by the hand, and said, Damsel, I bid thee arise.

Oh, sir, said she, I am faint; there is scarce life left in me. But he answered, That one once said, 'When my soul fainted within me, I remembered the Lord, and my prayer came in unto thee, into thy holy temple.' Fear not, but stand upon thy feet, and tell me wherefore thou art come. Jonah ii. 7.

MERCY. I am come for that unto which I was never invited, as my friend Christiana was. Hers was from the King, and mine was but from her: wherefore I fear I presume. The cause of her fainting.

Did she desire thee to come with her to this place?

MERCY. Yes; and as my Lord sees, I am come. And if there is any grace or forgiveness of sins to spare, I beseech that I, thy poor handmaid, may be partaker thereof.

Then he took her again by the hand, and led her gently in, and said, I pray for all them that believe on me, by what means soever they come unto me. Then said he to those that stood by, Fetch something, and give it Mercy to smell on, thereby to stay her fainting. So they fetched her a bundle of myrrh, and a while after she was revived. Mark this.

And now was Christiana, and her boys, and Mercy, received of the Lord at the head of the way, and spoke kindly unto by him.

Then said they yet further unto him, We are sorry for our sins, and beg of our Lord his pardon, and further information what we must do.

I grant pardon, said he, by word and deed: by word, in the promise of forgiveness; by deed, in the way I obtained it. Take the first from my lips with a kiss, and the other as it shall be revealed.

Song i. 2.
John xx. 20.

Now I saw in my dream, that he spake many good words unto them, whereby they were greatly gladded. He also had them up to the top of the gate, and showed them by what *deed* they were saved, and told them withal that that sight they would have again as they went along in the way, to their comfort.

Christ
Crucified
seen afar off.

So he left them a while in a summer-parlour below, where they entered into talk by themselves; and thus Christiana began: O Lord! how glad am I, that we are got in hither!

Talk
between the
Christians.

MERCY. So you well may; but I, of all, have cause to leap for joy.

CHRIS. I thought, one time, as I stood at the gate (because I had knocked and none did answer) that all our labour had been lost; specially when that ugly cur made such a heavy barking at us.

MERCY. But my worst fear was after I saw that you was taken into his favour, and that I was left behind. Now, thought I, 'tis fulfilled which is written, 'Two women shall be grinding together, the one shall be taken and the other left.' I

Matt. xxiv. 41.

had much ado to forbear crying out, Undone!
undone!

And afraid I was to knock any more; but when
I looked up to what was written over the gate, I Part I. page 29.
took courage. I also thought that I must either
knock again, or die; so I knocked, but I cannot
tell how, for my spirit now struggled betwixt life
and death.

CHRIS. Can you not tell how you knocked? I
am sure your knocks were so earnest, that the very
sound of them made me start; I thought I never
heard such knocking in all my life; I thought you
would have come in by violent hands, or a took the
kingdom by storm.

Christiana thinks her companion prays better than she.

Matt. xi. 12.

MERCY. Alas, to be in my case, who that so was
could but a done so? You saw that the door was
shut upon me, and that there was a most cruel
dog thereabout. Who, I say, that was so faint-
hearted as I, that would not a knocked with all
their might? But pray what said my Lord to my
rudeness? Was he not angry with me?

CHRIS. When he heard your lumbering noise, he
gave a wonderful innocent smile; I believe what
you did pleased him well enough, for he showed no
sign to the contrary. But I marvel in my heart
why he keeps such a dog; had I known that afore,
I fear I should not have had heart enough to have
ventured myself in this manner. But now we are
in, we are in, and I am glad with all my heart.

Christ pleased with loud and restless praises.

If the soul at first did know all it should meet with in its journey to heaven, it would hardly ever set out.

MERCY. I will ask, if you please, next time he
comes down, why he keeps such a filthy cur in his
yard. I hope he will not take it amiss.

The children
are afraid of
the dog.
Ay, do, said the children, and persuade him to
hang him, for we are afraid he will bite us when
we go hence.

So at last he came down to them again, and
Mercy fell to the ground on her face before him
and worshipped, and said, Let my Lord accept of
the sacrifice of praise which I now offer unto him,
with the calves of my lips.

So he said unto her, Peace be to thee; stand up.

But she continued upon her face and said,
Jer. xii. 1. 'Righteous art thou, O Lord, when I plead with
thee, yet let me talk with thee of thy judgments.'
Mercy
expostulates
about the
dog. Wherefore dost thou keep so cruel a dog in thy yard,
at the sight of which, such women and children
as we, are ready to fly from thy gate for fear?

Devil. He answered and said, That dog has another
owner; he also is kept close in another man's
ground, only my pilgrims hear his barking; he
Part i.
page 30. belongs to the castle which you see there at a
distance, but can come up to the walls of this
place.   He has frighted many an honest pilgrim
from worse to better, by the great voice of his
roaring.   Indeed, he that owneth him doth not
keep him of any goodwill to me or mine, but with
intent to keep the pilgrims from coming to me,
and that they may be afraid to knock at this gate
for entrance.   Sometimes also he has broken out,
and has worried some that I love; but I take all
A check to
the carnal
fear of the
pilgrims. at present patiently.   I also give my pilgrims
timely help, so they are not delivered up to his
power, to do to them what his doggish nature
would prompt him to.   But what! my purchased

one, I trow, hadst thou known never so much beforehand, thou wouldst not have been afraid of a dog.

The beggars that go from door to door will, rather than they will lose a supposed alms, run the hazard of the bawling, barking, and biting too of a dog; and shall a dog—a dog in another's man's yard, a dog whose barking I turn to the profit of pilgrims—keep any from coming to me? I deliver them from the *lions*, their darling from the power of the dog.

MERCY. Then said Mercy, I confess my ignorance; I spake what I understood not; I acknowledge that thou doest all things well.

Christians when wise enough acquiesce in the wisdom of their Lord.

CHRIS. Then Christiana began to talk of their journey, and to inquire after the way. So he fed them, and washed their feet, and set them in the way of his steps, according as he had dealt with her husband before.

Part I. page 32.

So I saw in my dream that they walked on their way, and had the weather very comfortable to them.

Then Christiana began to sing, saying :—

> Bless'd be the day that I began
>   A pilgrim for to be ;
> And blessed also be that man
>   That thereto moved me.
> 'Tis true, 'twas long ere I began
>   To seek to live for ever :
> But now I run fast as I can ;
>   'Tis better late than never.
> Our tears to joy, our fears to faith,
>   Are turned, as we see ;
> Thus our beginning (as one saith)
>   Shows what our end will be.

Now there was, on the other side of the wall that fenced in the way up which Christiana and her companions were to go, a garden, and that garden belonged to him whose was that barking dog of whom mention was made before. And some of the fruit-trees that grew in that garden shot their branches over the wall; and being mellow, they that found them did gather them up, and oft eat of them to their hurt. So Christiana's boys, as boys are apt to do, being pleased with the trees, and with the fruit that did hang thereon, did plash them, and began to eat. Their mother did also chide them for so doing, but still the boys went on.

Well, said she, my sons, you transgress, for that fruit is none of ours;—but she did not know that they did belong to the enemy; I'll warrant you if she had, she would have been ready to die for fear. But that passed, and they went on their way. Now, by that they were gone about two bows-shot from the place that led them into the way, they espied two very ill-favoured ones coming down apace to meet them. With that Christiana and Mercy her friend covered themselves with their veils, and so kept on their journey; the children also went on before; so that at last they met together. Then they that came down to meet them, came just up to the women as if they would embrace them; but Christiana said, Stand back, or go peaceably by as you should. Yet these two, as men that are deaf, regarded not Christiana's words, but began to lay hands upon them. At that Christiana, waxing very wroth, spurned at them with her feet. Mercy also,

The devil's garden.

The children eat of the enemy's fruit.

Two ill-favoured ones.

They assault Christiana.

as well as she could, did what she could to shift The pilgrims struggle with them. them. Christiana again said to them, Stand back, and be gone, for we have no money to lose, being pilgrims, as ye see, and such too as live upon the charity of our friends.

ILL-FAV. Then said one of the two of the men, We make no assault upon you for money, but are come out to tell you, that if you will but grant one small request which we shall ask, we will make women of you for ever.

CHRIS. Now Christiana, imagining what they should mean, made answer again, We will neither hear nor regard, nor yield to what you shall ask. We are in haste, cannot stay, our business is a business of life and death. So again she and her companions made a fresh assay to go past them, but they letted them in their way.

ILL-FAV. And they said, We intend no hurt to your lives, 'tis another thing we would have.

CHRIS. Ah, quoth Christiana, you would have us body and soul, for I know 'tis for that you are come; but we will die rather upon the spot than suffer ourselves to be brought into such snares as shall hazard our well-being hereafter. And with that they both shrieked out, and cried, Murder! She cries out. Deut. xxii. 23, 26, 27. murder! and so put themselves under those laws that are provided for the protection of women. But the men still made their approach upon them, with design to prevail against them. They therefore cried out again.

Now they being, as I said, not far from the gate 'Tis good to cry out when we are assaulted. in at which they came, their voice was heard from where they were, thither. Wherefore some of the house came out, and knowing that it was Christiana's tongue, they made haste to her relief. But by that they were got within sight of them the women were in a very great scuffle, the children also stood crying by. Then did he that came in for their relief call out to the ruffians, saying, What is that thing that you do? Would you make my Lord's people to transgress? He also attempted to take them, but they did make their escape over the wall into the garden of the man to whom the great dog belonged; so the dog became their protector. This Reliever then came up to the women, and asked them how they did. So they answered, We thank thy Prince, pretty well, only we have been somewhat affrighted; we thank thee also, for that thou camest in to our help, for otherwise we had been overcome.

REL. So after a few more words, this Reliever said as followeth: I marvelled much when you were entertained at the gate above, being ye knew that ye were but weak women, that you petitioned not the Lord there for a conductor; then might you have avoided these troubles and dangers, for he would have granted you one.

CHRIS. Alas! said Christiana, we were so taken with our present blessing, that dangers to come were forgotten by us; besides, who could have thought that so near the King's palace there should have lurked such naughty ones? Indeed it had been well for us had we asked our Lord for one; but since our Lord knew 'twould be for our profit, I wonder he sent not one along with us.

The Reliever comes.

The ill ones fly to the devil for relief.

The Reliever talks to the women.

Mark this.

REL. It is not always necessary to grant things We lose for want of asking for. not asked for, lest by so doing they become of little esteem; but when the want of a thing is felt, it then comes under, in the eyes of him that feels it, that estimate that properly is its due, and so consequently will be thereafter used. Had my Lord granted you a conductor, you would not neither so have bewailed that oversight of yours in not asking for one, as now you have occasion to do. So all things work for good, and tend to make you more wary.

CHRIS. Shall we go back again to my Lord, and confess our folly, and ask one?

REL. Your confession of your folly I will present him with. To go back again you need not; for in all places where you shall come, you will find no want at all; for in every of my Lord's lodgings which he has prepared for the reception of his pilgrims, there is sufficient to furnish them against all attempts whatsoever. But, as I said, he will be inquired of by them to do it for them: and 'tis a Ezek. xxxvi. 37. poor thing that is not worth asking for. When he had thus said, he went back to his place, and the pilgrims went on their way.

MERCY. Then said Mercy, What a sudden blank The mistake of Mercy. is here! I made account we had now been past all danger, and that we should never see sorrow more.

CHRIS. Thy innocency, my sister, said Christiana to Mercy, may excuse thee much; but as for me, Christiana's guilt. my fault is so much the greater, for that I saw this danger before I came out of the doors, and yet did not provide for it, where provision might have been had.   I am therefore much to be blamed.

MERCY.   Then said Mercy, How knew you this before you came from home?   Pray open to me this riddle.

CHRIS.   Why, I will tell you.   Before I set foot out of doors, one night, as I lay in my bed, I had a dream about this; for methought I saw two men, as like these as ever the world they could look, stand at my bed's feet, plotting how they might prevent my salvation.   I will tell you their very words.   They said ('twas when I was in my troubles), What shall we do with this woman? for she cries out, waking and sleeping, for forgiveness: if she be suffered to go on as she begins, we shall lose her as we have lost her husband.   This, you know, might a made me take heed, and have provided when provision might a been had.

Christiana's dream repeated.

MERCY.   Well, said Mercy, as by this neglect we have an occasion ministered unto us to behold our own imperfections, so our Lord has taken occasion thereby to make manifest the riches of his grace. For he, as we see, has followed us with unasked kindness, and has delivered us from their hands that were stronger than we, of his mere good pleasure.

Mercy makes good use of their neglect of duty.

Thus now, when they had talked away a little more time, they drew nigh to an house which stood in the way, which house was built for the relief of pilgrims; as you will find more fully related in the First Part of these records of the Pilgrim's Progress. So they drew on towards the house (the house of the Interpreter), and when they came to the door,

Part I. page 33.

they heard a great talk in the house. They then gave ear, and heard, as they thought, Christiana mentioned by name. For you must know that there went along, even before her, a talk of her and her children's going on pilgrimage. And this thing was the more pleasing to them, because they had heard that she was Christian's wife, that woman who was some time ago so unwilling to hear of going on pilgrimage. Thus, therefore, they stood still and heard the good people within commending her, who they little thought stood at the door. At last Christiana knocked as she had done at the gate before. Now when she had knocked, there came to the door a young damsel, and opened the door and looked, and behold two women were there.

Talk in the Interpreter's house about Christiana's going on pilgrimage.

She knocks at the door.

The door is opened to them by Innocent.

DAMSEL. Then said the damsel to them, With whom would you speak in this place?

CHRIS. Christiana answered, We understand that this is a privileged place for those that are become pilgrims, and we now at this door are such; wherefore we pray that we may be partakers of that for which we at this time are come; for the day, as thou seest, is very far spent, and we are loth to-night to go any farther.

DAMSEL. Pray what may I call your name, that I may tell it to my Lord within?

CHRIS. My name is Christiana; I was the wife of that pilgrim that some years ago did travel this way, and these be his four children. This maiden also is my companion, and is going on pilgrimage too.

INNOCENT. Then ran Innocent in (for that was

her name) and said to those within, Can you think who is at the door? There is Christiana and her children, and her companion, all waiting for enter-tainment here. Then they leaped for joy, and went and told their master. So he came to the door, and looking upon her, he said, Art thou that Christiana whom Christian, the good-man, left behind him when he betook himself to a pilgrim's life?

Joy in the house of the Interpreter that Christiana is turned pilgrim.

CHRIS. I am that woman that was so hard-hearted as to slight my husband's troubles, and that left him to go on in his journey alone, and these are his four children; but now I also am come, for I am convinced that no way is right but this.

INTER. Then is fulfilled that which also is written of the man that said to his son, Go, work to-day in my vineyard: and he said to his father, I will not; but afterwards repented and went.

Matt. xxi. 29.

CHRIS. Then said Christiana, So be it, Amen. God make it a true saying upon me, and grant that I may be found at the last of him in peace, without spot and blameless.

INTER. But why standest thou thus at the door? Come in, thou daughter of Abraham. We were talking of thee but now, for tidings have come to us before how thou art become a pilgrim. Come, children, come in; come, maiden, come in. So he had them all in to the house.

So when they were within, they were bidden sit down and rest them; the which when they had done, those that attended upon the pilgrims in the house, came into the room to see them. And one smiled, and another smiled, and they all smiled for

Old Saints glad to see the young ones walk in God's ways.

joy that Christiana was become a pilgrim. They also looked upon the boys; they stroked them over the faces with the hand, in token of their kind reception of them. They also carried it lovingly to Mercy, and bid them all welcome into their master's house.

After a while, because supper was not ready, the Interpreter took them into his significant rooms, and showed them what Christian, Christiana's husband, had seen some time before. Here therefore they saw the man in the cage, the man and his dream, the man that cut his way through his enemies, and the picture of the biggest of them all; together with the rest of those things that were then so profitable to Christian. The signifi-cant rooms. Part I. pages 34-44.

This done, and after these things had been somewhat digested by Christiana and her company, the Interpreter takes them apart again, and has them first into a room where was a man that could look no way but downwards, with a muck-rake in his hand. There stood also one over his head with a celestial crown in his hand, and proffered to give him that crown for his muck-rake; but the man did neither look up nor regard, but raked to himself the straws, the small sticks, and dust of the floor. The man with the muck-rake expounded.

Then said Christiana, I persuade myself that I know somewhat the meaning of this; for this is a figure of a man of this world, is it not, good sir?

INTER. Thou hast said the right, said he; and his muck-rake doth show his carnal mind. And whereas thou seest him rather give heed to rake up straws and sticks and the dust of the floor, than to what he says that calls to him from above with the celestial crown in his hand, it is to show that heaven is but as a fable to some, and that things here are counted the only things substantial.   Now whereas it was also showed thee, that the man could look no way but downwards, it is to let thee know that earthly things, when they are with power upon men's minds, quite carry their hearts away from God.

Christiana's prayer against the muck-rake.

CHRIS. Then said Christiana, O deliver me from this muck-rake!

Prov. xxx. 8.

INTER. That prayer, said the Interpreter, has lain by till 'tis almost rusty.   'Give me not riches,' is scarce the prayer of one of ten thousand.   Straws, and sticks, and dust, with most, are the great things now looked after.

With that Mercy and Christiana wept, and said, It is, alas! too true.

When the Interpreter had showed them this, he has them into the very best room in the house (a very brave room it was), so he bid them look round about and see if they could find anything profitable there.   Then they looked round and round, for there was nothing there to be seen but a very great spider on the wall, and that they overlooked.

MERCY. Then said Mercy, Sir, I see nothing; but Christiana held her peace.

INTER. But said the Interpreter, Look again. She therefore looked again and said, Here is not

Of the spider.

anything but an ugly spider, who hangs by her hands upon the wall.   Then said he, Is there but one spider in all this spacious room?   Then the water stood in Christiana's eyes, for she was a woman quick of apprehension; and she said, Yes, Lord, there is here more than one; yea, and spiders Talk about the spider. whose venom is far more destructive than that which is in her. The Interpreter then looked pleasantly upon her, and said, Thou hast said the truth. This made Mercy blush, and the boys to cover their faces, for they all began now to understand the riddle.

Then said the Interpreter again, 'The spider Prov. xxx. 28. taketh hold with her hands (as you see), and is in kings' palaces.' And wherefore is this recorded, but to show you that, how full of the venom of sin The interpretation. soever you be, yet you may by the hand of faith lay hold of, and dwell in the best room that belongs to the King's house above?

CHRIS. I thought, said Christiana, of something of this; but I could not imagine it all. I thought that we were like spiders, and that we looked like ugly creatures, in what fine room soever we were; but that by this spider, this venomous and ill-favoured creature, we were to learn how to act faith, came not into my mind. And yet she has taken hold with her hands, as I see, and dwells in the best room in the house. God has made nothing in vain.

Then they seemed all to be glad, but the water stood in their eyes; yet they looked one upon another, and also bowed before the Interpreter.

He had them then into another room where was Of the hen and chickens. a hen and chickens, and bid them observe a while. So one of the chickens went to the trough to drink, and every time she drank she lift up her head and her eyes towards heaven. See, said he, what this little chick doth, and learn of her to acknowledge whence your mercies come, by receiving them with looking up. Yet again, said he, observe and look; so they gave heed and perceived that the hen did Matt. xxiii. 37. walk in a four-fold method towards her chickens : 1. She had a common call, and that she hath all day long. 2. She had a special call, and that she had but sometimes. 3. She had a brooding note. And, 4. She had an outcry.

Now, said he, compare this hen to your King, and these chickens to his obedient ones. For answerable to her, himself has his methods which he walketh in towards his people. By his common call he gives nothing; by his special call he always has something to give; he has also a brooding voice, for them that are under his wing; and he has an outcry, to give the alarm when he sees the enemy come. I chose, my darlings, to lead you into the room where such things are, because you are women, and they are easy for you.

CHRIS. And, Sir, said Christiana, pray let us see some more. So he had them into the slaughter-house, where was a butcher a-killing of a sheep; and behold the sheep was quiet, and took her death patiently. Then said the Interpreter, You must learn of the sheep to suffer, and to put up wrongs without murmurings and complaints. Behold how quietly she takes her death, and, without objecting, she suffereth her skin to be pulled over her ears. Your King doth call you his sheep.

Of the butcher and the sheep.

Of the garden.

After this he led them into his garden, where was great variety of flowers, and he said, Do you see all these? So Christiana said, Yes. Then said he again, Behold, the flowers are diverse in stature, in quality, and colour, and smell, and virtue, and some are better than some; also where the gardener has set them, there they stand, and quarrel not one with another.

Again, he had them into his field, which he Of the field. had sowed with wheat and corn; but when they beheld, the tops of all were cut off, only the straw remained; he said again, This ground was dunged, and ploughed, and sowed; but what shall we do with the crop? Then said Christiana, Burn some, and make muck of the rest. Then said the Interpreter again, Fruit, you see, is that thing you look for, and for want of that you condemn it to the fire, and to be trodden under foot of men; beware that in this you condemn not yourselves.

Then, as they were coming in from abroad, they espied a little robin with a great spider in his mouth. Of the robin So the Interpreter said, Look here. So they looked, and the and Mercy wondered, but Christiana said, What a spider. disparagement is it to such a little pretty bird as the robin redbreast is, he being also a bird above many that loveth to maintain a kind of sociableness with man; I had thought they had lived upon crumbs of bread, or upon other such harmless matter. I like him worse than I did.

The Interpreter then replied, This robin is an emblem very apt to set forth some professors by; for to sight they are as this robin, pretty of note, colour, and carriage. They seem also to have a very great love for professors that are sincere; and above all other to desire to sociate with, and to be in their company, as if they could live upon the good man's crumbs. They pretend also that therefore it is that they frequent the house of the godly, and the appointments of the Lord; but when they are by themselves, as the robin, they can catch and gobble up spiders, they can change their diet, drink iniquity, and swallow down sin like water.

Pray, and you will get at that which yet lies un-revealed.

So when they were come again into the house, because supper as yet was not ready, Christiana again desired that the Interpreter would either show or tell of some other things that are profitable.

Then the Interpreter began and said: The fatter the sow is, the more she desires the mire; the fatter the ox is, the more gamesomely he goes to the slaughter; and the more healthy the lusty man is, the more prone he is unto evil.

There is a desire in women to go neat and fine, and it is a comely thing to be adorned with that that in God's sight is of great price.

'Tis easier watching a night or two, than to sit up a whole year together; so 'tis easier for one to begin to profess well, than to hold out as he should to the end.

Every shipmaster, when in a storm, will willingly cast that overboard that is of the smallest value in the vessel; but who will throw the best out first? None but he that feareth not God.

One leak will sink a ship, and one sin will destroy a sinner.

He that forgets his friend is ungrateful unto him, but he that forgets his Saviour is unmerciful to himself.

He that lives in sin, and looks for happiness here-after, is like him that soweth cockle, and thinks to fill his barn with wheat or barley.

If a man would live well, let him fetch his last day to him, and make it always his company-keeper.

Whispering, and change of thoughts, prove that sin is in the world.

If the world, which God sets light by, is counted a thing of that worth with men, what is heaven, that God commendeth?

If the life that is attended with so many troubles is so loth to be let go by us, what is the life above?

Everybody will cry up the goodness of men; but who is there that is, as he should, affected with the goodness of God?

We seldom sit down to meat but we eat and leave; so there is in Jesus Christ more merit and righteousness than the whole world has need of.

When the Interpreter had done, he takes them out into his garden again, and had them to a tree *Of the Tree* whose inside was all rotten and gone, and yet it grew *that is rotten at heart.* and had leaves. Then said Mercy, What means this? This tree, said he, whose outside is fair, and whose inside is rotten, it is to which many may be compared that are in the garden of God; who with their mouths speak high in behalf of God, but indeed will do nothing for him; whose leaves are fair, but their heart good for nothing but to be tinder for the devil's tinder-box.

Now supper was ready, the table spread, and all *They are at* things set on the board; so they sat down and did *supper.* eat when one had given thanks. And the Interpreter did usually entertain those that lodged with him with music at meals, so the minstrels played. There was also one that did sing, and a very fine voice he had. His song was this—

> The Lord is only my support,
>   And he that doth me feed;
> How can I then want anything
>   Whereof I stand in need?

Talk at supper.

When the song and music was ended, the Interpreter asked Christiana what it was that at first did move her to betake herself to a pilgrim's life.

A repetition of Christiana's experience.

Christiana answered: First, the loss of my husband came into my mind, at which I was heartily grieved; but all that was but natural affection. Then after that came the troubles and pilgrimage of my husband's into my mind, and also how like a churl I had carried it to him as to that. So guilt took hold of my mind, and would have drawn me into the pond, but that opportunely I had a dream of the well-being of my husband, and a letter sent me by the King of that country where my husband dwells, to come to him. The dream and the letter together so wrought upon my mind, that they forced me to this way.

INTER. But met you with no opposition afore you set out of doors?

CHRIS. Yes, a neighbour of mine, one Mrs. Timorous (she was akin to him that would have persuaded my husband to go back for fear of the lions). She all-to-be-fooled me for, as she called it, my intended desperate adventure; she also urged what she could to dishearten me to it, the hardship and troubles that my husband met with in the way: but all this I got over pretty well.   But a dream that I had, of two ill-looked ones, that I thought did plot how to make me miscarry in my journey, that hath troubled me much; yea, it still runs in my mind, and makes me afraid of every one that I meet, lest they should meet me to do me a mischief, and to turn me out of the way.   Yea, I may tell my Lord, though I would not have everybody know it, that between this and the gate by which we got into the way, we were both so sorely assaulted that we were made to cry out murder, and the two that made this assault upon us were like the two that I saw in my dream.

Then said the Interpreter, Thy beginning is good, thy latter end shall greatly increase.   So he addressed himself to Mercy, and said unto her, And what moved thee to come hither, sweetheart? *A question put to Mercy.*

Then Mercy blushed and trembled, and for a while continued silent.

INTER. Then said he, Be not afraid, only believe, and speak thy mind.

MERCY. So she began and said: Truly, Sir, my want of experience is that that makes me covet to be in silence, and that also that fills me with fears of coming short at last.   I cannot tell of visions and dreams as my friend Christiana can, nor know I what it is to mourn for my refusing of the counsel of those that were good relations. *Mercy's answer.*

INTER. What was it, then, dear heart, that hath prevailed with thee to do as thou hast done?

MERCY. Why, when our friend here was packing up to be gone from our town, I and another went accidentally to see her. So we knocked at the door and went in. When we were within, and seeing what she was doing, we asked what was her meaning. She said she was sent for to go to her husband; and then she up and told us how she had seen him in a dream, dwelling in a curious place, among immortals, wearing a crown, playing upon a harp, eating and drinking at his Prince's table, and singing praises to him for bringing him thither, etc. Now methought, while she was telling these things unto us, my heart burned within me; and I said in my heart, If this be true, I will leave my father and my mother, and the land of my nativity, and will, if I may, go along with Christiana.

So I asked her further of the truth of these things, and if she would let me go with her; for I saw now that there was no dwelling, but with the danger of ruin, any longer in our town. But yet I came away with a heavy heart, not for that I was unwilling to come away, but for that so many of my relations were left behind. And I am come, with all the desire of my heart, and will go, if I may, with Christiana unto her husband, and his King.

INTER. Thy setting out is good, for thou hast given credit to the truth. Thou art a Ruth, who did, for the love that she bore to Naomi, and to the Lord her God, leave father and mother, and the land of her nativity, to come out, and go with a people that she knew not heretofore. 'The Lord recompense thy work, and a full reward be given thee of the Lord God of Israel, under whose wing thou art come to trust.'

Ruth ii. 11, 12.

Now supper was ended, and preparations were made They address themselves for bed. for bed: the women were laid singly alone, and the boys by themselves. Now when Mercy was in bed, she could not sleep for joy, for that now her doubts Mercy's good night's rest. of missing at last were removed further from her than ever they were before. So she lay blessing and praising God, who had had such favour for her.

In the morning they rose with the sun, and prepared themselves for their departure; but the Interpreter would have them tarry a while, For, said he, you must orderly go from hence. Then said he to the damsel that at first opened unto them: Take them and have them into the garden to the bath, and there wash them, and make them clean from the soil which they have gathered by travelling. Then Innocent, the damsel, took them, and had them into the garden, and brought them to the bath; so she told them that there they must wash The bath Sanctification. and be clean, for so her master would have the women to do that called at his house as they were going on pilgrimage. They then went in and They wash in it. washed, yea, they and the boys and all; and they came out of that bath not only sweet and clean, but also much enlivened and strengthened in their joints. So when they came in they looked fairer a deal than when they went out to the washing.

When they were returned out of the garden from the bath, the Interpreter took them, and looked upon them, and said unto them, 'Fair as the moon.' Then he called for the seal, wherewith they used to be sealed that were washed in his bath. So the seal They are sealed. was brought, and he set his mark upon them, that they might be known in the places whither they were yet to go. Now the seal was the contents and sum of the passover which the children of Israel did

Exod. xiii. 8-10. eat when they came out from the land of Egypt; and the mark was set between their eyes. This seal greatly added to their beauty, for it was an ornament to their faces. It also added to their gravity, and made their countenances more like them of angels.

Then said the Interpreter again to the damsel that waited upon these women, Go into the vestry and fetch out garments for these people. So she

They are clothed. went and fetched out white raiment, and laid it down before him; so he commanded them to put it on. It was 'fine linen, white and clean.' When the women were thus adorned, they seemed to be a terror one to the other; for that they could not see that glory each one on herself, which they could see

True humility. in each other. Now therefore they began to esteem each other better than themselves. For, you are fairer than I am, said one; and, You are more comely than I am, said another. The children also stood amazed to see into what fashion they were brought.

The Interpreter then called for a man-servant of his, one Great-heart, and bid him take sword, and helmet, and shield; and take these my daughters, said he, and conduct them to the house called Beautiful, at which place they will rest next. So he took his weapons and went before them, and the Interpreter said, God speed. Those also that belonged to the family sent them away with many a good wish. So they went on their way, and sung—

This place has been our second stage;
  Here we have heard and seen
Those good things that, from age to age,
  To others hid have been.

The dunghill-raker, spider, hen,
  The chicken too to me
Hath taught a lesson; let me then
  Conformed to it be.

The butcher, garden, and the field,
  The robin and his bait,
Also the rotten-tree doth yield
  Me argument of weight

To move me for to watch and pray,
  To strive to be sincere,
To take my cross up day by day,
  And serve the Lord with fear.

Now I saw in my dream, that they went on, and Great-heart went before them. So they went and came to the place where Christian's burden fell off Part i. page 45. his back, and tumbled into a sepulchre. Here then they made a pause, and here also they blessed God. Now, said Christiana, it comes to my mind what was said to us at the gate, to wit, that we should have pardon, by word and deed; by word, that is, by the promise; by deed, to wit, in the way it was obtained. What the promise is, of that I know something; but what is it to have pardon by deed, or in the way that it was obtained, Mr. Great-heart, I suppose you know; wherefore, if you please, let us hear you discourse thereof.

GREAT-HEART. Pardon by the deed done, is pardon obtained by some one, for another that

A comment
upon what
was said at
the gate, or
a discourse
of our being
justified by
Christ.

hath need thereof: not by the person pardoned, but in the way, saith another, in which I have obtained it. So then, to speak to the question more large, the pardon that you and Mercy and these boys have attained, was obtained by another, to wit, by him that let you in at the gate: And he hath obtained it in this double way: He has performed righteousness to cover you, and spilt blood to wash you in.

CHRIS. But if he parts with his righteousness to us, what will he have for himself?

GREAT-HEART. He has more righteousness than you have need of, or than he needeth himself.

CHRIS. Pray make that appear.

GREAT-HEART. With all my heart; but first I must premise, that he of whom we are now about to speak is one that has not his fellow. He has two natures in one person, plain to be distinguished, impossible to be divided. Unto each of these natures a righteousness belongeth, and each righteousness is essential to that nature; so that one may as easily cause the nature to be extinct, as to separate its justice or righteousness from it. Of these righteousnesses, therefore, we are not made partakers so as that they, or any of them, should be put upon us that we might be made just, and live thereby. Besides these, there is a righteousness which this person hath, as these two natures are joined in one. And this is not the righteousness of the Godhead, as distinguished from the manhood; nor the righteousness of the manhood, as distinguished from the Godhead; but a righteousness which standeth in the union of both natures, and may properly be called, the righteousness that is essential to his being prepared of God to the capacity of the mediatory office which he was to be intrusted with. If he parts with his first righteousness, he parts with his Godhead; if he parts with his second righteousness, he parts with the purity of his manhood; if he parts with his third, he parts with that perfection that capacitates him to the office of mediation. He has therefore another righteousness, which standeth in performance, or obedience to a revealed will; and that is it that he puts upon sinners, and that by which their sins are covered. Wherefore he saith, 'As by one man's Rom. v. 19. disobedience many were made sinners, so by the obedience of one shall many be made righteous.'

CHRIS. But are the other righteousnesses of no use to us?

GREAT-HEART. Yes; for though they are essential to his natures and office and so cannot be communicated unto another, yet it is by virtue of them that the righteousness that justifies is for that purpose efficacious. The righteousness of his Godhead gives virtue to his obedience; the righteousness of his manhood giveth capability to his obedience to justify; and the righteousness that standeth in the union of these two natures to his office, giveth authority to that righteousness to do the work for which it is ordained.

So then, here is a righteousness that Christ, as God, has no need of, for he is God without it. Here is a righteousness that Christ, as man, has

no need of to make him so, for he is perfect man
without it.   Again, here is a righteousness that
Christ, as God-man, has no need of, for he is perfectly so without it.   Here then is a righteousness
that Christ, as God, as man, as God-man, has no
need of, with reference to himself, and therefore he
can spare it; a justifying righteousness, that he for
himself wanteth not, and therefore he giveth it
away; hence 'tis called the 'gift of righteousness.'
This righteousness, since Christ Jesus the Lord has
made himself under the law, *must* be given away;
for the law doth not only bind him that is under it
to do justly, but to use charity.   Wherefore he
must, he ought by the law, if he hath two coats,
to give one to him that hath none.   Now our Lord
indeed hath two coats, one for himself, and one to
spare; wherefore he freely bestows one upon those
that have none.   And thus, Christiana, and Mercy,
and the rest of you that are here, doth your pardon
come by deed, or by the work of another man.
Your Lord Christ is he that has worked, and given
away what he wrought for, to the next poor beggar
he meets.

But again, in order to pardon by deed, there must
something be paid to God as a price, as well as
something prepared to cover us withal.   Sin has
delivered us up to the just curse of a righteous law;
now from this curse we must be justified by way of
redemption, a price being paid for the harms we
have done; and this is by the blood of your Lord,
who came and stood in your place and stead, and
died your death for your transgressions.   Thus has

Margin notes: Rom. v. 17. · Rom. iv. 25. · Gal. iii. 13.

he ransomed you from your transgressions by blood, and covered your polluted and deformed souls with righteousness; for the sake of which, God passeth by you, and will not hurt you, when he comes to judge the world.

CHRIS. This is brave. Now I see that there was something to be learned by our being pardoned by *word* and *deed*. Good Mercy, let us labour to keep this in mind; and, my children, do you remember it also. But, Sir, was not this it that made my good Christian's burden fall from off his shoulder, and that made him give three leaps for joy? Christiana affected with this way of redemption.

GREAT-HEART. Yes, 'twas the belief of this that cut those strings that could not be cut by other means, and 'twas to give him a proof of the virtue of this, that he was suffered to carry his burden to the cross. How the strings that bound Christian's burden to him were cut.

CHRIS. I thought so; for though my heart was lightful and joyous before, yet it is ten times more lightsome and joyous now. And I am persuaded by what I have felt, though I have felt but little as yet, that if the most burdened man in the world was here, and did see and believe, as I now do, 'twould make his heart the more merry and blithe.

GREAT-HEART. There is not only comfort, and the ease of a burden brought to us, by the sight and consideration of these, but an endeared affection begot in us by it; for who can, if he doth but once think that pardon comes, not only by promise, but thus, but be affected with the way and means of his redemption, and so with the man that hath wrought it for him? How affection to Christ is begot in the soul.

CHRIS. True; methinks it makes my heart bleed

Part I.
page 45.

to think that he should bleed for me. Oh! thou
loving One! Oh! thou blessed One! thou deservest to have me, thou hast bought me: thou

Cause of
admiration.

deservest to have me all; thou hast paid for me ten
thousand times more than I am worth. No marvel
that this made the water stand in my husband's
eyes, and that it made him trudge so nimbly on.
I am persuaded he wished me with him; but, vile
wretch that I was! I let him come all alone. O
Mercy, that thy father and mother were here! yea,
and Mrs. Timorous also! nay, I wish now with all
my heart, that here was Madam Wanton too.
Surely, surely, their hearts would be affected; nor
could the fear of the one, nor the powerful lusts of
the other, prevail with them to go home again, and
to refuse to become good pilgrims.

GREAT-HEART. You speak now in the warmth of
your affections. Will it, think you, be always thus
with you? Besides, this is not communicated to
every one, nor to every one that did see your Jesus
bleed. There was that stood by, and that saw the
blood run from his heart to the ground, and yet

To be affected
with Christ,
and with
what he has
done, is a
thing
special.

were so far off this, that instead of lamenting, they
laughed at him; and instead of becoming his disciples, did harden their hearts against him. So that
all that you have, my daughters, you have by a
peculiar impression made by a divine contemplating
upon what I have spoken to you. Remember that
'twas told you, that the hen by her common call
gives no meat to her chickens. This you have,
therefore, by a special grace.

Now I saw still in my dream, that they went on until they were come to the place that Simple, and Sloth, and Presumption lay and slept in, when Christian went by on pilgrimage. And behold, they were hanged up in irons, a little way off on the other side. Simple, and Sloth, and Presumption hanged; and why.

MERCY. Then said Mercy to him that was their guide and conductor, What are those three men? and for what are they hanged there?

GREAT-HEART. These three men were men of very bad qualities, they had no mind to be pilgrims themselves, and whosoever they could they hindered. They were for sloth and folly themselves, and whoever they could persuade with, they made so too, and withal taught them to presume that they should do well at last. They were asleep when Christian went by, and now you go by they are hanged.[1]

MERCY. But could they persuade any to be of their opinion?

GREAT-HEART. Yes; they turned several out of the way. There was Slow-pace that they persuaded to do as they. They also prevailed with one Short-wind, with one No-heart, with one Linger-after-lust, and with one Sleepy-head, and with a young woman, her name was Dull, to turn out of the way and become as they. Besides, they brought up an ill report of your Lord, persuading others that he was Their crimes. Who they prevailed upon to turn out of the way.

---

[1] Behold here how the slothful are a sign,
   Hung up, 'cause holy ways they did decline.
   See here, too, how the child did play the man,
   And weak grow strong, when Great-heart leads the van.

a taskmaster. They also brought up an evil report of the good land, saying 'twas not half as good as some pretend it was. They also began to vilify his servants, and to count the very best of them meddlesome, troublesome busy-bodies. Further, they would call the bread of God husks; the comforts of his children, fancies; the travel and labour of pilgrims, things to no purpose.

CHRIS. Nay, said Christiana, if they were such, they shall never be bewailed by me. They have but what they deserve, and I think it is well that they hang so near the highway that others may see and take warning. But had it not been well if their crimes had been engraven in some plate of iron or brass, and left here, even where they did their mischiefs, for a caution to other bad men?

GREAT-HEART. So it is, as you well may perceive if you will go a little to the wall.

MERCY. No, no, let them hang, and their names rot, and their crimes live for ever against them. I think it a high favour that they were hanged afore we came hither; who knows else what they might have done to such poor women as we are? Then she turned it into a song, saying—

> Now then you three, hang there, and be a sign
> To all that shall against the truth combine.
> And let him that comes after, fear this end,
> If unto pilgrims he is not a friend.
> And thou, my soul, of all such men beware,
> That unto holiness opposers are.

Part I.
page 49. Thus they went on till they came at the foot of the Hill Difficulty, where, again, their good friend,

Mr. Great-heart, took an occasion to tell them of what happened there when Christian himself went by. So he had them first to the spring. Lo, saith he, this is the spring that Christian drank of before he went up this hill, and then 'twas clear and good, but now 'tis dirty with the feet of some that are not desirous that pilgrims here should quench their thirst. Thereat Mercy said, And why so envious, trow? But said their guide, It will do, if taken up and put into a vessel that is sweet and good; for then the dirt will sink to the bottom, and the water come out by itself more clear. Thus therefore Christiana and her companions were compelled to do. They took it up, and put it into an earthen pot, and so let it stand till the dirt was gone to the bottom, and then they drank thereof.

'Tis difficult getting of good doctrine in erroneous times. Ezek. xxxiv. 18.

Next he showed them the two by-ways that were at the foot of the hill, where Formality and Hypocrisy lost themselves. And, said he, these are dangerous paths. Two were here cast away when Christian came by; and although, as you see, these ways are since stopped up with chains, posts, and a ditch, yet there are that will choose to adventure here, rather than take the pains to go up this hill.

By-paths, tho' barred up, will not keep all from going in them. Part i. page 50.

CHRIS. 'The way of transgressors is hard.' 'Tis a wonder that they can get into those ways, without danger of breaking their necks.

Prov. xiii. 15.

GREAT-HEART. They will venture; yea, if at any time any of the King's servants doth happen to see them, and doth call unto them, and tell them that they are in the wrong ways, and do bid them beware

Jer xliv. 16, 17.
the danger, then they will railingly return them answer and say, 'As for the word that thou hast spoken unto us in the name of the King, we will not hearken unto thee; but we will certainly do whatsoever thing goeth out of our own mouths,' etc. Nay, if you look a little farther, you shall see that these ways are made cautionary enough, not only by these posts, and ditch, and chain, but also by being hedged up; yet they will choose to go there.

The reason why some do choose to go in by-ways. Prov. xv. 19.
CHRIS. They are idle, they love not to take pains, up-hill way is unpleasant to them. So it is fulfilled unto them as it is written, 'The way of the slothful man is as a hedge of thorns.' Yea, they will rather choose to walk upon a snare than to go up this hill, and the rest of this way to the city.

Then they set forward, and began to go up the hill, and up the hill they went; but before they got to the top, Christiana began to pant, and said, I The hill puts the pilgrims to it. dare say this is a breathing hill. No marvel if they that love their ease more than their souls, choose to themselves a smoother way. Then said Mercy, I must sit down; also the least of the children began to cry. Come, come, said Great-heart, sit not down here, for a little above is the Prince's arbour. Then took he the little boy by the hand, and led him up thereto.

They sit in the arbour. Part I. page 51.
Matt. xi. 28.
When they were come to the arbour, they were very willing to sit down, for they were all in a pelting heat. Then said Mercy, How sweet is rest to them that labour! And how good is the Prince of pilgrims, to provide such resting-places for them!

Of this arbour I have heard much, but I never saw it before. But here let us beware of sleeping; for, as I have heard, for that it cost poor Christian dear.

Then said Mr. Great-heart to the little ones, Come, my pretty boys, how do you do? What think you now of going on pilgrimage? Sir, said the least, I was almost beat out of heart, but I thank you for lending me a hand at my need. And I remember now what my mother has told me, namely, That the way to heaven is as up a ladder, and the way to hell is as down a hill. But I had rather go up the ladder to life, than down the hill to death. *The little boy's answer to the guide, and also to Mercy.*

Then said Mercy, But the proverb is, To go down the hill is easy. But James said (for that was his name), The day is coming, when, in my opinion, going down hill will be the hardest of all. 'Tis a good boy, said his master; thou hast given her a right answer. Then Mercy smiled, but the little boy did blush. *Which is hardest, up hill or down hill.*

CHRIS. Come, said Christiana, will you eat a bit, a little to sweeten your mouths, while you sit here to rest your legs? For I have here a piece of pomegranate, which Mr. Interpreter put in my hand, just when I came out of his doors. He gave me also a piece of an honeycomb, and a little bottle of spirits. I thought he gave you something, said Mercy, because he called you a to-side. Yes, so he did, said the other; but Mercy, it shall still be as I said it should, when at first we came from home: Thou shalt be a sharer in all the good that I have, *They refresh themselves.*

because thou so willingly didst become my companion. Then she gave to them, and they did eat, both Mercy and the boys. And said Christiana to Mr. Great-heart, Sir, will you do as we? But he answered, You are going on pilgrimage, and presently I shall return; much good may what you have do to you: at home I eat the same every day. Now when they had eaten and drank, and had chatted a little longer, their guide said to them, The day wears away; if you think good, let us prepare to be going. So they got up to go, and the little boys went before. But Christiana forgot to take her bottle of spirits with her, so she sent her little boy back to fetch it. Then said Mercy, I think this is a losing place. Here Christian lost his roll, and here Christiana left her bottle behind her: Sir, what is the cause of this? So their guide made answer and said, The cause is sleep or forgetfulness: some sleep, when they should keep awake; and some forget, when they should remember; and this is the very cause why often at the restingplaces some pilgrims in some things come off losers. Pilgrims should watch, and remember what they have already received under their greatest enjoyments; but for want of doing so, ofttimes their rejoicing ends in tears, and their sunshine in a cloud: Witness the story of Christian at this place.

When they were come to the place where Mistrust and Timorous met Christian to persuade him to go back for fear of the lions, they perceived as it were a stage, and before it, towards the road, a broad plate, with a copy of verses written thereon,

Christiana forgets her bottle of spirits.

Mark this.

Part 1. pages 51-54.

and underneath, the reason of raising up of that stage in that place, rendered. The verses were these—

> Let him that sees this stage take heed
> Unto his heart and tongue;
> Lest if he do not, here he speed
> As some have long agone.

The words underneath the verses were, This stage was built to punish such upon, who, through timorousness or mistrust, shall be afraid to go farther on pilgrimage. Also, on this stage both Mistrust and Timorous were burned through the tongue with an hot iron, for endeavouring to hinder Christian in his journey.

Then said Mercy, This is much like to the saying of the Beloved, 'What shall be given unto thee? or what shall be done unto thee, thou false tongue? Sharp arrows of the mighty, with coals of juniper.' Ps. cxx. 3, 4.

So they went on, till they came within sight of the lions. Now Mr. Great-heart was a strong man, so he was not afraid of a lion; but yet, when they were come up to the place where the lions were, the boys that went before were glad to cringe behind, for they were afraid of the lions; so they stepped back, and went behind. At this their guide smiled, and said, How now, my boys, do you love to go before, when no danger doth approach, and love to come behind so soon as the lions appear? Part I. pages 54, 55. *An emblem of those that go on bravely when there is no danger, but shrink when troubles come.*

Now as they went up, Mr. Great-heart drew his sword, with intent to make a way for the pilgrims in spite of the lions. Then there appeared one that, it seems, had taken upon him to back the lions; and *Of Grim the giant, and of his backing the lions.*

he said to the pilgrims' guide, What is the cause of your coming hither? Now the name of that man was Grim, or Bloody-man, because of his slaying of pilgrims, and he was of the race of the giants.

GREAT-HEART. Then said the pilgrims' guide, These women and children are going on pilgrimage, and this is the way they must go, and go it they shall in spite of thee and the lions.

GRIM. This is not their way, neither shall they go therein. I am come forth to withstand them, and to that end will back the lions.

Now to say truth, by reason of the fierceness of the lions, and of the *grim* carriage of him that did back them, this way had of late lain much unoccupied, and was almost all grown over with grass.

CHRIS. Then said Christiana, Though the highways have been unoccupied heretofore, and though the travellers have been made in time past to walk through by-paths, it must not be so now I am risen. Now ' I am risen a mother in Israel.'

Judges v. 6, 7.

GRIM. Then he swore by the lions, but it should; and therefore bid them turn aside, for they should not have passage there.

GREAT-HEART. But their guide made first his approach unto Grim, and laid so heavily at him with his sword, that he forced him to a retreat.

GRIM. Then said he (that attempted to back the lions), Will you slay me upon mine own ground?

A fight betwixt Grim and Great-heart.

GREAT-HEART. 'Tis the King's highway that we are in, and in his way it is that thou hast placed thy lions; but these women, and these children, though weak, shall hold on their way in spite of thy lions.

And with that he gave him again a downright blow, and brought him upon his knees. With this blow he also broke his helmet, and with the next he cut off an arm. Then did the giant roar so hideously, *The victory.* that his voice frighted the women; and yet they were glad to see him lie sprawling upon the ground. Now the lions were chained, and so of themselves could do nothing. Wherefore, when old Grim, that intended to back them, was dead, Mr. Great-heart said to the pilgrims, Come now and follow me, and no hurt shall happen to you from the lions. They therefore went on, but the women trembled as they passed by them; the boys also looked as if they *They pass by* would die, but they all got by without further *the lions.* hurt.

Now then they were within sight of the porter's *They come to* lodge, and they soon came up unto it; but they *the porter's* made the more haste after this to go thither, because *lodge.* 'tis dangerous travelling there in the night. So when they were come to the gate, the guide knocked, and the porter cried, Who is there? But as soon as the guide had said, It is I, he knew his voice, and came down (for the guide had oft before that come thither as a conductor of pilgrims). When he was come down, he opened the gate, and seeing the guide standing just before it (for he saw not the women, for they were behind him) he said unto him, How now, Mr. Great-heart? what is your business here so late to-night? I have brought, said he, some pilgrims hither, where, by my Lord's commandment, they must lodge. I had been here some time ago, had I not been opposed by the giant that did use to

back the lions ; but I, after a long and tedious combat with him, have cut him off, and have brought
the pilgrims hither in safety.

PORTER. Will you not go in, and stay till
morning ?

Great-heart
attempts to
go back.
The pilgrims
implore his
company
still.

GREAT-HEART. No; I will return to my Lord
to-night.

CHRIS. Oh, Sir, I know not how to be willing
you should leave us in our pilgrimage ; you have
been so faithful and so loving to us, you have fought
so stoutly for us, you have been so hearty in counselling of us, that I shall never forget your favour
towards us.

MERCY. Then said Mercy, O that we might have
thy company to our journey's end ! How can such
poor women as we, hold out in a way so full of
troubles as this way is, without a friend and
defender ?

JAMES. Then said James, the youngest of the
boys, Pray, Sir, be persuaded to go with us, and
help us, because we are so weak, and the way so
dangerous as it is.

GREAT-HEART. I am at my Lord's commandment.
If he shall allot me to be your guide quite through,

Help lost
for want of
asking for.

I will willingly wait upon you.   But here you failed
at first ; for when he bid me come thus far with you,
then you should have begged me of him to have
gone quite through with you, and he would have
granted your request.   However, at present I must
withdraw ; and so, good Christiana, Mercy, and my
brave children, Adieu.

Part I.
page 55.

Then the Porter, Mr. Watchful, asked Christiana

of her country, and of her kindred. And she said, I came from the City of Destruction, I am a widow woman, and my husband is dead, his name was Christian the pilgrim. How, said the porter; was he your husband? Yes, said she, and these are his children; and this, pointing to Mercy, is one of my townswomen. Then the porter rang his bell, as at such times he is wont, and there came to the door one of the damsels, whose name was Humble-mind. And to her the porter said, Go, tell it within, that Christiana, the wife of Christian, and her children, are come hither on pilgrimage. She went in, therefore, and told it. But oh! what a noise for gladness was there within, when the damsel did but drop that word out of her mouth.

Christiana makes herself known to the porter, he tells it to a damsel.

Joy at the noise of the pilgrims' coming.

So they came with haste to the porter, for Christiana stood still at the door. Then some of the most grave said unto her, Come in, Christiana; come in, thou wife of that good man; come in, thou blessed woman; come in, with all that are with thee. So she went in, and they followed her that were her children and her companions. Now when they were gone in, they were had into a very large room, where they were bidden to sit down; so they sat down, and the chief of the house was called to see, and welcome the guests. Then they came in, and understanding who they were, did salute each other with a kiss, and said, Welcome, ye vessels of the grace of God; welcome to us your friends.

Christians' love is kindled at the sight of one another.

Now because it was somewhat late, and because the pilgrims were weary with their journey, and also made faint with the sight of the fight, and of the terrible lions, therefore they desired, as soon as might be, to prepare to go to rest. Nay, said those of the family, refresh yourselves first with a morsel of meat. For they had prepared for them a lamb, with the accustomed sauce belonging thereto; for the porter had heard before of their coming, and had told it to them within. So when they had supped, and ended their prayer with a psalm, they desired they might go to rest. But let us, said Christiana, if we may be so bold as to choose, be in that chamber that was my husband's when he was here. So they had them up thither, and they lay all in a room. When they were at rest, Christiana and Mercy entered into discourse about things that were convenient.

CHRIS. Little did I think once, that when my husband went on pilgrimage, I should ever have followed.

MERCY. And you as little thought of lying in his bed, and in his chamber to rest, as you do now.

CHRIS. And much less did I ever think of seeing his face with comfort, and of worshipping the Lord the King with him, and yet now I believe I shall.

MERCY. Hark! don't you hear a noise?

CHRIS. Yes; 'tis, as I believe, a noise of music, for joy that we are here.

MERCY. Wonderful! Music in the house, music in the heart, and music also in heaven, for joy that we are here.

Thus they talked a while, and then betook themselves to sleep. So in the morning, when they were awake, Christiana said to Mercy:

Exod. xii. 38.

John i. 29.

Part i. page 64. Christ's bosom is for all pilgrims.

Music.

CHRIS. What was the matter, that you did laugh in your sleep to-night? I suppose you were in a dream. Mercy did laugh in her sleep.

MERCY. So I was, and a sweet dream it was; but are you sure I laughed?

CHRIS. Yes; you laughed heartily: but prithee, Mercy, tell me thy dream.

MERCY. I was a-dreaming that I sat all alone in a solitary place, and was bemoaning of the hardness of my heart. Mercy's dream.

Now I had not sat there long, but methought many were gathered about me, to see me, and to hear what it was that I said. So they hearkened, and I went on bemoaning the hardness of my heart. At this, some of them laughed at me, some called me fool, and some began to thrust me about. With that, methought I looked up, and saw one coming with wings towards me. So he came directly to me, and said, Mercy, what aileth thee? Now when he had heard me make my complaint, he said, 'Peace be to thee.' He also wiped mine eyes with his handkerchief, and clad me in silver and gold. He put a chain about my neck, and ear-rings in mine ears, and a beautiful crown upon my head. Then he took me by the hand, and said, Mercy, come after me. So he went up, and I followed, till we came at a golden gate. Then he knocked; and when they within had opened, the man went in and I followed him up to a throne, upon which one sat, and he said to me, Welcome, daughter. The place looked bright, and twinkling like the stars, or rather like the sun, and I thought that I saw your husband What her dream was. Ezek. xvi. 8-11.

there. So I awoke from my dream. But did I laugh?

CHRIS. Laugh! ay, and well you might, to see yourself so well. For you must give me leave to tell you, that I believe it was a good dream; and that, as you have begun to find the first part true, so you shall find the second at last. 'God speaks once, yea twice, yet man perceiveth it not. In a dream, in a vision of the night, when deep sleep falleth upon men, in slumbering upon the bed.' We need not, when a-bed, lie awake to talk with God; he can visit us while we sleep, and cause us then to hear his voice. Our heart ofttimes wakes when we sleep; and God can speak to that, either by words, by proverbs, by signs and similitudes, as well as if one was awake.

Job xxxiii. 14, 15.

Mercy glad of her dream.

MERCY. Well, I am glad of my dream, for I hope ere long to see it fulfilled, to the making of me laugh again.

CHRIS. I think it is now high time to rise, and to know what we must do.

MERCY. Pray, if they invite us to stay a while, let us willingly accept of the proffer. I am the willinger to stay a while here, to grow better acquainted with these maids; methinks Prudence, Piety, and Charity have very comely and sober countenances.

CHRIS. We shall see what they will do. So when they were up and ready, they came down; and they asked one another of their rest, and if it was comfortable or not.

MERCY. Very good, said Mercy; it was one

of the best night's lodging that ever I had in my life.

Then said Prudence and Piety, If you will be persuaded to stay here a while, you shall have what the house will afford.

CHAR. Ay, and that with a very good will, said Charity. So they consented, and stayed there about a month or above, and became very profitable one to another. And because Prudence would see how Christiana had brought up her children, she asked leave of her to catechise them. So she gave her free consent. Then she began at the youngest, whose name was James.

PRUD. And she said, Come, James, canst thou tell who made thee?

JAMES. God the Father, God the Son, and God the Holy Ghost.

PRUD. Good boy. And canst thou tell who saves thee?

JAMES. God the Father, God the Son, and God the Holy Ghost.

PRUD. Good boy still. But how doth God the Father save thee?

JAMES. By his grace.

PRUD. How doth God the Son save thee?

JAMES. By his righteousness, death, and blood, and life.

PRUD. And how doth God the Holy Ghost save thee?

JAMES. By his illumination, by his renovation, and by his preservation.

Then said Prudence to Christiana, You are to

They stay here some time.

Prudence desires to catechise Christiana's children.

James catechised.

be commended for thus bringing your children.   I suppose I need not ask the rest these questions, since the youngest of them can answer them so well.   I will therefore now apply myself to the youngest next.

PRUD. Then she said, Come, Joseph (for his name was Joseph), will you let me catechise you ?

JOSEPH. With all my heart.

PRUD. What is man ?

JOSEPH. A reasonable creature, so made by God, as my brother said.

PRUD. What is supposed by this word 'saved'?

JOSEPH. That man by sin has brought himself into a state of captivity and misery.

PRUD. What is supposed by his being saved by the Trinity ?

JOSEPH. That sin is so great and mighty a tyrant, that none can pull us out of its clutches but God ; and that God is so good and loving to man, as to pull him indeed out of this miserable state.

PRUD. What is God's design in saving of poor men ?

JOSEPH. The glorifying of his name, of his grace and justice, etc., and the everlasting happiness of his creature.

PRUD. Who are they that must be saved ?

JOSEPH. Those that accept of his salvation.

Good boy, Joseph ; thy mother has taught thee well, and thou hast hearkened to what she has said unto thee.

Then said Prudence to Samuel, who was the eldest but one :

PRUD. Come, Samuel, are you willing that I Samuel catechised. should catechise you also?

SAMUEL. Yes, forsooth, if you please.

PRUD. What is heaven?

SAM. A place and state most blessed, because God dwelleth there.

PRUD. What is hell?

SAM. A place and state most woeful, because it is the dwelling-place of sin, the devil, and death.

PRUD. Why wouldest thou go to heaven?

SAM. That I may see God, and serve him without weariness; that I may see Christ, and love him everlastingly; that I may have that fullness of the Holy Spirit in me, that I can by no means here enjoy.

PRUD. A very good boy also, and one that has learned well.

Then she addressed herself to the eldest, whose Matthew catechised. name was Matthew; and she said to him, Come, Matthew, shall I also catechise you?

MATT. With a very good will.

PRUD. I ask then, if there was ever anything that had a being antecedent to, or before God?

MATT. No, for God is eternal; nor is there anything excepting himself that had a being until the beginning of the first day: 'For in six days the Lord made heaven and earth, the sea, and all that in them is.'

PRUD. What do you think of the Bible?

MATT. It is the holy Word of God.

PRUD. Is there nothing written therein but what you understand?

MATT. Yes; a great deal.

PRUD. What do you do when you meet with such places therein that you do not understand?

MATT. I'think God is wiser than I. I pray also that he will please to let me know all therein that he knows will be for my good.

PRUD. How believe you as touching the resurrection of the dead?

MATT. I believe they shall rise, the same that was buried, the same in nature, though not in corruption. And I believe this upon a double account: First, because God has promised it; Secondly, because he is able to perform it.

Prudence's conclusion upon the catechising of the boys.

Then said Prudence to the boys, You must still hearken to your mother, for she can learn you more. You must also diligently give ear to what good talk you shall hear from others, for, for your sakes do they speak good things. Observe, also, and that with carefulness, what the heavens and the earth do teach you; but especially be much in the meditation of that book that was the cause of your father's becoming a pilgrim. I for my part, my children, will teach you what I can while you are here, and shall be glad if you will ask me questions that tend to godly edifying.

Mercy has a sweetheart.

Now by that these pilgrims had been at this place a week, Mercy had a visitor that pretended some good will unto her, and his name was Mr. Brisk; a man of some breeding, and that pretended to religion, but a man that stuck very close to the world. So he came once or twice or more to Mercy, and offered love unto her. Now Mercy was of a fair countenance, and therefore the more alluring.

Her mind also was, to be always busying of her- Mercy's
self in doing; for when she had nothing to do for temper.
herself, she would be making of hose and garments
for others, and would bestow them upon them that
had need. And Mr. Brisk, not knowing where or
how she disposed of what she made, seemed to be
greatly taken, for that he found her never idle.
I will warrant her a good housewife, quoth he to
himself.

Mercy then revealed the business to the maidens Mercy
that were of the house, and inquired of them con- inquires of
cerning him, for they did know him better than she. the maids
So they told her that he was a very busy young Mr. Brisk.
man, and one that pretended to religion, but was, as
they feared, a stranger to the power of that which
was good.

Nay then, said Mercy, I will look no more on
him; for I purpose never to have a clog to my soul.

Prudence then replied, that there needed no great
matter of discouragement to be given to him, her
continuing so as she had begun to do for the poor
would quickly cool his courage.

So the next time he comes, he finds her at her old Talk betwixt
work, a-making of things for the poor. Then said Mercy and
he, What! always at it? Yes, said she, either for Mr. Brisk.
myself, or for others. And what canst thou earn a
day? quoth he. I do these things, said she, 'that
I may be rich in good works, laying up in store a 1 Tim. vi.
good foundation against the time to come, that I 17-19.
may lay hold on eternal life.' Why, prithee, what

dost thou with them ? said he.   Clothe the naked,
said she.   With that his countenance fell.   So he

He forsakes
her, and why.

forbore to come at her again.   And when he was
asked the reason why, he said that Mercy was a
pretty lass, but troubled with ill conditions.

Mercy in
the practice
of mercy
rejected;
while Mercy
in the name
of mercy is
liked.

When he had left her, Prudence said, Did I not
tell thee that Mr. Brisk would soon forsake thee? yea,
he will raise up an ill report of thee; for notwithstanding his pretence to religion, and his seeming
love to Mercy, yet Mercy and he are of tempers
so different, that I believe they will never come
together.

MERCY. I might a had husbands afore now,
though I spake not of it to any; but they were such
as did not like my conditions, though never did any
of them find fault with my person.   So they and I
could not agree.

PRUD. Mercy in our days is little set by, any
further than as to its name : the practice, which
is set forth, by thy conditions, there are but few
that can abide.

Mercy's
resolution.

MERCY. Well, said Mercy, if nobody will have
me, I will die a maid, or my conditions shall be to
me as a husband.   For I cannot change my nature,
and to have one that lies cross to me in this, that I
purpose never to admit of, as long as I live.   I had
a sister named Bountiful, that was married to one
of these churls; but he and she could never agree;

How Mercy's
sister was
served by her
husband.

but because my sister was resolved to do as she had
begun, that is, to show kindness to the poor, therefore her husband first cried her down at the cross,
and then turned her out of his doors.

PRUD. And yet he was a professor, I warrant you?

MERCY. Yes, such a one as he was, and of such as he, the world is now full: but I am for none of them all.

Now Matthew, the eldest son of Christiana, fell sick, and his sickness was sore upon him, for he was much pained in his bowels, so that he was with it, at times, pulled as 'twere both ends together. There dwelt also not far from thence, one Mr. Skill, an ancient and well-approved physician. So Christiana desired it, and they sent for him, and he came. When he was entered the room, and had a little observed the boy, he concluded that he was sick of the gripes. Then he said to his mother, What diet has Matthew of late fed upon? Diet! said Christiana, nothing but that which is wholesome. The physician answered, This boy has been tampering with something that lies in his maw undigested, and that will not away without means. And I tell you that he must be purged, or else he will die. *Matthew falls sick.*

Gripes of conscience.

The physician's judgment.

SAM. Then said Samuel, Mother, mother, what was that which my brother did gather up and eat, so soon as we were come from the gate that is at the head of this way? You know that there was an orchard on the left hand, on the other side of the wall, and some of the trees hung over the wall, and my brother did plash and did eat. *Samuel puts his mother in mind of the fruit his brother did eat.*

CHRIS. True, my child, said Christiana, he did take thereof, and did eat; naughty boy as he was, I did chide him, and yet he would eat thereof.

SKILL. I knew he had eaten something that was

not wholesome food; and that food, to wit, that
fruit, is even the most hurtful of all. It is the fruit
of Beelzebub's orchard. I do marvel that none did
warn you of it; many have died thereof.

CHRIS. Then Christiana began to cry; and she
said, O naughty boy! and O careless mother! what
shall I do for my son?

SKILL. Come, do not be too much dejected; the
boy may do well again, but he must purge and
vomit.

CHRIS. Pray, sir, try the utmost of your skill with
him, whatever it costs.

SKILL. Nay, I hope I shall be reasonable. So he
made him a purge; but it was too weak. 'Twas
said it was made of the blood of a goat, the ashes of
an heifer, and with some of the juice of hyssop, etc.
When Mr. Skill had seen that that purge was too
weak, he made him one to the purpose, 'twas made
ex carne et sanguine Christi (you know physicians
give strange medicines to their patients), and it was
made up into pills, with a promise or two, and a
proportionable quantity of salt. Now he was to
take them three at a time fasting, in half a quarter
of a pint of the tears of repentance. When this
potion was prepared and brought to the boy, he was
loth to take it, though torn with the gripes, as if
he should be pulled in pieces. Come, come, said the
physician, you must take it. It goes against my
stomach, said the boy. I must have you take it,
said his mother. I shall vomit it up again, said the
boy. Pray, sir, said Christiana to Mr. Skill, how
does it taste? It has no ill taste, said the doctor;

Potion
prepared.

Heb. x. 1-4.

The Latin I
borrow.
Job vi. 54-57.

Mark ix. 49.

Heb. ix. 14.

The boy loth
to take the
physic.

Zech. xii. 10.

and with that she touched one of the pills with the tip of her tongue. Oh, Matthew, said she, this potion is sweeter than honey. If thou lovest thy mother, if thou lovest thy brothers, if thou lovest Mercy, if thou lovest thy life, take it. So with much ado, after a short prayer for the blessing of God upon it, he took it, and it wrought kindly with him. It caused him to purge, it caused him to sleep and rest quietly, it put him into a fine heat and breathing sweat, and did quite rid him of his gripes. The mother tastes it, and persuades him.

So in little time he got up, and walked about with a staff, and would go from room to room, and talk with Prudence, Piety, and Charity of his distemper, and how he was healed. A word of God in the hand of his faith.

So when the boy was healed, Christiana asked Mr. Skill saying, Sir, what will content you for your pains and care to and of my child? And he said, You must pay the Master of the College of Physicians, according to rules made, in that case, and provided. Heb. xiii. 11-15.

CHRIS. But, Sir, said she, what is this pill good for else?

SKILL. It is an universal pill; 'tis good against all the diseases that pilgrims are incident to, and when it is well prepared, it will keep good, time out of mind. This pill an universal remedy.

CHRIS. Pray, Sir, make me up twelve boxes of them, for if I can get these, I will never take other physic.

SKILL. These pills are good to prevent diseases, as well as to cure when one is sick. Yea, I dare say it, and stand to it, that if a man will but use

John vi. 50.

this physic as he should, it will make him live for ever.   But, good Christiana, thou must give these

In a glass of the tears of repentance.

pills no other way but as I have prescribed; for if you do, they will do no good.   So he gave unto Christiana physic for herself, and her boys, and for Mercy, and bid Matthew take heed how he eat any more green plums, and kissed them and went his way.

It was told you before that Prudence bid the boys, that if at any time they would, they should ask her some questions that might be profitable, and she would say something to them.

MATT. Then Matthew, who had been sick, asked

Of physic.

her, Why, for the most part, physic should be bitter to our palates?

PRUD. To show how unwelcome the Word of God and the effects thereof are to a carnal heart.

Of the effects of physic.

MATT. Why does physic, if it does good, purge, and cause that we vomit?

PRUD. To show that the Word, when it works effectually, cleanseth the heart and mind.   For look, what the one doth to the body, the other doth to the soul.

Of fire and of the sun.

MATT. What should we learn by seeing the flame of our fire go upwards? and by seeing the beams and sweet influences of the sun strike downwards?

PRUD. By the going up of the fire we are taught to ascend to heaven by fervent and hot desires; and by the sun sending his heat, beams, and sweet influences downwards, we are taught that the Saviour of the world, though high, reaches down with his grace and love to us below.

MATT. Where have the clouds their water ? *Of the clouds.*

PRUD. Out of the sea.

MATT. What may we learn from that ?

PRUD. That ministers should fetch their doctrine from God.

MATT. Why do they empty themselves upon the earth ?

PRUD. To show that ministers should give out what they know of God to the world.

MATT. Why is the rainbow caused by the sun ? *Of the rainbow.*

PRUD. To show that the covenant of God's grace is confirmed to us in Christ.

MATT. Why do the springs come from the sea to us through the earth ? *Of the springs.*

PRUD. To show that the grace of God comes to us through the body of Christ.

MATT. Why do some of the springs rise out of the tops of high hills ?

PRUD. To show that the spirit of grace shall spring up in *some* that are great and mighty, as well as in *many* that are poor and low.

MATT. Why doth the fire fasten upon the candle-wick ? *Of the candle.*

PRUD. To show that unless grace doth kindle upon the heart, there will be no true light of life in us.

MATT. Why is the wick, and tallow, and all, spent to maintain the light of the candle ?

PRUD. To show that body, and soul, and all, should be at the service of, and spend themselves to maintain in good condition that grace of God that is in us.

Of the
pelican.

MATT. Why doth the pelican pierce her own breast with her bill?

PRUD. To nourish her young ones with her blood, and thereby to show that Christ the blessed so loveth his young, his people, as to save them from death by his blood.

Of the cock.

MATT. What may one learn by hearing the cock to crow?

PRUD. Learn to remember Peter's sin, and Peter's repentance. The cock's crowing shows also that day is coming on; let then the crowing of the cock put thee in mind of that last terrible day of judgment.

Now about this time their month was out: wherefore they signified to those of the house that 'twas convenient for them to up and be going. Then said Joseph to his mother, It is convenient that you

The weak
may some-
times call
the strong
to prayers.

forget not to send to the house of Mr. Interpreter to pray him to grant that Mr. Great-heart should be sent unto us, that he may be our conductor the rest of our way. Good boy, said she, I had almost forgot. So she drew up a petition, and prayed Mr. Watchful the porter to send it by some fit man to her good friend Mr. Interpreter; who, when it was come, and he had seen the contents of the petition, said to the messenger, Go tell them that I will send him.

They provide
to be gone
on their way.

When the family where Christiana was saw that they had a purpose to go forward, they called the whole house together, to give thanks to their King for sending of them such profitable guests as these. Which done, they said to Christiana, And shall we not show thee something, according as our custom is to do to pilgrims, on which thou mayest meditate when thou art upon the way? So they took Christiana, her children, and Mercy, into the closet, and showed them one of the apples that Eve did eat of, and that she also did give to her husband, and that for the eating of which they both were turned out of Paradise, and asked her what she thought that was? Then Christiana said, 'Tis food or poison, I know not which. So they opened the matter to her, and she held up her hands and wondered.

Eve's apple.

A sight of sin is amazing. Gen. iii. 6. Rom. vii. 24.

Then they had her to a place, and showed her Jacob's ladder. Now at that time there were some angels ascending upon it. So Christiana looked, and looked, to see the angels go up; and so did the rest of the company. Then they were going into another place to show them something else; but James said to his mother, Pray bid them stay here a little longer, for this is a curious sight. So they turned again, and stood feeding their eyes with this so pleasant a prospect. After this, they had them into a place where did hang up a golden anchor, so they bid Christiana take it down; For, said they, you shall have it with you, for 'tis of absolute necessity that you should, that you may lay hold of that within the veil, and stand steadfast, in case you should meet with turbulent weather: So they were glad thereof. Then they took them, and had them to the mount upon which Abraham our father had offered up Isaac his son, and showed them the altar, the wood, the fire, and the knife, for

Jacob's ladder.

A sight of Christ is taking. Gen. xxviii. 12. John i. 51. Golden anchor.

Heb. vi. 19.

Of Abraham offering up Isaac. Gen. xxii. 9.

they remain to be seen to this very day. When they had seen it, they held up their hands and blessed themselves, and said, Oh, what a man for love to his Master, and for denial to himself, was Abraham. After they had showed them all these things, Prudence took them into the dining-room, where stood a pair of excellent virginals: so she played upon them, and turned what she had showed them into this excellent song, saying:

Prudence's virginals.

> Eve's apple we have showed you,
>   Of that be you aware ;
> You have seen Jacob's ladder, too,
>   Upon which angels are.
> An anchor you received here ;
>   But let not these suffice,
> Until with Abra'm you have gave
>   Your best, a sacrifice.

Now about this time one knocked at the door; so the porter opened, and behold Mr. Great-heart was there. But when he was come in, what joy was there! For it came now fresh again into their minds, how but a while ago he had slain old Grim Bloody-man the giant, and had delivered them from the lions.

Mr. Great-heart come again.

Then said Mr. Great-heart to Christiana, and to Mercy, My Lord has sent each of you a bottle of wine, and also some parched corn, together with a couple of pomegranates. He has also sent the boys some figs, and raisins to refresh you in your way.

He brings a token from his Lord with him.

Then they addressed themselves to their journey; and Prudence and Piety went along with them. When they came at the gate, Christiana asked the porter if any of late went by. He said, No, only one, some time since; who also told me that of late there had been a great robbery committed on the King's highway, as you go; but he saith the thieves are taken, and will shortly be tried for their lives. Then Christiana and Mercy were afraid; but Matthew said, Mother, fear nothing, as long as Mr. Great-heart is to go with us, and to be our conductor. Robbery.

Then said Christiana to the porter, Sir, I am much obliged to you for all the kindnesses that you have showed me since I came hither; and also for that you have been so loving and kind to my children. I know not how to gratify your kindness; wherefore pray, as a token of my respects to you, accept of this small mite. So she put a gold angel in his hand, and he made her a low obeisance, and said, Let thy garments be always white, and let thy head want no ointment. Let Mercy live, and not die, and let not her works be few. And to the boys he said, Do you fly youthful lusts, and follow after godliness with them that are grave and wise; so shall you put gladness into your mother's heart, and obtain praise of all that are sober-minded. So they thanked the porter, and departed. Christiana takes her leave of the porter. The porter's blessing.

Now I saw in my dream, that they went forward until they were come to the brow of the hill, where Piety, bethinking herself, cried out, Alas! I have forgot what I intended to bestow upon Christiana and her companions; I will go back and fetch it. So she ran and fetched it. While she was gone, Christiana thought she heard in a grove, a little way off, on the right hand, a most curious melodious note, with words much like these—

> Through all my life thy favour is
> So frankly show'd to me,
> That in thy house for evermore
> My dwelling-place shall be.

And, listening still, she thought she heard another answer it, saying—

> For why?   The Lord our God is good,
> His Mercy is for ever sure;
> His truth at all times firmly stood,
> And shall from age to age endure.

So Christiana asked Prudence what it was that made these curious notes? They are, said she, our country birds; they sing these notes but seldom, except it be at the spring, when the flowers appear, and the sun shines warm, and then you may hear them all day long. I often, said she, go out to hear them; we also ofttimes keep them tame in our house. They are very fine company for us when we are melancholy; also they make the woods, and groves, and solitary places, places desirous to be in.

Song ii. 11, 12.

By this time Piety was come again; so she said to Christiana, Look here, I have brought thee a scheme of all those things that thou hast seen at our house, upon which thou mayest look when thou findest thyself forgetful, and call those things again to remembrance for thy edification and comfort.

Piety bestoweth something on them at parting.

Now they began to go down the hill into the Valley of Humiliation. It was a steep hill, and the way was slippery; but they were very careful,

Part i. page 68.

so they got down pretty well. When they were down in the valley, Piety said to Christiana, This is the place where Christian your husband met with the foul fiend Apollyon, and where they had that dreadful fight that they had; I know you cannot but have heard thereof. But be of good courage; as long as you have here Mr. Great-heart to be your guide and conductor, we hope you will fare the better. So when these two had committed the pilgrims unto the conduct of their guide, he went forward, and they went after.

GREAT-HEART. Then said Mr. Great-heart, We need not to be so afraid of this valley, for here is nothing to hurt us, unless we procure it to ourselves. 'Tis true, Christian did here meet with Apollyon, with whom he also had a sore combat: but that fray was the fruit of those slips that he got in his going down the hill; for they that get slips *there*, must look for combats *here*. And hence it is that this valley has got so hard a name. For the common people, when they hear that some frightful thing has befallen such an one in such a place, are of an opinion that that place is haunted with some foul fiend or evil spirit; when, alas, it is for the fruit of their doing, that such things do befall them there.

This Valley of Humiliation is of itself as fruitful a place as any the crow flies over; and I am persuaded if we could hit upon it, we might find somewhere hereabouts something that might give us an account why Christian was so hardly beset in this place.

Mr. Great-heart at the Valley of Humiliation.

Part I. page 69.

The reason why Christian was so beset here.

A pillar with an inscription on it.

Then James said to his mother, Lo, yonder stands a pillar, and it looks as if something was written thereon; let us go and see what it is. So they went, and found there written, Let Christian's slips before he came hither, and the battles that he met with in this place, be a warning to those that come after. Lo, said their guide, did not I tell you that there was something hereabouts that would give intimation of the reason why Christian was so hard beset in this place? Then turning himself to Christiana, he said, No disparagement to Christian more than to many others whose hap and lot his was. For 'tis easier going up than down this hill; and that can be said but of few hills in all these parts of the world. But we will leave the good man, he is at rest, he also had a brave victory over his enemy: let Him grant that dwelleth above, that we fare no worse, when we come to be tried, than he.

This valley a brave place.

But we will come again to this Valley of Humiliation. It is the best and most fruitful piece of ground in all those parts. It is fat ground, and, as you see, consisteth much in meadows; and if a man was to come here in the summer-time, as we do now, if he knew not anything before thereof, and if he also delighted himself in the sight of his eyes, he might

Song ii. 1.

see that that would be delightful to him. Behold how green this valley is; also how beautiful with

Men thrive in the Valley of Humiliation. James iv. 6. 1 Pet. v. 5.

lilies! I have also known many labouring men that have got good estates in this Valley of Humiliation (for God resisteth the proud, but gives more, more grace to the humble); for indeed it is a very fruitful soil, and doth bring forth by handfuls. Some also have wished that the next way to their Father's house were here, that they might be troubled no more with either hills or mountains to go over: but the way is the way, and there's an end.

Now as they were going along and talking, they espied a boy feeding his father's sheep. The boy was in very mean clothes, but of a very fresh and well-favoured countenance, and as he sat by himself, he sang. Hark, said Mr. Great-heart, to what the shepherd's boy saith: so they hearkened, and he said:

> He that is down, needs fear no fall,
>   He that is low, no pride;
> He that is humble, ever shall
>   Have God to be his guide.
> I am content with what I have,
>   Little be it, or much;
> And, Lord, contentment still I crave,
>   Because thou savest such.
> Fullness to such a burden is
>   That go on pilgrimage;
> Here little, and hereafter bliss,
>   Is best from age to age.

Phil. iv 12, 13.

Heb. xiii. 5.

Then said their guide, Do you hear him? I will dare to say that this boy lives a merrier life, and wears more of that herb called heart's-ease in his bosom, than he that is clad in silk and velvet. But we will proceed in our discourse.

In this valley our Lord formerly had his country house. He loved much to be here; he loved also to walk these meadows, for he found the air was pleasant. Besides, here a man shall be free from the noise, and from the hurryings of this life.

Christ, when in the flesh, had his country house in the Valley of Humiliation.

All states are full of noise and confusion, only the Valley of Humiliation is that empty and solitary place. Here a man shall not be so let and hindered in his contemplation, as in other places he is apt to be. This is a valley that nobody walks in, but those that love a pilgrim's life. And though Christian had the hard hap to meet here with Apollyon, and to enter with him a brisk encounter, yet I must tell you, that in former times men have met with angels here, have found pearls here, and have in this place found the words of life.

Hos. xii. 4, 5.

Did I say our Lord had here in former days his country house, and that he loved here to walk? I will add, in this place, and to the people that live, and trace these grounds, he had left a yearly revenue, to be faithfully paid them at certain seasons, for their maintenance by the way, and for their further encouragement to go on in their pilgrimage.

Matt. xi. 29.

SAMUEL. Now, as they went on, Samuel said to Mr. Great-heart, Sir, I perceive that in this valley my father and Apollyon had their battle; but whereabout was the fight? for I perceive this valley is large.

GREAT-HEART. Your father had that battle with Apollyon at a place yonder, before us, in a narrow passage just beyond Forgetful Green. And indeed that place is the most dangerous place in all these parts. For if at any time the pilgrims meet with any brunt, it is when they forget what favours they have received, and how unworthy they are of them. This is the place also where others have been hard

Forgetful Green.

put to it. But more of the place when we are come to it; for I persuade myself, that to this day there remains either some sign of the battle, or some monument to testify that such a battle there was fought.

MERCY. Then said Mercy, I think I am as well in this valley, as I have been anywhere else in all our journey; the place methinks suits with my spirit. I love to be in such places where there is no rattling with coaches, nor rumbling with wheels. Methinks here one may, without much molestation, be thinking what he is, whence he came, what he has done, and to what the King has called him. Here one may think, and break at heart, and melt in one's spirit, until one's eyes become like the fish-pools of Hesbon. They that go rightly through this Valley of Baca make it a well; the rain that God sends down from heaven upon them that are here also filleth the pools. This valley is that from whence also the King will give to them vineyards; and they that go through it shall sing (as Christian did, for all he met with Apollyon).

Humility a sweet grace.

Song vii. 4.

Ps. lxxxiv. 5-7.

Hos. ii. 12.

GREAT-HEART. 'Tis true, said their guide. I have gone through this valley many a time, and never was better than when here.

An experiment of it.

I have also been a conductor to several pilgrims, and they have confessed the same, 'To this man will I look,' saith the King, 'even to him that is poor, and of a contrite spirit, and that trembles at my Word.'

Now they were come to the place where the afore-mentioned battle was fought. Then said the guide

The place
where
Christian
and the fiend
did fight.
Some signs
of the battle
remain.

to Christiana, her children, and Mercy, This is the
place; on this ground Christian stood, and up there
came Apollyon against him. And look, did not I
tell you? here is some of your husband's blood upon
these stones to this day! Behold, also, how here
and there are yet to be seen upon the place some
of the shivers of Apollyon's broken darts See also
how they did beat the ground with their feet as
they fought, to make good their places against each
other; how also, with their by-blows, they did split
the very stones in pieces. Verily Christian did here
play the man, and showed himself as stout, as could,
had he been there, even Hercules himself. When
Apollyon was beat, he made his retreat to the next
valley, that is called the Valley of the Shadow of
Death, unto which we shall come anon.

A monument
of the battle.

Lo, yonder also stands a monument, on which is
engraven this battle, and Christian's victory, to his
fame throughout all ages. So, because it stood just
on the wayside before them, they stepped to it, and
read the writing, which, word for word, was this—

A monument
of Christian's
victory.

Hard by, here was a battle fought,
  Most strange, and yet most true;
Christian and Apollyon sought
  Each other to subdue.
The man so bravely play'd the man,
  He made the fiend to fly;
Of which a monument I stand,
  The same to testify.

Part i.
page 74.

When they had passed by this place, they came
upon the borders of the Shadow of Death; and this
valley was longer than the other; a place also most

strangely haunted with evil things, as many are able to testify.   But these women and children went the better through it, because they had daylight, and because Mr. Great-heart was their conductor.

When they were entered upon this valley, they thought that they heard a groaning, as of dead men —a very great groaning.   They thought also they did hear words of lamentation spoken, as of some in extreme torment.   These things made the boys to quake, the woman also looked pale and wan; but their guide bid them be of good comfort.

Groanings heard.

So they went on a little further, and they thought that they felt the ground begin to shake under them, as if some hollow place was there ; they heard also a kind of hissing, as of serpents, but nothing as yet appeared.   Then said the boys, Are we not yet at the end of this doleful place ?   But the guide also bid them be of good courage, and look well to their feet, lest haply, said he, you be taken in some snare.

The ground shakes.

Now James began to be sick, but I think the cause thereof was fear; so his mother gave him some of that glass of spirits that she had given her at the Interpreter's house, and three of the pills that Mr. Skill had prepared ; and the boy began to revive. Thus they went on till they came to about the middle of the valley, and then Christiana said, Methinks I see something yonder upon the road before us, a thing of such a shape such as I have not seen.   Then said Joseph, Mother, what is it? An ugly thing, child, an ugly thing, said she.   But, mother, what is it like ? said he.   'Tis like I cannot

James sick with fear.

The fiend appears.

The pilgrims
are afraid.
tell what, said she. And now it was but a little
way off. Then said she, It is nigh.

Great-heart
encourages
them.
Well, well, said Mr. Great-heart, let them that
are most afraid keep close to me. So the fiend
came on, and the conductor met it; but when it
was just come to him, it vanished to all their sights.
Then remembered they what had been said some
James iv. 7. time ago: 'Resist the devil, and he will flee from
you.'

They went therefore on, as being a little refreshed;
but they had not gone far before Mercy, looking
behind her, saw, as she thought, something, most
A lion. like a lion, and it came a great padding pace after;
and it had a hollow voice of roaring, and at every
roar that it gave it made all the valley echo, and
their hearts to ache, save the heart of him that was
their guide. So it came up, and Mr. Great-heart
went behind, and put the pilgrims all before him.
The lion also came on apace, and Mr. Great-heart
1 Pet. v. 8, 9. addressed himself to give him battle. But when he
saw that it was determined that resistance should be
made, he also drew back and came no further.

Then they went on again, and their conductor
did go before them, till they came at a place where
A pit and
darkness. was cast up a pit, the whole breadth of the way,
and before they could be prepared to go over that,
a great mist and a darkness fell upon them, so that
they could not see. Then said the pilgrims, Alas!
now what shall we do? But their guide made
answer, Fear not; stand still and see what an end
will be put to this also. So they stayed there
because their path was marred. They then also

thought that they did hear more apparently the noise and rushing of the enemies, the fire also and the smoke of the pit was much easier to be discerned. Then said Christiana to Mercy, Now I see what my poor husband went through; I have heard much of this place, but I was never here afore now. Poor man! he went here all alone in the night; he had night almost quite through the way; also these fiends were busy about him, as if they would have torn him in pieces. Many have spoke of, but none can tell what the Valley of the Shadow should mean, until they come in it themselves. 'The heart knows its own bitterness, and a stranger intermeddleth not with its joy.' To be here is a fearful thing.

Christiana now knows what her husband felt.

GREAT-HEART. This is like doing business in great waters, or like going down into the deep; this is like being in the heart of the sea, and like going down to the bottoms of the mountains; now it seems as if the earth, with its bars, were about us for ever. 'But let them that walk in darkness, and have no light, trust in the name of the Lord, and stay upon their God.' For my part, as I have told you already, I have gone often through this valley, and have been much harder put to it than now I am, and yet you see I am alive. I would not boast, for that I am not mine own saviour; but I trust we shall have a good deliverance. Come, let us pray for light to Him that can lighten our darkness, and that can rebuke, not only these, but all the Satans in hell.

Great-heart's reply.

So they cried and prayed, and God sent light and deliverance, for there was now no let in their way;

They pray.

no, not there, where but now they were stopped with a pit. Yet they were not got through the valley; so they went on still, and, behold, great stinks and loathsome smells, to a great annoyance of them. Then said Mercy to Christiana, There is not such pleasant being here as at the gate, or at the Interpreter's, or at the house where we lay last.

One of the boys reply.

Oh, but, said one of the boys, it is not so bad to go through here as it is to *abide* here always, and for aught I know, one reason why we must go this way to the house prepared for us, is, that our home might be made the sweeter to us.

Well said, Samuel, quoth the guide, thou hast now spoke like a man. Why, if ever I get out here again, said the boy, I think I shall prize light and good way better than ever I did in all my life. Then said the guide, We shall be out by and by.

So on they went, and Joseph said, Cannot we see to the end of this valley as yet? Then said the guide, Look to your feet, for you shall presently be among the snares. So they looked to their feet, and went on; but they were troubled much with the snares. Now when they were come among the snares, they espied a man cast into the ditch on the left hand, with his flesh all rent and torn. Then

Heedless is slain, and Take-heed preserved.

said the guide, That is one Heedless, that was a-going this way; he has lain there a great while. There was one Take-heed with him, when he was taken and slain; but *he* escaped their hands. You cannot imagine how many are killed hereabout, and yet men are so foolishly venturous, as to set out lightly on pilgrimage, and to come without a guide.   Poor Christian! it was a wonder that he here escaped; but he was beloved of his God; also he had a good heart of his own, or else he could never have done it.   Now they drew towards the end of the way, and just there where Christian had seen the cave when he went by, out thence came forth Maul, a Giant.   This Maul did use to spoil young pilgrims with sophistry; and he called Great-heart by his name, and said unto him, How many times have you been forbidden to do these things? Then said Mr. Great-heart, What things?   What things! quoth the Giant, you know what things; but I will put an end to your trade.   But pray, said Mr. Great-heart, before we fall to it, let us understand wherefore we must fight.   Now the women and children stood trembling, and knew not what to do.   Quoth the Giant, You rob the country, and rob it with the worst of thefts.   These are but generals, said Mr. Great-heart, come to particulars, man.

Part i. pages 80, 81.

Maul, a Giant.

He quarrels with Great-heart.

Then said the Giant, Thou practisest the craft of a kidnapper, thou gatherest up women and children, and carriest them into a strange country, to the weakening of my master's kingdom.   But now Great-heart replied: I am a servant of the God of heaven; my business is to persuade sinners to repentance; I am commanded to do my endeavour to turn men, women, and children from darkness to light, and from the power of Satan to God; and if this be indeed the ground of thy quarrel, let us fall to it as soon as thou wilt.

God's ministers counted as kidnappers.

The Giant and Mr. Great-heart must fight.

Then the Giant came up, and Mr. Great-heart

went to meet him; and as he went he drew his sword, but the Giant had a club.   So without more ado they fell to it, and at the first blow the Giant struck Mr. Great-heart down upon one of his knees. With that the women and children cried out; so Mr. Great-heart, recovering himself, laid about him in full lusty manner, and gave the Giant a wound in his arm.   Thus he fought for the space of an hour, to that height of heat, that the breath came out of the Giant's nostrils as the heat doth out of a boiling caldron.

Weak folks' prayers do sometimes help strong folks' cries.

Then they sat down to rest them, but Mr. Great-heart betook him to prayer; also the women and children did nothing but sigh and cry all the time that the battle did last.

When they had rested them, and taken breath, they both fell to it again, and Mr. Great-heart, with a full blow, fetched the Giant down to the ground.   Nay, hold, and let me recover, quoth he. So Mr. Great-heart fairly let him get up.   So to it they went again, and the Giant missed but little of all-to breaking Mr. Great-heart's skull with his club.

The Giant struck down.

Mr. Great-heart, seeing that, runs to him in the full heat of his spirit, and pierceth him under the fifth rib; with that the Giant began to faint, and could hold up his club no longer.   Then Mr. Great-heart seconded his blow, and smit the head of the Giant from his shoulders.   Then the women and children rejoiced, and Mr. Great-heart also praised God for the deliverance he had wrought.

He is slain, and his head disposed of.

When this was done, they amongst them erected a pillar, and fastened the Giant's head thereon, and wrote underneath, in letters that passengers might read—

> He that did wear this head, was one
>   That pilgrims did misuse;
> He stopp'd their way, he spared none,
>   But did them all abuse;
> Until that I, Great-heart, arose,
>   The pilgrims' guide to be;
> Until that I did him oppose,
>   That was their enemy.

Now I saw, that they went to the ascent that was a little way off, cast up to be a prospect for pilgrims (that was the place from whence Christian had the first sight of Faithful, his brother). Wherefore here they sat down and rested; they also here did eat and drink, and make merry; for that they had gotten deliverance from this so dangerous an enemy. As they sat thus and did eat, Christiana asked the guide if he had caught no hurt in the battle. Then said Mr. Great-heart, No, save a little on my flesh; yet that also shall be so far from being to my determent, that it is at present a proof of my love to my Master, and you, and shall be a means by grace to increase my reward at last.

Part I. page 81.

2 Cor. iv.

CHRIS. But were you not afraid, good Sir, when you saw him come out with his club?

Discourse of the fights.

GREAT-HEART. It is my duty, said he, to distrust mine own ability, that I may have reliance on him that is stronger than all.

CHRIS. But what did you think when he fetched you down to the ground at the first blow?

GREAT-HEART. Why, I thought, quoth he, that so

my Master himself was served, and yet he it was that conquered at the last.

MATT. When you all have thought what you please, I think God has been wonderful good unto us, both in bringing us out of this valley, and in delivering us out of the hand of this enemy; for my part, I see no reason why we should distrust our God any more, since he has now, and in such a place as this, given us such testimony of his love as this.

Then they got up and went forward. Now a little before them stook an oak, and under it, when they came to it, they found an old pilgrim fast asleep. They knew that he was a pilgrim by his clothes, and his staff, and his girdle. So the guide, Mr. Great-heart, awaked him, and the old gentleman, as he lift up his eyes, cried out, What's the matter? who are you? and what is your business here?

GREAT-HEART. Come, man, be not so hot; here is none but friends. Yet the old man gets up and stands upon his guard, and will know of them what they were. Then said the guide, My name is Great-heart: I am the guide of these pilgrims, which are going to the Celestial Country.

HON. Then said Mr. Honest, I cry you mercy. I feared that you had been of the company of those that some time ago did rob Little-faith of his money; but now I look better about me, I perceive you are honester people.

GREAT-HEART. Why, what would or could you have done to have helped yourself, if we indeed had been of that company?

HON. Done! why, I would have fought as long

Mat. here admires goodness.

Old Honest asleep under an oak.

One saint sometimes takes another for his enemy.

Talk between Great-heart and he.

as breath had been in me; and had I so done, I am
sure you could never have given me the worst on 't;
for a Christian can never be overcome, unless he
shall yield of himself.

GREAT-HEART. Well said, Father Honest, quoth
the guide, for by this I know thou art a cock of the
right kind, for thou hast said the truth.

HON. And by this also I know that thou knowest
what true pilgrimage is, for all others do think that
we are the soonest overcome of any.

GREAT-HEART. Well, now we are so happily met,
pray let me crave your name, and the name of the
place you came from.

HON. My name I cannot: but I came from the
Town of Stupidity; it lieth about four degrees
beyond the City of Destruction.

Whence
Mr. Honest
came.

GREAT-HEART. Oh! are you that countryman
then? I deem I have half a guess of you: your
name is old Honesty, is it not?

So the old gentleman blushed, and said, Not
Honesty in the abstract, but Honest is my name,
and I wish that my nature shall agree to what I am
called.

HON. But, sir, said the old gentleman, how could
you guess that I am such a man, since I came from
such a place?

GREAT-HEART. I had heard of you before, by my
Master; for he knows all things that are done on the
earth: but I have often wondered that any should
come from your place, for your town is worse than
is the City of Destruction itself.

Stupefied
ones are
worse than
those merely
carnal.

HON. Yes; we lie more off from the sun, and so

are more cold and senseless; but was a man in a mountain of ice, yet if the Sun of Righteousness will arise upon him, his frozen heart shall feel a thaw; and thus it hath been with me.

GREAT-HEART. I believe it, Father Honest, I believe it; for I know the thing is true.

Then the old gentleman saluted all the pilgrims with a holy kiss of charity, and asked them of their names, and how they had fared since they set out on their pilgrimage.

Old Honest and Christiana talk.

CHRIS. Then said Christiana, My name I suppose you have heard of: good Christian was my husband, and these four were his children. But can you think how the old gentleman was taken, when she told them who she was! He skipped, he smiled, and blessed them with a thousand good wishes, saying:

HON. I have heard much of your husband, and of his travels and wars which he underwent in his days. Be it spoken to your comfort, the name of your husband rings all over these parts of the world: his faith, his courage, his enduring, and his sincerity under all, have made his name famous. Then he turned him to the boys, and asked them of their names, which they told him. And then said he unto them: Matthew, be thou like Matthew the publican, not in vice, but in virtue. Samuel, said he, be thou like Samuel the prophet, a man of faith and prayer. Joseph, said he, be thou like Joseph in Potiphar's house, chaste, and one that flies from temptation. And James, be thou like James the Just, and like James the brother of our Lord.

He also talks with the boys.
Old Mr. Honest's blessing on them.
Matt. x. 3.
Ps. xcix. 6.

Gen. xxxix.

Acts i. 13.

Then they told him of Mercy, and how she had

left her town and her kindred to come along with
Christiana and with her sons. At that, the old He blesseth
Mercy.
honest man said, Mercy is thy name? by Mercy
shalt thou be sustained, and carried through all those
difficulties that shall assault thee in thy way, till
thou shalt come thither where thou shalt look the
Fountain of Mercy in the face with comfort.

All this while the guide, Mr. Great-heart, was
very much pleased, and smiled upon his companion.

Now as they walked along together, the guide
asked the old gentleman if he did not know one Mr. Talk of one
Mr. Fearing.
Fearing, that came on pilgrimage out of his parts.

HON. Yes, very well, said he. He was a man that
had the root of the matter in him; but he was one
of the most troublesome pilgrims that ever I met
with in all my days.

GREAT-HEART. I perceive you knew him, for you
have given a very right character of him.

HON. Knew him! I was a great companion of
his; I was with him most an end; when he first
began to think of what would come upon us hereafter, I was with him.

GREAT-HEART. I was his guide from my Master's
house to the gates of the Celestial City.

HON. Then you knew him to be a troublesome one?

GREAT-HEART. I did so! but I could very well
bear it, for men of my calling are oftentimes intrusted with the conduct of such as he was.

HON. Well then, pray let us hear a little of him,
and how he managed himself under your conduct.

GREAT-HEART. Why, he was always afraid that Mr. Fearing's
troublesome
pilgrimage.
he should come short of whither he had a desire

to go. Everything frightened him that he heard
anybody speak of, that had but the least appearance
of opposition in it. I hear that he lay roaring at
the Slough of Despond for above a month together;
nor durst he, for all he saw several go over before
him, venture, though they, many of them, offered
to lend him their hand. *He would not go back
again neither.* The Celestial City, he said he should
die if he came not to it, and yet was dejected at
every difficulty, and stumbled at every straw that
anybody cast in his way. Well, after he had lain
at the Slough of Despond a great while, as I have
told you, one sunshine morning, I do not know how,
he ventured, and so got over. But when he was
over, he would scarce believe it. He had, I think,
a Slough of Despond in his mind, a slough that he
carried everywhere with him, or else he would never
have been as he was. So he came up to the gate,
you know what I mean, that stands at the head
of this way, and there also he stood a good while
before he would adventure to knock. When the
gate was opened he would give back, and give place
to others, and say that he was not worthy. For,
for all he got before some to the gate, yet many of
them went in before him. There the poor man
would stand shaking and shrinking; I dare say it
would have pitied one's heart to have seen him:
Nor would he go back again. At last he took the
hammer that hanged on the gate in his hand, and
gave a small rap or two; then one opened to
him, but he shrank back as before. He that opened
stept out after him, and said, Thou trembling

*His behaviour
at the Slough
of Despond.*

*His behaviour
at the gate.*

one, what wantest thou? With that, he fell to
the ground. He that spoke to him wondered to
see him so faint; so he said to him, Peace be to
thee; up, for I have set open the door to thee;
come in, for thou art blest. With that he got up,
and went in trembling, and when he was in, he was
ashamed to show his face. Well, after he had been
entertained there a while, as you know how the
manner is, he was bid go on his way, and also told
the way he should take. So he came till he came
to our house; but as he behaved himself at the
gate, so he did at my Master the Interpreter's door. His behaviour
He lay thereabout in the cold a good while, before at the Interpreter's door.
he would adventure to call; Yet he would not go
back. And the nights were long and cold then.
Nay, he had a note of necessity in his bosom to
my Master to receive him, and grant him the comfort of his house, and also to allow him a stout
and valiant conductor, because he was himself so
chicken-hearted a man; and yet, for all that, he
was afraid to call at the door. So he lay up and
down thereabouts, till, poor man, he was almost
starved. Yea, so great was his dejection, that
though he saw several others for knocking got in,
yet he was afraid to venture. At last, I think I
looked out of the window, and perceiving a man
to be up and down about the door, I went out to
him, and asked what he was; but, poor man, the
water stood in his eyes. So I perceived what he
wanted. I went therefore in, and told it in the
house, and we showed the thing to our Lord: so
he sent me out again, to entreat him to come in;

but I dare say I had hard work to do it. At last he came in, and I will say that for my Lord, he carried it wonderful lovingly to him. There were but a few good bits at the table, but some of it was laid upon his trencher. Then he presented the note, and my Lord looked thereon, and said his desire should be granted. So when he had been there a good while, he seemed to get some heart, and to be a little more comfortable. For my Master, you must know, is one of very tender bowels, specially to them that are afraid; wherefore he carried it so towards him, as might tend most to his encouragement. Well, when he had had a sight of the things of the place, and was ready to take his journey to go to the city, my Lord, as he did to Christian before, gave him a bottle of spirits, and some comfortable things to eat. Thus we set forward, and I went before him; but the man was but of few words, only he would sigh aloud.

When we were come to where the three fellows were hanged, he said that he doubted that that would be his end also. Only he seemed glad when he saw the Cross and the Sepulchre. There, I confess, he desired to stay a little to look, and he seemed for a while after to be a little cheery. When we came at the Hill Difficulty, he made no stick at that, nor did he much fear the lions: for you must know that his trouble was not about such things as those; his fear was about his acceptance at last.

I got him in at the house Beautiful, I think, before he was willing. Also, when he was in, I brought him acquainted with the damsels that were

---

Marginal notes:

How he was entertained there.

He is a little encouraged at the Interpreter's house.

He was greatly afraid when he saw the gibbet, cheery when he saw the Cross.

Dumpish at the house Beautiful

of the place; but he was ashamed to make himself much for company. He desired much to be alone; yet he always loved good talk, and often would get behind the screen to hear it. He also loved much to see ancient things, and to be pondering them in his mind. He told me afterwards that he loved to be in those two houses from which he came last, to wit, at the gate, and that of the Interpreter; but that he durst not be so bold to ask.

When we went also from the house Beautiful, down the hill, into the Valley of Humiliation, he went down as well as ever I saw a man in my life; for he cared not how mean he was, so he might be happy at last. Yea, I think there was a kind of a sympathy betwixt that valley and him; for I never saw him better in all his pilgrimage than when he was in that valley.

He went down into, and was very pleasant in, the Valley of Humiliation.

Here he would lie down, embrace the ground, and kiss the very flowers that grew in this valley. He would now be up every morning by break of day, tracing and walking to and fro in this valley.

Lam. iii. 27-29.

But when he was come to the entrance of the Valley of the Shadow of Death, I thought I should have lost my man: not for that he had any inclination to go back—that he always abhorred; but he was ready to die for fear. Oh, the hobgoblins will have me! the hobgoblins will have me! cried he; and I could not beat him out on 't. He made such a noise, and such an outcry here, that, had they but heard him, 'twas enough to encourage them to come and fall upon us.

Much perplexed in the Valley of the Shadow of Death.

But this I took very great notice of, that this

valley was as quiet while he went through it, as ever I knew it before or since. I suppose those enemies here had now a special check from our Lord, and a command not to meddle until Mr. Fearing was passed over it.

It would be too tedious to tell you of all. We will therefore only mention a passage or two more. When he was come at Vanity Fair, I thought he would have fought with all the men in the fair. I feared there we should both have been knocked on the head, so hot was he against their fooleries. Upon the Enchanted Ground he was also very wakeful. But when he was come at the river where was no bridge, there again he was in a heavy case. Now, now, he said, he should be drowned for ever, and so never see that face with comfort, that he had come so many miles to behold.

And here, also, I took notice of what was very remarkable: the water of that river was lower at this time than ever I saw it in all my life. So he went over at last, not much above wet-shod. When he was going up to the gate, Mr. Great-heart began to take his leave of him, and to wish him a good reception above. So he said, I shall, I shall. Then parted we asunder, and I saw him no more.

HON. Then, it seems, he was well at last.

GREAT-HEART. Yes, yes; I never had doubt about him; he was a man of a choice spirit, only he was always kept very low, and that made his life so burdensome to himself, and so troublesome to others. He was, above many, tender of sin. He was so afraid of doing injuries to others, that he

His behaviour at Vanity Fair.

His boldness at last.

Ps. lxxxviii.
Rom. xiv. 21.

often would deny himself of that which was lawful, 1 Cor. viii. 13. because he would not offend.

Hon. But what should be the reason that such a good man should be all his days so much in the dark?

Great-heart. There are two sorts of reasons for it. One is, the wise God will have it so: some must pipe, and some must weep. Now Mr. Fearing was one that played upon this bass. He and his fellows found the sackbut, whose notes are more doleful than the notes of other music are; though indeed some say, the bass is the ground of music. And, for my part, I care not at all for that profession that begins not in heaviness of mind. The first string that the musician usually touches is the bass, when he intends to put all in tune. God also plays upon this string first, when he sets the soul in tune for himself. Only here was the imperfection of Mr. Fearing, he could play upon no other music but this, till towards his latter end. Reason why good men are so in the dark. Matt. xi. 16-18.

I make bold to talk thus metaphorically, for the ripening of the wits of young readers, and because, in the book of the Revelations, the saved are compared to a company of musicians that play upon their trumpets and harps, and sing their songs before the throne. Rev. viii. 2. Chap. xiv. 2, 3.

Hon. He was a very zealous man, as one may see by what relation you have given of him. Difficulties, lions, or Vanity Fair, he feared not at all. It was only sin, death, and hell that was to him a terror, because he had some doubts about his interest in that celestial country.

A close
about him.

GREAT-HEART. You say right; those were the things that were his troublers: and they, as you have well observed, arose from the weakness of his mind thereabout, not from weakness of spirit as to the practical part of a pilgrim's life. I dare believe that, as the proverb is, he could have bit a firebrand, had it stood in his way; but the things with which he was oppressed no man ever yet could shake off with ease.

Christiana's
sentence.

CHRIS. Then said Christiana, This relation of Mr. Fearing has done me good. I thought nobody had been like me, but I see there was some semblance 'twixt this good man and I; only we differed in two things: his troubles were so great, they brake out; but mine I kept within. His also lay so hard upon him, they made him that he could not knock at the houses provided for entertainment; but my trouble was always such as made me knock the louder.

Mercy's
sentence.

MERCY. If I might also speak my heart, I must say something of him has also dwelt in me. For I have ever been more afraid of the lake, and the loss of a place in Paradise, than I have been of the loss of other things. Oh, thought I, may I have the happiness to have a habitation there! it is enough, though I part with all the world to win it.

Matthew's
sentence.

MATT. Then said Matthew, Fear was one thing that made me think that I was far from having that within me that accompanies salvation; but if it was so with such a good man as he, why may it not also go well with me?

James's
sentence.

JAMES. No fears, no grace, said James. Though

there is not always grace where there is the fear of hell, yet to be sure there is no grace where there is no fear of God.

GREAT-HEART. Well said, James, thou hast hit the mark, 'for the fear of God is the beginning of wisdom'; and, to be sure, they that want the beginning have neither middle nor end. But we will here conclude our discourse of Mr. Fearing, after we have sent after him this farewell—

> Well, Master Fearing, thou didst fear
> Thy God, and wast afraid
> Of doing anything, while here,
> That would have thee betray'd.
> And didst thou fear the lake and pit?
> Would others did so too!
> For, as for them that want thy wit,
> They do themselves undo.

Their farewell about him.

Now I saw, that they still went on in their talk. For after Mr. Great-heart had made an end with Mr. Fearing, Mr. Honest began to tell them of another, but his name was Mr. Self-will. He pretended himself to be a pilgrim, said Mr. Honest, but I persuade myself he never came in at the gate that stands at the head of the way.

Of Mr. Self-will.

GREAT-HEART. Had you ever any talk with him about it?

HON. Yes, more than once or twice; but he would always be like himself, self-willed. He neither cared for man, nor argument, nor yet example: what his mind prompted him to, that he would do, and nothing else could he be got to.

Old Honest had talked with him.

GREAT-HEART. Pray what principles did he hold? for I suppose you can tell.

320 THE PILGRIM'S PROGRESS

Self-will's
opinions.

HON. He held that a man might follow the vices as well as the virtues of the pilgrims; and that if he did both, he should be certainly saved.

GREAT-HEART. How! If he had said, 'tis possible for the best to be guilty of the vices, as well as to partake of the virtues of pilgrims, he could not much have been blamed; for indeed we are exempted from no vice absolutely, but on condition that we watch and strive. But this, I perceive, is not the thing; but if I understand you right, your meaning is, that he was of that opinion, that it was allowable so to be?

HON. Ay, ay, so I mean; and so he believed and practised.

GREAT-HEART. But what ground had he for his so saying?

HON. Why, he said he had the Scripture for his warrant.

GREAT-HEART. Prithee, Mr. Honest, present us with a few particulars.

HON. So I will. He said, To have to do with other men's wives had been practised by David, God's beloved; and therefore he could do it. He said to have more women than one, was a thing that Solomon practised; and therefore he could do it. He said that Sarah and the godly midwives of Egypt lied, and so did saved Rahab; and therefore he could do it. He said that the disciples went at the bidding of their Master, and took away the owner's ass; and therefore he could do so too. He said that Jacob got the inheritance of his father in a way of guile and dissimulation; and therefore he could do so too.

GREAT-HEART. High base! indeed; and you are sure he was of this opinion?

HON. I have heard him plead for it, bring Scripture for it, bring argument for it, etc.

GREAT-HEART. An opinion that is not fit to be, with any allowance, in the world.

HON. You must understand me rightly. He did not say that any man might do this; but, that those that had the virtues of those that did such things might also do the same.

GREAT-HEART. But what more false than such a conclusion? For this is as much as to say, that because good men heretofore have sinned of infirmity, therefore he had allowance to do it of a presumptuous mind. Or if because a child, by the blast of the wind, or for that it stumbled at a stone, fell down and defiled itself in mire, therefore he might wilfully lie down and wallow like a boar therein. Who could have thought that any one could so far have been blinded by the power of lust? But what is written must be true, 'They stumble at the word, being disobedient; whereunto also they were appointed.' 1 Pet. ii. 8.

His supposing that such may have the godly man's virtues, who addict themselves to their vices, is also a delusion as strong as the other. 'Tis just as if the dog should say, I have, or may have, the qualities of the child, because I lick up its stinking excrements. To eat up the sin of God's people is no sign of one Hos. iv. 8. that is possessed with their virtues. Nor can I believe that one that is of this opinion can at present have faith or love in him. But I know you have made strong objections against him; prithee what can he say for himself?

HON. Why, he says, to do this by way of opinion seems abundance more honest, than to do it, and yet hold contrary to it in opinion.

GREAT-HEART. A very wicked answer; for though to let loose the bridle to lusts, while our opinions are against such things, is bad; yet to sin, and plead a toleration so to do, is worse. The one stumbles beholders accidentally, the other pleads them into the snare.

HON. There are many of this man's mind that have not this man's mouth; and *that* makes going on pilgrimage of so little esteem as it is.

GREAT-HEART. You have said the truth, and it is to be lamented. But he that feareth the King of Paradise shall come out of them all.

CHRIS. There are strange opinions in the world; I know one that said, 'twas time enough to repent when they came to die.

GREAT-HEART. Such are not over-wise. That man would have been loth, might he have had a week to run twenty miles in for his life, to have deferred that journey to the last hour of that week.

HON. You say right; and yet the generality of them that count themselves pilgrims do indeed do thus. I am, as you see, an old man, and have been a traveller in this road many a day; and I have taken notice of many things.

I have seen some that have set out as if they would drive all the world afore them, who yet have, in few days, died as they in the wilderness, and so never got sight of the promised land.

I have seen some that have promised nothing, at the first setting out to be pilgrims, and that one would have thought could not have lived a day, that have yet proved very good pilgrims.

I have seen some that have run hastily forward, that again have, after a little time, run as fast just back again.

I have seen some who have spoken very well of a pilgrim's life at first, that, after a while, have spoken as much against it.

I have heard some, when they first set out for Paradise, say positively there is such a place, who, when they have been almost there, have come back again and said there is none.

I have heard some vaunt what they would do in case they should be opposed, that have even at a false alarm fled faith, the pilgrim's way, and all.

Now as they were thus in their way, there came one running to meet them, and said, Gentlemen, and you of the weaker sort, if you love life, shift for yourselves, for the robbers are before you. *Fresh news of trouble.*

GREAT-HEART. Then said Mr. Great-heart, They be the three that set upon Little-faith heretofore. Well, said he, we are ready for them. So they went on their way. Now they looked at every turning, when they should have met with the villains; but whether they heard of Mr. Great-heart, or whether they had some other game, they came not up to the pilgrims. *Part i. page 155. Great-heart's resolution.*

Christiana then wished for an inn for herself and

Christiana
wisheth for
an inn.
Rom. xvi. 23.
Gaius.

her children, because they were weary. Then said Mr. Honest, There is one a little before us, where a very honourable disciple, one Gaius, dwells. So they all concluded to turn in thither; and the rather, because the old gentleman gave him so good a report. So when they came to the door, they went in, not knocking, for folks use not to knock at the door of an inn. Then they called for the master of the house, and he came to them. So they asked if they might lie there that night.

They enter
into his
house.

GAIUS. Yes, gentlemen, if you be true men, for my house is for none but pilgrims. Then was Christiana, Mercy, and the boys the more glad, for that the innkeeper was a lover of pilgrims. So they called for rooms, and he showed them one for Christiana and her children and Mercy, and another for Mr. Great-heart and the old gentleman.

Gaius
entertains
them, and
how.

GREAT-HEART. Then said Mr. Great-heart, Good Gaius, what hast thou for supper? for these pilgrims have come far to-day, and are weary.

GAIUS. It is late, said Gaius, so we cannot conveniently go out to seek food; but such as we have you shall be welcome to, if that will content.

GREAT-HEART. We will be content with what thou hast in the house; forasmuch as I have proved thee, thou art never destitute of that which is convenient.

Gaius his
cook.

Then he went down and spake to the cook, whose name was Taste-that-which-is-good, to get ready supper for so many pilgrims. This done, he comes up again, saying, Come, my good friends, you are welcome to me, and I am glad that I have an house to entertain you; and while supper is making ready, if you please, let us entertain one another with some good discourse. So they all said, Content.

GAIUS. Then said Gaius, Whose wife is this aged matron? and whose daughter is this young damsel?

Talk between Gaius and his guests.

GREAT-HEART. The woman is the wife of one Christian, a pilgrim of former times, and these are his four children. The maid is one of her acquaintance, one that she hath persuaded to come with her on pilgrimage. The boys take all after their father, and covet to tread in his steps; yea, if they do but see any place where the old pilgrim hath lain, or any print of his foot, it ministereth joy to their hearts, and they covet to lie or tread in the same.

Mark this.

GAIUS. Then said Gaius, Is this Christian's wife? and are these Christian's children? I knew your husband's father, yea, also his father's father. Many have been good of this stock; their ancestors dwelt first at Antioch. Christian's progenitors (I suppose you have heard your husband talk of them) were very worthy men. They have, above any that I know, showed themselves men of great virtue and courage for the Lord of the pilgrims, his ways, and them that loved him. I have heard of many of your husband's relations that have stood all trials for the sake of the truth. Stephen, that was one of the first of the family from whence your husband sprang, was knocked on the head with stones. James, another of this generation, was slain with the edge of the sword. To say nothing of Paul and Peter, men anciently of the family from whence your husband came, there was Ignatius, who was cast to

Acts xi. 26.

Of Christian's ancestors.

Acts vii. 59, 60.

Acts xii. 2.

the lions; Romanus, whose flesh was cut by pieces from his bones; and Polycarp, that played the man in the fire. There was he that was hanged up in a basket in the sun for the wasps to eat, and he whom they put into a sack and cast him into the sea to be drowned. 'Twould be impossible utterly to count up all of that family that have suffered injuries and death, for the love of a pilgrim's life. Nor can I but be glad to see that thy husband has left behind him four such boys as these. I hope they will bear up their father's name, and tread in their father's steps, and come to their father's end.

GREAT-HEART. Indeed, Sir, they are likely lads; they seem to choose heartily their father's ways.

GAIUS. That is it that I said. Wherefore Christian's family is like still to spread abroad upon the face of the ground, and yet to be numerous upon the face of the earth; wherefore let Christiana look out some damsels for her sons, to whom they may be betrothed, etc., that the name of their father and the house of his progenitors may never be forgotten in the world.

Advice to Christiana about her boys.

HON. 'Tis pity this family should fall, and be extinct.

GAIUS. Fall it cannot, but be diminished it may; but let Christiana take my advice, and that's the way to uphold it.

And Christiana, said the innkeeper, I am glad to see thee and thy friend Mercy together here, a lovely couple. And may I advise, take Mercy into a nearer relation to thee. If she will, let her be given to Matthew, thy eldest son; 'tis the way to preserve you a posterity in the earth. So this match was concluded, and in process of time they were married. But more of that hereafter.

Mercy and Matthew marry.

Gaius also proceeded, and said, I will now speak on the behalf of women, to take away their reproach. For as death and the curse came into the world by a woman, so also did life and health: 'God sent forth his Son, made of a woman.' Yea, to show how much those that came after did abhor the act of their mother, this sex in the Old Testament coveted children, if haply this or that woman might be the mother of the Saviour of the world.

Gen. iii.
Gal. iv. 4.

Why women of old so much desired children.

I will say again, that when the Saviour was come, women rejoiced in him before either man or angel. I read not that ever any man did give unto Christ so much as one groat; but the women followed him, and ministered to him of their substance. It was a woman that washed his feet with tears, and a woman that anointed his body to the burial. They were women that wept when he was going to the cross, and women that followed him from the cross, and that sat by his sepulchre when he was buried. They were women that were first with him at his resurrection-morn, and women that brought tidings first to his disciples that he was risen from the dead. Women, therefore, are highly favoured, and show by these things that they are sharers with us in the grace of life.

Luke ii.

Chap viii. 2, 3.

Chap. vii. 37, 50. John xi. 2. Chap. xii. 3. Luke xxiii. 27. Matt. xxvii. 55, 56, 61.

Luke xxiv. 22, 23.

Now the cook sent up to signify that supper was almost ready, and sent one to lay the cloth, the trenchers, and to set the salt and bread in order.

Supper ready.

Then said Matthew, The sight of this cloth and

of this forerunner of the supper begetteth in me a greater appetite to my food than I had before.

GAIUS. So let all ministering doctrines *to* thee in this life, beget *in* thee a greater desire to sit at the supper of the great King in his kingdom; for all preaching, books, and ordinances here, are but as the laying of the trenchers, and as setting of salt upon the board, when compared with the feast that our Lord will make for us when we come to his house.

What to be gathered from laying of the board with the cloth and trenchers.

So supper came up, and first a heave-shoulder and a wave-breast was set on the table before them, to show that they must begin their meal with prayer and praise to God. The heave-shoulder David lifted his heart up to God with, and with the wave-breast, where his heart lay, with that he used to lean upon his harp when he played. These two dishes were very fresh and good, and they all ate heartily well thereof.

Lev. vii. 32-34. Chap. x. 14, 15. Ps. xxv. 1. Heb. xiii. 15.

The next they brought up was a bottle of wine, red as blood. So Gaius said to them, Drink freely; this is the juice of the true vine, that makes glad the heart of God and man. So they drank and were merry.

Deut. xxxii. 14. Judges ix. 13. John xv. 1.

The next was a dish of milk, well crumbed. But Gaius said, Let the boys have that, that they may grow thereby.

1 Pet. ii. 1, 2. A dish of milk.

Then they brought up in course a dish of butter and honey. Then said Gaius, Eat freely of this; for this is good to cheer up and strengthen your judgments and understandings. This was our Lord's dish when he was a child: 'Butter and honey shall

Of honey and butter.

Isa. vii. 15.

he eat, that he may know to refuse the evil and choose the good.'

Then they brought them up a dish of apples, A dish of and they were very good-tasted fruit. Then said apples. Matthew, May we eat apples, since they were such by and with which the serpent beguiled our first mother?

Then said Gaius—

> Apples were they with which we were beguiled,
> Yet sin, not apples, hath our souls defiled.
> Apples forbid, if eat, corrupt the blood;
> To eat such, when commanded, does us good.
> Drink of his flagons, then, thou church, his dove,
> And eat his apples, who are sick of love.

Then said Matthew, I made the scruple because I, a while since, was sick with eating of fruit.

GAIUS. Forbidden fruit will make you sick, but not what our Lord has tolerated.

While they were thus talking, they were presented Song vi. 11. with another dish, and it was a dish of nuts. Then A dish of said some at the table, Nuts spoil tender teeth, nuts. specially the teeth of children; which when Gaius heard, he said—

> Hard texts are nuts (I will not call them cheaters),
> Whose shells do keep their kernels from the eaters.
> Ope then the shells, and you shall have the meat;
> They here brought are for you to crack and eat.

Then were they very merry, and sat at the table a long time, talking of many things. Then said the old gentleman, My good landlord, while we are cracking your nuts, if you please, do you open this riddle—

A riddle put forth by old Honest.

> A man there was, though some did count him mad,
> The more he cast away, the more he had.

Then they all gave good heed, wondering what good Gaius would say; so he sat still a while, and then thus replied—

Gaius opens it.

> He that bestows his goods upon the poor,
> Shall have as much again, and ten times more.

Joseph wonders.

Then said Joseph, I dare say, Sir, I did not think you could have found it out.

Oh, said Gaius, I have been trained up in this way a great while; nothing teaches like experience. I have learned of my Lord to be kind, and have found by experience that I have gained thereby. 'There Prov. xi. 24. is that scattereth, yet increaseth; and there is that withholdeth more than is meet, but it tendeth to Chap. xiii. 7. poverty.' 'There is that maketh himself rich, yet hath nothing; there is that maketh himself poor, yet hath great riches.'

Then Samuel whispered to Christiana his mother, and said, Mother, this is a very good man's house; let us stay here a good while, and let my brother Matthew be married here to Mercy before we go any further.

The which Gaius the host overhearing, said, With a very good will, my child.

Matthew and Mercy are married.

So they stayed there more than a month, and Mercy was given to Matthew to wife.

While they stayed here, Mercy, as her custom was, would be making coats and garments to give to the poor, by which she brought up a very good report upon the pilgrims.

But to return again to our story.   After supper the lads desired a bed, for that they were weary with travelling.   Then Gaius called to show them their chamber; but said Mercy, I will have them to bed.   So she had them to bed, and they slept well: but the rest sat up all night, for Gaius and they were such suitable company that they could not tell how to part.   Then after much talk of their Lord, themselves, and their journey, old Mr. Honest, he that put forth the riddle to Gaius, began to nod. Then said Great-heart, What, Sir, you begin to be drowsy; come, rub up, now here's a riddle for you. Then said Mr. Honest, Let's hear it.

The boys go to bed, the rest sit up.

Old Honest nods.

Then said Mr. Great-heart—

> He that will kill, must first be overcome:
> Who live abroad would, first must die at home.

A riddle.

Ha! said Mr. Honest, it is a hard one; hard to expound, and harder to practise.   But come, land-lord, said he, I will, if you please, leave my part to you; do you expound it, and I will hear what you say.

No, said Gaius, 'twas put to you, and 'tis expected that you should answer it.

Then said the old gentlemen—

> He first by grace must conquer'd be,
>   That sin would mortify:
> And who, that lives, would convince me,
>   Unto himself must die.

The riddle opened.

It is right, said Gaius; good doctrine and experience teaches this. For first, until grace displays itself, and overcomes the soul with its glory, it is altogether without heart to oppose sin. Besides, if sin is Satan's cords, by which the soul lies bound, how should it make resistance, before it is loosed from that infirmity?

Secondly, nor will any, that knows either reason or grace, believe that such a man can be a living monument of grace, that is a slave to his own corruptions.

A question worth the minding.

And now it comes in my mind, I will tell you a story worth the hearing. There were two men that went on pilgrimage, the one began when he was young, the other when he was old. The young man had strong corruptions to grapple with, the old man's were decayed with the decays of nature. The young man trod his steps as even as did the old one, and was every way as light as he. Who now, or which of them, had their graces shining clearest, since both seemed to be alike?

A comparison.

HON. The young man's, doubtless. For that which heads it against the greatest opposition, gives best demonstration that it is strongest. Specially when it also holdeth pace with that that meets not with half so much, as to be sure old age does not.

A mistake.

Besides, I have observed that old men have blessed themselves with this mistake, namely, taking the decays of nature for a gracious conquest over corruptions, and so have been apt to beguile themselves. Indeed, old men that are gracious are best able to give advice to them that are young, because they have seen most of the emptiness of things. But yet, for an old and a young to set out both together, the young one has the advantage of the fairest discovery of a work of grace within him, though the old man's corruptions are naturally the weakest.

Thus they sat talking till break of day. Now when the family was up, Christiana bid her son James that he should read a chapter; so he read the fifty-third of Isaiah. When he had done, Mr. Honest asked why it was said that the Saviour is said to come ' out of a dry ground,' and also that ' he had no form nor comeliness in him.' Another question.

GREAT-HEART. Then said Mr. Great-heart, To the first I answer, Because the church of the Jews, of which Christ came, had then lost almost all the sap and spirit of religion. To the second I say, The words are spoken in the person of the unbelievers, who, because they want that eye that can see into our Prince's heart, therefore they judge of him by the meanness of his outside: just like those that know not that precious stones are covered over with a homely crust; who, when they have found one, because they know not what they have found, cast it again away, as men do a common stone.

Well, said Gaius, now you are here, and since, as I know, Mr. Great-heart is good at his weapons, if you please, after we have refreshed ourselves, we will walk into the fields, to see if we can do any good. About a mile from hence there is one Slay-good, a giant that doth much annoy the King's highway in these parts; and I know whereabout his haunt is. He is master of a number of thieves. 'Twould be well if we could clear these parts of him. Giant Slay-good assaulted and slain.

So they consented and went; Mr. Great-heart with his sword, helmet, and shield, and the rest with spears and staves.

He is found with one Feeble-mind in his hand. When they came to the place where he was, they found him with one Feeble-mind in his hands, whom his servants had brought unto him, having taken him in the way. Now the giant was rifling of him, with a purpose after that to pick his bones; for he was of the nature of flesh-eaters.

Well, so soon as he saw Mr. Great-heart and his friends at the mouth of his cave, with their weapons, he demanded what they wanted.

GREAT-HEART. We want thee; for we are come to revenge the quarrel of the many that thou hast slain of the pilgrims, when thou hast dragged them out of the King's highway, wherefore come out of thy cave. So he armed himself and came out; and to a battle they went, and fought for above an hour, and then stood still to take wind.

SLAY-GOOD. Then said the Giant, Why are you here on my ground?

GREAT-HEART. To revenge the blood of pilgrims as I also told thee before. So they went to it again, and the Giant made Mr. Great-heart give back; but he came up again, and in the greatness of his mind he let fly with such stoutness at the Giant's head and sides, that he made him let his weapon fall out of his hand. So he smote him and slew him, and cut off his head, and brought it away to the inn. He One Feeble-mind rescued from the Giant. also took Feeble-mind the pilgrim, and brought him with him to his lodgings. When they were come home, they showed his head to the family, and then set it up, as they had done others before, for a terror to those that should attempt to do as he, hereafter.

Then they asked Mr. Feeble-mind how he fell into his hands.

FEEBLE. Then said the poor man, I am a sickly man, as you see; and, because death did usually once a day knock at my door, I thought I should never be well at home; so I betook myself to a pilgrim's life, and have travelled hither from the town of Uncertain, where I and my father were born. I am a man of no strength at all, of body, nor yet of mind, but would, if I could, though I can but crawl, spend my life in the pilgrim's way. When I came at the gate that is at the head of the way, the Lord of that place did entertain me freely, neither objected he against my weakly looks, nor against my feeble mind, but gave me such things that were necessary for my journey, and bid me hope to the end. When I came to the house of the Interpreter, I received much kindness there, and, because the Hill Difficulty was judged too hard for me, I was carried up that by one of his servants. Indeed, I have found much relief from pilgrims, though none was willing to go so softly as I am forced to do; yet still, as they came on, they bid me be of good cheer, and said that it was the will of their Lord that comfort should be given to the feeble-minded, and so went on their own pace. When I was come up to Assault Lane, then this Giant met with me, and bid me prepare for an encounter; but, alas! feeble one that I was, I had more need of a

How Feeble-mind came to be a pilgrim.

1 Thess. v. 14.

cordial. So he came up and took me. I conceited

Mark this.

he should not kill me. Also, when he had got me into his den, since I went not with him willingly, I believed I should come out alive again; for I have heard, that not any pilgrim that is taken captive by violent hands, if he keep heart-whole towards his Master, is, by the laws of Providence, to die by the hand of the enemy. Robbed, I looked to be, and robbed to be sure I am; but I am, as you see, escaped with life, for the which I thank my King as author, and you as the means. Other brunts I also

Mark this.

look for, but this I have resolved on, to wit, to *run* when I can, to *go* when I cannot run, and to *creep* when I cannot go. As to the main, I thank Him that loves me, I am fixed. My way is before me, my mind is beyond the river that has no bridge, though I am, as you see, but of a feeble mind.

HON. Then said old Mr. Honest, Have not you, some time ago, been acquainted with one Mr. Fearing, a pilgrim?

FEEBLE. Acquainted with him! yes; he came from the town of Stupidity, which lieth four degrees to the northward of the City of Destruction, and as

Mr. Fearing Mr. Feeble-mind's uncle.

many off of where I was born; yet we were well acquainted, for indeed he was mine uncle, my father's brother. He and I have been much of a temper. He was a little shorter than I, but yet we were much of a complexion.

Feeble-mind has some of Mr. Fearing's features.

HON. I perceive you know him, and I am apt to believe also that you were related one to another; for you have his whitely look, a cast like his with your eye, and your speech is much alike.

FEEBLE. Most have said so that have known us both: and besides, what I have read in him, I have for the most part found in myself.

GAIUS. Come, Sir, said good Gaius, be of good cheer, you are welcome to me, and to my house, and what thou hast a mind to, call for freely; and what thou wouldest have my servants do for thee, they will do it with a ready mind.

Gaius comforts him.

FEEBLE. Then said Mr. Feeble-mind, This is unexpected favour, and as the sun shining out of a very dark cloud. Did Giant Slay-good intend me this favour when he stopped me, and resolved to let me go no further? Did he intend that after he had rifled my pockets I should go to Gaius mine host? Yet so it is.

Notice to be taken of providence.

Now just as Mr. Feeble-mind and Gaius were thus in talk, there comes one running, and called at the door, and told, that about a mile and a half off there was one Mr. Not-right, a pilgrim, struck dead upon the place where he was, with a thunderbolt.

Tidings how one Not-right was slain with a thunderbolt, and Mr. Feeble-mind's comment upon it.

FEEBLE. Alas! said Mr. Feeble-mind, is he slain? He overtook me some days before I came so far as hither, and would be my company-keeper. He also was with me when Slay-good, the giant, took me; but he was nimble of his heels, and escaped. But it seems he escaped to die, and I was took to live.

What, one would think, doth seek to slay outright,
Ofttimes delivers from the saddest plight.
That very providence, whose face is death,
Doth ofttimes to the lowly life bequeath.
I taken was, he did escape and flee,
Hands cross'd gives death to him, and life to me.

Now about this time, Matthew and Mercy were married : also Gaius gave his daughter Phebe to James, Matthew's brother, to wife ; after which time they yet stayed above ten days at Gaius's house, spending their time, and the seasons, like as pilgrims used to do.

The pilgrims prepare to go forward.

When they were to depart, Gaius made them a feast, and they did eat and drink, and were merry. Now the hour was come that they must be gone ; wherefore Mr. Great-heart called for a reckoning. But Gaius told him that at his house it was not the custom for pilgrims to pay for their entertainment. He boarded them by the year, but looked for his

Luke x. 33-35. How they greet one another at parting.

pay from the good Samaritan, who had promised him at his return, whatsoever charge he was at with them, faithfully to repay him. Then said Mr. Great-heart to him—

3 John v. 6.

GREAT-HEART. 'Beloved, thou dost faithfully whatsoever thou dost, to the brethren and to strangers, which have borne witness of thy charity before the church; whom if thou (yet) bring forward on their journey after a godly sort, thou shalt do well.'

Gaius's last kindness to Feeble-mind.

Then Gaius took his leave of them all, and of his children, and particularly of Mr. Feeble-mind. He also gave him something to drink by the way.

Now Mr. Feeble-mind, when they were going out of the door, made as if he intended to linger. The which, when Mr. Great-heart espied, he said, Come, Mr. Feeble-mind, pray do you go along with us, I will be your conductor, and you shall fare as the rest.

FEEBLE. Alas! I want a suitable companion; you are all lusty and strong, but I, as you see, am weak. I choose therefore rather to come behind, lest by reason of my many infirmities I should be both a burden to myself and to you. I am, as I said, a man of a weak and feeble mind, and shall be offended and made weak at that which others can bear. I shall like no laughing, I shall like no gay attire, I shall like no unprofitable questions. Nay, I am so weak a man as to be offended with that which others have a liberty to do. I do not yet know all the truth; I am a very ignorant Christian man; sometimes, if I hear some rejoice in the Lord, it troubles me because I cannot do so too. It is with me as it is with a weak man among the strong, or as with a sick man among the healthy, or as a lamp despised ('He that is ready to slip with his feet, is as a lamp despised in the thought of him that is at ease'); so that I know not what to do.

Feeble-mind for going behind.

His excuse for it.

Job xii. 5.

GREAT-HEART. But, brother, said Mr. Great-heart, I have it in commission, to comfort the feeble-minded, and to support the weak. You must needs go along with us; we will wait for you, we will lend you our help, we will deny ourselves of some things, both opinionative and practical, for your sake; we will not enter into doubtful disputations before you, will be made all things to you rather than you shall be left behind.

Great-heart's commission.

1 Thess. v. 14.

Rom. xiv.

1 Cor. viii.

A Christian spirit.
Chap. ix. 22.

Now all this while they were at Gaius's door; and, behold, as they were thus in the heat of their discourse, Mr. Ready-to-halt came by, with his

Ps. xxxviii. 17.
Promises.

crutches in his hand; and he also was going on pilgrimage.

Feeble-mind
glad to see
Ready-to-
halt come by.

FEEBLE. Then said Mr. Feeble-mind to him, Man, how camest thou hither? I was but just now complaining that I had not a suitable companion, but thou art according to my wish. Welcome, welcome, good Mr. Ready-to-halt, I hope thee and I may be some help.

READY. I shall be glad of thy company, said the other; and, good Mr. Feeble-mind, rather than we will part, since we are thus happily met, I will lend thee one of my crutches.

FEEBLE. Nay, said he, though I thank thee for thy goodwill, I am not inclined to halt before I am lame. Howbeit, I think, when occasion is, it may help me against a dog.

READY. If either myself or my crutches can do thee a pleasure, we are both at thy command, good Mr. Feeble-mind.

Thus therefore they went on; Mr. Great-heart, and Mr. Honest went before, Christiana and her children went next, and Mr. Feeble-mind, and Mr. Ready-to-halt came behind with his crutches. Then said Mr. Honest—

New talk.

HON. Pray, sir, now we are upon the road, tell us some profitable things of some that have gone on pilgrimage before us.

GREAT-HEART. With a good will. I suppose you have heard how Christian of old did meet with Apollyon in the Valley of Humiliation, and also what hard work he had to go through the Valley of the Shadow of Death. Also I think you cannot

Part I.
pages 68-74,
76.

but have heard how Faithful was put to it with Madam Wanton, with Adam the first, with one Discontent, and Shame; four as deceitful villains as a man can meet with upon the road.

Hon. Yes, I have heard of all this; but indeed, good Faithful was hardest put to it with Shame: he was an unwearied one.

Great-heart. Ay; for as the pilgrim well said, he of all men had the wrong name.

Hon. But pray, Sir, where was it that Christian and Faithful met Talkative? That same was also a notable one. Part i. page 92.

Great-heart. He was a confident fool; yet many follow his ways.

Hon. He had like to have beguiled Faithful.

Great-heart. Ay, but Christian put him into a way quickly to find him out. Thus they went on till they came at the place where Evangelist met with Christian and Faithful, and prophesied to them of what should befall them at Vanity Fair. Part i. page 106.

Great-heart. Then said their guide, Hereabouts did Christian and Faithful meet with Evangelist, who prophesied to them of what troubles they should meet with at Vanity Fair.

Hon. Say you so? I dare say it was a hard chapter that then he did read unto them.

Great-heart. 'Twas so; but he gave them encouragement withal. But what do we talk of them? They were a couple of lion-like men, they had set their faces like flint. Don't you remember how undaunted they were when they stood before the judge? Part i. page 115.

HON. Well, Faithful bravely suffered!

GREAT-HEART. So he did, and as brave things came on 't; for Hopeful and some others, as the story relates it, were converted by his death.

HON. Well, but pray go on; for you are well acquainted with things.

Part I.
page 122.
GREAT-HEART. Above all that Christian met with after he had passed through Vanity Fair, one By-ends was the arch one.

HON. By-ends! what was he?

GREAT-HEART. A very arch fellow, a downright hypocrite. One that would be religious which way ever the world went; but so cunning, that he would be sure neither to lose nor suffer for it. He had his *mode* of religion for every fresh occasion, and his wife was as good at it as he. He would turn and change from opinion to opinion, yea, and plead for so doing too. But so far as I could learn, he came to an ill end with his by-ends; nor did I ever hear that any of his children were ever of any esteem with any that truly feared God.

They are
come within
sight of
Vanity.
Now by this time they were come within sight of the town of Vanity, where Vanity Fair is kept. So when they saw that they were so near the town, they consulted with one another how they should pass through the town, and some said one thing, and some another. At last Mr. Great-heart said, I have, as you may understand, often been a conductor of pilgrims through this town; now I am acquainted
They enter
into one
Mr. Mnason's
to lodge.
Acts xxi. 16.
with one Mr. Mnason, a Cyprusian by nation, an old disciple, at whose house we may lodge. If you think good, said he, we will turn in there?

Content, said old Honest; Content, said Christiana; Content, said Mr. Feeble-mind: and so they said all. Now you must think it was eventide by that they got to the outside of the town, but Mr. Great-heart knew the way to the old man's house. So thither they came; and he called at the door, and the old man within knew his tongue so soon as ever he heard it; so he opened, and they all came in. Then said Mnason their host, How far have ye come to-day? So they said, From the house of Gaius our friend. I promise you, said he, you have gone a good stitch, you may well be a-weary; sit down. So they sat down.

GREAT-HEART. Then said their guide, Come, what cheer, sirs? I dare say you are welcome to my friend.

They are glad of entertainment.

MNASON. I also, said Mr. Mnason, do bid you welcome; and whatever you want, do but say, and we will do what we can to get it for you.

HON. Our great want, a while since, was harbour, and good company, and now I hope we have both.

MNASON. For harbour, you see what it is; but for good company, that will appear in the trial.

GREAT-HEART. Well, said Mr. Great-heart, will you have the pilgrims up into their lodging?

MNASON. I will, said Mr. Mnason. So he had them to their respective places, and also showed them a very fair dining-room, where they might be and sup together, until time was come to go to rest.

Now when they were set in their places, and were a little cheery after their journey, Mr. Honest asked his landlord if there were any store of good people in the town?

MNASON. We have a few; for indeed they are but a few, when compared with them on the other side.

They desire to see some of the good people in the town.

HON. But how shall we do to see some of them? for the sight of good men to them that are going on pilgrimage, is like to the appearing of the moon and the stars to them that are sailing upon the seas.

Some sent for.

MNASON. Then Mr. Mnason stamped with his foot, and his daughter Grace came up. So he said unto her, Grace, go you tell my friends, Mr. Contrite, Mr. Holyman, Mr. Love-saint, Mr. Dare-not-lie, and Mr. Penitent, that I have a friend or two at my house, that have a mind this evening to see them.

So Grace went to call them, and they came; and, after salutation made, they sat down together at the table.

Then said Mr. Mnason, their landlord, My neighbours, I have, as you see, a company of strangers come to my house: they are pilgrims; they come from afar, and are going to Mount Zion. But who, quoth he, do you think this is? pointing with his finger to Christiana. It is Christiana, the wife of Christian, that famous pilgrim, who with Faithful his brother were so shamefully handled in our town. At that they stood amazed, saying, We little thought to see Christiana, when Grace came to call us; wherefore this is a very comfortable surprise. Then they asked her of her welfare, and if these young men were her husband's sons.   And when she had them told they were, they said, The King whom you love and serve make you as your father, and bring you where he is in peace.

HON. Then Mr. Honest (when they were all sat down) asked Mr. Contrite and the rest in what posture their town was at present.

CONTRITE. You may be sure we are full of hurry in fair-time.   It is hard keeping our hearts and spirits in any good order when we are in a cumbered condition.   He that lives in such a place as this is, and that has to do with such as we have, has need of an item, to caution him to take heed, every moment of the day.

HON. But how are your neighbours for quietness?

CONTRITE. They are much more moderate now than formerly.   You know how Christian and Faithful were used at our town; but of late, I say, they have been far more moderate.   I think the blood of Faithful lieth with load upon them till now; for since they burned him, they have been ashamed to burn any more.   In those days we were afraid to walk the streets, but now we can show our heads.   Then the name of a professor was odious; now, specially in some parts of our town (for you know our town is large) religion is counted honourable.

Then said Mr. Contrite to them, Pray, how fareth it with you in your pilgrimage?   How stands the country affected towards you?

HON. It happens to us as it happeneth to way-faring men — sometimes our way is clean, some-

Some talk betwixt Mr. Honest and Contrite.

The fruit of watchfulness.

Persecution not so hot at Vanity Fair as formerly.

times foul, sometimes up-hill, sometimes down-hill; we are seldom at a certainty; the wind is not always on our backs, nor is every one a friend that we meet with in the way. We have met with some notable rubs already, and what are yet behind we know not, but for the most part we find it true, that has been talked of, of old, A good man must suffer trouble.

CONTRITE. You talk of rubs; what rubs have you met withal?

HON. Nay, ask Mr. Great-heart our guide, for he can give the best account of that.

GREAT-HEART. We have been beset three or four times already. First, Christiana and her children were beset with two ruffians, that they feared would a took away their lives. We were beset with Giant Bloody-man, Giant Maul, and Giant Slay-good. Indeed, we did rather beset the last, than were beset of him. And thus it was: After we had been some time at the house of 'Gaius, mine host, and of the whole church,' we were minded upon a time to take our weapons with us, and so go see if we could light upon any of those that were enemies to pilgrims (for we heard that there was a notable one thereabouts). Now Gaius knew his haunt better than I, because he dwelt thereabout, so we looked, and looked, till at last we discerned the mouth of his cave; then we were glad and plucked up our spirits. So we approached up to his den; and, lo, when we came there, he had dragged by mere force into his net this poor man, Mr. Feeble-mind, and was about to bring him to his end. But when he saw us, supposing, as we thought, he had had another prey, he left the poor man in his hole, and came out. So we fell to it full sore, and he lustily laid about him; but in conclusion, he was brought down to the ground, and his head cut off, and set up by the wayside for a terror to such as should after practice such ungodliness. That I tell you the truth, here is the man himself to affirm it, who was as a lamb taken out of the mouth of the lion.

FEEBLE. Then said Mr. Feeble-mind, I found this true to my cost, and comfort: to my cost, when he threatened to pick my bones every moment; and to my comfort, when I saw Mr. Great-heart and his friends with their weapons approach so near for my deliverance.

HOLY-MAN. Then said Mr. Holy-man, There are two things that they have need to be possessed with that go on pilgrimage: courage, and an unspotted life. If they have not courage, they can never hold on their way; and if their lives be loose, they will make the very name of a pilgrim stink. *Mr. Holy-man's speech.*

LOVE-SAINT. Then said Mr. Love-saint, I hope this caution is not needful amongst you. But truly there are many that go upon the road, that rather declare themselves strangers to pilgrimage, than strangers and pilgrims in the earth. *Mr. Love-saint's speech.*

DARE-NOT-LIE. Then said Mr. Dare-not-lie, 'Tis true, they neither have the pilgrim's weed, nor the pilgrim's courage; they go not uprightly, but all awry with their feet; one shoe goes inward, another outward, and their hosen out behind; there a rag, and there a rent, to the disparagement of their Lord. *Mr. Dare-not-lie his speech.*

PENITENT. These things, said Mr. Penitent, they ought to be troubled for, nor are the pilgrims like to have that grace put upon them and their pilgrim's progress as they desire, until the way is cleared of such spots and blemishes.

Thus they sat talking and spending the time, until supper was set upon the table; unto which they went and refreshed their weary bodies; so they went to rest. Now they stayed in this fair a great while, at the house of this Mr. Mnason, who in process of time gave his daughter Grace unto Samuel, Christiana's son, to wife, and his daughter Martha to Joseph.

The time, as I said, that they lay here was long (for it was not now as in former times). Wherefore the pilgrims grew acquainted with many of the good people of the town, and did them what service they could. Mercy, as she was wont, laboured much for the poor; wherefore their bellies and backs blessed her, and she was there an ornament to her profession. And to say the truth for Grace, Phebe, and Martha, they were all of a very good nature, and did much good in their place. They were also all of them very fruitful, so that Christian's name, as was said before, was like to live in the world.

While they lay here, there came a monster out of the woods, and slew many of the people of the town. It would also carry away their children, and teach them to suck its whelps. Now no man in the town durst so much as face this monster; but all men fled when they heard of the noise of his coming.

The monster was like unto no one beast upon

Mr. Penitent his speech.

A monster.

Rev. xvii. 3.

the earth; its body was like a dragon, and it had His shape.
seven heads and ten horns. It made great havoc His nature.
of children, and yet it was governed by a woman.
This monster propounded conditions to men, and
such men as loved their lives more than their souls,
accepted of those conditions. So they came under.

Now this Mr. Great-heart, together with these
that came to visit the pilgrims at Mr. Mnason's
house, entered into a covenant to go and engage
this beast, if perhaps they might deliver the people
of this town from the paw and mouths of this so
devouring a serpent.

Then did Mr. Great-heart, Mr. Contrite, Mr. How he is
Holy-man, Mr. Dare-not-lie, and Mr. Penitent, engaged.
with their weapons, go forth to meet him. Now
the monster at first was very rampant, and looked
upon these enemies with great disdain; but they
so belaboured him, being sturdy men at arms, that
they made him make a retreat. So they came home
to Mr. Mnason's house again.

The monster, you must know, had his certain
seasons to come out in, and to make his attempts
upon the children of the people of the town; also
these seasons did these valiant worthies watch him
in, and did still continually assault him, insomuch
that in process of time he became not only wounded,
but lame; also, he has not made that havoc of the
townsmen's children as formerly he has done; and it
is verily believed by some that this beast will die of
his wounds.

This therefore made Mr. Great-heart and his
fellows of great fame in this town; so that many

of the people that wanted their taste of things yet had a reverent esteem and respect for them. Upon this account, therefore, it was that these pilgrims got not much hurt here. True, there were some of the baser sort that could see no more than a mole, nor understand more than a beast; these had no reverence for these men, nor took they notice of their valour or adventures.

Well, the time grew on that the pilgrims must go on their way; wherefore they prepared for their journey. They sent for their friends, they conferred with them, they had some time set apart, therein to commit each other to the protection of their Prince. There was again that brought them of such things as they had, that were fit for the weak and the Acts xxviii. 10. strong, for the women and the men, and so laded them with such things as were necessary.

Then they set forwards on their way; and their friends accompanying them so far as was convenient, they again committed each other to the protection of their King, and parted.

They, therefore, that were of the pilgrims' company went on, and Mr. Great-heart went before them. Now, the women and children being weakly, they were forced to go as they could bear; by this means Mr. Ready-to-halt and Mr. Feeble-mind had more to sympathise with their condition.

When they were gone from the townsmen, and when their friends had bid them farewell, they quickly came to the place where Faithful was put to death. There therefore they made a stand, and thanked Him that had enabled him to bear his cross

so well; and the rather, because they now found
that they had a benefit by such a manly suffering
as his was.

They went on therefore after this, a good way
further, talking of Christian and Faithful, and how
Hopeful joined himself to Christian after that Faithful was dead.

Now they were come up with the Hill Lucre, Part i. page 131.
where the silver mine was which took Demas off
from his pilgrimage, and into which, as some think,
By-ends fell and perished; wherefore they considered
that. But when they were come to the old monument that stood over against the Hill Lucre, to wit,
to the Pillar of Salt, that stood also within view of
Sodom and its stinking lake, they marvelled, as did
Christian before, that men of that knowledge and
ripeness of wit as they were should be so blinded
as to turn aside here. Only they considered again,
that nature is not affected with the harms that others
have met with, specially if that thing upon which
they look has an attracting virtue upon the foolish
eye.

I saw now that they went on till they came at Part i. page 136.
the river that was on this side of the Delectable
Mountains;—to the river where the fine trees grow
on both sides, and whose leaves, if taken inwardly,
are good against surfeits; where the meadows are
green all the year long; and where they might lie Ps. xxiii.
down safely.

By this river-side, in the meadow, there were cotes
and folds for sheep, an house built for the nourishing
and bringing up of those lambs, the babes of those

women that go on pilgrimage. Also there was here One that was intrusted with them, who could have compassion, and that could gather these lambs with his arm and carry them in his bosom, and that could gently lead those that were with young. Now to the care of *this man*, Christiana admonished her four daughters to commit their little ones, that by these waters they might be housed, harboured, succoured, and nourished, and that none of them might be lacking in time to come. This man, if any of them go astray or be lost, he will bring them again : he will also bind up that which was broken, and will strengthen them that are sick. Here they will never want meat, and drink, and clothing ; here they will be kept from thieves and robbers ; for this man will die before one of those committed to his trust shall be lost. Besides, here they shall be sure to have good nurture and admonition, and shall be taught to walk in right paths—and that, you know, is a favour of no small account. Also here, as you see, are delicate waters, pleasant meadows, dainty flowers, variety of trees, and such as bear wholesome fruit—fruit, not like that that Matthew eat of, that fell over the wall out of Beelzebub's garden, but fruit that procureth health where there is none, and that continueth and increaseth it where it is.

So they were content to commit their little ones to him ; and that which was also an encouragement to them so to do was, for that all this was to be at the charge of the King, and so was as an hospital to young children and orphans.

Now they went on ; and when they were come to

Heb. v. 2.
Isa. xl. 11.

Jer. xxiii. 4.
Ezek. xxxiv.
11-16.

By-path Meadow, to the stile over which Christian went with his fellow Hopeful, when they were taken by Giant Despair and put into Doubting Castle; they sat down and consulted what was best to be done; to wit, now they were so strong, and had got such a man as Mr. Great-heart for their conductor, whether they had not best to make an attempt upon the Giant, demolish his castle, and, if there were any pilgrims in it, to set them at liberty, before they went any further.   So one said one thing, and another said the contrary.   One questioned if it was lawful to go upon unconsecrated ground, another said they might, provided their end was good; but Mr. Great-heart said, Though that assertion offered last cannot be universally true, yet I have a commandment to resist sin, to overcome evil, to fight the good fight of faith; and I pray, with whom should I fight this good fight, if not with Giant Despair?   I will therefore attempt the taking away of his life, and the demolishing of Doubting Castle. Then said he, Who will go with me?   Then said old Honest, I will.   And so will we too, said Christiana's four sons, Matthew, Samuel, James, and Joseph; for they were young men and strong. So they left the women in the road, and with them Mr. Feeble-mind, and Mr. Ready-to-halt with his crutches, to be their guard until they came back; for in that place, though Giant Despair dwelt so near, they keeping in the road, a little child might lead them.

So Mr. Great-heart, old Honest, and the four young men went to go up to Doubting Castle to look for Giant Despair.   When they came at the

They being come to By-path stile, have a mind to have a pluck with Giant Despair. Part i. pages 138-147.

1 John ii. 13, 14.

Isa. xi 6.

Castle gate, they knocked for entrance with an unusual noise. At that the old Giant comes to the gate, and Diffidence his wife, follows. Then said he, Who, and what is he that is so hardy, as after this manner to molest the Giant Despair? Mr. Great-heart replied, It is I, Great-heart, one of the King of the Celestial Country's conductors of pilgrims to their place; and I demand of thee that thou open thy gates for my entrance. Prepare thyself also to fight, for I am come to take away thy head and to demolish Doubting Castle.

Despair has overcome Angels.

Now Giant Despair, because he was a giant, thought no man could overcome him: and again, thought he, Since heretofore I have made a conquest of angels, shall Great-heart make me afraid? So he harnessed himself and went out. He had a cap of steel upon his head, a breastplate of fire girded to him, and he came out in iron shoes, with a great club in his hand. Then these six men made up to him, and beset him behind and before; also when Diffidence the giantess came up to help him, old Mr. Honest cut her down at one blow. Then they fought for their lives, and Giant Despair

Despair is loth to die.

was brought down to the ground, but was very loth to die. He struggled hard, and had, as they say, as many lives as a cat, but Great-heart was his death, for he left him not till he had severed his head from his shoulders.

Then they fell to demolishing Doubting Castle,[1]

---

[1] Though Doubting Castle be demolished,
And the Giant Despair hath lost his head,
Sin can rebuild the castle, make't remain,
And make Despair the giant live again.

and that, you know, might with ease be done, since Doubting
Castle
demolished. Giant Despair was dead. They were seven days in destroying of that ; and in it of pilgrims they found one Mr. Despondency, almost starved to death, and one Much-afraid, his daughter ; these two they saved alive. But it would have made you a-wondered to have seen the dead bodies that lay here and there in the castle-yard, and how full of dead men's bones the dungeon was.

When Mr. Great-heart and his companions had performed this exploit, they took Mr. Despondency and his daughter Much-afraid into their protection, for they were honest people, though they were prisoners in Doubting Castle to that tyrant Giant Despair. They therefore, I say, took with them the head of the Giant (for his body they had buried under a heap of stones), and down to the road and to their companions they came, and showed them what they had done. Now when Feeble-mind and Ready-to-halt saw that it was the head of Giant Despair indeed, they were very jocund and merry. Now Christiana, if need was, could play upon the viol, and her daughter Mercy upon the lute ; so, They have since they were so merry disposed, she played them music and a lesson, and Ready-to-halt would dance. So he joy. took Despondency's daughter, named Much-afraid, by the hand, and to dancing they went in the road. True, he could not dance without one crutch in his hand, but I promise you he footed it well : also the girl was to be commended, for she answered the music handsomely.

As for Mr. Despondency, the music was not much

to him, he was for feeding rather than dancing, for that he was almost starved. So Christiana gave him some of her bottle of spirits for present relief, and then prepared him something to eat; and in little time the old gentleman came to himself, and began to be finely revived.

Now I saw in my dream, when all these things were finished, Mr. Great-heart took the head of Giant Despair, and set it upon a pole by the high-way-side, right over against the pillar that Christian erected for a caution to pilgrims that came after, to take heed of entering into his grounds.

Then he writ under it, upon a marble stone, these verses following :—

A Monument of deliverance.

This is the head of him, whose name only
In former times did pilgrims terrify.
His Castle's down; and Diffidence, his wife,
Brave Master Great-heart has bereft of life.
Despondency, his daughter Much-afraid,
Great-heart for them also the man has play'd.
Who hereof doubts, if he'll but cast his eye
Up hither, may his scruples satisfy.
This head also, when doubting cripples dance,
Doth show from fears they have deliverance.

When these men had thus bravely showed themselves against Doubting Castle, and had slain Giant Despair, they went forward, and went on till they came to the Delectable Mountains, where Christian and Hopeful refreshed themselves with the varieties of the place. They also acquainted themselves with the Shepherds there, who welcomed them, as they had done Christian before, unto the Delectable Mountains.

Now the Shepherds seeing so great a train follow Mr. Great-heart (for with him they were well acquainted), they said unto him, Good Sir, you have got a goodly company here; pray where did you find all these?

Then Mr. Great-heart replied—

First, here is Christiana and her train,
Her sons, and her sons' wives, who, like the wain,
Keep by the pole, and do by compass steer
From sin to grace, else they had not been here:
Next, here's old Honest, come on pilgrimage,
Ready-to-halt too, who I dare engage
True-hearted is, and so is Feeble-mind,
Who willing was not to be left behind;
Despondency, good man, is coming after,
And so also is Much-afraid his daughter.
May we have entertainment here, or must
We further go? Let's know whereon to trust.

The guide's speech to the Shepherds.

Then said the Shepherds, This is a comfortable company. You are welcome to us; for we have for the feeble, as for the strong. Our Prince has an eye to what is done to the least of these; therefore infirmity must not be a block to our entertainment. So they had them to the palace door, and then said unto them, Come in, Mr. Feeble-mind; come in Mr. Ready-to-halt; come in, Mr. Despondency, and Mrs. Much-afraid his daughter. These, Mr. Great-heart, said the Shepherds to the guide, we call in by name, for that they are most subject to draw back; but as for you, and the rest that are strong, we leave you to your wonted liberty. Then said Mr. Great-heart, This day I see that grace doth shine in your faces, and that

Their entertainment.

Matt. xxv. 40.

A description of false Shepherds.

Ezek. xxxiv. 21. you are my Lord's Shepherds indeed; for that you have not pushed these diseased neither with side nor shoulder, but have rather strewed their way into the palace with flowers, as you should.

So the feeble and weak went in, and Mr. Greatheart and the rest did follow. When they were also set down, the Shepherds said to those of the weakest sort, What is it that you would have? for, said they, all things must be managed here to the supporting of the weak, as well as the warning of the unruly.

So they made them a feast of things easy of digestion, and that were pleasant to the palate, and nourishing; the which, when they had received, they went to their rest, each one respectively unto his proper place. When morning was come, because the mountains were high, and the day clear, and because it was the custom of the Shepherds to show to the pilgrims, before their departure, some rarities; therefore, after they were ready, and had refreshed themselves, the Shepherds took them out into the fields, and showed them first what they had showed to Christian before.

Then they had them to some new places. The Mount Marvel. first was to Mount Marvel, where they looked, and behold a man at a distance, that tumbled the hills about with words. Then they asked the Shepherds what that should mean? So they told them that that man was the son of one Great-grace, of whom you read in the first part of the records of the Part i page 156. Pilgrim's Progress. And he is set there to teach pilgrims how to believe down, or to tumble out of their ways, what difficulties they shall meet with, Mark xi. 23, 24. by faith.   Then said Mr. Great-Heart, I know him: he is a man above many.

Then they had them to another place, called Mount Innocent; and there they saw a man clothed all in white, and two men, Prejudice and Ill-will, continually casting dirt upon him.   Now behold the dirt, whatsoever they cast at him, would in little time fall off again, and his garment would look as clear as if no dirt had been cast thereat. *Mount Innocent.*

Then said the pilgrims, What means this?   The Shepherds answered, This man is named Godly-man, and this garment is to show the innocency of his life.   Now those that throw dirt at him, are such as hate his well doing; but, as you see, the dirt will not stick upon his cloths, so it shall be with him that liveth truly innocently in the world.   Whoever they be that would make such men dirty, they labour all in vain; for God, by that a little time is spent, will cause that their innocence shall break forth as the light, and their righteousness as the noonday.

Then they took them, and had them to Mount Charity, where they showed them a man that had a bundle of cloth lying before him, out of which he cut coats and garments for the poor that stood about him; yet his bundle or roll of cloth was never the less. *Mount Charity.*

Then said they, What should this be?   This is, said the Shepherds, to show you, that he that has a heart to give of his labour to the poor, shall never want wherewithal.   He that watereth shall be watered himself. And the cake that the widow gave to the prophet did not cause that she had ever the less in her barrel.

The work of one Fool, and one Want-wit.

They had them also to a place where they saw one Fool, and one Want-wit, washing of an Ethiopian, with intention to make him white; but the more they washed him the blacker he was. They then asked the Shepherds what that should mean. So they told them, saying, Thus shall it be with the vile person; all means used to get such an one a good name shall in conclusion tend but to make him more abominable. Thus it was with the Pharisees, and so shall it be with all hypocrites.

Mercy has a mind to see the hole in the hill. Part I. page 151.

Then said Mercy, the wife of Matthew, to Christiana her mother, Mother, I would, if it might be, see the hole in the hill; or that commonly called the by-way to hell. So her mother brake her mind to the Shepherds. Then they went to the door. It was in the side of a hill, and they opened it, and bid Mercy hearken a while. So she hearkened, and heard one saying, Cursed be my father for holding of my feet back from the way of peace and life! And another said, O that I had been torn in pieces before I had, to save my life, lost my soul! And another said, If I were to live again, how would I deny myself, rather than come to this place! Then there was as if the very earth had groaned and quaked under the feet of this young woman for fear. So she looked white, and came trembling away, saying, Blessed be he and she that is delivered from this place.

Now when the Shepherds had showed them all these things, then they had them back to the palace, and entertained them with what the house would afford. But Mercy, being a young and breeding woman, longed for something that she saw there, but was ashamed to ask. Her mother-in-law then asked her what she ailed, for she looked as one not well. Then said Mercy, There is a looking-glass hangs up in the dining-room, off of which I cannot take my mind; if therefore I have it not, I think I shall miscarry. Then said her mother, I will mention thy wants to the Shepherds, and they will not deny it thee. But she said, I am ashamed that these men should know that I longed. Nay, my daughter, said she, it is no shame, but a virtue, to long for such a thing as that. So Mercy said, Then, mother, if you please, ask the Shepherds if they are willing to sell it. Mercy longeth, and for what.

Now the glass was one of a thousand. It would present a man one way, with his own features exactly, and, turn it but another way, and it would show one the very face and similitude of the Prince of pilgrims himself. Yea, I have talked with them that can tell, and they have said they have seen the very crown of thorns upon his head, by looking in that glass; they have therein also seen the holes in his hands, in his feet, and his side. Yea, such an excellency is there in that glass, that it will show him to one where they have a mind to see him, whether living or dead, whether in earth or heaven, whether in a state of humiliation or in his exaltation, whether coming to suffer or coming to reign. It was the Word of God.

James i. 23.

1 Cor. xiii. 12.

2 Cor. iii. 18.

Part i.
page 148.

Christiana therefore went to the Shepherds apart (now the names of the Shepherds are Knowledge, Experience, Watchful, and Sincere), and said unto them, There is one of my daughters a breeding woman, that I think doth long for something that she hath seen in this house, and she thinks she shall miscarry if she should by you be denied.

She doth
not lose
her longing.

EXPERIENCE. Call her, call her ; she shall assuredly have what we can help her to. So they called her, and said to her, Mercy, what is that thing thou wouldest have ? Then she blushed and said, The great glass that hangs up in the dining-room. So Sincere ran and fetched it, and with a joyful consent it was given her. Then she bowed her head, and gave thanks, and said, By this I know that I have obtained favour in your eyes.

They also gave the other young women such things as they desired, and to their husbands great commendations, for that they joined with Mr. Great-heart to the slaying of Giant Despair, and the demolishing of Doubting Castle.

How the
Shepherds
adorn the
pilgrims.

About Christiana's neck the Shepherds put a bracelet, and so they did about the necks of her four daughters ; also they put earrings in their ears, and jewels on their foreheads.

Part i.
page 152.

When they were minded to go hence, they let them go in peace, but gave not to them those certain cautions which before were given to Christian and his companion. The reason was, for that these had Great-heart to be their guide, who was one that was well acquainted with things, and so could give them their cautions more seasonably, to wit, even then when the danger was nigh the approaching.

What cautious Christian and his companions had Part I. page 165. received of the Shepherds, they had also lost, by that the time was come that they had need to put them in practice. Wherefore here was the advantage that this company had over the other.

From hence they went on singing, and they said—

> Behold, how fitly are the stages set
> For their relief that pilgrims are become :
> And how they us receive without one let,
> That make the other life our mark and home !
>
> What novelties they have, to us they give,
> That we, though pilgrims, joyful lives may live :
> They do upon us, too, such things bestow,
> That show we pilgrims are, where'er we go.

When they were gone from the Shepherds, they quickly came to the place where Christian met with Part I. page 154. one Turn-away, that dwelt in the town of Apostacy. Wherefore of him Mr. Great-heart their guide did now put them in mind, saying, This is the place where Christian met with one Turn-away, who carried with him the character of his rebellion at his back.   And this I have to say concerning this man ; He would hearken to no counsel, but once a-falling, How one Turn-away managed his apostacy. persuasion could not stop him.   When he came to the place where the Cross and the Sepulchre was, he did meet with one that did bid him look there ; but he gnashed with his teeth, and stamped, and said he was resolved to go back to his own town.   Before he came to the gate, he met with Evangelist, who Heb. x. 26 29. offered to lay hands on him to turn him into the

way again. But this Turn-away resisted him, and
having done much despite unto him, he got away
over the wall, and so escaped his hand.

Then they went on; and just at the place where
Little-faith formerly was robbed, there stood a man
with his sword drawn, and his face all bloody. Then
said Mr. Great-heart, What art thou? The man
made answer, saying, I am one whose name is
Valiant-for-truth. I am a pilgrim, and am going
to the Celestial City. Now as I was in my way,
there were three men did beset me, and propounded
unto me these three things: 1. Whether I would
become one of them? 2. Or go back from whence
I came? 3. Or die upon the place? To the first I
answered, I had been a true man a long season, and
therefore it could not be expected that I now should
cast in my lot with thieves. Then they demanded
what I would say to the second. So I told them
that the place from whence I came, had I not found
incommodity there, I had not forsaken it at all; but
finding it altogether unsuitable to me, and very unprofitable for me, I forsook it for this way. Then
they asked me what I said to the third. And I told
them, my life cost more dear far, than that I should
lightly give it away. Besides, you have nothing to
do thus to put things to my choice; wherefore, at
your peril be it if you meddle. Then these three,
to wit, Wild-head, Inconsiderate, and Pragmatic,
drew upon me, and I also drew upon them.

So we fell to it, one against three, for the space of
above three hours. They have left upon me, as you
see, some of the marks of their valour, and have also

One Valiant-
for-truth
beset with
thieves.

Prov. i. 10-14.

How he
behaved
himself, and
put them to
flight.

carried away with them some of mine. They are but just now gone: I suppose they might, as the saying is, hear your horse dash, and so they betook them to flight.

GREAT-HEART. But here was great odds, three against one. Great-heart wonders at his valour.

VALIANT. 'Tis true, but *little* and *more* are nothing to him that has the truth on his side. 'Though an host should encamp against me,' said one, 'my heart shall not fear: though war should rise against me, in this will I be confident,' etc. Besides, said he, I have read in some records, that one man has fought an army; and how many did Samson slay with the jawbone of an ass? Ps. xxvii. 3.

GREAT-HEART. Then said the guide, Why did you not cry out, that some might have come in for your succour?

VALIANT. So I did—to my King, who I knew could hear, and afford invisible help, and that was sufficient for me.

GREAT-HEART. Then said Great-heart to Mr. Valiant-for-truth, thou hast worthily behaved thyself: let me see thy sword. So he showed it him. When he had taken it in his hand, and looked thereon a while, he said, Ha! it is a right Jerusalem blade. Isa. ii. 3.

VALIANT. It is so. Let a man have one of these blades, with a hand to wield it, and skill to use it, and he may venture upon an angel with it. He need not fear its holding, if he can but tell how to lay on. Its edges will never blunt. It will cut flesh and bones, and soul, and spirit and all. Eph. vi. 12-17. Heb. iv. 12.

GREAT-HEART. But you fought a great while; I wonder you were not weary.

2 Sam. xxiii. 10.

VALIANT. I fought till my sword did cleave to my hand; and when they were joined together, as if a sword grew out of my arm, and when the blood ran through my fingers, then I fought with most courage.

The Word.
The Faith.
Blood.

GREAT-HEART. Thou hast done well. Thou hast resisted unto blood, striving against sin. Thou shalt abide by us, come in and go out with us; for we are thy companions.

Then they took him, and washed his wounds, and gave him of what they had to refresh him; and so they went on together. Now as they went on, because Mr. Great-heart was delighted in him (for he loved one greatly that he found to be a man of his hands), and because there were with his company them that were feeble and weak, therefore he questioned with him about many things; as, first, what countryman he was?

VALIANT. I am of Dark-land; for there I was born, and there my father and mother are still.

GREAT-HEART. Dark-land, said the guide; doth not that lie upon the same coast with the City of Destruction?

VALIANT. Yes, it doth. Now, that which caused me to come on pilgrimage was this: We had one Mr. Tell-true came into our parts, and he told it about what Christian had done, and went from the City of Destruction; namely, how he had forsaken his wife and children, and had betaken himself to a pilgrim's life. It was also confidently reported how

How Mr.
Valiant came
to go on
pilgrimage.

he had killed a serpent that did come out to resist him in his journey, and how he got through to whither he intended. It was also told what welcome he had at all his Lord's lodgings, specially when he came to the gates of the Celestial City; for there, said the man, he was received with sound of trumpet by a company of Shining Ones. He told it also how all the bells in the city did ring for joy at his reception, and what golden garments he was clothed with; with many other things that now I shall forbear to relate. In a word, that man so told the story of Christian and his travels, that my heart fell into a burning haste to be gone after him; nor could father or mother stay me: so I got from them, and am come thus far on my way.

GREAT-HEART. You came in at the gate, did you not?

VALIANT. Yes, yes; for the same man also told us that all would be nothing, if we did not begin to enter this way at the gate. *He begins right.*

GREAT-HEART. Look you, said the guide to Christiana, the pilgrimage of your husband, and what he has gotten thereby, is spread abroad far and near. *Christian's name famous.*

VALIANT. Why, is this Christian's wife?

GREAT-HEART. Yes, that it is; and these are also her four sons.

VALIANT. What! and going on pilgrimage too?

GREAT-HEART. Yes, verily; they are following after.

VALIANT. It glads me at heart! Good man! how joyful will he be, when he shall see them *He is much rejoiced to see Christian's wife.*

that would not go with him, yet to enter after him in at the gates into the city!

GREAT-HEART. Without doubt it will be a comfort to him; for, next to the joy of seeing himself there, it will be a joy to meet there his wife and his children.

VALIANT. But now you are upon that, pray let me hear your opinion about it. Some make a question, whether we shall know one another when we are there?

GREAT-HEART. Do they think they shall know themselves then? or that they shall rejoice to see themselves in that bliss? And if they think they shall know and do these, why not know others, and rejoice in their welfare also?

Again, since relations are our second self, though that state will be dissolved there, yet why may it not be rationally concluded that we shall be more glad to see them there, than to see they are wanting?

VALIANT. Well, I perceive whereabouts you are as to this. Have you any more things to ask me about my beginning to come on pilgrimage?

GREAT-HEART. Yes. Were your father and mother willing that you should become a pilgrim?

VALIANT. O no! They used all means imaginable to persuade me to stay at home.

GREAT-HEART. Why, what could they say against it?

The great stumbling-blocks that by his friends were laid in his way.

VALIANT. They said it was an idle life; and if I myself were not inclined to sloth and laziness, I would never countenance a pilgrim's condition.

GREAT-HEART. And what did they say else?

VALIANT. Why, they told me that it was a dangerous way; yea, the most dangerous way in the world, said they, is that which the pilgrims go.

GREAT-HEART. Did they show wherein this way is so dangerous?

VALIANT. Yes, and that in many particulars.

GREAT-HEART. Name some of them.

VALIANT. They told me of the Slough of Despond, where Christian was well-nigh smothered. They told me that there were archers standing ready in Beelzebub Castle to shoot them that should knock at the Wicket-gate for entrance. They told me also of the wood, and dark mountains, of the Hill Difficulty, of the lions, and also of the three giants, Bloody-man, Maul, and Slay-good. They said moreover, that there was a foul fiend haunted the Valley of Humiliation; and that Christian was by him almost bereft of life. Besides, said they, you must go over the Valley of the Shadow of Death, where the hobgoblins are, where the light is darkness, where the way is full of snares, pits, traps, and gins. They told me also of Giant Despair, of Doubting Castle, and of the ruins that the pilgrims met with there. Further they said I must go over the Enchanted Ground, which was dangerous. And that after all this, I should find a river, over which I should find no bridge, and that the river did lie betwixt me and the Celestial Country. *The first stumbling-block.*

GREAT-HEART. And was this all?

VALIANT. No. They also told me that this way was full of deceivers, and of persons that lay await there, to turn good men out of the path. *The second.*

GREAT-HEART. But how did they make that out?

The third. VALIANT. They told me that Mr. Worldly-Wiseman did there lie in wait to deceive. They also said that there was Formality and Hypocrisy continually on the road. They said also that By-ends, Talkative, or Demas would go near to gather me up; that the Flatterer would catch me in his net; or that, with green-headed Ignorance, I would presume to go on to the gate, from whence he always was sent back to the hole that was in the side of the hill, and made to go the by-way to hell.

GREAT-HEART. I promise you this was enough to discourage. But did they make an end here?

The fourth. VALIANT. No; stay. They told me also of many that had tried that way of old, and that had gone a great way therein, to see if they could find something of the glory there, that so many had so much talked of from time to time; and how they came back again, and befooled themselves for setting a foot out of doors in that path, to the satisfaction of all the country. And they named several that did so, as, Obstinate and Pliable, Mistrust and Timorous, Turn-away and old Atheist, with several more, who, they said, had, some of them, gone far to see if they could find, but not one of them found so much advantage by going, as amounted to the weight of a feather.

GREAT-HEART. Said they anything more to discourage you?

The fifth. VALIANT. Yes, they told me of one Mr. Fearing, who was a pilgrim, and how *he* found this way so solitary that he never had comfortable hour therein;

also that Mr. Despondency had like to have been starved therein; yea, and also which I had almost forgot, that Christian himself, about whom there has been such a noise, after all his ventures for a celestial crown, was certainly drowned in the Black River, and never went foot further, however it was smothered up.

GREAT-HEART. And did none of these things discourage you?

VALIANT. No; they seemed but as so many nothings to me.

GREAT-HEART. How came that about?

VALIANT. Why, I still believed what Mr. Telltrue had said; and that carried me beyond them all.

How he got over these stumbling-blocks.

GREAT-HEART. Then this was your victory, even your faith.

VALIANT. It was so. I believed, and therefore came out, got into the way, fought all that set themselves against me, and by believing am come to this place.

> Who would true valour see,
>   Let him come hither;
> One here will constant be,
>   Come wind, come weather.
> There's no discouragement
> Shall make him once relent,
> His first avow'd intent
>   To be a pilgrim.
>
> Whoso beset him round
>   With dismal stories,
> Do but themselves confound,—
>   His strength the more is.

No lion can him fright,
He'll with a giant fight,
But he will have a right
To be a pilgrim.

Hobgoblin nor foul fiend
Can daunt his spirit;
He knows he at the end
Shall life inherit.
Then fancies fly away;
He'll fear not what men say;
He'll labour night and day
To be a pilgrim.

Part I.
Page 168.

By this time they were got to the Enchanted Ground, where the air naturally tended to make one drowsy. And that place was all grown over with briars and thorns, excepting here and there, where was an enchanted arbour, upon which if a man sits, or in which if a man sleeps, 'tis a question, say some, whether ever they shall rise or wake again in this world. Over this forest, therefore, they went, both one with another, and Mr. Great-heart went before, for that he was the guide; and Mr. Valiant-for-truth, he came behind, being there a guard, for fear lest peradventure some fiend, or dragon, or giant, or thief, should fall upon their rear, and so do mischief. They went on here each man with his sword drawn in his hand, for they knew it was a dangerous place. Also they cheered up one another as well as they could: Feeble-mind, Mr. Great-heart commanded should come up after him; and Mr. Despondency was under the eye of Mr. Valiant.

Now they had not gone far, but a great mist and

a darkness fell upon them all; so that they could scarce, for a great while, see the one the other. Wherefore they were forced, for some time, to feel for one another by words; for they walked not by sight.

But any one must think that here was but sorry going for the best of them all, but how much worse for the women and children, who both of feet and heart were but tender. Yet so it was, that through the encouraging words of him that led in the front, and of him that brought them up behind, they made a pretty good shift to wag along.

The way also was here very wearisome, through dirt and slabbiness. Nor was there on all this ground so much as one inn or victualling-house, therein to refresh the feebler sort. Here, therefore, was grunting, and puffing, and sighing. While one tumbleth over a bush, another sticks fast in the dirt; and the children, some of them, lost their shoes in the mire. While one cries out, I am down; and another, Ho, where are you? and a third, The bushes have got such fast hold on me, I think I cannot get away from them.

Then they come at an arbour, warm, and promising much refreshing to the pilgrims; for it was finely wrought above-head, beautified with greens, furnished with benches and settles. It also had in it a soft couch, whereon the weary might lean. This, you must think, all things considered, was tempting, for the pilgrims already began to be foiled with the badness of the way; but there was not one of them that made so much as a motion to stop

An arbour on the Enchanting Ground.

there. Yea, for aught I could perceive, they continually gave so good heed to the advice of their guide, and he did so faithfully tell them of dangers, and of the nature of dangers when they were at them, that usually, when they were nearest to them, they did most pluck up their spirits, and hearten one another to deny the flesh. This arbour was called the Slothful's Friend, on purpose to allure, if it might be, some of the pilgrims there to take up their rest when weary.

The name of the arbour.

I saw then in my dream, that they went on in this their solitary ground, till they came to a place at which a man is apt to lose his way. Now, though when it was light, their guide could well enough tell how to miss those ways that led wrong, yet in the dark he was put to a stand; but he had in his pocket a map of all ways leading to or from the Celestial City; wherefore he struck a light (for he never goes also without his tinder-box) and takes a view of his book or map, which bids him be careful, in that place, to turn to the right-hand way. And had he not here been careful to look in his map, they had all, in probability, been smothered in the mud; for just a little before them, and that at the end of the cleanest way too, was a pit, none knows how deep, full of nothing but mud, there made on purpose to destroy the pilgrims in.

The way difficult to find.

The guide has a map of all ways leading to or from the city.

Then thought I with myself, Who that goeth on pilgrimage but would have one of these maps about him, that he may look when he is at a stand, which is the way he must take?

God's Book.

They went on then in this Enchanted Ground till

they came to where was another arbour, and it was built by the highway-side. And in that arbour An arbour, there lay two men, whose names were Heedless and and two asleep Too-bold. These two went thus far on pilgrimage; therein. but here, being wearied with their journey, they sat down to rest themselves, and so fell fast asleep. When the pilgrims saw them, they stood still and shook their heads, for they knew that the sleepers were in a pitiful case. Then they consulted what to do, whether to go on and leave them in their sleep, or to step to them and try to awake them. So they concluded to go to them and wake them,—that is, if they could; but with this caution, namely, to take heed that themselves did not sit down nor embrace the offered benefit of that arbour.

So they went in and spake to the men, and called The pilgrims try to wake them. each by his name (for the guide, it seems, did know them); but there was no voice nor answer. Then the guide did shake them, and do what he could to disturb them. Then said one of them, I will pay you when I take my money. At which the guide shook his head. I will fight so long as I can hold my sword in my hand, said the other. At that one of the children laughed.

Then said Christiana, What is the meaning of Their endeavour is fruitless. this? The guide said, They talk in their sleep. If you strike them, beat them, or whatever else you do to them, they will answer you after this fashion; or as one of them said in old time, when the waves of the sea did beat upon him, and he slept as one upon the mast of a ship, 'When I awake, I will seek it Prov. xxiii. 34, 35. again.' You know, when men talk in their sleep, they say anything; but their words are not governed either by faith or reason.   There is an incoherency in their words now, as there was before, betwixt their going on pilgrimage, and sitting down here. This, then, is the mischief on 't, when heedless ones go on pilgrimage, 'tis twenty to one but they are served thus.   For this Enchanted Ground is one of the last refuges that the enemy to pilgrims has; wherefore it is, as you see, placed almost at the end of the way, and so it standeth against us with the more advantage.   For when, thinks the enemy, will these fools be so desirous to sit down as when they are weary? and when so like to be weary as when almost at their journey's end?   Therefore it is, I say, that the Enchanted Ground is placed so nigh to the land of Beulah, and so near the end of their race.   Wherefore let pilgrims look to themselves, lest it happen to them as it has done to these, that, as you see, are fallen asleep, and none can wake them.

Then the pilgrims desired with trembling to go forward, only they prayed their guide to strike a

The light of the Word.

light, that they might go the rest of their way by the help of the light of a lanthorn.   So he struck a light, and they went by the help of that through

2 Pet. i. 19.

the rest of this way, though the darkness was very great.

The children cry for weariness.

But the children began to be sorely weary, and they cried out unto Him that loveth pilgrims to make their way more comfortable.   So by that they had gone a little further, a wind arose, that drove away the fog; so the air became more clear.

Yet they were not off (by much) of the Enchanted Ground ; only now they could see one another better, and the way wherein they should walk.

Now when they were almost at the end of this ground, they perceived that, a little before them, was a solemn noise, as of one that was much concerned. So they went on and looked before them ; and, behold, they saw, as they thought, a man upon his knees, with hands and eyes lift up, and speaking, as they thought, earnestly to one that was above. They drew nigh, but could not tell what he said ; so they went softly till he had done. When he had done, he got up and began to run towards the Celestial City. Then Mr. Great-heart called after him, saying, So-ho ! friend, let us have your company, if you go, as I suppose you do, to the Celestial City. So the man stopped, and they came up to him. But so soon as Mr. Honest saw him, he said, I know this man. Then said Mr. Valiant-for-truth, Prithee, who is it ? 'Tis one, said he, that comes from whereabouts I dwelt. His name is Stand-fast : he is certainly a right good pilgrim.

So they came up one to another ; and presently Stand-fast said to old Honest, Ho, Father Honest, are you there ? Ay, said he, that I am, as sure as you are there. Right glad am I, said Mr. Stand-fast, that I have found you on this road. And as glad am I, said the other, that I espied you upon your knees. Then Mr. Stand-fast blushed, and said, But why, did you see me ? Yes, that I did, quoth the other, and with my heart was glad at the sight. Why, what did you think ? said Stand-fast.

Stand-fast upon his knees in the Enchanted Ground.

The story of Stand-fast.

Talk betwixt him and Mr. Honest.

Think! said old Honest; what should I think. I thought we had an honest man upon the road, and therefore should have his company by and by. If you thought not amiss, how happy am I! But if I be not as I should, I alone must bear it. That is true, said the other; but your fear doth further confirm me that things are right betwixt the Prince of pilgrims and your soul; for he saith, ' Blessed is the man that feareth always.'

They found him at prayer.

VALIANT. Well, but brother, I pray thee, tell us what was it that was the cause of thy being upon thy knees even now? Was it for that some special mercy laid obligations upon thee, or how?

STAND-FAST. Why, we are, as you see, upon the Enchanted Ground ; and as I was coming along, I was musing with myself of what a dangerous road

What it was that fetched him upon his knees.

the road in this place was, and how many that had come even thus far on pilgrimage had here been stopped, and been destroyed. I thought also of the manner of the death here with which this place destroyeth men. Those that die here die of no violent distemper. The death which such die is not grievous to them ; for he that goeth away in a sleep begins that journey with desire and pleasure ; yea, such acquiesce in the will of that disease.

HON. Then Mr. Honest, interrupting of him, said, Did you see the two men asleep in the arbour?

Prov. x. 7.

STAND-FAST. Ay, ay, I saw Heedless and Too-bold there, and for aught I know, there they will lie till they rot. But let me go on in my tale. As I was thus musing, as I said, there was one in very pleasant attire, but old, that presented herself unto me, and offered me three things, to wit, her body, her purse, and her bed. Now the truth is, I was both a-weary and sleepy; I am also as poor as an owlet, and that, perhaps, the witch knew. Well, I repulsed her once and twice, but she put by my repulses, and smiled. Then I began to be angry, but she mattered that nothing at all. Then she made offers again, and said, If I would be ruled by her, she would make me great and happy; for, said she, I am the mistress of the world, and men are made happy by me. Then I asked her name, and she told me it was Madam Bubble. This set me further from her; but she still followed me with enticements. Then I betook me, as you see, to my knees, and with hands lift up and cries, I prayed to Him that had said he would help. So, just as you came up, the gentlewoman went her way. Then I continued to give thanks for this my great deliverance; for I verily believe she intended no good, but rather sought to make stop of me in my journey.

Madam Bubble, or this vain world.

HON. Without doubt her designs were bad. But stay, now you talk of her, methinks I either have seen her, or have read some story of her.

STAND-FAST. Perhaps you have done both.

HON. Madam Bubble! is she not a tall, comely dame, something of a swarthy complexion?

STAND-FAST. Right, you hit it; she is just such an one.

HON. Doth she not speak very smoothly, and give you a smile at the end of a sentence?

STAND-FAST. You fall right upon it again, for these are her very actions.

HON. Doth she not wear a great purse by her side, and is not her hand often in it, fingering her money, as if that was her heart's delight ?

STAND-FAST. 'Tis just so ; had she stood by all this while, you could not more amply have set her forth before me, nor have better described her features.

HON. Then he that drew her picture was a good limner, and he that wrote of her said true.

GREAT-HEART. This woman is a witch, and it is by virtue of her sorceries that this ground is enchanted. Whoever doth lay their head down in her lap, had as good lay it down upon that block over which the axe doth hang; and whoever lay their eyes upon her beauty, are counted the enemies of God. This is she that maintaineth in their splendour all those that are the enemies of pilgrims ; yea, this is she that has bought off many a man from a pilgrim's life. She is a great gossiper ; she is always, both she and her daughters, at one pilgrim's heels or other, now commending, and then preferring the excellencies of this life. She is a bold and impudent slut ; she will talk with any man. She always laugheth poor pilgrims to scorn, but highly commends the rich. If there be one cunning to get money in a place, she will speak well of him from house to house. She loveth banqueting and feasting mainly well ; she is always at one full table or another. She has given it out in some places that she is a goddess, and therefore some do worship her. She has her times and open places of cheating ; and she will say and avow it, that none can show a good

The world.

James iv. 4.
1 John ii. 15.

comparable to hers. She promiseth to dwell with
children's children, if they will but love and make
much of her. She will cast out of her purse gold like
like dust, in some places, and to some persons. She
loves to be sought after, spoken well of, and to lie
in the bosoms of men. She is never weary of commending her commodities, and she loves them most
that think best of her. She will promise to some
crowns and kingdoms if they will but take her
advice, yet many has she brought to the halter,
and ten thousand times more to hell.

STAND-FAST. Oh! said Stand-fast, what a mercy
is it that I did resist her; for whither might she
have drawn me?

GREAT-HEART. Whither! nay, none but God
knows whither. But in general, to be sure, she
would have drawn thee 'into many foolish and 1 Tim. vi. 9.
hurtful lusts, which drown men in destruction and
perdition.'

'Twas she that set Absalom against his father,
and Jeroboam against his master. 'Twas she that
persuaded Judas to sell his Lord; and that prevailed with Demas to forsake the godly pilgrim's
life. None can tell of the mischief that she doth.
She makes variance betwixt rulers and subjects,
betwixt parents and children, betwixt neighbour
and neighbour, betwixt a man and his wife, betwixt a man and himself, betwixt the flesh and
the heart.

Wherefore, good master Stand-fast, be as your
name is, and when you have done all, *stand*.

At this discourse there was among the pilgrims a

mixture of joy and trembling, but at length they
brake out, and sang—

> What danger is the pilgrim in !
>   How many are his foes !
> How many ways there are to sin
>   No living mortal knows.
> Some of the ditch shy are, yet can
>   Lie tumbling on the mire :
> Some, though they shun the frying-pan,
>   Do leap into the fire.

Part i.
Page 191.

After this I beheld, until they were come unto
the land of Beulah, where the sun shineth night and
day. Here, because they were weary, they betook
themselves a while to rest. And because this
country was common for pilgrims, and because the
orchards and vineyards that were here belonged to
the King of the Celestial Country, therefore they
were licensed to make bold with any of his things.
But a little while soon refreshed them here ; for the
bells did so ring, and the trumpets continually sound
so melodiously, that they could not sleep ; and yet
they received as much refreshing as if they had slept
their sleep never so soundly. Here also all the
noise of them that walked the streets was, More
pilgrims are come to town. And another would
answer, saying, And so many went over the water,
and were let in at the golden gates to-day. They
would cry again, There is now a legion of Shining
Ones just come to town, by which we know that
there are more pilgrims upon the road, for here they
come to wait for them, and to comfort them after
all their sorrow. Then the pilgrims got up and

walked to and fro; but how were their ears now filled with heavenly noises, and their eyes delighted with celestial visions! In this land they heard nothing, saw nothing, felt nothing, smelt nothing, tasted nothing, that was offensive to their stomach or mind: only when they tasted of the water of the river, over which they were to go, they thought that tasted a little bitterish to the palate, but it proved sweeter when it was down.

Death bitter to the flesh, but sweet to the soul.

In this place there was a record kept of the names of them that had been pilgrims of old, and a history of all the famous acts that they had done. It was here also much discoursed how the river to some had had its *flowings*, and what *ebbings* it has had while others have gone over. It has been in a manner *dry* for some, while it has overflowed its banks for others.

Death has its ebbings and flowings like the tide.

In this place, the children of the town would go into the King's gardens and gather nosegays for the pilgrims, and bring them to them with much affection. Here also grew camphire with spikenard, and saffron, calamus, and cinnamon, with all its trees of frankincense, myrrh, and aloes, with all chief spices. With these the pilgrims' chambers were perfumed, while they stayed here; and with these were their bodies anointed, to prepare them to go over the river when the time appointed was come.

Now, while they lay·here, and waited for the good hour, there was a noise in the town that there was a post come from the Celestial City, with matter of great importance, to one Christiana, the

A messenger
of Death sent
to Christiana.
wife of Christian the pilgrim. So inquiry was made
for her, and the house was found out where she was.
So the post presented her with a letter, the contents
His message. whereof was, Hail, good woman, I bring thee tidings
that the Master calleth for thee, and expecteth that
thou shouldest stand in his presence in clothes of
immortality, within this ten days.

How welcome
is death to
them that
have nothing
to do but to
die.
    When he had read this letter to her, he gave her
therewith a sure token that he was a true messenger,
and was come to bid her make haste to be gone.
The token was, an arrow with a point sharpened
with love, let easily into her heart, which by degrees
wrought so effectually with her, that at the time
appointed she must be gone.

    When Christiana saw that her time was come,
and that she was the first of this company that was
Her speech
to her guide.
to go over, she called for Mr. Great-heart, her guide,
and told him how matters were. So he told her he
was heartily glad of the news, and could have been
glad had the post come for him. Then she bid that
he should give advice how all things should be
prepared for her journey. So he told her, saying,
Thus and thus it must be, and we that survive will
accompany you to the river-side.

To her
children.
    Then she called for her children, and gave them
her blessing, and told them that she yet read with
comfort, the mark that was set in their foreheads,
and was glad to see them with her there, and that
they had kept their garments so white. Lastly,
she bequeathed to the poor that little she had,
and commanded her sons and her daughters to be
ready against the messenger should come for them.

When she had spoken these words to her guide and to her children, she called for Mr. Valiant-for-truth, and said unto him, Sir, you have in all places showed yourself true-hearted; be faithful unto death, and my King will give you a crown of life. I would also entreat you to have an eye to my children, and if at any time you see them faint, speak comfortably to them. For my daughters, my sons' wives, they have been faithful, and a fulfilling of the promise upon them will be their end. But she gave Mr. Stand-fast a ring. *To Mr. Valiant.* *To Mr. Stand-fast.*

Then she called for old Mr. Honest, and said of him, Behold an Israelite indeed, in whom is no guile. Then said *he*, I wish you a fair day when you set out for Mount Zion, and shall be glad to see that you go over the river dry-shod. But she answered, Come wet, come dry, I long to be gone; for however the weather is in my journey, I shall have time enough when I come there to sit down and rest me, and dry me. *To old Honest.*

Then came in that good man, Mr. Ready-to-halt, to see her. So she said to him, Thy travel hither has been with difficulty, but that will make thy rest the sweeter. But watch and be ready, for at an hour when you think not, the messenger may come. *To Mr. Ready-to-halt.*

After him came in Mr. Despondency, and his daughter Much-afraid, to whom she said, You ought with thankfulness, for ever to remember your deliverance from the hands of Giant Despair, and out of Doubting Castle. The effect of that mercy is, that you are brought with safety hither. Be ye *To Despondency and his daughter.*

watchful, and cast away fear; be sober, and hope to the end.

To Feeble-mind.

Then she said to Mr. Feeble-mind, Thou wast delivered from the mouth of Giant Slay-good, that thou mightest live in the light of the living for ever, and see thy King with comfort. Only I advise thee to repent thee of thy aptness to fear and doubt of his goodness before he sends for thee; lest thou shouldest, when he comes, be forced to stand before him for that fault with blushing.

Her last day and manner of departure.

Now the day drew on that Christiana must be gone. So the road was full of people to see her take her journey. But behold all the banks beyond the river were full of horses and chariots, which were come down from above to accompany her to the city gate. So she came forth and entered the river, with a beckon of farewell to those that followed her to the river-side. The last word she was heard to say here was, I come, Lord, to be with thee, and bless thee.

So her children and friends returned to their place, for that those that waited for Christiana had carried her out of their sight. So she went and called, and entered in at the gate with all the ceremonies of joy that her husband Christian had done before her.

At her departure her children wept, but Mr. Great-heart and Mr. Valiant played upon the well-tuned cymbal and harp for joy. So all departed to their respective places.

Ready-to-halt summoned.

In process of time there came a post to the town again, and his business was with Mr. Ready-to halt.

So he inquired him out, and said to him, I am come to thee in the name of Him whom thou hast loved and followed, though upon crutches; and my message is to tell thee that he expects thee at his table to sup with him in his kingdom, the next day after Easter; wherefore prepare thyself for this journey.

Then he also gave him a token that he was a true messenger, saying, I have broken thy golden bowl, Eccles. xii. 6. and loosed thy silver cord.

After this Mr. Ready-to-halt called for his fellow-pilgrims, and told them, saying, I am sent for, and God shall surely visit you also. So he desired Mr. Valiant to make his will. And because he had nothing to bequeath to them that should survive him but his crutches, and his good wishes, therefore Promises. thus he said: These crutches I bequeath to my His will. son that shall tread in my steps, with an hundred warm wishes that he may prove better than I have done.

Then he thanked Mr. Great-heart for his conduct and kindness, and so addressed himself to his journey. When he came at the brink of the river, he said, Now I shall have no more need of these crutches, since yonder are chariots and horses for me to ride on. The last words he was heard to say His last words. were Welcome life! So he went his way.

After this Mr. Feeble-mind had tidings brought Feeble-mind summoned. him, that the post sounded his horn at his chamber-door. Then he came in and told him, saying, I am come to tell thee that thy Master has need of thee, and that in very little time thou must behold his

face in brightness.   And take this as a token of the
Eccles. xii. 3. truth of my message: Those that look out at the
windows shall be darkened.

Then Mr. Feeble-mind called for his friends, and
told them what errand had been brought unto him,
and what token he had received of the truth of the
He makes no will. message.   Then he said, Since I have nothing to
bequeath to any, to what purpose should I make
a will? As for my feeble mind, that I will leave
behind me; for that I have no need of that in the
place whither I go; nor is it worth bestowing upon
the poorest pilgrim; Wherefore, when I am gone,
I desire that you, Mr. Valiant, would bury it in a
dunghill.   This done, and the day being come in
which he was to depart, he entered the river as the
His last words. rest.   His last words were, Hold out, faith and
patience.   So he went over to the other side.

When days had many of them passed away, Mr.
Mr. Despondency's summons. Despondency was sent for.   For a post was come,
and brought this message to him: Trembling man,
these are to summon thee to be ready with thy
King by the next Lord's day, to shout for joy for
thy deliverance from all thy doubtings.

And, said the messenger, that my message is true,
Eccles. xii. 5. take this for a proof: so he gave him, 'The Grasshopper to be a burden unto him.' Now Mr. Despon-
His daughter goes too. dency's daughter, whose name was Much-afraid, said,
when she heard what was done, that she would go
with her father.   Then Mr. Despondency said to his
friends, Myself and my daughter, you know what
we have been, and how troublesomely we have
behaved ourselves in every company. My will and

my daughter's is, that our desponds, and slavish His will.
fears, be by no man ever received, from the day of
our departure, for ever; for I know that after my
death they will offer themselves to others. For, to
be plain with you, they are ghosts, the which we
entertained when we first began to be pilgrims, and
could never shake them off after; and they will
walk about and seek entertainment of the pilgrims;
but for our sakes shut ye the doors upon them.

When the time was come for them to depart,
they went to the brink of the river. The last words
of Mr. Despondency were, Farewell night; welcome
day! His daughter went through the river singing, His last words.
but none could understand what she said.

Then it came to pass, a while after, that there was Mr. Honest summoned.
a post in the town that inquired for Mr. Honest.
So he came to his house where he was, and delivered
to his hand these lines: Thou art commanded to be
ready against this day seven-night; to present thy
self before thy Lord at his Father's house. And
for a token that my message is true, 'All thy Eccles. xii. 4.
daughters of music shall be brought low.' Then
Mr. Honest called for his friends, and said unto
them, I die, but shall make no will. As for my He makes no will.
honesty, it shall go with me; let him that comes
after be told of this. When the day that he was to
be gone was come, he addressed himself to go over
the river. Now the river at that time overflowed
the banks in some places, but Mr. Honest in his
lifetime had spoken to one Good-conscience to meet Good-conscience helps Mr. Honest over the river.
him there, the which he also did, and lent him his
hand, and so helped him over. The last words of

Mr. Honest were, Grace reigns! So he left the world.

Mr. Valiant summoned.

After this it was noised abroad that Mr. Valiant-for-truth was taken with a summons, by the same post as the other, and had this for a token that the

Eccles. xii. 6.

summons was true: 'That his pitcher was broken at the fountain.' When he understood it, he called for his friends and told them of it. Then said he, I am going to my fathers, and though with great difficulty I am got hither, yet now I do not repent me of all the trouble I have been at to arrive where

His will.

I am. My sword I give to him that shall succeed me in my pilgrimage, and my courage and skill to him that can get it. My marks and scars I carry with me, to be a witness for me that I have fought His battles who now will be my rewarder. When the day that he must go hence was come, many accompanied him to the river-side, into which as he

His last words.

went he said, 'Death, where is thy sting?' And as he went down deeper, he said, 'Grave, where is thy victory?' So he passed over, and all the trumpets sounded for him on the other side.

Mr. Stand-fast is summoned.

Then there came forth a summons for Mr. Stand-fast (this Mr. Stand-fast was he that the rest of the pilgrims found upon his knees in the Enchanted Ground), for the post brought it him open in his hands. The contents whereof were, That he must prepare for a change of life, for his Master was not willing that he should be so far from him any longer. At this Mr. Stand-fast was put into a muse. Nay, said the messenger, you need not doubt of the truth of my message, for here is a token of the truth thereof,

'Thy wheel is broken at the cistern.' Then he called to him Mr. Great-heart, who was their guide, and said unto him, Sir, although it was not my hap to be much in your good company in the days of my pilgrimage, yet, since the time I knew you, you have been profitable to me. When I came from home, I left behind me a wife and five small children; let me entreat you at your return (for I know that you will go and return to your Master's house, in hopes that you may yet be a conductor to more of the holy pilgrims) that you send to my family, and let them be acquainted with all that hath and shall happen unto me. Tell them, moreover, of my happy arrival to this place, and of the present late blessed condition that I am in. Tell them also of Christian and Christiana his wife, and how she and her children came after her husband. Tell them also, of what a happy end she made, and whether she is gone. I have little or nothing to send to my family, except it be prayers and tears for them; of which it will suffice if thou acquaint them, if peradventure they may prevail.

When Mr. Stand-fast had thus set things in order, and the time being come for him to haste him away, he also went down to the river. Now there was a great calm at that time in the river; wherefore Mr. Stand-fast, when he was about half way in, he stood a while, and talked to his companions that had waited upon him thither. And he said:

This river has been a terror to many; yea, the thoughts of it also have often frighted me. But now methinks I stand easy; my foot is fixed upon

Eccles. xii. 6.

He calls for Mr. Great-heart.

His speech to him.

His errand to his family.

His last words.

that upon which the feet of the priests that bare the ark of the covenant stood, while Israel went over this Jordan. The waters, indeed, are to the palate bitter, and to the stomach cold; yet the thoughts of what I am going to, and of the conduct that waits for me on the other side, doth lie as a glowing coal at my heart.

I see myself now at the end of my journey, my toilsome days are ended. I am going now to see *that* head that was crowned with thorns, and *that* face that was spit upon, for me.

I have formerly lived by hearsay, and faith, but now I go where I shall live by sight, and shall be with Him in whose company I delight myself.

I have loved to hear my Lord spoken of, and wherever I have seen the print of his shoe in the earth, there I have coveted to set my foot too.

His name has been to me as a civet-box; yea, sweeter than all perfumes. His voice to me has been most sweet, and his countenance I have more desired than they that have most desired the light of the sun. His Word I did use to gather for my food, and for antidotes against my faintings. He has held me, and I have kept me from mine iniquities; yea, my steps hath he strengthened in his way.

Now, while he was thus in discourse, his countenance changed, his strong man bowed under him; and after he had said, Take me, for I come unto thee, he ceased to be seen of them.

But glorious it was, to see how the open region was filled with horses and chariots, with trumpeters and pipers, with singers and players on stringed instruments, to welcome the pilgrims as they went up, and followed one another in at the beautiful gate of the city.

As for Christian's children, the four boys that Christiana brought with her, with their wives and children, I did not stay where I was till they were gone over. Also, since I came away, I heard one say that they were yet alive, and so would be for the increase of the Church in that place where they were for a time.

Shall it be my lot to go that way again, I may give those that desire it an account of what I here am silent about. Meanwhile I bid my reader Adieu.